Body
CHECK

BODY CHECK

A BLADES HOCKEY NOVEL

MARIA LUIS

ALKMINI BOOKS, LLC

Eleven years ago, I married the hockey player who swept me off my feet in college. A year ago, we sat opposite each other and finalized our divorce.

I've tried to move on.
I've tried to *forget* him.

But even when we were drowning at rock bottom, *Jackson Carter has always owned my heart.*

From the outside looking in, we're both doing just fine.

He's the beloved captain of the Boston Blades.
I'm hustling my way to success with my photography business.

Then Jackson comes crashing back into my world, netting me a once-in-a-lifetime opportunity that can take my career to new heights.

Suddenly, I'm traveling with the Blades while desperately trying to keep my heart intact.

Hotel rooms. One-on-one interviews. Cross-country flights. Everywhere I turn, Jackson is there, a temptation I'm barely able to resist.

Until I stop resisting altogether.

One heart-wrenching kiss. One forbidden touch. We may not be married anymore but one thing still hasn't changed—Jackson is mine.

And I'm forever his.

Cover Design & Artwork: Najla Qamber, Qamber Designs

Editing: Kathy Bosman, Indie Editing Chick

Proofreaders: Tandy Proofreads; Dawn Black

❀ Created with Vellum

To all the badass players of the NHL.
To their equally badass girlfriends and wives and mothers and
sisters who support them on the ice and off.
And to Celine Dion -
This one's for you.

Good job, honey.

CHAPTER 1
HOLLY
BOSTON, MASSACHUSETTS

The groom is sporting hard wood.

And I'm not referring to the hockey stick he wields around TD Garden for the Boston Blades. No, I'm talking about the metaphorical type of wood—the one that sprang to life in his black tuxedo pants the minute his bride, Zoe, began the walk of all walks down the center aisle of Boston's historical Trinity Church.

My knees burn against the scratchy red rug as I angle my camera to snap a photo of the groom's awestruck expression. While Andre Beaumont—King Sin Bin to hockey fans across the country—may have hired me as his wedding photographer, I'm pretty sure he's not interested in having his erection memorialized in between pictures of Zoe's gorgeous, ivory lace gown and the flower girl prancing down the aisle like a cotton ball made of tulle.

Then again, it's the ball-busting kind of photo that his teammates and brothers-in-hockey-gear would kill to get their hands on, and Andre should have known better than to rope me into this gig.

Swallowing an ill-timed laugh, my fingers slide over the camera's familiar black, plastic frame.

1

Click.

One inappropriate photo down. Only one hundred-plus elegant ones to go.

Wedding photography isn't my thing. And, sure, maybe it's because I lived the Happily Ever After fairytale and came out on the other side with my gold band tucked away in my dresser and my newly signed divorce papers doused in wine, sweet-and-sour sauce, and dried tears.

It was a rough night.

Scratch that—it's been a rough three years.

Like a moth to a flame, I lower the camera and slide my gaze to the second groomsman standing to the right of Andre. My grandmother once called him "strapping." Accurate, I'll admit, albeit begrudgingly. He's built like a linebacker: tall and broad with muscular thighs that strain the fabric of his tuxedo pants. Dark brown hair that's casually tousled in the same style he's worn for years now. Even when he graced the glossy front page of *Sports Illustrated* last February, he looked exactly the same.

Some things change . . . he hasn't.

Hard, square jaw. Formidable body. Shrewd brown eyes that I imagine terrify his opponents on the ice when he comes barreling toward them.

Jackson Carter.

Captain of the Boston Blades.

Otherwise known as my ex-husband.

Those astute dark eyes meet mine now, and I wait for the rush of familiar emotions to hit me like a freight train. Only, before I have the chance to do my usual shushing of my heart, Jackson's full lips part and he mouths something that looks *suspiciously* like, "Did you just take a picture of his dick?"

And that right there, *that's* the reason why I've felt so lost for the last three years.

Our marriage didn't crumble because one of us cheated.

Jackson isn't that sort of guy, and I've always been a one-man kind of woman.

It didn't combust in a ball of fiery flames because we fought like we were prepping our audition tapes for that trashy reality TV show *Marriage Boot Camp*.

No, we simply . . . grew apart.

He passed out on the couch.

I slept in the bed.

He ate meals with his teammates.

I chowed down on mine alone at my desk, late into the evening hours after my employees had already gone home to their families.

He reached out to Andre or the Blades goalie, Duke Harrison, when he needed to talk.

I acted like smothering my emotions was as easy as breathing.

Eleven years ago, I married the man who swept me off my feet during my first semester at Cornell University.

A year ago, we sat opposite each other at a wooden table, our feet locked on our respective sides instead of tangling together the way we'd always done, nothing but our signatures standing in the way of a divorce.

The cry fest with the Chinese food and wine came later that night. No matter how alone I'd felt prior to finalizing our divorce, spending that first night in our house—empty but for the select furniture I'd kept—had been a hard pill to swallow. Accepting the fact that we'd failed at the *till death do us* part of our vows was even more difficult.

Camera feeling heavy in my hands, I lift my gaze from Jackson's mouth and return silently: "Blackmail."

His eyes crinkle at the corners, and my pathetic heart dives into an incessant *thud-thud-thud* that could rival the quick-paced tempo of an EDM song. *Dammit.* Those creasing laugh lines are more attractive than they have any right to be. Hell, the fact that I still find Jackson attractive at all feels like unjust punishment, doled out for some unknown bad misdeed I've committed in life. Considering my worst transgression of late is accidentally tossing half a burger into a recycling bin, the unyielding attraction seems a bit unfair.

He drags his thumb across his bottom lip, in that revealing way of his that tells me he's trying to wrestle back a grin, and I nearly hurl my camera at his head in retribution.

I can just imagine the newspaper headlines now: *Ex-wife of Famous NHL Player Interrupts Wedding of the Season by Flying Camera—Updates to Follow.*

Once upon a time, I'd made it my mission to make Jackson's infamous steel resolve disintegrate in inappropriate places. He always got me back—generally in bed with me fisting the sheets and his tight body powering into mine.

Now, I swallow hard at the memories and divert my attention to the bride.

Zoe radiates warmth and happiness. When her lips turn up behind the gossamer fabric of her veil, I readjust my grip on the camera and rise to my haunches. Knees cracking, I scoot back to avoid blocking someone's view. The five bridesmaids to my left all smile, as if on cue, and I catch a shot of them, too.

The light streaming in through the stained-glass windows paints them in a mural of jeweled tones, and I know—even if I make my living taking photos of professional athletes—that the picture will be one that's kept on their walls for years to come.

I get Zoe next, just as she steps up to meet Andre and her father gives her away.

Whether or not Andre is still sporting wood, I've got no idea. I keep my gaze above the belt, so to speak, as I step into the dance that's become as familiar to me as breathing over the last number of years: finding the best angles for the best photos.

Beaumont looks down at his bride like she's his greatest

gift, and then he throws tradition out the window by lifting the veil and smoothing it back over her head with a mammoth-sized hand.

The Blades' toughest son of a bitch grins, looks at the priest, and announces, "Sorry, Father, I'll always be the worst kind of sinner."

"Andre—" Zoe's hands flutter upward.

He promptly cradles her face with one hand, binds an arm around her back, and, without giving anyone the chance to object, drops a heady kiss onto her mouth.

"Hell fucking yeah!" shouts one of the guys from the groom's side. "Get it, man. Get. It!"

Someone in the pews follows up with an equally boisterous, "Don't get her pregnant in the church, dude!"

The guests roar with laughter, palms kissing with thunderous applause.

I capture it all on camera:

Zoe's wide gaze as her fiancé steals a kiss before the ceremony officially begins.

The top of Andre's dark head as he glides his mouth over his bride's, his hand flexing at the small of her back, as though he's desperate to strip her out of the gown and touch her bare skin.

The bridesmaids whistling.

Father Christopher's red face and twitching lips.

My lens finds Jackson.

Click.

His hands dive into the pockets of his well-tailored pants.

Click.

He grazes his teeth over his lower lip.

Click.

Familiar brown eyes land on my face, startling in their intensity.

Click.

Long ago, he'd look at me just like he is now and whisper in that rough, endearing Texas drawl of his, "Always you."

The sentiment used to send my heart soaring.

Now he only averts his gaze, stubbled cheeks hollowing with a heavy breath, and turns back to the bride and groom.

Click.

The final shutter of the camera mimics the steady rhythm of my heart.

One inappropriate photo down.

Five too many pictures of my ex-husband already catalogued.

Father Christopher clears his throat. "Perhaps we can hold off on the impregnating until after we exchange vows?"

I snort.

And then the four-year-old ring bearer seals Andre Beaumont's sinner status for good. Thrusting one little arm up in the air as Andre releases Zoe and steps back, the kid shouts, "Mommy! Mommy, Mr. Beaumont has a sword in his pants! *I* want one that big!"

I find Andre's shocked expression with my lens.

Click.

I may not have the husband or the white picket fence or the two-point-five kids, but goddamn it, I love my job.

Some days, it feels like enough.

CHAPTER 2
HOLLY

I hate my job.

Beneath my office desk, my bare toes curl into the area rug I picked out five years ago when Carter Photography became something more concrete than an idea percolating in my head. I've had staff come and go, but this rug has been a constant through it all.

Why are you thinking about the damn rug?

Ahem. Probably because I don't want to contemplate the proposition Steven Fairfax has laid out for me. A proposal that . . . oh God, it'd be *hell*. Like, 'jump feet first into a vat of molten lava and then roll around in the sand' sort of hell.

Black eyes blink back at me from across my desk. "Do you want me to go over all of that again, Ms. Carter?"

Snagging a pen off the top of my planner, I tap the butt against the desk. "I'm going to shoot it straight with you, Steven—do you mind if I call you Steven?"

The producer from ESPN's top competitor, Sports 24/7, continues his one-sided staring contest. More rapid blinking ensues, and I'm forced to consider being a good Samaritan and offer my eye drops. Or maybe I threw him for a loop by not leaping for joy ten minutes ago when he broke out the projector and analytical graphs to brag about his TV network's annual audience numbers compared to ESPN's. Honestly, it was all very reminiscent of a whose-dick-is-bigger competition.

According to Steven Fairfax's presentation, Sports 24/7 would be the uncomfortably large variety only found in pornos.

Either way, not even a symbolic ten-inch penis can change my mind.

See: the vat of molten lava and sand bit.

He treats me to a creepy tongue swipe, along with another round of robust blinking. "Will you take the offer?"

Over my dead body.

I shove one foot into a ballet slipper, then do the same with the other. Time for business. "Listen, Steven, it's quite an honor that you flew out here from L.A. to talk to me about your new show—"

"Getting Pucked."

Adding insult to injury, the show's name is downright cringeworthy despite the intentional pun. And, if memory serves me well, my grandmother also had a hockey romance novel on her bookshelf by the same name.

The depressing fact is, "getting pucked" in reality isn't as amazing as fiction makes it out to be—although is reality ever better?

At Steven's impatient drumming of his fingers on my desk, I force a tight smile. "Right, *Getting Pucked*." More smiling on my part; my lips peel back from my teeth and I briefly worry that I look positively feral. When Steven doesn't shirk back in fear, I let out a controlled sigh of relief. "Listen, it sounds like a great premise. It really does, but—"

"Nothing's been done like this for hockey before. Football? There's *Hard Knocks* over on HBO and *A Football Life* televised by the NFL Network, but *Getting Pucked* has the ability to blow those successes out of the water. It's a gamechanger for Sports 24/7." Steven's dark eyes brighten with excitement as he fidgets with the stiff collar of his dress shirt. "Can you imagine it? An intimate camera crew following the players of the Boston Blades—getting in their heads, observing their daily lives, showing the world what it really means to play for the NHL."

I'm not buying it. Yes, I have my own reasons for not wanting Carter Photography to act as a sacrificial lamb for the cause but, ignoring the elephant in the room named Jackson Carter for a hot second, Steven has yet to answer one pressing question . . .

"Why the Blades?" I ask. "Why not the Kings since your studios are in L.A? Or even the Blackhawks? Let's get real—Chicago won the Cup last year, not us."

I say "us" like I still watch the Blades, which I don't.

Seeing Jackson in his element does funny things to my stomach and inevitably leads to devouring a gallon of Moose Tracks ice cream in a single sitting.

It's not a pretty sight to behold.

Steven sits back, hands interlacing over his round belly. "You want to get real, *Holly*?" His mouth curls in a smarmy grin. "The truth is, everyone knows the Blades are on the verge of a complete overhaul. Half their first line is predicted to retire this year. Duke Harrison, for one. Who knows what'll happen next season with him gone—the Blades have operated on a we-have-the-Mountain-and-we're-good rationale for at least four years, and it's no secret that Tommy Kase isn't ready to fill Harrison's shoes. Then there's talks of Weston Cain bowing out. Man's already got one reconstructed hip on the books."

I wince at the mention of the Blades' defenseman. At twenty-eight, Cain is still young, but the sport doesn't play nice when you've got a penchant for dropping gloves and throwing fists. The body might be a temple, but on the ice, it's a punching bag on the best of days and roadkill on the worst.

"And then there's Jackson Carter."

My gaze cuts to Steven's, even as my stomach twists with unease. "Oh? What about him?"

"There're *rumors*."

He says it like I should know what he's talking about. Me, the wife. The *ex*-wife. Jackson and I might be friendly whenever we cross paths—like we were at Andre and Zoe's wedding two weekends ago—but we don't talk otherwise. I don't pick up my phone to send him a *how are you?* text, and he definitely doesn't reach out either.

The Cold War has reached Boston, Massachusetts, my friends.

Appropriate, I think, since it's so damn cold out for half the year. Which couldn't be more different than my hometown of Natchitoches, Louisiana—a small, historical blip on the map some three hours outside of New Orleans. Living in New England for more than a decade, though, has thickened my blood in more ways than one.

I set the pen down and push away from my desk to stand. "Steven, personal reasons aside"—it's not like he didn't blatantly check out my bare ring finger when he first walked in—"Carter Photography isn't equipped to handle the scale of a production like *Getting Pucked*. We're a small company that packs a big punch, but we have our limits."

"That's what we want."

Yeah, sure he does. I resist the urge to roll my eyes. "Right now, you *think* that's what you want. But when we're knee-deep in preseason, and there are multiple players' storylines to relay to the viewers, whose do we prioritize?" Folding my arms over my pink knit dress, I tilt my head and study him. "I know where you're going with this—you want the ex-wife of the Blades' beloved captain trailing him and making you some damn good TV. If you wanted this to succeed, you would have approached a media firm that's as deep as the Blades' roster." My chin lifts. "Instead, you chose me. Us.

Carter Photography. Ten employees total—three of which are strictly admin."

Not even an eye twitch from the peanut gallery. Watching me steadily, Steven says, "Carter Photography has won multiple awards in the last few years. Your photos have graced the front page of every big-time sports magazine in the States. Every pro-sports team in the Boston area has you on their payroll because of the quality that you deliver—you and your nine other employees."

He's not wrong.

In the last few years, the company has skyrocketed to heights I never even allowed myself to consider tangible. Carter Photography started as nothing more than a hobby. It was my way of discovering what made *me* happy when faced day in and day out with the fire Jackson applied to his career. Living with a formidable force like my ex-husband . . . Well, it was either start a fire of my own or be swept up in the maelstrom that was his everyday life.

I opted for the former at the risk of being destroyed by the latter.

Turns out, my knack for taking pictures was something others appreciated. The New England Patriots have us creating visual anecdotes that they use on their social media platforms. The Boston Celtics have us on speed dial—every time they want innovation in the form of commercials or mini-documentaries about their players, Carter Photography is the first firm they call.

I might not be able to spiral a football or shoot a free throw, but I've spent the latter part of my twenties and early thirties making Carter Photography indispensable to New England's professional sports teams.

And it cost you everything, didn't it?

My lids fall shut, and I rock back on my heels as though experiencing the blow of my failed marriage all over again.

Where's Ben & Jerry when you need them?

"I won't lie," Steven says, "your rocky relationship with Jackson Carter only makes this all the more interesting. But your divorce isn't why I flew out to Boston, Holly." When I look his way, he plants his hand down on the spreadsheets he laid out earlier in our meeting. "The teams love you and your company, and if you ever opened Carter Photography to franchises outside of the Northeast, you'd be swamped with offers. So, we're bringing L.A. and Sports 24/7 to you here in Beantown."

I swallow, my mouth feeling parched like I've skipped the liquids and have gone straight for sawdust. "Only tourists call Boston Beantown."

"Right." He raps his knuckles on the desk, once, twice. "Whaddaya say? You agree to be the director of photography behind *Getting Pucked* and we'll supply any additional staff you need to make this happen—their wages on us. We need your eye for storytelling—the way you instinctively know where the camera needs to be—and the guys feel comfortable with you."

It's on the tip of my tongue to say that the guys are comfortable because they've known me as Jackson's wife for far longer than they've known me as the ex. At the end of the day, though, if there's anyone who can convince them to open up their lives on TV, it's me.

"Did the board sign off on production already?" I ask, moving to the floor-to-ceiling glass window that overlooks Arlington Street and Boston Common. If I stare hard enough through the clusters of trees, I can spot tourists meandering through the park.

Behind me, Steven grunts his affirmation. "Already done. Contracts have been signed for months now—we were only waiting till the beginning of preseason to start. Other shows film training during the summer but we want in on the real action. That's priority, and you're the missing puzzle piece to the master plan."

Preseason begins in less than three weeks, which means Sports 24/7 sure waited a long time before approaching me. With a timeline like theirs, it doesn't take a rocket scientist to figure out that, despite the silver-tongued bullshit being spewed, Carter Photography was not their first choice. Might not have been their second or third either.

I'm the farthest thing from a rocket scientist.

Unfortunately for Mr. Steven Fairfax, however, I'm no pushover. I learned from the best—my grandmother who raised my brother and me, all while owning and solely operating a corner store after my granddaddy died. Once, she even pulled a gun on a man who dared rob *her* store. She fired, too. Caught him right in the ass as he was fleeing the scene.

Crazy woman ruled with an iron fist until her death this year, and I like to think that some of that bullheadedness trickled down to me.

In droves.

I rest my backside against the windowpane and stare at the gussied-up L.A. businessman seated at my desk. Unlike him, I don't bother beating around the bush. "Let's talk pay."

Steven's brows shoot up at my boldness. It takes him a second to recover, but then he's leaning forward to riffle through his papers. He slips one sheet from the rest and slides it across the desk with the tip of one finger. "I think you'll be pleased with the number we've come up with for you."

I kill the immediate eagerness in my chest. *Don't let him read you like that.* Until recently, my emotions were as transparent as the swirling winds just before a hurricane. I hid nothing. I lived my life in unedited freedom, always convinced that every person I met was just another friendship waiting to be started.

Learning the truth about my parents in my grandmother's will changed all that.

But only the living can adjust to what secrets the dead

reveal. Time *that* particular revelation with my divorce, and is it any wonder why my heart went on lockdown?

I approach the desk and quickly scan the contract. My jaw hardens when I spot the number that's highlighted and bolded. Underlined twice, too, just in case I couldn't see it otherwise. There could be unicorn stickers on that sheet and it still wouldn't impress me.

It's just like a ten-inch dick to be all show and no delivery.

Steven mistakes my silence for shock. "Exciting, I know. That's a healthy price for four months of work," Steven murmurs like we're in on our own little secret. "And, of course, all of your expenses will be compensated for by the network. Travel, accommodations, dining. We pay the best *for* the best."

"Double it and I'll sign the contract today."

"*What*?"

I meet his gaze without flinching. "You said that the contracts with the Blades were signed months ago. And yet, you're here just three weeks before preseason starts. The first game is on September fifteenth. A network like yours wouldn't show up so close to deadline unless you were in a tough spot." Knuckles planted on the desk, I try to look more intimidating than my five-foot-one frame will ever be. "I can read between the lines, Steven. You tried to hire other companies first. For whatever reason, they turned you down. And so here you are."

His Adam's apple dodges down his throat. "And so here I am," he rasps, the rapid blinking resuming once again.

He's out of luck—there's no way I'm offering my eye drops now.

Sorry, not sorry, buddy.

"You're out of options and signing this contract puts me in an unfavorable position." Let's face it, spending hours upon hours in Jackson's company will send me into diabetic shock. I'll be lucky if I don't drive good ol' Moose Tracks into early extinction. "Here's how this is going to work. Double it, or Carter Photography is off the table and you're back to square one."

Checkmate.

As I wait for Steven Fairfax to answer, I make a point to keep my expression neutral.

He makes another pass of his tongue along his bottom lip. Then reaches into his briefcase to pull out yet another folder. Setting it on the desk, he flicks it open and spins it around so that the words are legible from where I stand.

"You know," he drawls with a subtle edge, "your ex-husband warned us that you wouldn't agree to our first offer. Seems he still knows you pretty well."

Every thought scatters on my next exhale.

I shake my head, mouth parting and then snapping closed as the words sink in. *Jackson* spoke to him? It sounds so utterly ludicrous that laughter bubbles to life in my chest, demanding to be released in all of its sarcastic, bitter glory.

Not now. Be professional!

"I'm sorry"—my gaze falls to the contract pinned to the desk under my palm—"but did you say that *Jackson* told you that I'd ask for more money? When in the world . . . why would he—"

"We were required to meet with every player to re-verify that they would allow us to film them. The owner's request when we first did our rounds. Same with the coaches." Sports 24/7's producer only shrugs. "Only this time, Carter wouldn't sign unless you were the one who . . . Well, you can see where I'm going with this."

You can see where I'm going with this.

Oh yeah. I can *absolutely* see where Steven Fairfax is going with this, and my professional veneer cracks a little more. So, it wasn't at all that Sports 24/7 had gone through other companies before arriving at mine. Or maybe they had. Hell, maybe they'd even gone so far as to sign on one of the countless firms across the country—until Jackson threw a goddamn wrench in their plans and had them spinning a complete one-eighty in the opposite direction.

A direction that points unfailingly at me.

My fingers clench at my sides, nails carving half-moons into my palms.

I'm going to kill him—and I'm going to make it hurt, too.

His precious hockey stick right to the twin pucks between his legs.

It'd serve him right for interfering with my life after we made the *joint* decision to go our separate ways.

I stride to my office door and yank it open so hard that Shelby, my poor assistant, flings herself at the wall. The folder she was holding drops to the floor and her hands lift in the air as if to shield her face.

After three years of working together, her reaction doesn't come as a shock. She's an aspiring actress with a love for drama, even if she's never had a single callback. Every few months she tells me that her big break is coming and that she's preparing her resignation letter—and every time, she waltzes back into the office the very next morning like nothing happened.

Even so, I'm totally going to have to pick up her favorite peanut butter brownies from Mike's Pastry on the way in tomorrow or she'll be giving me the stink eye for the rest of the week.

When Steven calls out my name, I glance over my shoulder at him.

He gestures to the papers spread about my desk. "Do we have a deal? You take the six-figures and you sign on with *Getting Pucked* for four short months. This will be *massive* exposure for your business. Massive."

Thirty minutes ago, I'd been hesitant to sign onto a project that would have me working in close spaces with Jackson for months. Hesitant, but still intrigued, despite my reservations.

A job like this could be the difference between keeping the business relegated to New England or expanding across the country.

But knowing what I do now—that Jackson won't even commit to the show unless Carter Photography is involved—my answer is a lot firmer than a *maybe*.

My fingers circle the doorknob. "No deal, Mr. Fairfax. You can tell Jackson Carter that I don't need his pity. Better yet, I'll tell him myself."

The Cold War is about to come to a boiling, explosive end.

Damn you, Jackson. Damn. You.

CHAPTER 3
JACKSON

I 'm eating baked chicken at my kitchen island when I hear it.

Or, should I say, when I hear *her*.

"Jackson!"

Puncturing the chicken with my fork, I lean back on my stool and eye the front door like there's a mythical Yeti on the other side instead of a slip of a woman whose head doesn't even reach my chin.

I wait for her Southern drawl to holler again as I chew . . . and nearly choke swallowing the chicken down.

Shit, that's awful.

After thirty-four years of drawing air into my lungs, there's no hiding from the fact that my skills don't extend to the kitchen.

Holly knew it.

I know it.

My goddamn stomach knows it.

I eye my dinner with distaste. *I should have ordered takeout.*

"Jackson!" she shouts, voice tinny as it echoes through the front wall of my Back Bay condo, followed by the insistent hammering of her fist on the door. "Jackson, open up right now or I'll-I'll—"

There really should be a rulebook on dealing with ex-wives. Then again, I've never been all that good at following the rules—not when it comes to Holly, the only woman I've ever loved. She had me wrapped around her finger the minute we met at Cornell during my junior year and not much has changed since then. Divorced or not, there's not a damn thing I wouldn't do for her if she needed me.

But there's only one reason she'd show up unannounced today, which means she's out for blood. Once upon a time, Pissed-Off Holly came in second place only to Sexed-Up Holly, our limbs tangled together after a round of hard sex.

Since the sex is off the table and has been for the better part of two years, I set down my fork and ditch dinner in favor of heading for the front door. *Time to face the music . . .*

And prepare for the knife that's bound to be angled for my jugular the moment we're face to face.

I catch sight of my reflection in the mirror opposite the door. Thanks to extra physical conditioning at practice today —one of the guys decided to mouth back to Coach Hall—I look like hell. Not that it matters much.

Holly isn't here to do the admiring stint.

More heavy knocking that's loud enough for my neighbors on the floor below to hear. Then, "*Jack—*"

The rest of my name is swallowed by a short-lived shriek when I swing open the door and catch her off guard. She rights herself at the last moment, color blooming on her cheeks as her fingers accidentally graze my chest in her struggle to keep from wiping out. *My* fingers twitch at my sides, which is better than giving into the disastrous urge to haul her upright and touch my skin to hers. Would she feel the same? Taste the same? I've got no shame in admitting that the questions haunt me more nights than not.

Keeping my treacherous fingers to myself, I give her a

quick once-over that's done sooner than it began. Wavy, long, blond hair tucked behind her ears. Blue eyes that have always —*always*—reminded me of the Texas sky in my hometown, Zachsville. A trim body: small breasts, nipped in waist, narrow hips. Holly has always been small in everything but personality, graceful entrances notwithstanding.

Dipping my chin, I look down and meet her gaze. "You stop by for dinner?"

We both know that she didn't stop by for my half-assed cooking, and she does that Holly thing where she scrapes the inside of her thumb with the nail of her index finger. When she's pissed, the finger scraping commences.

Willing to press my luck so I can see her all fired up, I casually lean against the doorjamb, arms linked over my chest. "Havin' baked chicken in case you were wondering what's on the menu."

Her glossy, pink lips part. Clamp closed a second later.

"Gotta give you a disclaimer, though." I lift my left hand, index finger and thumb millimeters apart. "It's about *this* dry."

More finger scraping. And then she ups the ante by blowing out a long breath that does nothing to alleviate the stick from her ass that's keeping her back ramrod straight. "You set the temperature on four-fifty again. Didn't you."

Not a question. She knows me too well.

She was *your wife.*

Was. Operative word there.

"You caught me." In another life, I would have winked and turned up the charm. Had her laughing hard enough at my pathetic cooking skills that she'd drag me down for a kiss and simply order pizza instead. I don't wink now. I do, however, turn up the charm, knowing that it'll drive her up a wall and I'll reap the benefits when her cheeks turn rosy and her eyes darken from a sky blue to the turbulent navy hue of Boston's harbor. Shrugging, I drawl, "Never fails that I forget I'm cooking in the first place."

"Too busy watching clips again?"

Always. You don't get to where I'm at in the NHL by not making the most out of every hour of the day—and, for over a decade, I've done nothing but breathe in hockey and exhale league-crushing stats. I'm the two-time winner of the Art-Ross trophy for most points scored during the regular season, once during my short, one-year stint with the Dallas Stars and the other time with the Boston Bruins, and am *also* the winner of The Conn Smythe award. I've hoisted the Stanley Cup up in the air with the aid of my former team, the Bruins, and have made the playoffs every year that I've been with the Blades. "Watching clips" is my adaptation of scrolling through Facebook or Buzzfeed.

I'm a man with tunnel vision, but sometimes that tunnel vision has got faulty wiring.

And I'm not blind to the fact that my dedication to the sport robbed me of a balanced life outside the rink. More specifically, it robbed me of a lifetime with Holly. I don't regret much in life, but . . . Well, let's just say that I've got a first-class ticket on the Wishful Thinking train. Here's to hoping that one day I'll be able to look at the woman in front of me and not feel the needle of regret pricking my calloused skin.

Hands empty, I settle for another shrug. "Nothing a little BBQ sauce can't fix. Trust me, you can't even see the chicken at this point."

Her nose wrinkles. "I'm not even going to respond to that."

"Disgusting, I know."

She rolls her eyes, and then, without waiting for me to do the whole welcome to my humble abode bit, shoulders past me and enters the condo I purchased six months ago. I'm not surprised that she knows where I moved to, considering that I know that she opted for a modern apartment overlooking the Charles River after she sold our historic Cambridge triple-decker.

The money from the sale spontaneously appeared in my bank account a few weeks after we finalized our divorce. Along with a short email that got straight to the point: *I know the lawyers gave me the house, but it's not right for me to keep the money from it. You purchased it. Not me. We'll call it even.*

Even.

I almost snort.

Holly and I aren't even *close* to being even. Not in this lifetime.

"You've got a lot of nerve, you know that?" Her flats squeak against the marble flooring as she whirls around to face me, hands balled into fists at her sides. "So much goddamned nerve."

I jut my chin in the direction of my abandoned dinner. "I promise the chicken isn't protesting the smothering. It was a unanimous decision—mutually beneficial to us both."

Her jaw visibly tightens. "You have no idea how tempted I am to—"

"Eat with me? There's a lone chicken breast on the stove, begging to be dressed with ketchup, just the way you like it." I'm fucking with her, riling her up in the way that I know throws her off course.

She doesn't disappoint.

Cheeks flushing, Holly drags in a deep breath. Smooths her perfectly blown-out hair behind her ears. Sets her hands on her hips and squares off against me like some sort of Texan daredevil from the old Western days, pistol strapped to her thigh and a corset cinched around her waist.

"You knew that I'd find out and you meddled anyway."

Guess we're doing this.

I spin on my heel and head for the kitchen. If you were to Google "open floor plan," my condo would fit the bill.

Exposed brick walls. Not a single doorway in sight when you first enter. The living room and kitchen make up some eight-hundred square feet. The floor-to-ceiling windows on the far side of the room allow for natural light and offer a gorgeous view of the harbor.

There's no way I'll ever give up living on the coast. Not even for the chance to return to good ol' landlocked Zachsville once I retire—I've been gone from Texas almost longer than I lived there.

Holly's shoes echo off the marble as she trails me.

"Jackson, can we not do the avoidance thing for once?"

Pulling open the top cupboard, I palm a plate and glance over my shoulder to look at the woman who stole my heart within weeks of meeting her. "We're gonna have this conversation like civilized people," I mutter, not missing the way her blue eyes skirt down my body.

I hate that I can't read her worth a damn. Though the stiff expression she's rocking is all I need to know that she's shut herself off from me. *What else did you expect? Y'all aren't married anymore.*

Reflexively, my grip tightens on the plate.

"I'm not in the mood for wine," she tells me after a minute.

"No wine." I pick up the tongs and slide the chicken from pan to plate. "Baked chicken for one coming up." I spoon mashed potatoes next to the chicken, then follow up with a helping of baked beans reheated straight from a can. *Welcome to the Culinary House of Carter: Yelp Rated, 1.7-stars.* Setting the plate onto the kitchen island next to mine, I move to the fridge and grab the ketchup while I'm at it.

Never let it be said that I don't have Holly's best interests at heart.

"Jackson—"

I lift my brows at her as I settle on the stool again. "Want to talk? Eat some dinner and we'll talk."

26

"I really—"

I don't even hesitate to cut her off with a lifted hand. Give Holly the chance, and she'll talk my head off for the next ten hours straight. Only now I can't invent creative ways to shut her up. Can't swallow her words with a hot kiss that'll make her legs quiver and her lids fall shut as she sinks into my frame. *She doesn't belong to you anymore.* Yeah, as if I could ever forget.

"I'm takin' a guess—you didn't eat lunch today?"

She squirms at that, fingers plucking fruitlessly at her pretty pink dress. "I was busy."

"You're always busy." I gesture to the stool next to mine. "What do the Italians say again? *Mangia?*"

Cringing at my horrid pronunciation, she mutters, "Something like that."

Holly's short and the stool is tall, and I don't bother to hide a grin when she tries to primly hop up—and subsequently bounces right off. The hem of her dress reveals a strip of smooth skin that I stare at a little too long. Flashing me an accusatory glance, she yanks on the fabric and hauls herself up for a second try. She succeeds, just barely, hands fluttering around her dress to hide the goods away from the likes of me.

When her blue eyes find my face, I purposely cast my gaze down to her ass. "You're the very picture of grace, Holls."

Nostrils flaring, she snags the knife off my plate and the fork from hers and proceeds to cut into the dry chicken. Sans ketchup. Bless her heart.

She pops the bite into her mouth, not an inkling of dread underlining her expression. I steel my shoulders and bide my time by taking a pull from my water bottle. Count down the seconds in my head like a ticking time bomb until she realizes she made a grave error in ignoring the peace offering that came in the form of Heinz ketchup.

One . . .

Two . . .

A gurgling sound rumbles in her throat as utensils clatter to the granite. Hands lifting to her collarbone, she coughs like she's just inhaled her very first cigarette.

"Holy cr—"

She barely gets the words out before erupting into a coughing fit so volatile I'm surprised the windows don't rattle.

Because I'm a gentleman, I uncap my water bottle and silently hand it over. Then I make a point to *s-l-o-w-l-y* swirl my next piece of chicken through a puddle of BBQ sauce. Her color high, she eyes me like she's seconds away from stealing my fork and stabbing me with the tines.

I smile, just a little. "I promise that it wasn't my plan to avoid talking about *Getting Pucked* by killin' you."

Droplets of water glisten on her lips when she gulps down another fistful of water. "You can be such a jerk," she mutters.

At one point in time, she thought my jokes and dry humor were hilarious. We clearly aren't those same people anymore, and so I shake off the ashes of our failed marriage from my heart and hunker down to business.

It's what she came here for, after all.

Propping an elbow on the kitchen island, I angle my body to face her completely. "You're really that pissed off that I did you a solid?"

"Did me a *solid*?" She shoves the plate away and spins her stool so that we're eye-to-eye. Or, as much as we can ever be eye-to-eye, considering I dwarf her by a foot and some change. Shaking her head, she snorts out her disbelief. "You didn't do me a solid, Jackson. You practically blackmailed Sports 24/7 into hiring me!"

"I wouldn't use the word 'blackmail.'"

Her blond brows arch high. "No? What word would you use then? *Browbeat?*"

I lean my weight into the hand on my thigh so that we are,

in fact, eye-to-eye. Her nose is inches from mine when I counter, "Negotiate works."

This close, I can see that her pupils are dilated. Anger, not lust. Her cheeks are tinged the same hue as her pink dress.

"*Negotiate* implies that you gave them a choice in the matter. But you didn't give them that choice—either they hired me or you walked out."

If I'd known Holly would freak out over this, I would have kept my damn mouth shut. *And this is why you can't be friends with your exes. Nothing good ever comes of it.*

I move my hand from my thigh to my knee. Edge a smidge closer to her because I've never been one to avoid using my size to press my case. "They could have let me walk. They could have opted for another team, but they didn't. Sports 24/7 wants me—"

"God, your ego knows no bounds, does it?"

"—and to have me, they had to have you, too."

CHAPTER 4
HOLLY

Jackson is a stubborn son of a gun.

This is the same man who, seven years back, brought the Boston Bruins to a Stanley Cup victory on a broken patella (*not* the same thing as *paella*, the delicious Spanish seafood dish). It was game seven, down to the last period, and he clinched the win with the dirtiest slapshot in NHL history that's *still* shown on highlight reels years later.

He played through the pain, never revealing the magnitude of his agony until the final buzzer sounded and he was ensconced safely in the locker room.

Full disclosure, that damn knee cap was threatening to pull a peep show out of his skin. A sight that had me seeing triple when I fought my way to his side and took one look at him, hockey pants stripped off his muscular form and perspiration dotting his temple. He took my hand and comforted *me* when my legs turned into cooked spaghetti. Me, as though I was the one with a broken *paella*. Patella. Whatever.

Every sports journalist loved him that spring. They nicknamed him the Badass of Hockey. The Beast of the Northeast. The one man who'd put the victory of his team above his own health.

It's not in his DNA to give up or step down when confronted with adversity.

Except with us.

I shove the errant thought away like a fly zipping annoyingly around my head.

Fix my attention on the face that's as familiar to me as my own. My fingers clench together in my lap. "It was a pity negotiation and you know it. But I don't need your help. I'm good on my own. I'm *succeeding* on my own." At the vehemence in my tone, his dark eyes turn flinty and unapproachable. "I don't want your handouts, Jackson, you know that."

When he says nothing at all, my stupid mouth gets the best of me—as it always does—and I seek to fill the silence. "I spent so many years living on your income, on the perks of you playing for the NHL, and I was so, so clear that I didn't want that to continue. I'm not trying to be ungrateful, or sound like a spoiled brat, but I need to stand on my own. Can't you see that? I need to know that my success comes from my own drive and ambition, and not because of what connections you've made in *your* career."

Those connections may have helped me in the very beginning, but I've come so far since then. I would never interfere with his relationship with the Blades. Is it so wrong to expect that level of respect in return?

Jackson lifts a hand to his face, thumb scrubbing along his lower lip.

He's not trying to hold back a smile right now. His expression is grave. The smile lines at the corners of his eyes almost smooth—or as smooth as they'll ever be. Then he speaks, his voice such a low timbre that I nearly tip forward in my need to hear what he has to say.

"You ever think that maybe me *blackmailing* Sports 24/7 has nothing to do with pity and everything to do with needing *you* on the other side of that camera?"

My heart gives a wild, traitorous thump. Stupid, stupid organ. "I . . . Jackson, I don't even know what to—"

"Say?" He shakes his head, his dark hair flopping forward over his forehead. Long, blunt-tipped fingers roughly shove the thick strands back into place. "I won't lie—I knew this gig would be good for the business. You're big in New England, Holls, but this would do some serious legwork for your reach across the country."

I can sense the *but* coming along, and it's on the tip of my tongue to tell him to hurry it up already. *Patience, girl, have some damn patience.* Unsurprisingly, patience has never been a virtue of mine.

"But, and I'm sorry to disappoint, I didn't throw down for you in Coach's office because *Getting Pucked* would open doors for Carter Photography—not completely." Dark eyes lift to my face, unwavering in their intensity. "I did it for me."

His words aren't registering, not over the loud ringing in my ears. I swallow hard, then press my tongue against the back of my teeth as I wrack my brain for something to say— something that isn't, "Come again?"

In the end, my response isn't all that much better than the one voiced in my head. Nor does it sound any less incredulous. "How in the world would *me* being the one behind the camera help *you*?"

He shifts his large frame off the stool, and I know he's about to pace. A troubled Jackson is a pacing Jackson. I watch as he fists his hands behind his head, then I struggle to avert my gaze when the cotton clinging to the hard muscles of his torso lifts with his upraised arms.

My life would be so much easier if Jackson weren't at the top of his game and probably bench-pressing weights that are double my size—he looks way too good for my peace of mind.

Jaw ticking with an unnamed emotion, Jackson grinds out, "I need someone to run interference with what gets filmed.

The network required everyone's signature on a contract or the entire production was a bust. No matter how much I'd like to give Sports 24/7 the middle finger, the Blades need *Getting Pucked*. A show like this can lead to all sorts of sponsorships—a spotlight on our charities, cash in the bank for the team. I'd be an asshole to strip my guys of the opportunity because I want nothing to do with this shit."

Steven Fairfax's mention about the Blades overhauling the roster flits through my head, and I can't help but ask . . . "Are you retiring?"

"*What*?"

"Retiring," I repeat, lowering myself off the stool so I can step near him. "Are you planning to retire after this season?"

"Fuck no." He narrows his eyes, brows knitting together. His raised arms fall back to his sides when he demands, "Why the hell would you even ask that?"

"It was something the show's producer, Steven Fairfax, said to me today—about why Sports 24/7 wants the Blades on *Getting Pucked*'s first season." Needing to do something with my hands, I lock them over my chest and rock back on my heels. "They think Harrison is retiring this year, along with Weston Cain . . . and you."

Muscles balled tight under his T-shirt, Jackson prowls through the kitchen without sparing me a glance. "See?" he growls, and I'm not even sure he's speaking to me at this point. "*This* is the shit I'm talking about. They're vultures— analysts, journalists, Hollywood. All of them. Imagine if they saw one of the guys at the hospital or something, they'd already be marking me—any of *us*—as good-as-fucking-gone."

Snagging the plates off the kitchen island, he moves swiftly, aggressively, toward a trash can near the fridge and drops the dry chicken into the garbage. He sets the plates in the sink, then locks his hands on the lip of the counter, his back to me.

Shoulders hunched.

His sweatpants hanging low on his hips to reveal a quarter-inch of skin between his T-shirt and his waistband. That quarter-inch is tan, taut, and so incredibly tempting.

Nope, nope. Not happening!

Especially since my heart is warring a battle of its own: keep the space between us or rush forward and offer comfort with my arms linked around his waist and a kiss pressed to his back. Decisions, decisions, and only one is acceptable given the circumstances of our non-existent relationship.

Retreat now.

I take a tentative step back.

"It's the media, Jackson," I say, voice huskier than it has any right to be. I clear my throat. "They're going to say what they want to say, regardless of whether or not you participate in a reality show."

He leans his weight back on his heels, hands still locked on the edge of the counter. The T-shirt rides higher on his back, exposing twin dimples at the base of his spine.

Seriously? My gaze flits to the ceiling, then returns. A peek won't hurt, right? Not when he isn't even looking at me? For memory's sake, of course. Nothing more.

"Trust me," Jackson mutters, "I know what they're going to say after watching this season." He glances at me over his shoulder, his dark eyes pinning me in place. "I'm not retiring, Holls. Not yet, not until I'm ready."

"Then you're all set. If you're not planning to retire, then what secrets of yours am I keeping from the public? None. You can do this on your own. You're a big boy, Jackson."

Hands falling from the counter, he faces me completely. Thick, muscular legs spread to balance his weight. Strong chest stretching the fabric of his T-shirt. That elusive strip of bare skin now gone since he's standing upright.

If he's trying to prove that he's not a "big boy" but rather "all man," he's unfortunately missed his window of opportunity. I became aware of *that* particular fact years ago. Physically, he's massive—and the energy he radiates, just by breathing, only makes him seem that much more intimidating.

"Take the gig," he orders, voice low and compelling.

My chin lifts defiantly. "Regardless of how you feel about the show, the fact remains that Carter Photography wouldn't even be on Sports 24/7's radar if it weren't for you *needing* me behind the camera."

"And yet, me needing you entails a six-figure check landing in your bank account. Explain to me how you're on the bad end of this bargain again?"

Right or wrong, Jackson's manipulation of Sports 24/7's interest makes me feel . . . God, it makes me feel as though I'm right back where I started, scraping together a business on the back of someone else's success—*his* success, considering he was the one to beg the Blades' management to let me photograph the team in the first place. More specifically, though, it's a sharp reminder of the sacrifices I made to be with him.

Dropping out of Cornell—to my grandmother's horror—so that I could follow him to Boston after the Bruins drafted him.

Finishing my degree online at UMass Boston, so that I never worried over missed classes when I flew across the country to each and every one of his games.

Marriage is compromise in its greatest form. Our last-hurrah therapist told us that, but she was wrong. Marriage is compromise, yes, but never at the expense of who you are. Which is where I failed. Me, not Jackson. I lost myself so deeply that by the time I realized there might be a problem, I was already on the verge of drowning.

Jackson wasn't a bad husband.

He was good down to his core; always wanting to help others, to help me, but in living within his shadow for so many years, I became a returning secondary character on the Jackson Carter Show, simply known as "the wife."

Now I'm "the ex-wife," so I guess not much has changed.

Taking the *Getting Pucked* gig is the equivalent of starting all over again and I can't do that.

Not even for him.

Meeting his gaze, I say the words that I know he doesn't want to hear: "I don't need the six-figure check. Not everything is about the money."

I turn on the balls of my feet, ready to get the hell out of his condo before I do something I'll regret—like caving in to the vulnerability heating Jackson's gaze.

I don't get far.

A masculine hand wraps around my forearm, dragging me to a halt. Limiting my escape. And then he's right there, big body popping my personal bubble, spinning me around so that, to make eye contact, I've got to tip my head back, back, back because I'm so dang short.

Dark eyes flit over my face, searching. "If it's not about the money, then what are you lookin' for?"

"Happiness." I clasp my hand over his and peel his fingers off my arm, one by one, until I'm free. "It's staring at yourself in the mirror and knowing that you got to where you are on your own merits and not on bargained favors. It's knowing" —I draw in a deep, grounding breath—"that sometimes what's in your heart and what's in your head aren't the same, but you're making a life change . . . you're going to let reason take charge, for once, instead of the damn organ that's failed you countless times over."

His expressionless mask cracks. Splintering right there in front of me as he reaches for me and I scoot out of the way. "Fuck, Holly—"

"All these years," I say, cutting him off, "I've done what's best for *you*. I don't regret it. I don't regret *us*. But I can't—I can't be at your beck and call when you need me to put out your fires. We're not married. We're not together. And it's unfair of you to ask me to take one for the team simply because you think I'll be swayed by dollar signs."

Hurt creeps into my heart and I stamp it mercilessly into the ground. "I can't be won over by a check, no matter how big. There's no amount of money in the world that would convince me that it's a good idea to put myself back in your orbit day in and day out. We didn't work, Jackson, and I won't risk getting my heart all tangled up in you again."

I don't give him the opportunity to convince me otherwise.

What good would it do, anyway?

I don't regret loving Jackson Carter.

I don't even regret giving him every last corner of my soul, knowing that the alternative would mean giving up everything that I am now, my role as CEO of Carter Photography being at the top of the list. Perspective and personal growth, I try to remind myself when the gray clouds cling a little too tightly to my soul, is worth the heartache.

But I'll be damned if I take a backseat to Jackson's career all over again, just because he needs me to act as "interference" against a TV production he doesn't want sniffing around his personal life. I've had enough perspective and personal growth for one lifetime, thank you very much.

The money isn't worth it.

The potential fame isn't worth it.

Losing my heart, being sucked back into the downward spiral of depression, isn't worth it.

Not with Jackson. Not again.

CHAPTER 5
JACKSON

"**L**et's do another take. Jackson, can you, uh—"

The director's sentence withers when I glare in his direction, my helmet clasped between my hands as I rest my elbows on the boards at TD Garden.

First day of production for *Getting Pucked* and I'm *this* close to blowing my lid. Instead of training, me and my guys have been forced into a rotation of introductions for the camera. Some of my teammates, like Marshall Hunt, are natural-born charmers—they grin and speak eloquently and they sure as hell don't lose their temper.

The crew saved me for last. Either they're a bunch of sadists or they know I only signed the contract because I wouldn't let my team down, and have decided to punish me for, quite literally, holding up the show.

The director of photography, whose name I don't remember, but who looks like he's spent the last twenty years in the arctic tundra, tries again. "Listen, Mr. Carter." Desperation thickens his voice as he slides a glance to his camera guy. "I'm sure you'd like to go home, right? We just need you to cooperate with us. Give us your name, hometown, the position you play, and two facts you think the fans will be surprised to learn about you."

As captain for the Blades, I'm never the troublemaker.

I enforce the rules.

I keep the shitheads in line, twenty-four-seven.

I lead by example, even when that means I come across looking like an arrogant, uptight prick.

But there's nothing about *Getting Pucked* that sits right with me. I'm not interested in having the curtains pulled back on my life. Some shit isn't meant to be aired out as dirty laundry, particularly when said dirty laundry could end my career before I'm ready to retire my skates.

The fact that the show won't televise later this year but within the same week as filming? That's the cherry on top of the shittastic sundae I'm being forced to swallow.

Welcome to the hell that is Steven Fairfax's ingenious creation, where the NHL blends with reality TV and emerges feeling like a cross between *Survivor* and *Real World: Road Rules*.

Sensing Coach's eyes on me from across the rink, I grit out a strained smile and attempt to play nice. "Hey." *Fuck, man, not so growly.* I clear my throat. Try again. "I'm Jackson Carter. Texas-bred, and captain for the Blades."

The director's pale face glows with excitement as he flashes me two thumbs-up like I'm a toddler learning how to shit in the toilet for the first time.

Go, me.

I angle my body to face the camera fully. "I'm on the frontline, in the right-wing slot."

The director nods eagerly, then rolls his hand in a *keep going* gesture. He flips me the peace sign, which I guess is his reminder for "two facts."

Unblinking, I meet the camera lens head-on. "Two random facts about me . . . when I'm home alone at night, there's nothing I like more than to play a little *My Heart Will*

Go On from Celine Dion while I soak in a bubble bath of champagne." The director's grin falters, and I press onward, completely straight-faced. "I also recently adopted a pig named 'Fact Number Two.' Don't know what happened to Number One." I grin. "Might have turned out to be someone's dinner."

"*Cut!*"

I shove away from the boards, my skates gliding across the ice.

I should apologize for being a Class-A dick—if my Texan mom heard me just now, she'd waste no time in pinching my ear and giving it a hard twist. An apology isn't what escapes when I ask the director, "Think y'all can work with what I gave you?"

I think I've been played.

No shit, tears are gathering in his eyes. Tears that he doesn't bother to sop up with the sleeve of his cashmere sweater as he clamps a hand over his heart in full *Pledge of Allegiance* mode. "Yes. *Oh*, so much yes. Have you been to her show in Vegas? It's amazing. My husband is obsessed. We've gone four times already this year and I swear to you, it feels like a religious awakening each and every time."

My shit-eating grin, already dying a slow death, disintegrates completely when he tacks on, "I'm sure fans will be *so* pleased to discover that you know the worth of Celine Dion. Just imagine the new types of fan-mail you'll get after the pilot episode. Brilliant, Carter, just brilliant!"

He winks, tears magically gone, and I briefly deliberate on the ramifications of ramming my fist into his smirking face.

"You a fan of Celine now, Carter? Never would have pegged you for a romantic."

At Andre Beaumont's dry tone, I crane my neck to stare up at the Garden's ceiling, hundreds of feet above the ice. Cupping my helmet between my hands, I lift it to my chest like a hockey version of a rosary bead, and mock-pray, "God, give me strength to not take this man's hockey stick and shove it so far up his ass, he'll be waddling for weeks." A minute pause. "Amen."

Beaumont's shoulder collides with mine as he skates past. "Asshole."

Shuffling my helmet to one hand, I flip him the bird with the other. "Could have said the same for you. And here I was thinkin' that you'd still be in your post-honeymoon bliss, attitude checked at the door."

The NHL's top enforcer blinds me with a rare grin. "Boston feeds the darkness of my soul—I can't stop the assholery the minute I come back, any more than you can stop being a prick twenty-four-seven."

I don't want to laugh but I do. It boils deep in my chest, and as the blades of my skates push against the ice to propel me forward, I mutter, "I'm honestly surprised you're even down for any of this."

Beaumont's dark head swivels in my direction. "*Getting Pucked*, you mean?"

"Yeah." After we unhinge the waist-high door in the boards, it's a matter of trucking it through the tunnel to the locker rooms where we're due to have a meeting with Coach Hall sans TV production. Thank fuck. "It wasn't that long ago that you had your own showdown with the media. Can't imagine why you'd voluntarily sign up for this shit after everything that happened."

Hockey stick perched over his shoulder, Beaumont ambles down the tunnel like a Viking gearing up for battle instead of a hockey player off to face the people who sign our paychecks. "I didn't want to, but Zoe . . ." He shrugs, switching the stick to the other shoulder. "Zoe made a good point—I'll probably be out of the game by the time we have kids. Can't play forever, eh? Anyway, she thinks doing something like this will be good for the little Beaumonts one day. They'll be able to see this part of my life, and maybe I'll be lucky enough to have a son or a daughter who loves the sport as much as I do."

Kids. Family.

My heart gives a dull thud, like a knock on my ribcage to remind myself that I'm not, in fact, dead. Since my divorce, I've certainly felt that way a time or two. Throat tight, I grind out, "Yeah, makes sense."

All my teammates have their own reasons for signing the *Getting Pucked* contracts, and I need to get my head out of my own ass before I screw it up for them. *Do it for your boys. Don't be a goddamn prick.*

I swallow, hating the panic that twines down my spine like claws scraping into my flesh. All it would take is one wrong clip being shown on TV to change the trajectory of my plans for the season. One too nosey cameraman who digs a little too deep, and suddenly I won't be known as the Badass of Hockey anymore but the player who—

Inhaling sharply, I breathe through the spike of anxiety and focus on palming the locker-room door open.

The guys are mostly changed out of their uniforms already, which the producers wanted us in for the sake of "TV authenticity," whatever the hell that means. They nod as I pass them, some offering a two-fingered salute and others giving me a curt chin-nod.

These guys are my family, but as captain, I operate out of a strange focal point. They respect me. They'll cover me on the ice and are always up for grabbing dinner or playing poker. But at the end of the day, they've got to own up to me. I'm the gateway to the big guns on the board, which means that while my teammates will do anything for me, the slight fracture in our relationship won't ever be mended.

It's the one thing I miss most about life before the "C" was stitched onto my jersey. When you're Captain, there's a whole lot of ass-kissing going around. Except for Beaumont and our assistant captain, Duke Harrison—they don't give a fuck who

I am, and, in return, they're as close to brothers as I'll ever have in the rink. Outside of it, too.

I plunk my helmet onto the top shelf in my stall, next to my gloves, then reach behind my neck to fist my jersey and pull it over my head. Slipping the material onto the metal hook, I focus on removing the rest of my uniform and pads instead of the low pulse of anxiety that's yet to dissipate. No one spares me a second glance, and I'm sure that to my team-mates I look the same as always: stone-faced, reserved, completely in control.

It's better for team morale if that's all they see.

My ass is on the bench, my shoulders hunched as I unlace my skates when I hear her.

Holly.

"Coach, always good to see you."

Spine snapping straight, I make a mental note to slow the immediate rush of my breath as I wait for her to speak again. *What the fuck is she doing here?*

"Holly," Coach says warmly, "I'm so glad you called."

Called?

I give up any pretense of staying in my own zone and swing my legs over the side of the bench. Dressed in nothing but my compression shorts and Under Armour leggings, I watch as my ex-wife leans in for a hug from one of the NHL's most popular coaches. Holly smiles prettily, all pink-painted lips and straight, white teeth, and then gives a small tug on the hem of her deep blue sweater. Tight skinny jeans complete the look, along with knee-high black boots. Slung across her chest is a dainty silver purse that doesn't even look like it could fit my wallet.

I blink.

Blue sweater. Silver purse.

Blades' colors.

What the hell is she doing?

Like she's got a homing beacon on me, her blond head

turns in my direction. Blue eyes pin me in place. That is, before her gaze drops to my bare chest and lingers a touch too long. Call it primal nature or what have you, but I have the most absurd urge to stretch my arms above my head and gauge her reaction.

Since our divorce, exercise has been my singular outlet for every emotion under the sun. I've always been big—journalists don't call me the Beast of the Northeast just because of that time I played with a shattered knee cap—but I know what I look like now. I know that all those extra curls and burpees and miles-long runs have thickened my arms and strengthened my core.

As her cheeks pinken, I drop my elbows to my thighs and kick up my chin to keep my gaze locked on her face. On her parted lips.

Her fingers lurch to the chain-link strap of her purse like she's holding on for dear life. A heartbeat later, she whirls away, presenting me with her trim back and small, perky ass, and—

I slam my eyes shut.

Stop right there, man. Go no further.

A big body slides onto the bench beside me. "What's Holly doing here?"

My fingertips dig into the spandex leggings, grounding myself against the heat sparking to life in my groin. To Duke, I mutter, "No idea. We don't talk."

"You did at Beaumont's wedding," comes his dry reply.

"Let me rephrase. We don't talk on a regular—"

"Make sure your dicks are in your cups, gentlemen, we've got a visitor!"

At Coach Hall's half-assed joke, my teammates grumble loudly about wanting the opportunity to let their dicks fly free, but everyone laughs, and no one takes offense, least of all my ex-wife. They know Holly well—she's been the lead photographer behind the Blades for a number of years now.

47

She's done engagement pictures, graduation photos, and even baptism shoots for some of the new Blades babies.

But nothing has been scheduled for today, which means her presence comes with a giant question mark.

"Put them away," she says now, mock-shielding her eyes, "I don't need to see any of y'all's micro-penises, trust me."

"Having flashbacks to Carter's small dick?" shouts an asshole from the opposite corner of the locker room.

Let me repeat: Beast of the Northeast.

Suffice as it is to say, the guys know I don't put up with Holly being dragged into their gutter talk. Not when we were married; not now either.

Josh Kammer, as a rookie, hasn't been dealt that lesson yet.

I tilt my head in his direction, my hands hanging loosely between my knees. "Josh?"

Beside me, Duke mutters "here we go" under his breath.

"Yeah, Cap?" the rookie left-wing asks blithely.

"Do me a favor and meet me an hour before practice tomorrow, will you?" The vets on the team all trade glances, and I don't even bother to stand and get a good look at the kid. They all know I'm about to make his life hell tomorrow.

I like to think of it as a rite of passage to learning how *not* to be a dick.

And if he's curled over a trash can after our one-on-one workout, heaving out his guts, because he's had a miraculous understanding that playing for The Show means more than just putting on the uniform, then I'll have done my job right.

Respect. Ambition. Teamwork.

Playing for the Blades means doing it all—and it's the latter part of the trifecta that had me caving in to Sports 24/7 two weeks ago.

The rookie utters out an obliviously eager, "Fuck yeah, I'll meet you, Cap!" and then even Coach is shaking his head like he can't believe he drafted a naïve idiot like Josh Kammer.

Hopefully the kid's a lot smarter when it comes to doing his job on the ice.

I look to Holly, a little surprised to find that her eyes are locked on me. Despite the twenty feet or so separating us, I don't mistake the way she mouths, "Thank you."

Familiar words I've confessed to no one but myself bubble up in my chest, each clawing their way up my throat in an attempt to pull free. In the end, I swallow over them all, shoving them down deep where they belong, and give her a curt nod that reveals nothing as to how I truly feel about her. About our broken vows.

She'd been right, what she said the other day.

We aren't married. We aren't together.

Having her back is where the line gets drawn, starting now.

"All right, you assholes," says Coach, puffing out his chest in that way he only does when we've got company in the house, "how did all of you feel about *Getting Pucked* today?" When some of the guys begin to complain, he fingers the lanyard around his neck and sucks a whistle between his lips, blowing loudly. "That was a rhetorical question! I don't give a damn if your panties are all in a twist"—his head pivots in my direction, eyes narrowed and accusing—"but I've got great news for you."

"They're getting us blow jobs?"

There's a smack on the head, and then our star center, Marshall Hunt, grunts out, "Use your brain, Kammer, or I'll make sure the only blow job you get for the rest of your life comes from a flushlight."

Coach Hall keeps talking like the interruption didn't even happen. "I know that some of you have reservations about *Getting Pucked* and I get it. We're a team. We keep shit between us . . . our personal lives, the way we operate, fail-ures and successes." Coach steps forward, and I see some of the guys shift their legs so that he has ample space to pace back and forth, as he's known to do. "In case you've been unconscious for the last two months, this is the year we take the Cup. This is the year we dominate every game and every pass and every save. I want it documented. I want other teams to worry. I want us to *win*."

Unable to stop myself, I look to Holly again.

This time, she doesn't glance in my direction.

Not when Coach ushers her forward.

Not when her fingers fist the chain of her purse strap where it hangs between her breasts.

Not when her Southern drawl rings loud and clear in the locker room: "I want all of those things, too, Coach. I'm already dreaming of taking pictures of y'all with the Cup."

That earns her a roar of applause and even Kammer the Idiot hollers, "Fuck yeah, Mrs. Carter. Fuck yeah!"

She's not Mrs. Carter, not anymore, but she smiles kindly at him anyway because that's the sort of person she is. "I want more than that, though. I know y'all—I know your families and your wives and your kids and, hell, Henri, I even know your mother and she doesn't even live in the States!"

Henri Bordeaux, our resident French-Canadian from Montreal, waves at her enthusiastically.

Holly waves back, the tension visibly lessening in her frame.

As for me, I can't tear my gaze away from her, in part because I have a gut feeling that I know where she's going with this and I have no idea what sort of game she's playing.

The other part of me . . . Well, I've always loved watching her command a room. Always.

"I was approached by Sports 24/7, initially, to work on *Getting Pucked* as the director of photography. I turned that offer down."

When the griping begins, my voice cuts through the noise like steel: "Let her talk."

Silence greets me, and yet Holly still doesn't look my way.

She balls her hair up into a messy bun, which she leaves twisted at the nape of her neck. Like being in this room has skyrocketed her nerves as well as her temperature, and she's in desperate need of cooling off.

I'm not enough of an idiot to assume that it's my presence throwing her off.

Aside from the one or two times at the end of our marriage when she emotionally crumpled before me, she's always been tougher than anyone else I know.

That toughness lifts her chin now as she says, "I've been through a lot with you guys over the last few years, and the more I thought about it, the worse I felt about not joining this venture with all of you." She glances at Hall. "I've talked it out with Coach, as well as the other board members. They, in turn, approached Sports 24/7 with a compromise."

A compromise.

My fingers slide down over the curve of my knees, my back hunching as I drop my gaze to the floor between my feet. I focus on a speck of dust on the thin, old carpet. Zero in on it as Holly informs us that while she won't be in charge of the overall direction of the show, she and her team will personally be responsible for any one-on-one interviews that occur outside of the arena or practice. The ice will remain Sports 24/7's domain.

Duke's shoulder knocks into mine. "You good, man?"

I nod. "All good."

Not quite the truth.

The truth is that I'm hovering in that space between grateful and agitated, my emotions a tumultuous wreck in much the same way that they've been for a year and counting.

She's doing this for her career, jackass, not for you.

I wait as everyone gives Holly a hug on their way out the door.

And then I wait some more until Coach and our GM are

shaking her hand and then following out behind the rest of my teammates.

I sit on that bench until Holly and I are the only ones left.

The door shuts behind Duke, leaving us alone, and then Holly and I are speaking over each other:

"We need to talk."

"Can you please put a shirt on?"

CHAPTER 6
HOLLY

A year without seeing Jackson's bare chest is like a year without basking in sunlight.

You can get through it.

Hell, some days you might even relish the murky, gray skies and the heavy snowfall.

Until you get a glimpse of what you've been missing. It's straight downhill from there.

"Can you please put a shirt on?"

I hear the words leave my mouth as I visually soak up the panther-like way Jackson's hands move to the bench on either side of his hips. Jackson's always been ripped, but this is . . . just *wow*. His arm muscles flex, the visible tendons that run along his biceps and down over his forearms visibly rippling. I bet if I were to *Urban Dictionary* "arm porn," I'd find Jackson's picture as the only definition.

Down, girl.

Dark eyes flit over my body, lingering on my thighs and waist before returning to my face. His grin is slow, knowing. "You look flushed, Holls. Feelin' overheated?"

Unfortunately.

I trace my fingers over the cool metal strap of my purse

and cling tightly to the linked chain. Since approaching Coach Hall, I've combed through this conversation with Jackson a million times over in my head. I've pictured him falling at my feet, grateful as all get-out for doing him a *solid.* I've imagined him turning ambivalent, like I'm a little too late to the cause. I've even played out entire scenarios where he's so overcome with happiness that he twirls me around in the air like I'm some sort of Disney princess on ice.

In none of those versions of the conversation, however, do the following words even *consider* being uttered: "Your nipples are hard."

Except that's what I say.

Your. Nipples. Are. Hard.

Oh my God, someone kill me.

Jackson's dark brows shoot up. "Excuse me?"

"Your nipples," my stupid mouth utters without my support, "they're hard as diamonds."

Eyebrows still arched high, he sits up a little. Glances down at his chest and rock-hard abs. Like a woman possessed, I count each abdominal ridge as though I'm in pre-K and learning how to count on my fingers with the Count from *Sesame Street*: *one delicious ab, two delicious abs, three delicious abs, ah ah ah.*

Girl, you are losing it.

Jackson tilts his head, clearly trying to eyeball his pecs. "How many carats you thinkin'?"

I cannot believe I'm having this conversation right now.

I slam my eyes shut. "One."

"Yeah?" The blatant humor in his voice is nearly tangible, and I get the feeling that he's dragging his thumb along his bottom lip, trying to keep a lid on fully-blown laughter. "Just one?"

"Cubic zirconia. Off the shelf of Target."

"Fitting," he husks out, "since you'd live in Target if they let you."

Too true. It's hard to resist the lure of a place where I can literally buy whatever I want in one store. Growing up in Natchitoches, department stores weren't a thing—not until I was older and already had one foot out the door. It's not my fault if I choose to make up for lost time now.

The sound of the bench creaking under his weight has me opening my eyes again.

I watch as he searches through his stall for a shirt. He's given me a prime view of the slope of his taut back and the faded pink lines that stretch horizontally across his flesh. Stretch marks, he once told me. Growth spurt after growth spurt as a kid carved their memories into his back forever.

For years, I'd trail my fingertips over each one, memorizing the feel of the raised, puckered flesh, so very different from the youthful pictures his mother once showed me.

Tall. Strapping. The Beast of the Northeast.

He slips a gray T-shirt over his head now, and the stretch marks and his hard nipples and the muscles-on-muscles disappear from sight.

"You changed your mind," he says casually as he pulls a pair of sweats up his legs. I do my best to ignore the fact that if he were alone, he'd probably shuck off the compression shorts and leggings before pulling on a fresh set of briefs and jeans. *He's trying to be respectful.* Maybe. I'm not sure. "Did you take the six-figs?" he asks.

I didn't take anything from Sports 24/7. Not a dime.

Instead, I asked the Blades to cover the basic expenses required by my team. "This way you'll know that I'm working for *you* and not some TV producer," I'd told the board of directors for the Blades. "Ensuring that the guys come out of this with the same reputation as they had going in is my top priority."

They accepted.

The pay was infinitely less, much closer to my usual rate, but I didn't make a fuss.

I meet Jackson's gaze. Try to get a read on his emotions. Finally, I answer his question with one of my own: "Would you believe me if I said no?"

For a moment, he says nothing at all. He ruffles his brown hair with one hand. Loops the string at his waistband into a tight knot. Then, "You're an entrepreneur, Holls. A better one than I'll ever be, which means I know you're being compensated for the gig at whatever amount you feel makes it a worthwhile venture."

He steps forward, and I'm ashamed to say that I step back in response. It's instinctual, self-preservation at the most basic level. A need to keep him at arm's length before the steel walls around my heart soften and cave in to futile hopes and desperate dreams. "This is what you wanted . . . for me to take the gig."

Like we're embarking on a dance that I never received an invitation to, he risks another step forward again. There's a glint in his dark eyes, a silent challenge that dares me to hold my ground and let him approach.

I swallow, hard.

Then fasten my gaze on his broad chest as he ambles closer with his long-legged gait. "True," he murmurs, "it *was* what I wanted. But I specifically remember you sayin' that I've got to bank my own fires. Call me curious—what changed for you? And don't tell me nothing. Don't lie."

He stops in front of me, less than a foot away, and I lift my gaze from his chest to his throat to his rugged face. "It's exactly as I said to the team," I lie smoothly, "it feels wrong not to take this step with y'all, considering I've been around for half the lifespan of the franchise." I offer a delicate shrug. "I don't want to live with regrets."

Slowly, as though he doesn't believe me, Jackson asks, "So, you'd regret not doing this?"

"Yes."

"And you don't regret leaving the heftier salary on the table?"

Without a doubt, he's trying to get a read on me. He stands with his shoulders rounded and his gaze locked on my face, and I fight the urge to squirm under his unwavering stare. One heartbeat. That's all I last before I'm averting my gaze and glancing past him to the row of stalls along the back wall.

"Holls."

At the determined grit in his voice, I fold my arms across my belly and cup my opposite elbows. "Do we have to go there?" I draw in a sharp breath. "Can't we just, for once, let a decision stand without dissecting it a million times over? I'm taking the job for the Blades organization. I'm doing this for me." I fall back a step. "Not for you."

My feet move without my conscious realization of it, backpedaling me all the way up until my hand is on the doorknob and my heart feels like it's lodged in my throat.

"Tell me to my face that you're not doing *Getting Pucked* for me."

Like my body has a will of its own, my forehead gently kisses the cool, metal door that's my escape from the locker room. My escape from *him.*

Why.

Why can't he just let me leave without tearing all of our carefully sewn scars back open?

Why does he always have to *push*?

Shoulders straightening, I press my back to the door. "All those trophies you've won are inflating your ego, Jackson." God, I hate the way he watches me now—like he knows what I don't want to admit, like he'll stop at nothing until I give him what he wants. *Like he's locked in the same hell that I've been in for the last year without him.* "The universe doesn't revolve around you."

And because Jackson has never been good with boundaries, he eclipses the space between us until his masculine scent is infiltrating my senses and all I see are his broad shoulders and hard chest.

The back of my head collides with the door as I stare him down. "Stop pushing," I edge out, my voice sounding breathless even to my own ears. *So pathetic.* "For God's sake, just—"

His thumb catches on my lower lip in a silent order for me to shut up.

I gulp at the intimate—*unexpected*—contact.

Audibly.

Ridiculously.

Embarrassment seeps into my veins.

And then I shove at his bulky chest, finally earning myself some much-needed breathing room. "You're crossing boundaries."

Jaw visibly clenched, he balls his hands into fists and sets them on his hips. On me, that pose would look like I'm throwing a tantrum. On him, a pro-hockey player and a man who has always kept a tight leash on his emotions, he looks like he's on the verge of blowing a gasket.

I don't blame him.

My temper is . . . God, it's *boiling.*

Behind my back, I fist the doorknob. "You want the truth, Captain?" I lower my voice, fury lacing every word. "The truth is that no matter how much I wish I could toss you to the wolves and not care, I can't do that. Your words got to me, I admit it. They got to me so damn badly that I pulled out our wedding album and realized that, for better or worse, I can't walk away from you when I should—when it's in my best interest to lay down the sword and get the hell out of dodge. I hope you're pleased with yourself."

His lips part on a sharp breath. "Holls—"

"Don't touch me." *Don't touch me or I'll shatter.* I yank open the door with more force than necessary. "You want to know if I regret taking on *Getting Pucked*?" I shake my head, my hair catching on my chin. I shove the strands back with a rough, shaky hand. "I don't regret working with the Blades. I don't regret turning down that six-figure check. But I regret that even after all this time, I can't tell you no."

I don't wait for him to say my name or plead his case before bolting out the door.

He pushed, and he got his answer, but I can't guarantee that he'll like what I had to say.

I can't tell you no.

I'm going to need some crash 101 courses in doing just that if I plan to survive the next four months. Otherwise, I'll be right back with the wine, the tears, and the Chinese food all over again.

And something tells me that I won't survive another round of heartbreak with Jackson Carter.

CHAPTER 7
JACKSON

"**C**ap, take your turn or I'm forcing you to buy me some fancy-ass steak when we land in Nashville."

My gaze snaps from the front of the airplane to Weston Cain, who's seated across the aisle from me. With his suit undone at the neck and his blond hair slicked back all prim and tidy, you'd never guess that he has an obsession with the board game Battleship.

But here we are: him handing me my ass so swiftly my ships are going down in lightning speed, and me constantly glancing for sight of Holly making her way onto the team's jet for our first preseason game against the Nashville Predators.

I clear my throat, my back pressed to the window as I sit facing the aisle, my long legs sprawled out in what little space the row allots. "Rules were that loser buys the steak. I'm not losin'." I stare down at my grid, then look to the plastic backing of Cain's board. "D-4."

Cain's mouth lifts in a smug smile. "Miss."

"Fucker," I grunt, fitting a white pin in the corresponding slot in my grid.

Beaumont's dark head pops up from the row behind me. Forearms pressed into my chair's headrest, he leans forward and sweeps his gaze over my spread. "What kind of fancy-ass steak you thinking about, Cain?"

"Wagyu. I like it when my meat is massaged."

I cock a brow. "You like it when it's chopped off, too? Because after you're done with your massage and your specialty diet of grass and ice beer, that little bastard is gone and being served on a porcelain plate with potatoes au gratin."

"Maybe he likes the pain," Beaumont muses, rubbing his chin dramatically. "You like pain, Cain?"

"I like free steak." Cain twirls a finger in the air, not even perturbed by the shift in conversation and his impending lack of dick, and then adds, "C-3."

One glance down at my grid and I'm tempted to do the cock-hacking for him. "Dammit."

"Is that a hit, Cap?"

Beaumont snaps up one of my red pins before slipping it into the second hole of my Destroyer. "He's been hit!"

Narrowing my eyes, I glare up at our enforcer. "Why the fuck are you so chipper? It's four in the goddamn morning and you're wearing a suit."

He only flashes me a grin. "I took a hit, if you know what I mean."

From the row behind him, Josh Kammer jumps up like a mole emerging from compact dirt. "You really want to be talking about weed like that, Sin? Pretty sure that shit's against protocol."

Beaumont's dark brows furrow as the easygoing expression on his face dies a quick death. "Someone tell the rookie to take a seat before I help him do so."

"What? All I'm saying is—"

"He's talking about sex," I cut in, meeting Kammer's gaze. "He got laid. Now sit down unless you're up for another round of rope climbing."

I swallow a chuckle when the kid promptly collapses back

into his seat. It's safe to say that he's not in the mood to press his luck so soon after our last one-on-one. I'm not into hazing the newbies, but I sure as hell will put them in their place when they start talking shit—especially if it involves Holly.

As though thinking her name has conjured her up, I hear the strains of her voice as she enters the plane, and *goddamn*, it takes every inch of self-control not to lift my ass off the cushioned seat and scope her out.

"Matt," she says to the attendant, "it's so good to see you again!" There's quiet murmuring, and then, "For me? Are you sure?"

Fuck, I want to see her face when Matt hands over the goods. It's nothing big, nothing monumental, but it's a peace offering I know she'll appreciate. If we're going to be dancing around each other for the next few months, I need her on my side. I need her to know that I'm not the prick who'll take her for granted when she's doing it all for me—however much she wants to pretend otherwise.

"Carter."

I flick my gaze up to Beaumont, who's watching me with narrowed eyes. "Yeah?" My voice is gruffer than I'd like, and I grab my water bottle from the back of the seat in front of me and take a swig. "What's up?"

He leans down as far as he can go, his chest crushing my seat back. "You look like you want to take a *hit*, buddy. Simmer down or you're going to poke a hole in the bottom of Battleship."

"Pretty sure this game is supposed to be G-rated," pipes up Cain from across the aisle, just as I glance down at my crotch and . . . fuck me, but Andre is right.

I'm sporting wood.

For my ex-wife.

In a plane surrounded by my teammates.

Christ, it's going to be a long four months.

Needing to get the conversation off me and my ill-timed

hard-on, I pick up the board game and shove it at Beaumont as I climb to my feet. "Take this, will you?"

His fingers wrap around the sharp, plastic edges, his dark eyes flitting down before zeroing in on my face. "Masturbation in the bathroom won't get you into the Mile High Club, Carter. Plus, no one on this plane wants to sleep with you."

Cain chokes on a boisterous laugh when I narrow my eyes at him. To Andre, I drawl, "That's not what you were telling me before Zoe entered the picture."

Pure. Silence.

Beaumont lasts a total of four seconds before his neutral expression cracks and he's bent over the board game, laughing so hard that heads swivel in our direction to see what's going on. Including Holly's.

She's holding her gift bag to her chest as she stares down the aisle, some ten rows separating us. Blond hair pulled up in a ponytail. Black, rimmed glasses perched on her nose. Yoga pants and a blue Blades sweatshirt complete the outfit.

She looks fresh-faced and young, and I'm momentarily hit with memory after memory of waking up to her beside me in bed, her face smashed in the pillow, one arm splayed across my face. I can't count the number of mornings I've woken her up by nipping at her arm, after being almost smothered by its weight in my sleep.

Sometimes romance isn't cuddle sessions and lingerie—it's clinging to the edge of the mattress and praying you don't topple over when your wife decides to hog the entire bed.

Without giving myself the chance to switch gears, I duck my head to avoid smacking it on the overhead bins, and step into the aisle. The team is settling in for our flight to Nashville. Some of the guys are sleeping, heads propped awkwardly in the small confines of the seats; others quietly play on their phones. A few issue me their usual two-fingered salute as I pass them.

Matt, our regular attendant, smiles when he sees me approach. "Do you need something, Mr. Carter?"

I've told the guy hundreds of times to call me Jackson, but he always laughs me off. Short, thin, and with a mop of red hair on his head, he could be anywhere between forty and sixty as well as a stand-in for Ronald McDonald.

"Nah, I'm good, man. Just gotta piss real fast."

Almost comically, he leans his slender frame to the left, his blue eyes no doubt landing on the bathroom at the back of the plane, close to where I was seated. When he looks my way again, I lift my brows, silently daring him to call me out on my bullshit.

But just like he's always called me Mr. Carter, Matt's the sorta guy who will always keep his nose out of people's business. Without a word, he slips into the empty seat to his left to let me edge past him.

I give him a nod.

His mouth pulls wide. "Don't piss on the floor, Mr. Carter, or you'll be the one cleaning it up."

And *that's* why the Blades will pay the guy whatever he wants: he gives as much shit as he takes, and like a momma bear, he's never shy about putting us all in our places if the situation calls for it.

Hard-Ass Matt, the guys call him.

Matt's shoulders never fail to inch back with pride whenever they do.

Holly has already taken her seat by the time I reach her side. Her camera girl, Carmen, sits beside her. I've known Carmen since she came on board with Carter Photography. Nice girl. Quirky. She hasn't exactly been a cheerleader in my court since the divorce.

Not that I've ever worried about divided courts—I think it's safe to say that both Holly and I have always wanted the people in our lives to feel okay with talking to us both.

No picking sides.

No feeling guilty.

I set my hand on the back of Holly's seat, consciously aware that I can't crowd her or tease her into glancing up and having my crotch at eye level. In a relationship, it would be funny, maybe even sexy, depending on the mood. While divorced, it's pushing boundaries.

And she's already warned me that I push those enough already.

As if sensing my presence, she glances up, gaze skimming up my body until she arrives at my face. Behind the black frames of her glasses, her blue eyes are bright and beautiful. "I'm going to assume you're the one behind the gift?"

I shift my weight back, giving us space, and rest my ass against the seat opposite hers. "It's a peace offering." Perched in her lap, the bag sits unopened, the black tissue paper still spiking up in the air from when I tried to make it look half-decent this morning. "I think you'll like it."

Her fingers trail up the side, then tug down on the bag. The tissue paper crinkles but remains in place. Probably because I stuffed an entire package in there—like cooking, wrapping presents isn't my thing. Making assists on the ice? Scoring goals and watching the lamp light up? That's more my speed.

"Black like your soul, I see." She says it with a teasing glint before plucking the black tissue paper from the bag and tucking it between her knees. Blond ponytail swinging forward, she peers inside and promptly lets loose a low, husky laugh. "Are you trying to tell me something?"

I watch as she pulls out the noise-cancellation headphones that I bought for her. Against my will, my chest tightens when faced with the small smile curving her lips. Fuck me, but the tightening sensation feels a lot more like strangulation when she flicks her gaze up to my face, a question in her blue eyes.

"We're noisy bastards, if you remember," I say gruffly.

"Figure with all the traveling you'll be doing with us over the next few months, it might be something you'd like to keep on hand."

On the other side of Holly, Carmen snorts—derisively, no doubt—and makes a show of whipping out a pair of small earbuds and sticking them in her ears.

I open my mouth, prepared to apologize for not bringing her something, too, when Matt taps me on the shoulder. "Take a seat, Mr. Carter. We're ready to get a move-on."

"Right," I mutter, "sorry for the hold up."

Holly's cheeks flush and she drops her gaze. "Thanks for the gift, Jackson." Her fingers drum along the headset's cushioned ear padding. "It's great. And I'm sure we'll see each other later on today, but—"

I sit.

What the hell are you doing, man?

Clearly, Holly has the same idea because her lips purse. "What're you doing?"

Hell if I know.

If I were smart, I'd tromp right back to where I'd been sitting with Beaumont and Cain.

If I were smart, I wouldn't give a shit if I watched her discover what else I put in the bag.

If I were smart, I'd do everything in my power to get it in my skull that Holly and I didn't work for a million and one different reasons, and I'd be an idiot to let myself linger now. To let myself soak up her scent, her beauty, the sweet pitch of her voice.

Holly was equal parts my strength and my weakness, and in this moment, I can't resist the pull—*her* pull.

I snap the seat belt together across my hips. Pinch my suit at the knees and get comfortable, my left leg sprawled in the aisle and my right spread wide and bent at the knee to fit in the narrow row.

"Jackson?"

I slide the blind down over the oval window, blocking out the sights of Logan International Airport and eclipsing my two seats in relative darkness. "Open up the rest of your peace offerings, Holls. I want to see your face."

CHAPTER 8
HOLLY

I *want to see your face.*

There's no time to respond or still my rapidly beating heart before the cabin lights flicker and dim, and Matt's smooth voice echoes over the speakers: "Hello, my dear Blades. So good to see you all again! It's been too long."

A chorus of male voices rise up behind me:

"We missed you, Hard-Ass!"

"It's been *months*, man! You been laid yet?"

"Matt, what'll I have to pay to exchange the shitty crackers you're about to give me for a big, juicy steak?"

There's a strangled chuckle, and then, "Mr. Harrison, I've missed you too. Mr. Hartwell, that answer is between me and my nonexistent partner, thank you very much. And, Mr. Cain, you'll eat the crackers and you'll like it." The sounds of masculine groaning at the back of the plane makes me grin. This back-and-forth ribbing has run rampant for years now. Luckily, Matt knows how to hold his own. Something he proves when he adds, "You all know that I won't be repeating myself when I say, if I catch any of you watching porn on this flight, I'll kick you off while flying thirty-thou-sand feet in the air. No parachute. Your fans will be disappointed—don't test me. Our travel time is a few minutes shy of three hours, and we'll have you ready for the Predators by 8 a.m. Sit back and enjoy, gents. It's good to see you again for another season."

The speaker clicks off and chatter resumes. Quieter now, due to the lack of light and the gentle classical music Matt enjoys playing just to get under the team's skin.

If he weren't beloved by every player, he'd probably have been fired by now.

As Debussy drowns out male voices, I'm acutely aware of the fact that I'm not alone. To my left, Carmen reads on her phone, earphones plugged in to avoid the classical music. I know Jackson isn't her favorite person—since I brought her on as an additional camera on my team, she's always been fiercely loyal to me. She had little credentials when she applied to the job listing but I took a chance on her anyway. And when her ex-husband turned out to be a cheating schmuck, I found myself blurring the lines between boss and friend.

As far as the latter goes, Carmen is as close to a bestie that I have, and I know that watching me fall apart with Jackson over the last year has been just another bullet point in her long list about why men are assholes.

Jackson isn't an asshole.

We just couldn't find a way to meet in the middle.

The gift bag sits heavy in my lap, the expensive head-phones he purchased resting on my stomach. They feel like a brand against the fabric of my shirt—a brand of failed dreams and bitter hopes and nonexistent reconciliations. Stupid, I know, to want something back that didn't work in the first place, but emotions are rarely logical.

"Open it, Holls."

His deep Texan drawl curls around me like wisps of heavy smoke, warming me up from my toes to that forever-tingly spot behind my ear. The spot that Jackson once loved to kiss, knowing that it made my fingers twitch and my skin leap and my heart thud a little faster.

I switch on the light above my head just as the jet's engine begins to hum and the aircraft jerks forward. "You should sit with the guys," I mutter, desperate to draw the line back in the sand between us.

"I will—after you see what else is in there."

Forget the line—there's a damn aisle dividing us, and yet I *still* feel like he's right there, pressed against me, surrounding me.

There's no more tissue paper to remove, so I tilt the bag and shove my fingers inside, grasping around for whatever else he purchased. Plastic meets my fingertips, and I draw the yellow package out and tilt it under the light to better read the font scrolled across.

My heart squeezes. "Jackson—"

"Sour Patch Watermelon candies," he murmurs, "your favorite."

Beside me, Carmen slumps farther down in her seat. I get the feeling she's listening to us and not whatever playlist she selected. Part of me—the young girl who once loved a boy more than anything else in the world—wishes that Jackson and I could be alone. But that wouldn't be smart—it wouldn't be *logical*—and so the thirty-two-year-old divorcee takes center stage and tries to not read between the lines when there *are* no lines to be read.

"Stress and candy go hand-in-hand for me. Thanks for saving me a trip to a corner store at midnight when Carmen and I are editing film till we can't see."

I finally cave and glance his way. Sparse light dances across his features, splicing over his crooked nose and giving way to shadows for the lower part of his face. His dark eyes, however, remain visible—and they're locked on me.

"I figured that'd be the case," he says, the smoky tendrils of his voice skipping along my spine as though it's a physical touch, "so I've got a supply loaded and ready in my suitcase for you."

Carmen turns her body, shifting in the seat beside mine to give me her back.

Some privacy.

Slick sweat licks at my palms. Space, I need space. To breathe, to remember the downward spiral of our marriage, to remind myself that I'm allowed to regret what could have been but shouldn't uncap the bottle of *what-ifs*.

What-ifs are dangerous.

Jackson's long leg enters my periphery as he changes positions. The armrest goes up so he can face me as much as possible with the seat belt locking him in place. "There's one more thing in the bag for you, Holls. One last peace offering and then I'll go back to my seat."

Because the noise-cancelling headphones and my stress-eating candies aren't enough?

Carefully, I dig into the bag, feeling around. Nothing. Emptiness. I use the overhead light to glance inside, only to note a small card lying flat against the bottom. *What are you doing to me, Jackson?* With shaky fingers, which I'll deny to my dying day, I slip the card out from the bottom of the bag and peel open the red envelope.

Inside are two tickets to I'm-not-really-sure.

"There's an event tomorrow morning at an art gallery," Jackson says as I squint to read the text on the tickets. "A National Geographic photography showcase." He pauses, and each indrawn breath that I hear him pull into his chest is mimicked by my own as I struggle not to let my scattering emotions wear me down.

I want to cry.

I want to throw the damn tickets at his face.

I want to hop into his lap and tell him thank-you in the way he's always appreciated most—with my lips wrapped around his cock and my hands cupping his balls.

"Figured you and Carmen can slip away for an hour before you have to report for duty," he continues. "Sports 24/7 will have us covered at morning practice. Y'all can swoop in later tomorrow night and do what you gotta do with the team."

"Jackson, you didn't have to do this."

I wish he hadn't. I want that dividing line. I want a permanent aisle.

He's slow to answer. Seconds tick past, and then he's moving his big body into the aisle. He lifts a hand. I'm halfway convinced that he's about to graze his knuckles along my cheek, but then his hand drops back to his side. His fingers curl into a tight fist that he knocks twice against his outer thigh. "Thank you for comin' on board with this, Holls. Just"—he exhales, and it sounds as though he's physically removing the pressure off his shoulders—"thank you."

He's gone before I can edge out another word.

The back of my skull collides with the headrest and I lift the envelope again to stare at the two tickets peeking out. Photography. My favorite candy. Headphones. If I didn't know any better, I'd say that Jackson is trying to woo me.

It's such a ludicrous thought that I snort out loud.

Our divorce was a mutual agreement, but he was the one to bring it into the discussion first.

With two fingers, I tap the tickets back into the envelope— and then spot my ex-husband's handwriting on the inner flap. The black ink against the red envelope is tough to read in the dim light and I poke Carmen in the shoulder.

"Give me your phone," I whisper, "I know you've been listening this whole time."

She doesn't even bother to deny it as she sits up. "Get those romantic thoughts out of your mind, girl. He's not the guy for you."

He was, once.

"Phone, Carmen. You can lecture me after I've had coffee."

With a grumble, she slips me her phone, and I turn on the flashlight app and aim it at the envelope.

My chest inflates with a sharp breath as I read the words he's written for me:

We aren't married, not anymore. But I won't forget what you're doing for me, Holly. I needed this and I needed you. When you need me next, don't hesitate to ask. We're family, even if it's not the way we always envisioned, and I learned a long time ago to never take family for granted. Jackson.

I'm ashamed to admit that my nose grows itchy and tears tease at the corners of my eyes, demanding release into the world.

We're family.

For as long as I can remember, my family was a unit of four with my grandparents at the helm and my brother, Sam, and I taking up the rear. I have no disillusions that I was loved, though it was the sort of love ruled with an iron thumb and a stern voice and a warning to not turn out like my irresponsible parents. Affection wasn't something I knew firsthand until Jackson came into my life.

He knows how much that F-word means to me, and I hate him for utilizing it now and for bending my steel resolve. More than anything, though, I hate the warmth that fills my chest as I clutch the envelope to my chest.

That warmth feels like hope, and I refuse to feed it any more life than Jackson already has this morning.

CHAPTER 9
JACKSON

The Nashville Predators are playing like a bunch of pussies tonight.

It might be preseason, and there might be more rookies than vets on the ice, but, fuck. It's like they're dainty ballerinas being forced to crawl through the mud during army basic training and are terrified of getting their damn slippers wet. They dance out of the way when Beaumont comes barreling toward them; drop out of a scuffle for the puck against the boards with Henri Bordeaux way too easily.

They're looking to avoid injury, and we're out to dominate and draw blood.

I'm on the bench tonight, as I always am for the first game of preseason. Watching and analyzing alongside Coach Hall to scope out our weak spots and discuss what we can do to bolster our lines. It's a proposal I made a few years back with the Blades—a tip I picked up from the captain of the Stars when I played for them—and it's something that has always helped me to counterattack when I'm in the rink.

Only, tonight we look like vultures swarming in for the kill.

I don't know whether to applaud or wince when Marshall

Hunt, our top-notch center, nails the puck in at the net's junction, lighting the lamp a half-second later.

4-1 is now 5-1.

And we're only in the second period with another six minutes to go before the third.

"This is getting ugly," I mutter. I'm in a suit, just like Coach, and the hem of my tailored jacket lifts as I fit my hands on my hips and stare resolutely at the ice. "If this is any indication as to how their season is gonna go, they're either fucked or scared to make big moves."

Coach watches as our guys thump Hunt on the back before tossing his clipboard on the bench beside Cain. "Maybe we're just that good."

"You think?"

"Not even a little." Rubbing his mustache, he adds, "But I do think we're playing a little harder now that we've got *Getting Pucked* hovering around us all the time. No one wants to look like shit when you have a TV crew ready to catch you looking like shit."

That, I can believe.

In the last few weeks, the *Getting Pucked* production crew has been everywhere. In the locker rooms after practice. In the stands *during* practice. Shoving microphones in our faces whenever we pause long enough to guzzle Gatorade when we're switching lines. I've even been approached while pissing in one of the arena's urinals, my dick clamped in hand.

If there wasn't an official end date to the madness, I'd be concerned that *Getting Pucked* is a bit like contracting herpes —once you're infected, it's yours for life.

The Predators make a call to switch from first to second lines, and Coach snaps at Josh Kammer and Daxton Garrett to get in there and sub out Bordeaux and Hunt. They do, and the rest of the game passes exactly as the first two periods have. I'm halfway convinced Harrison let a goal slip in the five-hole, during the last twenty seconds of the game, out of pure pity.

The final score? 7-2.

Talk about a massacre on the ice—but instead of entrails being swept up by the Zamboni after the game, there are hats and towels.

I trail my teammates as they tromp on their skates back to the locker room, but I don't get far. *Getting Pucked*'s director—Mark Fillmore, a.k.a the Celine Dion enthusiast—cuts me off just before the locker room.

"Mind if we hit you with some questions before you join the team?" he asks, jerking a thumb to his camera and sound guys. "We want to capture your initial reaction to what you saw on the ice." With a snap of his fingers, his two guys move forward and get in my face. "How do you feel about taking home the first preseason win?"

Play nice, man. Don't be a dick.

It's my job to watch my boys on the ice and study their every last move, just like it's this guy's job to make good TV. I get that. I know that. And it's the only reason that I shove my hands deep into the front pockets of my slacks and get comfortable, resigned to doing what needs to be done.

"Naturally, I'm excited to see the team play well." I let out a low chuckle, hoping that it doesn't sound strained. "But at the end of the day, it's preseason, which means it doesn't really matter how well we did. It's practice on a larger scale, nothin' more."

Fillmore's eyes pop open wide, as though my willingness to talk has surprised him, and he rolls his fingers in the air, urging me to continue.

My cheeks pinch as I force a smile. "Nashville played soft. They're working a different game than we are right now, and that's not an indicator that they'll do shitty this season or that we'll win every game." I'm not so much of an idiot that I'll trash talk another team in an interview that'll be seen by the masses in a week's time. Offering a casual shrug, I say, "Every team has different tactics."

"But with seven goals on the Blades' end, that's a rather bold statement to make for a first game."

I stare at the camera. "What's bolder? Protecting your best players from injury? Or putting your first line out on day one with the hope that you can see where your weak points sit?"

The camera breaks from me and swings to *Getting Pucked*'s director. It's easy to see that he's pondering what I've said—he pinches the collar of his dress shirt, popping the top button free like he's either overheated or buying himself some time before answering. And then he verbally swivels in another direction when he says, "Before you were traded to the Blades, you were the assistant captain for the Boston Bruins for two seasons. Do you think that experience put you in place to do well in the Blades franchise?"

"I think my love for the sport put me in a good position to do well with the Blades. Experience gets you far, but an innate understanding of the game gets you further."

"And you have this . . . *innate* understanding, yes?"

When you've lived and breathed something for thirty years of your life, it's no longer an "understanding." It's something much bigger, something I could never put into words, even if I tried.

At the end of the day, I *am* hockey.

It's what I think about when I roll out of bed.

It's what I think about when I'm in the gym, pumping iron three times my weight.

It's what I think about when I'm in the shower, rinsing away the sweat and exhaustion after pushing myself to the brink each and every day, worry always lingering in the back of my head on those *what-ifs*.

Those *what-ifs*, more than anything, bring the anxiety swiftly back.

I shove the depressing thought away ruthlessly, but it's

poignant enough to ruin my mood and erase the fake-it-for-TV smile on my face. "Any hockey player will be able to read between the skates—I'm no exception." It's a complete brush-off response, but I wave at the camera like I'm the goddamned king of England and back up out of the frame. "You good with all that?" I ask Fillmore, hoping he won't need more from me. "Don't have time for Celine Dion chitchat tonight."

By some twist of fate, he gives me a double thumbs-up and motions me into the locker room as though I've been dismissed.

I'll take the dismissal—it beats letting the darkness drag me under, the way it's done for the last year. It creeps into my chest, spiraling to my extremities like an infection running through my veins, paralyzing in its toxicity.

Deep breaths, man.

A hand claps down on my shoulder. "Want to grab celebratory wings and beer with the guys?"

I glance back at Harrison. "It's not really a celebration when the opposing team played it safe and kept their first line off the ice. We both know you let that last snipe in."

"I felt bad. Their rookies were slow as hell." His mouth quirks up. "I sure as fuck won't be lenient the next time we see them. Let's just say that I did it for rookie encouragement."

"What a giver," I drawl, cracking a grin as the pressure eases off my chest.

"My girl tells me the same thing in bed." With a wink, he steers me toward his stall with a hand to my shoulder, so he can change out of his gear and into street clothes. "I'm hoping she'll be saying the same thing when I pop the question."

The question.

I blink. Then blink again. "Holy shit, man, you finally proposing? Only took you what . . . like five years?"

Harrison grunts, flips me the bird, then draws a black

sweater over his head. "Somewhere around there. We've just been enjoying life."

It took me less than three to propose and marry Holly. We got married during my first season with the Bruins—a small, intimate wedding with just my mom, her grandmother and younger brother, and a select handful of friends present. We did it here in Boston, near the harbor with the lights from the ships twinkling a stone's throw away, and a tepid fall breeze teasing the strands of her blond hair.

Our wedding was beautiful. Elegant. Just like her.

Out of habit, I look at my left hand. It's unadorned, as it's been for months now, my platinum wedding band tucked away in a safe inside my condo. Balling my hand into a fist, I shake it out. Sometimes, in my weak moments, I can still feel Holly slipping the ring onto my finger. Can still see the way she smiled brightly, and whispered fervently, "Always you, Jackson."

Fuck me.

I brush aside my suit jacket, then slip my hand back into my pants pocket as I yank my head out of the past. "She'll say yes. Charlie loves you."

The goalie laughs. "Of course she'll say yes. Soulmates, man." He steps into a pair of black dress shoes, then hauls his big-ass duffel over his shoulder. "Anyway, you coming with us? The guys want wings, and I'm in the mood to play some darts and kick more ass than I already have tonight."

"If Charlie tells you to screw off when you get on one knee, it's because your ego is the size of Texas."

"So's my dick."

I roll my eyes. "Fat and squat, then? Lucky lady."

"What's fat and squat?" Hunt asks as he approaches us, his duffel—like Harrison's—hiked over one shoulder.

"Harrison's dick."

Hunt grins wickedly. "You in the fat-and-squat-cock club,

buddy?" He lifts a hand, palm out. "Give it, here, my man. It's a party of one—you're the first to join."

Harrison throws out a fist and punches our center in the arm. "Asshole."

The two bicker like an old married couple while we head for the bus parked outside of Bridgestone Arena. We all pile in, one after another, and I choose an empty seat toward the front. Stripping off my jacket, I lay it across my lap and watch as my guys file in past my row.

When Josh Kammer moves past me, I call him out. "Sit with me, rookie."

His eyes shoot to the back of the bus and then down at the aisle seat next to mine. "Yeah?" He sounds hesitant, uncertain. Fingers dive into his shorn hair, scratching behind his ear. "That cool?"

"It's cool if I say it is."

"Right." His ass collides with the seat, knees pinned together like he's scared shitless and trying to make himself disappear into thin air. Doesn't make his case any stronger when he wrings his hands and picks at his nails, head down like he's fascinated with the skin flaking off.

With my gaze on the seat in front of me, I give him a second to get a grip. Kammer was a first-round draft pick out of Rhode Island—a rookie that Coach, our GM, and I envisioned completing a power forward that could do real damage on the ice, alongside myself and Hunt, should something happen to Henri Bordeaux.

At URI, Kammer was quick on his feet, a player with little fear and a knack for making filthy moves that made the crowd roar with approval. Tonight, I didn't see any of that potential the team doled out so much money for. It's a problem. Kammer's contract is worth more than many veterans' and all eyes are on him to make that same magic happen for the Blades as he did for his alma mater.

"You played sloppy tonight," I finally murmur, not wanting to level him down to the quick by being brutally honest. Being brutally honest? Kammer was a damn pigeon out on the ice, always waiting to be fed the puck instead of making those same moves that earned him a spot on the team in the first place.

He's quiet for a moment, still fidgeting in his seat. "We won, Cap."

At his defensive tone, I set my ankle on my opposite knee, then lace my fingers over my shin. Casual to the very end. I learned long ago that yelling got me nowhere. What's that saying? Patience is a virtue? I'm an impulsive man in every aspect of life but with my team.

I tap my fingers on my leg. "Wrong answer, kid." His head jerks in my direction, and I lift a brow, daring him to challenge me. "Want to try again without the pissy attitude?"

"I'm just saying," he mutters, "we *won* and it's preseason. I'll do better next time."

"There won't be a next time if you show up like you did tonight." When he opens his mouth to argue, I stampede right over him: "Part of being a team is transparency. If you're nervous, say so. If your ankle feels like Satan just took a piss on it, mention it to John over in therapy. What you did tonight was stand there and skate like you've never played hockey before. The team won, but you didn't touch the puck once."

"Sometimes players don't get the biscuit. It happens—"

"Russell needed you to make an assist and you watched the puck fly past you."

His shoulders crumple at my mention of the second-line right-winger, my backup. "Fuck, Cap, I just—"

I don't pat his arm or hug him like I'm some mother hen tending to her chicks, but I do him one better. Shifting my hands from my shin to my knee, I say, "My first game with the NHL, I threw up in the locker room during our pep talk. I was so fuckin' nervous. I envisioned everything going wrong that could go wrong—me slipping when climbing over the boards, the Jumbotron catching me eating the bench when I wiped out. Anything and everything went through my head and I let that shit get to me."

"You *puked*?"

He sounds absolutely horrified, and I chuckle. "Right on the floor. Didn't even make it to the garbage can. You can ask my wi"—I clear my throat—"*ex*-wife when you see her. I'm sure she'd be all too happy to relay how I made a fool of myself."

Kammer's hands loosen and land on his thighs. "What'd your coach say?"

"Told me to clean the shit up while the rest of my team went out for the National Anthem. I was on my knees, trying not to hurl some more, while they were all out there, hands over their hearts and ready to play a killer game."

He whistles sharply. "Damn, that blows."

It'd been even worse when I finally got my ass to my team. I felt queasy, looked like shit, and proceeded to play the worst hockey of my career. "My coach benched me for the first three games of the season."

This time, Kammer says nothing and I can almost hear the wheels spinning in his head, no doubt worrying that *I'm* about to bench him right now. End of the day, Coach Hall makes the final decision on who plays or doesn't play, but I've got input and I've always had more control with the playbook than I've seen of other captains and their coaches.

The bus's engine hums to life, then rolls forward without further delay. The guys fuck around behind us, talking about darts and puck bunnies and the seven-motherfucking-goals they scored tonight.

I tip my head back. "I'm not gonna tell Coach to bench you, kid. You'd only be more nervous when you came back." It'd been that way for me. My first season with the Bruins had been an up-and-down relationship that could have been a showcase for a new TV show, When Jackson Carter Loses Everything. It'd resulted in me being traded to the Dallas Stars before, miracle of all miracles, the Bruins signed me back on after I got my ass in line. "You need to get the nerves out of your system while it's preseason because if you pull this shit during an actual game, you'll find yourself on the farm team so fast you won't even know what happened. This is our year to win the Cup, and you're either leading the pack with your line or you're the anchor around our neck that we need to cut loose. Which one is it going to be?"

"I want to be a part of the pack, Cap."

"Then go back to the hotel and find tonight's game online. Analyze every time you screwed up and be prepared to tell me everythin' you did wrong when we're back at practice in two days."

"But the guys are going out—"

"Not the rookies." I gesture for him to vacate the seat. "Y'all don't have the luxury of wings and beer and pussy until you're not slowing us down on the ice and letting two shots on the net go unchecked." I leave out mention of Harrison's pity goal; the Mountain has been in the NHL longer than I have and I'm not about to call him to task. "Send me Kase."

Grumbling, Kammer clambers to his feet. Throws me a glance as he turns for the back of the bus. "The guys are right," he grunts, "you're a fucking hard-ass."

My reputation precedes me.

I almost grin.

"I play to win, kid." I drop my foot to the floor and sit up. "And I accept nothing less from my team. If hockey isn't on the brain twenty-four-seven, then you don't want this bad enough—and I can guaran-goddamn-tee that someone else will want it more than you do."

Almost resentfully, he snips, "I want it, Cap."

"Then enjoy your night of watching clips and eating room

service. I'll be at the hotel's bar if you're feelin' the need to vent about how I'm an asshole for not letting you party with the vets."

His cheeks go red and he drops a fist on his vacated seat's headrest. "I'll get you Kase."

"Good choice."

As the bus barrels down the highway, toward the airport hotel where we're staying, I manage to squeeze in a talk with Kase, our backup goalie, and two other rookies who played decent tonight but not great.

The rookies are the first to scurry off the bus when we pull up at the hotel.

Welcome to my life—Captain of the Blades, babysitter to the newbies, and all-around asshole when anyone gets in my way of what I crave most: the Stanley Cup.

As I step down onto the cement, the gravel crackling under the soles of my leather shoes, I can't shake the fact that Holly never got on the bus with Carmen. Either she had plans afterward and took a cab or she simply wanted to avoid me after I gave her my peace offering on the plane.

I don't let either option bother me.

Captain.

Babysitter.

Hard-ass.

Nowhere on that list is "husband."

What she does in her spare time is not my business, and I'd be smart to do as I preach.

Eyes on the Cup.

Heart in the game.

But I'd be lying to myself if I said that I don't search for her in the hotel lobby when I make my way inside. Or that, when I come up empty, disappointment sinks into my bones.

Lucky for me, it's not the first time I've lied to myself—and after a year, I've gotten real good at smothering the truths deep down in the shadows of my soul.

Truth: letting Holly walk away is the hardest thing I've ever done.

Truth: I may have brought up divorce first but only because Holly had lost her spark, her luster, and I wasn't enough anymore to rekindle her fire.

Lie: I've moved on.

CHAPTER 10
HOLLY

I t's close to midnight by the time I make it back to the hotel with Carmen. After spending the last two hours at the bar with the Blades, pulling them to the side individually to get in our first round of personal interviews, I'm ready to hit the sack.

My feet hurt from standing.

My back aches from it being the dreaded time of the month again. Considering that I haven't had sex since Jackson, I wish I could at least flip an OFF switch on the period bit. Since my body has never reacted well to birth control, my only savior is Midol and even that doesn't do the trick most of the time.

Cramps 'R Us, you're the real devil incarnate.

All I want is a bed, some pillows to smash my face against, and a shower—not exactly in that order.

"How do you think we did without Adam tonight?" Carmen asks as we lug our equipment through the rotating front doors. "I know you usually don't hop on sound."

She's right.

As Carter Photography has grown over the years, I've expanded my knowledge to more than photography. I can work a camera just as well as any other videographer and know how to edit footage and get the best shots. Sound, however, has never been a passion of mine. In comes Adam, our resident sound mixer.

"We did fine." Shouldering my heavy backpack, I rearrange my grip on the equipment that wouldn't fit in our bags—my tripod and light reflector—and duck my head as we enter the hotel's lobby. "Plus, Adam would have been with us if he could."

"You mean it's not every day his wife gives birth to their first child?"

I grin at Carmen's teasing. "Just think, maybe if Sports 24/7 had approached us months ago like they did for the rest of the team, we could have told Adam to strap up one last time to keep the little guys from zipping to ground zero."

Carmen doesn't even bat an eye. "We're talking about his sperm now, aren't we?"

With the heavy weight on my back, I can't even roll my shoulders in a shrug. "More like we're talking about him deciding the wrong time to have sex. He should have waited for a full moon or the sign of a new zodiac or—"

"Waiting on an astrological sign to decide when to forego the condom? I know why *I'm* childless, but now it all makes sense for you."

Jackson and I were always way too busy with our careers to even think about adding a baby into the mix. Still, I only laugh off Carmen's comment, knowing that her teasing doesn't come from a place of ill-will, as we wait for the elevator to *ding!* and open up its glossy, reflective doors.

Turning my back on the elevator, I skim my gaze over the lobby. For a cheapo airport hotel, this one isn't too shabby. During my marriage, I stayed in countless throughout the country while I tagged along for game after game. It's my first time visiting this one.

A beautiful fountain bubbles to life to my right, positioned beneath a skylight some four stories above. Stone benches sit around it, as though encouraging visitors to take a seat and bask in the tranquil sounds of the fountain. Beyond it, a floor-to-ceiling window awaits, overlooking a gorgeous pool that I noted when we first arrived. Now, in the darkness, fairy lights twinkle outside the window, and I can almost imagine late-night swimmers paddling about in the pool.

Off to my left is a restaurant, and beside it, a bar.

My grip tightens on the tripod as I note the single figure seated at the far end. With his back to me, there's nothing particularly identifiable about him. Solid black T-shirt, backward ball-cap—solid black, too—gray sweatpants that could just as easily be from Walmart as they could be a designer brand.

I see nothing of his profile from where I stand.

And yet I know instinctively that it's him—Jackson—and I must be crazy because the only thought crossing my mind as I stare at him is, *He looks so lonely sitting there by himself.*

"Holly?"

My shoulders flinch at Carmen's inquiring tone. "Go up without me," I hear myself say, even though internally I'm shouting, *Stop what you're doing! Nuh-uh, don't do it, don't you do it.* I do it. "I need to . . ."—*think!*—"change my tampon."

Oh. Good. Lord.

"You can't wait until you get to your room?"

The elevator alerts its arrival with a *ding!* that sounds altogether more damning than me admitting, out loud, that seeing Jackson by himself at the bar twists at my insides in a way that I wish I could ignore.

"It's real heavy this month."

"At least you know you can't be pregnant."

I whip my head around to look at Carmen. "How would I be pregnant? I haven't had sex since Jackson—"

"Let me rephrase," she murmurs, a sly smile curving her lips, "at least you know that when you walk over to that bar and sit down next to that man you're eyeing, you can't have sex. We both know how you feel about getting it on when you're on your period."

I want to die of mortification, both because Carmen caught me staring at Jackson—though I guess I should feel thankful that she didn't recognize him—and since she's well-aware of the fact that when my period has taken up residency, my vagina gets a DO NOT DISTURB sign in the interim.

What can I say?

If *I* don't want to be down there during this time of the month, I don't want anyone else to be down there either.

When the elevator doors begin to slip shut, Carmen shoves an arm out to stop them. She walks backward into the brightly lit space, never taking her eyes off my face. "Do what you gotta do, girl," she tells me after reaching forward to hit the floor button she needs. "No judgment here."

"It's nothing."

The last thing I hear before the elevator doors close is, "Tell Jackson I say hi!"

Tell Jackson I say hi.

Dammit. I hate that Carmen knows me way too well. And that smug tone in her voice? Oh yeah, she knows exactly where my brain went when I spotted Jackson.

My shoulders slump, both from the weight of the bag strapped to my back, as well as with the internal battle I war with myself. I should go up to my room. Shower. Take out my contacts. Jump in bed in preparation for the 5 a.m. wake-up call we've all been handed in order to make our flight back to Boston.

My body will thank me for the sleep.

My damn cramps will weep with relief as soon as I retrieve my heating pad from my suitcase and put it to good use.

My feet, however, have different plans, and I find myself heading straight for Jackson. I try not to dwell on the fact that I could be heading into awkward territory—when was the last time either of us sought each other out for more than just a quick, business-worthy conversation?

Ages ago.

It honestly feels as though a time never existed where I

could leap into his embrace and freely wrap my arms around his solid mass, my palms rubbing the hard muscles of his back.

Nerves collect in my belly like hundreds of butterflies set in a jar with the lid sealed tight. I feel their silky wings whispering against my skin, somehow ending up in my chest, pushing at my throat until I'm right there, standing just behind him, trying to think of something witty to say.

"Want some company?"

There's no mirror along the bar, and he's at a complete disadvantage.

I can see him, but he has nothing to go on besides my voice—and in that quiet place where my weaknesses live, I wonder if we've been strangers for so long that he doesn't immediately recognize the sound of my voice anymore.

His ball-cap-covered head lifts and his shoulders visibly stiffen, and I worry that I've made a critical error in judgement. *Crap, crap, crap.* I silently order my feet to move, to hustle me back to the elevator where I can pretend that none of this happened. They're rooted to the carpet where I stand.

Jackson swivels on the barstool, his shoe hooking on the neighboring stool's foot rung. His elbows land on the bar behind him, and his biceps curl and flex under the thin fabric of his T-shirt—the thin fabric which has lifted far enough to give me a glimpse of his skin and the beginnings of a happy trail.

When I jerk my gaze up, my cheeks flushed, there's nothing in his expression to indicate that he feels the same chaotic pull that exists within me. And when he speaks in that gravel-pitch drawl of his, he's as smooth and as unaffected as I've ever heard him.

"You lost, Holls?" His dark eyes flit to the elevator behind me. "Or are you needin' some help with all your gear?"

I want to take that stool next to yours. I don't want you to look so alone.

Sometimes talking doesn't cut it and so I say nothing at all.

Instead, I set the tripod and light reflector down on the floor and suck back a pained moan when I slip the backpack from my shoulders and lower it next to the tripod. Unzipping the front pocket, I pull out my wallet and keep my gaze on the bar as I lift myself onto the stool.

"What're you drinking?" I ask my ex-husband as I flag down the bartender. "Beam and Coke?"

It's his usual—the same thing he's been ordering since we met so many years ago.

"Just Coke tonight."

Or *was* his usual.

I stave off a wave of disappointment that even his love for Beam and Coke has changed.

As Jackson turns on his stool, and as his knee grazes the outside of my left thigh, I smile brilliantly at the bartender when he stops to ask what I'm having. If Jackson had been drinking whiskey, I would have matched him with a cocktail to settle my nerves. As it is, I reach for a black beverage napkin and murmur, "Do you have any hot tea on hand? Green or jasmine? I'm not picky."

The bartender slides me a small, flirty smile. "Can I see your ID, miss? Just gotta check to see that you're of legal age." He leans in, his blue eyes locked on my face and that flirtatious grin still playing at his lips. "Don't need you stumbling your way back to your room after living so dangerously with your drink of choice."

Living so dangerously.

He couldn't be more accurate, especially given the way that Jackson straightens his back. With a growl that widens my gaze, he snaps, "She's knocking on social security's door, she's so old. Get her the damn tea before she expires and we're debatin' between a coffin or cremation."

The bartender glances from me to Jackson, and mutters, "Asshole," before beating it down the length of the bar.

I don't know whether to laugh or reprimand the man simmering beside me. "That was rude," I finally settle on, figuring it's the easy way out of a potentially awkward conversation.

Jackson wraps a hand around his glass, then tosses back half the soda like it's straight whiskey instead. "He was staring at your tits."

So much for avoiding the awkwardness.

I fold the napkin in half, then fold it again. "He was flirting."

"I'm aware."

I glance over at him, keenly cognizant of his surly tone. With his shoulders hunched and his hat pulled low to shield the upper part of his face, all I see is a clenched jaw and a set of full, pursed lips.

The bartender reappears, kettle in hand and tea cup sliding across the oak bar. "Your tea, miss. Do you want to pay now or open a tab—"

"Put it on mine."

"Jackson—" I cut off because there's no point in arguing. The bartender is already spinning in the opposite direction, away from us, and anything I'd say would be heard on deaf ears.

When Jackson wants to be an asshole, he's top of the line.

I swear it's the reason the Bruins were so hesitant about trading him to the Blades—it's not every day that you come across a player like the man seated beside me who's both admired and feared in the very same breath.

Cupping the teacup with both hands, I breathe out a sigh of relief at the warmth radiating from the porcelain. Not as good as a heating pad directly on my stomach, but it'll do for now. After a sip, I lower the cup. "Your team won and you're sitting here brooding. Pretty sure Harrison didn't stop bitching about you not being at the bar to one-up him in darts for almost an hour."

Jackson shifts on the stool, his legs spreading wide.

His knee touching mine.

I suck in another mouthful of tea to distract myself with a safer, more reliable sort of heat that has nothing to do with ex-husbands.

"Harrison would be bitching even more if I were there to take him out in darts," he murmurs, turning so that we're no longer quite shoulder-to-shoulder. He props one forearm on the bar, while his free hand, still holding onto his half-full glass, rests on his right knee. "Did you get the footage you needed?"

"I did." Grimacing, I shrug. "Well, mostly. I'll need to meet with the rookies to kick off their storylines but since they weren't—"

"I held them hostage."

I blink. "What?"

"It's tradition." Casually, he brings his glass up to his mouth, then watches me over the rim. "No rookie goes out after the first game of preseason."

Tradition?

Swiping my finger along the warm porcelain, I center my gaze on the cubes of ice floating in his soda. Much easier than looking him in the eye. "Can it really be considered a tradition when you've only just started it?"

He freezes mid-sip. Drops the soda back to his knee. I still see nothing of his eyes, thanks to the brim of his hat, but there's no missing how his lips part, then press back together like he's trying to gather his thoughts. Then, "We've been doin' it this way for three years now, Holls."

Three years.

My stomach lurches at the implication riding his tone—three years was before our divorce, before our separation, which means he's probably told me this before and I . . .

I wish I had a hat of my own to hide behind.

Since I don't, I avert my gaze and bring my teacup to my mouth. I ignore the scalding of hot liquid on my tongue as I draw the tea into my system and attempt to push the conversation forward. "So, you what? Keep them from having fun with the rest of the guys? Stand outside their guestrooms to make sure they stay locked inside?"

The firm line of his mouth relaxes. "I teach them that hockey will always come first. For as long as they're in this game, they've got to live and breathe it—over going out, over picking up women, over everything."

CHAPTER 12
JACKSON

I regret the words immediately, especially when Holly's pretty blue eyes drop to her lap in clear disappointment.

And no wonder, jackass, you pretty much told her that hockey came before her and your marriage.

Fuck.

"Holls—"

She shakes her head, her usual blond ponytail swinging, and sets her teacup back on the bar. If we were the old us, I'd cup her face, slide my knuckle under her chin and force her to look at me.

To *see* me.

The man who loved her more than life itself.

The man who's drowning under an awkward concoction of pride and anxiety, so much so that I can hardly see straight anymore.

"Let's get this on camera?" she murmurs, jumping off the stool to start pulling at her gear. "Tell me all about what the rookies have to learn, but just"—she unzips her backpack and pulls out a fancy-ass camera that I can't even begin to name—"hold on a minute while I set everything up."

After placing my soda next to her tea, I move to where

she's hooked the camera onto the tripod. When she bends over to grab something else, my hand catches on her arm and I pull her back up.

"Holly."

Blue eyes lift to meet my gaze. "Almost done. One sec."

Her skin feels hot as fire beneath my palm, smooth as the finely worn rocks I used to skip back home in the small pond that sat on the edge of our family property. *Let her go.* I ignore reason, just for a moment, and sweep my thumb back and forth over her arm.

Holly Belliveaux Carter has always been my weakness.

I have no interest in speaking to her for the camera, for the public, but it's the reason why she's here in this hotel in the first place. *Remember that—she chose to help you but not because she was all excited to do so. Or because she's hoping to get back together with you. This is business, nothing more.*

Releasing her, I step back and drag my thumb across my bottom lip. "What can I do to help?"

I'm not even sure she's aware of glancing down at where I touched her, but then she's smiling—as genuine as the fake smile she gave to the bartender—and pointing at her gear and instructing me on how to get it all set up.

Five minutes later, my ass is on the barstool again and she's hovering by the camera, all professional, with her hair bundled on the top of her head and her shirt half-tucked into her pants. She looks a little tired, a little worn out, and it's on the tip of my tongue to tell her that we can do this another day when she doesn't look half-dead on her feet.

"You ready?" she asks.

No. "Yeah."

"Perfect!" Flashing me another of those bright-but-not-real smiles, she steps away from the camera to watch me with her hips squared off and her hands by her sides. "Okay, we're going to jump right in. I'll edit out all the extras, so let's ignore the camera—"

"Hard to do that with all that light shining on me." I slip my fingers through my hair, all too aware that the strands feel flat now that I've discarded my hat.

"Just think of it like . . ." Holly's fingers tap on her thigh. "Ah, I got it. Just think of it like God's coming down to judge you for all your sins."

I bark out a laugh. "*That's* supposed to make me feel better?"

"I'm rarely in the hot seat, but I figure that if I were, it'd be a bit like confession." Her voice drops to a playful cadence. "Tell me all of the things, Captain Carter."

If it were only her I was telling, I'd be a hell of a lot more tempted to open my pie-hole and do some confessing. As it is, I palm a fist over my thigh and then dip my head in acquiescence. "I've only been to confession once in my life."

"Have you? I don't think I've heard this story before."

She moves into the light, a bright halo surrounding the crown of her head and casting her features in shadows. But I can practically hear her smile—and, this time, I know without doubt that it's real. Wanting to keep the ease of the conversation going, a first for us in so long, I drag the heel of my palms down the length of my thighs. "And"—I draw in a deep, dramatic breath—"I lied."

"*What*?"

I nod sagely. "Crazy, right? I went willingly into confession because my momma demanded it of me. We were one of the only Catholic families in Zachsville, so it's not like I had much of a choice in the matter."

"How old were you?"

Scrubbing the day-old scruff on my jawline, I make a show of thinking real hard. "Twelve? Maybe thirteen?"

There's a small hesitation, and then she murmurs, "And you lied?"

"Oh yeah. See, it was Christmas time, and my dad asked me if I'd help with getting the lights for the tree out of the attic. I said yes—he bribed me with the lure of pizza—and all I had to do was stand at the bottom of the ladder as he slid me down a box to catch."

Holly steps forward, arms over her chest, a smile tugging at her lips. "I'm already scared on your behalf."

"You should be, swee—" I break off, clearing my throat, hand moving from my jaw to ease against my mouth. *Shut up, man, don't even go there.* I reach blindly behind me, my fingers grasping the cup she abandoned, and I suck down what's left of the tea. I hate tea to the core of my soul, but God knows it's better to pretend that I'm afflicted by a random bout of coughing than to confess that I almost called her *sweetheart.*

Some habits are impossible to break.

"*Anyway,*" I continue, the cup clasped between my hands, "there I am, ready to catch this box that my dad says will have everything we need—and then it rips in half as he's lowering it down the ladder toward me."

She barely covers up a shocked burst of laughter. "Please tell me you didn't get hurt."

Warmth spreads in my chest that she would be concerned in the first place, and then I'm shoving it away to keep on with the story. "Depends on the way you look at it," I murmur with an easy roll of my shoulders. "All I remember is my dad shouting, "oh, hell," and then the next minute it was raining down old-fashioned glass Christmas lights and *Playboy* magazines."

I watch as her blue eyes go wide and her cheeks, even with the glare of the lights we've set, turn pink. She's biting down so hard on her lower lip that I'm surprised she doesn't draw blood. "Jackson," she manages to work out in between gusts of laughter, "oh, my God."

"Trust me," I mutter, enjoying her joy way too much for my own good, "God wouldn't have wanted any part of that scene. I don't know which one of us was more embarrassed— my dad as he stared down at me hopping around, trying to avoid shattered glass and old-as-fuck magazines, or me, when I realized that everywhere I looked were breasts."

"Looks like Santa came early that year."

Laughter climbs my throat at her blasé tone, and it takes everything in my power to maintain a straight face. Thumb sweeping across my bottom lip, I feel my lips curve into the first real smile I've had in months—despite the light hitting me square in the face and turning my vision splotchy.

I couldn't look away from Holly if I tried.

"My dad was horrified, naturally, and I was a preteen with sudden access to all these naked women on the pages."

"You didn't."

I lift my arms wide, palms up, tea cup clasped in my right hand. "I did."

"I don't know whether to slap you on the back and tell you congrats or shut my eyes and try not to think about where this story is going."

"It gets worse," I offer happily.

She shakes her head. "Of course it does."

"I don't know how many times I jerked off to those magazines. My dad even had the very first issue, and let's be honest, it would have been a crime *not* to take advantage of what Santa had given to me as an early present." I pause, waiting for her to hurry me along, and when she does, I drawl, "Only, my mother caught me one night."

"Poor Momma Martha," Holly whispers, a smile barely contained on her face. "I can only imagine how loud she must have shrieked."

"The neighbors called the cops."

"I'm surprised she didn't drop dead of a heart attack right then and there."

"Oh, she tried, trust me, but nothing a little cold water couldn't remedy."

When I wink, Holly only presses her fingers to her lips again to hold back another laugh. "You're awful."

And it feels so damn good to be laughing with you again.

"Guilty as charged." Setting the teacup down, I lean back, elbows on either side of me on the bar. "When she asked where the magazine came from, I wouldn't answer. Didn't want to do that to Pops, y'know, even if he had just been deployed, halfway across the world, for his tour of duty. The very next day, she dragged me straight to confession. Told me in that proper Texan drawl of hers that I'd tell the priest exactly what I'd done."

"So, you told him that you . . . that you . . ." She trails off, uncertainty crossing her face for the first time since she first sat down, and then huffs out, "masturbated" all prim and proper.

"Nah," I say, "I turned my pops right in. Lied and told him that my dad handed me that *Playboy* and said, 'now's your turn to learn how to be a man.' The priest laughed, told me to recite some Hail Mary's for as many times as I'd jerked off, and then sent me on my way."

"Your mother must have been ready to kill you *and* your dad."

"She still doesn't know." I let out a low chuckle. "The priest never told her, and I didn't want her getting mad, so I kept it all to myself . . . until now."

Our easy back-and-forth slips into a small silence, and then Holly murmurs, "I'm not even sure if I want to know this . . . but how many Hail Mary's did you have to say?"

I grin, and I know it's a wicked one just based on the way Holly's eyes go wide. "I wasn't done until Lent was over."

It's an exaggeration by far but it has the result I want.

Holly's blond head tips back as peals of laughter strip from her soul and dance in the space between us. "You're so bad," she whispers, flicking a tear away from the corner of her eye, "so, so bad."

Familiar heat settles low in my gut as I climb to my feet,

and I catch myself just before I would have swooped in and wrapped my arms around her, binding her to me.

She told you not to cross boundaries.

I want to reject that voice of reason. I want to press my lips to hers and claim her the way I did for all those years that we were married.

But we aren't married, not anymore.

The reality of our situation crashes down on me like tons —literal tons—being heaped on my shoulders. The reality of our situation is that we tried to meet in the middle and failed. The reality of our situation is that she deserves more than a man who prioritized hockey over everything else in his life.

Funny how, when it comes to hockey, I'm the force no one wants to reckon with, but with my own wife, I broke the second she looked at me from across the table at our favorite restaurant and said, "We need to talk."

Fact is, I'm that pathetic sack of shit who let Holly slip through my fingers. She didn't leap for joy when I mentioned divorce, but she sure as hell didn't deny that maybe it was for the best, that maybe we'd simply grown apart.

You can't "grow apart" from somebody when they've got your heart in a vice. At least, that's how it's always felt for me, even now.

I rake my fingers through my hair, turning my body slightly, so that the glare of the light isn't shining directly on my face and in my eyes.

"Oh, crap."

My gaze leaps to her heart-shaped face. "What?"

She edges past me to reach for the camera, then flashes me a sheepish grin. "Accidentally got all that on camera. I totally forgot that we were filming once you got into your story."

Well, damn.

She presses a button, bottom lip sucked behind her front teeth, and then pumps a fist in the air. "All right, we're good."

"We are?" And damn me if my brain doesn't automatically transcribe her words to mean that *we're* good, as in us, our relationship, what little we have of it left.

"Yep!" She grins, then reaches up to tug on her ponytail. "You, Captain, have been deleted from my memory card."

Deleted.

So fucking final—how incredibly ironic.

I force a grin to match the one she's sporting. "Thanks for looking out."

"*Pshhh.*" Winking at me, she begins to disassemble her setup. "I did it for Momma Martha, Jackson. Can you imagine if she saw all that on TV next week with the season's pilot episode? She'd have a conniption. We'll get a more . . . *professional* interview another day."

If my mom witnessed that confession on TV, she'd fly to Boston, thwack me with her slipper, and then drag my ass back to Texas, kicking and screaming the whole way. If there is any luck in the world, she'd bring her best friend Honey, and Honey would at least laugh about it with me on the flight —even while my dear mother prayed for my soul.

Holly bends over, tucking the camera back into her backpack, flashing me her round ass—and I cut my gaze to the ceiling.

Don't look. She's not yours. Don't you dare —

I look, like a starved man who's been hooked on the same diet for over a decade.

A diet that I've refused to give up even though my sex life with Holly dried up years ago.

Before I'm aware of speaking, I hear the rasp in my voice when I say, "Can I ask you something?"

Still bent over, still testing the limits of my control, Holly glances back at me, her ponytail swinging down to point at the floor. "Sure?"

I clear my throat. Swipe my clammy hands against my sweats. "You were done for the evenin' and you still came over to me. Why?"

She drops to her haunches, knees cracking the way they've always done after an early career in gymnastics and dance, before meeting my gaze head-on.

Hell, her eyes are so blue. It seems incredible that it feels like I'm seeing them now for the very first time, noting their exact hue: a dark navy rim, a brighter, more cerulean center. My dick stiffens in my pants, and I ignore the bastard like he's a traitor on the verge of mutiny.

"Holls?"

She doesn't smile this time, as sober as I've quite literally been for almost a year, and then tears my heart in two with only four words: "You looked so alone."

CHAPTER 13
HOLLY

"**W**ho made the jalapeño poppers?"

At Carmen's question, I lift my glass of merlot in salutation. "You're looking at her," I say with a grin, plucking one off the tray on the table before us. Cheesy goodness oozes from the hot pepper (sans seeds, of course), and with a toast to Carmen, I pop it into my mouth and squeeze my eyes shut in culinary bliss. "Oh, man, perfect amount of cream—"

"You think that's her O face?" Shelby, my assistant, asks the room.

My eyes fly open. "*Shelby.*"

She blinks back at me. "What? Like we weren't all already thinking it with you moaning like that over there."

By *we*, she means all ten staffers of Carter Photography. In honor of *Getting Pucked*'s two-hour season premiere tonight, I decided to host a watch-party in our office. And I've brought all of the necessary supplies to keep us entertained: appetizers, pizza, wine and beer, dessert.

And, apparently, the O face.

Cue: instant mortification.

In my defense, I'm a total foodie. I'd eat my way through a

city if given the opportunity. If it weren't for finding my calling with photography, I'd have dug straight into the cooking world.

Cooking—not baking—feeds my soul. Literally.

Downing a gulp of wine, I mutter, "How about we act like we're professionals? No talking about orgasms."

Shelby trades a glance with Carmen. "We're off the clock, which means that orgasms can be on the table."

God, not this conversation again. Since my divorce, Shelby has made it her mission—in between auditions for whatever latest show she wants a role in—to get me a man. A *new* man. Really, any man that isn't Jackson Carter. The fact that I'm not interested in dating? Not a problem, the way she sees it. In her mind, I'm sure, I'm just ready to be plucked up by the next eligible Boston bachelor.

I glance up at the flat-screen TV mounted on the wall, wishing that the show would start so I can avoid this conversation once again. When the commercial cuts to yet another commercial, I accept temporary defeat with another pull of my wine. "I don't think Adam wants to listen to us talk about orgasms."

Naturally, my sound guy only offers a shrug that's both bashful and ambivalent. "You could talk about whatever you wanted—I'm still riding on the high of my wife giving birth."

"Perfect!" Shelby exclaims, clapping her hands together. "Orgasms it is!" She leans forward in her chair, then drops her elbows on the oak table that stretches nearly the length of the conference room. Brown hair hanging in wavy curls, she tucks the strands behind her ears and resumes her position.

God help me.

I nudge Carmen in the side. "More wine," I mutter out of the corner of my mouth, handing her my glass. "Better yet, pass over the bottle instead."

Carmen ignores my plea for all of the wine and only pours me another glass of red. "You don't have the luxury of getting sloppy tonight. You told me that we had to take notes on the show—see what we can improve on for next week."

She's right, I know she's right.

While we spent the latter part of last week editing footage and corresponding with *Getting Pucked*'s TV producers about the highlight reels they wanted for their clips, we've yet to see the entire episode from start to finish. Tonight is the night, for better or for worse, and our gathering is as much of a team-bonding exercise as it is analyzing every aspect of our contribution to the episode to see what we can work on.

Which is sort of the issue with me signing with the Blades and not Sports 24/7.

I no longer have the upper hand, and whatever their producers decide is the end of the road. For a control freak like myself, my new situation isn't ideal, but I meant what I said to the team: my loyalty will always be with the Blades and not some sports network.

Still, nerves balloon in my belly as I try to keep my focus locked on my employees and not scoping out the clock on the wall every two minutes, waiting for 8 p.m. to strike on the dot.

"The thing is," Shelby is saying now, "you want to open your mouth a little more for the moan. Like, make your cheeks all hollow and don't forget to flare your nostrils maybe a half-centimeter or something, just for show." When she demonstrates, I don't even bother to pay her any attention. She's a boss when it comes to administrative work, but I'll be dead before I start taking advice about how to look in the throes of orgasm from an actress.

Who also just so happens to be a virgin.

I may be in a years' long dry spell, but at least I've done the deed before, thank you very much.

Carmen snorts into her drink beside me, just as Adam shouts, "Guys, guys, opening credits are on!"

My gaze leaps to the TV as the male narrator announces,

"You think you know us, but you haven't seen us like this before. For the next two hours, I'll be taking you behind the scenes with the Boston Blades. We're the NHL's biggest threat . . . but only if we can work together to take the Cup home at the end of the season."

Hold on . . .

I don't even have the chance to say a word before one of my photographers, Maisey, shouts, "Wait, hold the goddamn phone. Was that *Jackson* doing the voiceover?"

I open my mouth and . . . and . . .

For the first time in my life, I have no words.

None. Zilch. Nada.

Someone's cell phone *pings!* with an incoming message, but I can't tear my focus away from the TV. Jackson—*my* Jackson—is the one narrating the entire season?

He's not yours anymore.

Whatever. Semantics.

Regardless, how in the world did he go from not wanting to do *Getting Pucked* at all to signing up for the show's narration?

"Phone," Carmen says at my side, dropping my cell into my lap. "You might want to look at it."

I glance down, heart rate spiking at the name on the glass screen.

JACKSON:

I'm sorry in advance.

He's sorry? What the hell does that mean? I mean, logistically, there are a lot of things he could be sorry for, starting with the two of us and ending with apologizing for who the hell knows what.

Swiping my thumb across the screen to unlock the phone, I tap on my ex-husband's text message and am promptly bombarded with text after text.

BEAUMONT:

Carter, man, did you add her?

HARRISON:

Seconding that. You added Holly to Safe Space, right?

JACKSON:

She's in.

Bless her heart.

HUNT:

Holly!!!! Welcome!

HARRISON:

Hunt, dude, we agreed to let Carter roll out the proverbial red carpet. Wait your turn.

UNKNOWN NUMBER:

She hasn't said anything yet…you think we scared her off?

UNKNOWN NUMBER:

If we did, I blame Kammer.

UNKNOWN NUMBER:

What the fuck, Cain?? I didn't do shit. Calm your tits.

UNKNOWN NUMBER:

My tits are calm, asshole. Stop looking at them.

UNKNOWN NUMBER:

I'm not even in the same building as you!!

UNKNOWN NUMBER:

Stop thinking about them, then.

BEAUMONT:

Children, behave—before I take my stick and
shove it where the sun don't shine.

HUNT:

This conversation went downhill so fast.

Tearing my gaze from what is clearly some sort of group chat for the Blades players, I hop off the couch with a mutter that I'll be back. Shelby protests that I'm leaving in the middle of a segment of us interviewing Henri Bordeaux, but I have bigger fish to fry right now.

Like figuring out why I've been added to the so-called "Safe Space."

The same elusive group chat Jackson spent all of his time in while we were married.

At least, I've got a feeling it's the same one.

Shutting the door behind me, I step into the hall and head for my office. The floor is devoid of all light, but I've spent so many late hours here that it's no problem at all to feel my way to my office and let myself in.

City lights dance through my window, giving the room an almost ethereal glow.

All the while, my phone continues to vibrate in my hand like it's a ticking time bomb. I scan the group text once more, the phone's luminous screen making it easy to read the messages:

JACKSON:

Cain, calm your tits. Kammer, stop being a
bitch. Beaumont, for fuck's sake, man, leave
the stick talk to your wife or on the ice.

HARRISON:

Guys, show just started.

BEAUMONT:

Holy shit, Carter, you sound like a frog.
Scratch that, you sound like you swallowed a
dick.

UNKNOWN NUMBER:

What size dick?

HUNT:

Medium. Not girthy. Big, fat head though.
Wicked veiny.

JACKSON:

Y'all are a bunch of idiots. Also, can we
PLEASE watch the language now that y'all
begged me to add Holly?

UNKNOWN NUMBER:

Oh, shit, I forgot already. Sorry Holly!

UNKNOWN NUMBER:

Sorry Holly

BORDEAUX:

I miss everything, yes?

No doubt about it, their group thread is a disaster zone and a PR catastrophe in the waiting.

And, somehow, I've found myself in the thick of it all.

With sweaty palms, I scroll through my contacts for the one person I haven't called directly in a year. I wait, heart in my throat, for Jackson to answer, torn between hoping that he picks up and praying that he doesn't.

My emotions, just like the Safe Space thread, are as chaotic as an Irish pub here in Boston on St. Patty's Day.

By the fourth ring, disappointment thickens the lump in my throat. Convinced that he has no plans to answer, I pull the phone from my ear and hover my thumb over the red telephone button.

"Idiot," I mutter to myself. I stare at the time stamp rolling at the top of the screen, mocking me with how many seconds I've waited.

Thirty-one seconds, that's how long.

Thirty seconds too—

"Holly?"

His voice is tinny, small.

My thumb switches angles from the red button to tapping the speakerphone option.

"Holls, you there?"

Over the phone, his voice is pitched lower. Rougher. During the early days when we first dated, I used to live for him calling me just so I could hear him as he sounds now. I'm only a little ashamed to admit that the timbre of his voice still twists my insides and curls my toes.

One day, I tell myself, *one day that'll all just stop.*

Because if I'm forced to spend the rest of my life lusting after my ex-husband's voice, I'm calling it right now: in a previous life, I must have screwed someone over real bad. Worse than a burger in a recycling bin. What other reason would I have to pay this sort of penance now?

"Hey." I clear my throat, laying waste to the lump that just won't go away. "I'm here."

The line dips into short, uncomfortable silence. Then, "Is everything okay?"

In the darkness of my office, with only the scant cityscape to create shadows, it's so damn easy to support the illusion that this phone call is like any other we used to have. I can picture me sitting on the white, plush sofa that I've got pressed against the far wall, my skirt lifted to my hips and my fingers playing between my legs as Jackson whispers dirty, feverish words over the phone.

On the few occurrences when I couldn't make his games, he never let the distance stop him from making me cry out his name. Or from him ducking into the hotel bathroom to keep his teammates clueless as to what he was up to.

"Holly, are you there?"

His voice is sharp now, not the seductive growl that tips me over the edge. It's sharp enough to send me tumbling from the memories and back into reality.

With shaky fingers, I slip my hair behind my ears and drop my chin with a heavy breath. "Yeah, I'm sorry. I'm here." *Be normal. Don't be awkward!* "Why did—"

"Look," he says, and I can almost picture him leaning his head back against the cushions while he reclines on his couch, "I should have told you the guys wanted you in the group chat, so I'm sorry if that caught you off guard. They're persistent assholes."

"Trust me, I'm aware." If I wasn't already, that group text definitely solidified it for me. *Persistent* might actually be an understatement. "Why add me at all?"

His breath crackles over the phone, and I remove him from speakerphone to press the cell to my ear. "They said that you're a part of the team now that you're filming us for the next few months." He pauses, and then adds, "You can mute them."

"Mute them?" I ponder out loud, my thumb caressing the smooth edge of my phone case, "or you, too?"

Laughter greets me, deep and gritty. "Is that a dig at my voiceover skills?"

Even though he can't see me, my shoulders lift in a shrug. "I'd say don't quit your day job any time soon for acting, but it seems you're heading in that direction anyway."

This time, there's no pause on his end. I hear rustling like he's getting comfortable—on the couch? In his bed?—and then he's speaking again: "It was cheesy, huh?"

I smile, just a little. "Now don't go putting words in my mouth, Captain."

He laughs again, and the sound heats me like basking

under the sun after months of winter. "Don't give me open-ings like that, Holls. You know I can't resist the pull to make you blush."

Only then do I realize the *exact* opening he's talking about.

Oh, God. Talk about embarrassing innuendos.

"I didn't mean—"

"I know you didn't," he says, cutting me off. "You're safe from my teasing—don't stress about it. Boundaries, right?"

Pushing off from the desk, I move toward the window. I press my fingertips to the cool glass, then glance down at the bustle of a Friday night in Boston. Car lights zoom down Arlington Street, and I think of all the evenings I spent here at the office instead of at home with the man on the other end of the line.

Curiosity pushes the words up and out of my mouth: "Why aren't y'all watching the episode together? There's no game tonight."

A pause. Then, "Most of them opted to watch it with their families."

My heart twists at everything he isn't saying. The guys are with their wives, their girlfriends, their families, and he's . . . "Are you at home?"

His home, girl, not yours.

I shove the thought away, refusing to give it any weight. I sold *our* home almost a year ago when the memories proved to be too heartbreaking. I'm not someone who loves self-torture, and living in the same house that we bought together when we moved to Boston? It was torture at the ultimate level.

Not that being on the phone with him now is any better. Not for my peace of mind, at least.

"Jackson?"

"Yeah," he finally says, "I'm home. Me, my takeout from Sam's, and a bottle of water."

At the mention of Sam's Italian Cuisine, I can't stop the

moan from slipping out. Thinly woven dough with butter slathered over the toasted crust, and prosciutto tucked inside like a treasure of meat heaven. My mouth waters as though I'm starved, even though I scarfed down two slices of pizza less than an hour ago. "Oh my God, I haven't had Sam's in so long. I miss it."

Like a lot of my other favorite things in life, I've avoided Sam's since our divorce. It was the first restaurant we tried together here in Boston, and the same restaurant where we sat when Jackson first brought up that we might not be able to work out for the long haul. That night, I'd wanted to talk to him about the tension I felt growing between us. The words were barely out of my mouth before he was giving voice to the word no married person ever wants to hear.

Divorce.

I hadn't wanted to hear it.

But deep down, behind the tears, I'd also known that we'd reached an irreversible place. We were strangers who no longer had any common ground between us beyond our wedding bands and our memories.

Good memories. Bad memories.

My forehead tips forward and kisses the window. I clutch the phone in my hand like a lifeline as I watch the activity beyond the glass—watching life pass me by as I'm forever hooked on the past.

On my ex-husband.

There's more rustling, and then Jackson's gravel-pitched voice drawls, "I got those little dough things you like so much."

I can't help but chuckle. "Rub it in my face, why don't you." The bastard. He *knows* how much I love them.

I hear what sounds like foam containers being pried open. Hushed chewing as though he's pulled the phone away from his mouth. A sex-on-a-stick groan that sends a spark of lust and need straight to my core.

"Damn," he growls, "only one more left. I was going to save it for tomorrow, but I think . . ."

My mouth goes dry. "You think what?"

"I think I'll eat it just for you, Holls. No need to thank me." My stomach lets out a growl of its own when he tacks on, "I wouldn't do this for just anyone, you know, especially when I'm already stuffed."

Listening to my ex-husband eat my favorite food shouldn't be sexy, but here I am. Rock meet bottom: feeling hot and bothered as he tempts me with groans and happy sighs over the phone.

Figures that the sounds he's making are as close to sex as I've gotten since the last time *we* were in bed together.

"You're a real gentleman, Captain."

I hear him swallow, probably polishing off the last of the doughy treats at my expense. "I'm a lot of things, but—"

"Don't say it."

He doesn't heed my warning. "—I prefer to think of myself as a king."

I shake my head, hating the way I can't help but smile at his dry tone. "Your ego, Jackson."

"It's big, I know."

"I was going to say that it's impenetrable, actually."

"And big." Maybe it's just my imagination, but I swear he's grinning. "Big like my—"

"Don't you dare go there."

"What?" He's all boyish innocence now. "Big *heart*, Holls, that's where I was going. Damn, would you get your mind out of the gutter?"

My heart beats a quick tattoo, and I pull back from the window a scant few inches. Focus on my hazy reflection staring back at me in the glass instead of the cityscape beyond it. I'm grateful for the shadows—without them, I'm sure it'd be hard to ignore the blush that's warming my cheeks, thanks to his playful teasing.

Since I've always given as good as I've gotten, I don't stop now. "My mind is being airlifted out as we speak, thank you so much for your concern." I lower my voice. "I'm glad to be rescued. It was scary down there—downright terrifying."

"Yeah?"

"Oh yeah." I meet my gaze in my reflection, the blue of my eyes muted to a dull gray in the shadows. "There was chanting and incense and hockey players galore, and in the very center of it all . . . their king."

He pauses. Then, "How did I look?"

"A lot like Andre Beaumont."

Surprised laughter erupts on the other end of the line. "Touché. My ego deserved that."

I push away from the window. "It probably deserves a lot more if we're going for full transparency. It's out of control."

"Comes with the territory of being captain."

"Comes with the territory of you being *you*." I tuck my hair behind my ear, then pause at my office door, reluctant to get off the phone when I've . . . *Be honest with yourself at least.* And the honest truth is—I've missed this. The quick back-and-forth, the laughter, the feeling that someone out there gets me and my humor. I miss *him.*

There, I said it.

I miss him, Jackson, my ex-husband.

"I should probably go," he says softly. "We've got an early flight tomorrow."

Right. Of course. Two days ago, the Blades went skate to skate against Toronto at home, but starting tomorrow, it's two straight away games to wrap up preseason. First up, the Philadelphia Flyers and then the Chicago Blackhawks. Carmen, Adam, and I will no doubt be quarantined to our hotel rooms in order to get all footage edited ahead of our deadline or face the wrath of Mark Fillmore.

I scrub my hand over my jaw, swiping it down over my mouth as dread filters in. "I hate early mornings."

"I remember."

My chest inflates with a deep inhale. "Some things never change."

"No, some things don't." The line goes silent, and I'm pulling open the door when he adds, "In case I haven't mentioned it yet, I'm proud of you, Holls. What you're doing with the team? The show? I'm just . . . yeah, I just wanted you to know. You're doin' great."

Maybe I shouldn't let his praise swell my lungs with air and push my shoulders back with confidence, but I do. "Thank you," I whisper, my fingers tightening their hold on my phone, "that means a lot to me."

"Good." More silence. "Okay, right. I'll see you in the morning. Night, Holly."

"Night, Jackson."

Pulling my phone away from where it's been cradled against my ear, I finally click the red telephone—but not until I note the time we spent talking on the phone together.

Thirty-one minutes and one second.

Something about that makes me grin. I've missed a decent chunk of *Getting Pucked*'s first episode, and as I wait for the sting of regret to settle in, I pull open the Safe Space group chat that Jackson added me to. My grin only widens.

HARRISON:

Holly? Are you there? Did we scare you off?

BEAUMONT:

Pretty sure that Jackson can take the blame for that one. Him and his clogged throat on TV.

HUNT:

Look at that massive forehead. Jesus, Mary, and Joseph, Andre—you park cars on that thing???

UNKNOWN NUMBER:

Park or pahk the cah?

HUNT:

The rookie thinks he's got Boston jokes.

UNKNOWN NUMBER:

I DO have jokes.

HUNT:

How's this for a joke, Kammer? Me, you, at dawn, pisto

UNKNOWN NUMBER:

Pisto? Is that a new pasta sauce?

HUNT:

No, it's called my wife asking me to let the dog out and I couldn't threaten you and be a good dog-dad all at once.

UNKNOWN NUMBER:

#whipped

BEAUMONT:

#dontbejealousrookie

UNKNOWN NUMBER:

I don't know about Kammer, but I'm jealous about the dog. I need a new apartment that allows animals.

HARRISON:

Anyone notice that Jackson has disappeared and Holly has yet to comment?

UNKNOWN NUMBER:

Maybe she muted us.

HUNT:

I noticed.

BORDEAUX:

I notice.

BEAUMONT:

Bets, right now, that they're on the phone.

HARRISON:

Ten bucks.

BEAUMONT:

Cheap bastard.

HUNT:

Fifty.

God, they're ridiculous.

And after so many years of knowing them, they're family, too. But like with all family, sometimes what they don't know won't hurt them.

ME:

Hello boys. Unfortunately for all of you, I've been watching the episode with my team. Not sure about Jackson, but if you want to transfer that money over to me . . . I wouldn't be opposed to the extra cash ;-)

I pocket my phone, then head back to where I left Carmen and the rest of my staff.

My talk with Jackson tonight . . . the way my heart felt lighter than it has in years? I'm not willing to share any of that, not just yet.

CHAPTER 14
JACKSON

My eyes are locked on the puck when I'm hit by a goddamn tank.

Fitzgerald, one of Philly's D-men, cedes no mercy as stars dance and black webs crawl across my vision. The force of his body check slams me into the boards, my helmet glancing off the Plexiglas, the crowd beyond it roaring with applause as I blink rapidly.

In a sea of tangerine orange, I spot a lone blue-and-silver jersey.

Blades fans representing in enemy territory—gotta love them.

"Might want to sit down, old man. Wouldn't want you embarrassing yourself on reality TV," Fitzgerald grunts by my ear as he tries to hook the biscuit and steal it away.

Not happening.

Vision still swirling, head still pounding, I hunch my shoulders and bulldoze my way out of the hole with enough force that Fitzgerald falls back. I skim my gaze over the ice, the players flying toward me from all angles as nausea rips up my throat and everything goes topsy-turvy.

Not right now, not right now.

By sheer force of will, I keep my protein shake down and feed the puck to Bordeaux where he's waiting outside the crease. Fitzgerald curses behind me, knocking into my shoulder as he flies toward the net. I follow a heartbeat later, fully prepared to tackle the asshole if he so much as—

Bordeaux lines up the shot and snaps the puck forward.

—*fuck.*

Fitzgerald's partner-in-crime clears the puck, stopping what would have been a filthy clapper, and proceeds to hustle down the rink.

Unlike when we played Nashville, the Philadelphia Flyers aren't jerking around.

The fierce competitor in me demands that we switch lines and get Beaumont and Cain on the ice to do their job. Losing isn't an option, not even in preseason, but neither is keeping the rookies off the ice until game day hits, when we all realize that they're timid and nervous and un-fucking-capable of protecting Harrison in the net.

Today doesn't count. I tell that to myself when Kammer misses an opportunity to gain possession of the puck. I repeat the same mantra when, in the next period, our rookie center loses the face-off. I curse under my breath, repeating it once more, when the Flyers' forward successfully drops a pass and our second-line defenseman, Quinton Dennis, falls for the ploy. A second later, the Flyers swoop up the temporarily discarded puck and head straight for Harrison.

Stick back.

Head down.

They score.

Even though the scoreboard doesn't lie about our 2-2 tie, as the last few seconds of the game tick away, I'm on the verge of sitting every one of my players down and having a come-to-Jesus moment about how much they fucking sucked tonight.

A tie is not a win—it's a glorified participation ribbon for those over the age of fifteen.

As we shake hands with the Flyers after the buzzer sounds off, I can't ignore that the pressure from helmet-meets-Plexiglas has yet to disperse. It only worsens when we head to the locker room, the crew of *Getting Pucked* already there and waiting to go all psychoanalyst on us and decipher what exactly it was that had us falling apart on the ice.

My vision softens, turning the crispness of life into a blurry mosaic of different colors when I reach my stall. *Focus, focus, focus.* With shaky fingers, I drop my stick on the bench and then tear into my duffel.

Side-panel. Zipper closed.

It's gaping open a second later, my bare hand diving in to find the bottle of painkillers that I've tucked away for cases like these.

Cases like when I just don't feel right, when my head feels like it's been submerged in an unrelenting fog, when my knees quiver and the thought of holding myself up on my skates for any length of time seems like a dauntless, unachievable task.

Planting a stabilizing hand on the stall, I toss back the pills and swallow them dry.

Three pills, as prescribed by my primary-care doctor when I told him about my migraines months ago. The dosage was only meant to tide me over until my appointment with Dr. Mebowitz, he said. I went to that lucrative appointment . . . I just never went back after that.

So, the three pills it is. I never take more, always too aware that many a great hockey player has come before me—and many will follow—who have succumbed to addiction. That's not me: the rehab, the addiction.

But, holy hell, Fitzgerald hit me like a damn giant chasing down a tiny, porcelain figurine.

In this scenario, I'm the porcelain figurine.

Lucky me.

The guys filter into the locker room, stripping off their jerseys and their pads, and I do, too, at a much slower pace. Slower, a little less coordinated. Gloves in the duffel; jersey over my head; compression shorts and hockey pants in the bag. Briefs and sweats are yanked up my legs.

"Captain? A minute before you get on the bus and head back to the hotel?"

Pain cleaves my head in two, but I signed a contract. I agreed to this. So I turn to face Fillmore with what I hope is a friendly grin. "Yeah, sure. Here?"

When I indicate the bench, he nods. "It'll do. Yeah, sit just like that with your back to the stalls. We want to get a few quick moments with you for this week's episode, and then we'll be out of your hair."

Relief eases into my system when my ass meets the bench. Grounded. That's how I feel, like if I wait only another beat, maybe two, the pulsing in my head will flick off and the shortness of my breath will soothe out. Get back to normal. For years, my "normal" seems to be constantly shifting into something new and, sometimes, something unrecognizable.

"You took a major hit out there, Carter," Fillmore starts, dropping to his haunches behind the camera guy so that he's at eye level with me. "How's the head?"

Feels like a freight train collided with my skull and then backed up right over me for shits and giggles. "Normal," I lie, looking straight at the camera, "it'd take a lot more than a bump like that to bring me down."

Fillmore laughs, his palm dropping on his thigh. "I think that was a little more than a bump."

It wasn't how hard Fitzgerald hit me but rather the angle that my helmet hit the boards. After two-decades-plus of being on the receiving end of body checks like the one tonight, I know all about those bad angles. "Have you ever played hockey before, Fillmore?"

He trades a glance with one of his crew members. "Nothing more than a recreational pickup game back in grade school. Nothing like how you all play on the ice."

"We grow up getting slammed into the boards," I say, wishing that I had an energy drink or something else to replenish my electrolytes. It's been a long day, more than a few hours since I last ate, and I played hard out there—even if we didn't pull out a win. "It's what we do. Wake up, get slammed or do the slamming. Then you get up and do it all over again."

"Any concussions?"

"Two." *Officially*. Two concussions that officially went on the records. As for the rest . . . who knows, really? Could be five, ten, thirty. For most of my career, the NHL has never required a checkup with a neurologist after having your bell rung. Ignoring the insistent, but low, ringing in my ears, I add, "The first one was back in my third season with the Bruins. Funnily enough, it came from Andre Beaumont when he still played for the Red Wings."

Fillmore cracks a smile at that, clearly sensing a story there. "And how'd you feel when he was traded to the Blades years later?"

"Like I wanted to pummel his ugly mug in." I set my palms on my thighs. "I was out for twelve or thirteen games after that hit."

Fillmore glances over his shoulder. "Hey, Beaumont! Come over here a sec!"

Half-dressed in street clothes, Andre ambles over and plunks down next to me. "What's up?"

"We were discussing that time you gave Carter a concussion," the director says with the same glimmer in his eyes that he had when he raved about Celine Dion. Honestly, it's a little disturbing. "How'd it happen?"

There are videos aplenty online, but Beaumont has never been shy about his role on the ice. He's huge, bigger than me, with arms the size of tree trunks and fists the size of boulders. And that's saying a lot since I'm easily over six-foot-four and close in at almost two-fifty.

Beaumont nudges me in the side. "I want it on the record that we're best buds now."

A chuckle reverberates in my chest. "That's because I don't have to worry about you busting my cheek anymore."

"*Breaking*," he corrects, meeting the camera's lens with a wicked grin. "I clocked him so hard his cheekbone literally cracked and shifted out of place. Not that I meant to—wrong place, wrong time. Our Jackson isn't a fighter, not like me."

My stomach heaves as I let out a hard laugh. "That's not saying much. *No* one fights like you do." As a right-winger on the front line, it's not my job to fight or start shit and intimidate the other team just by existing. I score goals, not turn into the Hulk on Ice. "There was a brawl—both teams got in on it—and one minute I had Bear Rawley in a headlock and the next I was being carried off the ice on a stretcher."

"Holly threatened me at the hospital," Beaumont drawls, reaching up to tug on his ear, "told me that if you weren't the same after that hit she'd personally cut off my dick and feed it to the wolves."

I don't remember that at all, but then again, I'd been put under as soon as we rolled up to Mass General. Still, the visual of petite Holly throwing down against the big, bad Andre Beaumont has me running a hand over my heart without even realizing that I'm doing it.

"What wolves was she planning on finding in the middle of Boston?" I ask.

"Hell if I know." Beaumont thumps me on the shoulder, then turns back to Fillmore. "Anyway, Carter and I had to sort out our . . . *differences* once I showed up, but now we're all good. It's part of the game. You injure something and get right back up again. Like Cap, here"—he jerks a thumb at me

—"no doubt he had his brains rattled out there on the ice tonight, but you're fine, eh?"

I make sure to look in the camera directly when I lie, "Yeah, I'm all good."

"See?" Beaumont, my best friend, slings an arm around my shoulders. "Nothing keeps Carter down—not for long, anyway. He's center gravity for this team. We'd be fucked without him. Can I say fucked? Is that not kosher for TV?"

"We'll bleep it out."

"Fucking perfect, then," he goes on, giving my head a pat, like I'm a good dog, before climbing to his feet. "Another thing about hockey? There are always shit nights, but it's the way you approach the next game that truly makes the difference. No celebrating tonight. We don't deserve all that."

"And you think you'll win against the Blackhawks?" Fillmore asks, his voice curious.

I ignore the persistent ringing in my ears and vow, "We'll decimate them."

CHAPTER 15
HOLLY

" One weird thing that Marshall does at home that no one knows about . . ." Gwen, Marshall Hunt's wife, stares back at me from the laptop screen where we've set up a video chat for the sake of a family-esque interview. My tripod and camera are angled to catch both Hunt and the laptop in the frame. "That's a tough one," Gwen muses.

Despite the fact that she's hundreds of miles away, Marshall shoots his wife a flirty look. "Is it really that tough? You know me better than anyone else."

"I'm trying not to embarrass you on national television. Trust me, you give me enough ammunition that I could answer this question for the next seven days." She tucks her red hair behind her ears, then combs her fingers through their fur baby's black fur, where the pup is all curled up on her lap.

"I don't embarrass easily," Hunt says with a casual shrug. "Do your worst, honey."

"You asked for it." She winks, and I'm sure it was aimed at me and not her husband, before continuing, "He talks in his sleep. A *lot*."

I can't help but grin. Marshall Hunt is a pretty boy

through and through—the one magazines want for his face and his abs, before finishing the article with a quick reference of his stellar stats on the ice. "What's he talking about?" I ask. "Hockey? Game play?"

"Oh, no." Gwen's grin widens. "In his sleep, Marshall is *all* about the scandal. Except that he's always an observer looking in. It's the strangest thing, honestly. The first time I heard him sleep-talking, he sounded horrified by what had to be some Jerry-Springer-level stuff in his dreams. He was all, 'oh *no*, she didn't!'" She presses a hand to her chest, all offended-like. "And some very concerned, 'That is *so* not okay. Dump his ass.'"

I look to Marshall with a raised brow, but he only grins. "I think it's all the Bravo TV I watch when I'm at home. *Vanderpump Rules* is my jam. I've even got some of the guys hooked on it—we watch it while we work out in the mornings."

"You landed a weird one," I tell Gwen, "you know that, right?"

Her entire expression softens. "I'm just as weird, trust me. I couldn't imagine my life without him."

Considering that I knew both Gwen and Hunt when they were on the outs and finding their way back together again, I'm so happy to see *them* happy. This interview will be the perfect clip to round out next week's episode, especially as the Blades got their asses handed to them by the Flyers last night. When I spoke with Mark Fillmore about what we needed for this episode, we unanimously agreed that showing the players with their families during an away game stretch would go miles toward demonstrating to the world that while the Blades may have a single-track mindset on the ice, off it, they're family men—husbands, brothers, fathers, sons.

Carmen, Adam, and I split up today, each of us tackling as many interviews with the players and their families as we could since the game with the Blackhawks isn't for another day.

After seven interviews on my own, and hours' worth of time lugging around equipment from hotel room to hotel room, I'm beat and ready for bed.

Glancing down at my wristwatch, I push to my feet and say my good-nights. Gwen and I agree to get together for lunch when I'm back in town. We're overdue for a catch-up anyway—she's our publicist and is crazy good at what she does.

With my backpack slung over my shoulder, I step into the hotel's hallway and try to get my bearings straight. Second floor. Fifth floor. Third floor. I've been *everywhere*, and if I were the sort of person to chart my number of steps for the day, I have no doubt it'd be in the thousands.

The Chicago airport hotel is beyond massive.

"Fourth floor," I mutter to myself, "that's yours."

I hike my backpack up some, readjusting the weight, and turn for the elevator that's down the hall and somewhere off to the right. I think. Or maybe it's the other way? Screw it. I'll find it when I find it.

Nothing like a little hotel adventure when all you want to do is get frisky with your sheets and block out the outside world for five hours of uninterrupted—

"Jackson?"

My ex-husband snaps up straight from where he's feeding change into a vending machine. His dark hair is a mess like he's combed his fingers through the strands countless times today, and . . . well, he's barefoot.

Not that I'm a foot-lover or anything like that, but Jackson's feet have always stunned me. Mainly because they're huge, and you know what they say about the size of a guy's . . .

My stomach nose-dives as the rest of Jackson comes into focus.

Oh.

Oh.

I jerk my gaze from the drawstring pants slung low around his waist to his shirtless torso. His tanned skin gleams under the florescent lighting, all bulging muscles and surly confidence.

"Do you ever wear a shirt anymore?"

His palm comes up to rub the center of his naked chest. "They're confining."

"They're appropriate for public places," I shoot back, feeling altogether way too warm. Maybe I'm developing a fever. I mean, my hands are clammy and my head feels a little heavy with pressure, but I'll persevere. A fever can't hold me back.

Jackson selects a button, collects his drink when the machine spits it out a moment later, and then steps to the left.

Blocking my path down the hallway that'll lead me to the elevator.

Dammit.

"You've been avoidin' me, Holls."

God, he's so persistent. *Even if he is a little bit right.*

I step to the right, prepared to dart around him toward freedom. "We've both been busy. Do you know how many minutes I've filmed today? *Hours'* worth of minutes. Then there's getting with Carmen and Adam to edit them all, and you've been at practice . . ."

Because Jackson knows me way too well, he does nothing but stand there, legs spread like he's a gladiator prepared to fight to the death—or keep me from escaping. His soda can *pops!* as he thumbs open the aluminum tab.

Never mind, persistent no longer covers it, not when he's clearly waiting me out.

Like he's been yanked straight from a commercial on TV, he tips the soda can up to his mouth and takes a long pull, looking rugged and handsome and too masculine for comfort. His brown eyes never leave my face.

I fidget with the straps of my bag—and then I cave, miserably. "So, okay, maybe I've been . . . ensuring that we don't cross paths."

"Why?"

Because . . .

My eyes slam shut so I don't have to make eye contact with the man who's haunted my dreams these last few nights. I like to think that I've matured over the last year into a woman who doesn't need a man's approval. Not that I've ever really needed a man's approval because I haven't, but . . . Well, I've always loved *Jackson's* approval, and hearing him tell me how proud he is of me shifted something in my heart. Made me wonder all about those *what-ifs* for far longer than is socially acceptable when you're talking about your ex-husband.

I need space, which is nearly impossible when we're stuck in the same vicinity for days on end, with no reprieve in sight until we're boarding the plane back home to Boston.

"Some things," I finally mutter, "are better left unsaid."

There's a hollow *thud* sound, and then pressure is at my back, fingers slipping under the straps of the bag. *Jackson.*

Whirling around, I put one palm up, face out, and take two quick steps back. "What're you doing?"

His mouth curls, not quite a smile but not so tight-lipped either. "Taking the weight off your shoulders."

I stare at him. "Going for double entendres now?"

"Just being a gentleman."

"I thought you were aiming high for a chance at playing king?"

"Well, that was the plan," he says, catching me off guard when he pushes at the backstraps at my shoulders, "but that was before you told me Beaumont was already wearin' the crown."

My backpack slips down, and I make a move to stop its downward trajectory, bending my elbows.

Jackson is faster.

He tugs on the straps, sending them down to my wrists, where he hooks a finger under each plush arm. My tripod and light reflector fall to the thin carpet with a quiet *thud.* His warm breath wafts over my face, and it's only then that I realize the position we're in: his arms looped around me, forearms resting on the curve of my butt, my hands palming his chest as I try to maintain my balance.

His *naked* chest.

I swallow. "Your nipples are hard again."

Jackson's cheeks hollow out with an indrawn breath as he tips his head back to stare at the ceiling. His arms don't move from their place around me. "We're standing under an air vent."

"A convenient excuse."

"It's called talking facts. I'm feeling a little chilled."

"Talking facts?" My eyebrows shoot up in disbelief. "*Fact* is, you've never been chilled a day in your life."

Brown eyes zero in on my face. "I'm a hockey player, sweetheart. You think my nuts don't shrivel and duck for cover every time I step out on the ice?"

Sweetheart.

Holy crap, holy crap, holy—

Jackson's mouth firms and, before I can prepare for it, he swoops the backpack out from around me and slings it onto his back, letting it hang unceremoniously by one strap. He turns on his heel. The florescent lighting does nothing but illuminate each and every one of the scars that mark his spine like a mother celebrates her child's growth with penciled lines on a spare wall in a childhood home.

The stretchmarks always marked a silent vulnerability that's otherwise nonexistent in my ex-husband's nature.

"Jackson. Jackson, where are you going?" Grabbing my

other gear off the floor, my sneakered feet pick up the pace as I trail him. "And, excuse me, but can you give me my backpack? That's theft."

He doesn't even glance back over his shoulder. "It's not theft if I plan to return it."

A groan slips from my mouth. "No," I mutter, my hands lifting even though he can't see me . . . which might be a good thing as I'm making a strangling sort-of gesture with them, the tripod and light reflector clashing against one another. Louder, I go on, "I'm not doing it."

"Doing what?"

"The word games! The theft versus borrowing or the blackmail versus negotiating."

Without warning, he turns left at the end of the hallway, away from where the elevators are located. "Holls, we aren't playing games. We stopped all that a long time ago."

Then what the hell are we doing here?

Pausing at a door, he digs around in his sweatpants and reveals a plastic key card that he swipes over the lock. An echoing *click* sounds louder than it should, but I suppose that its only competition is the thudding of my heart.

When I don't move to follow him into his hotel room, Jackson pauses within the frame, looking large and imposing and unfamiliar as he stares down at me. I blink, and recognize the crooked slope of his nose. I blink again, and know the specific sharpness of his jaw and the heavy slant of his brows. I blink once more, and there is not a hue in this world that I know better than the brown of his eyes.

And yet, he's never seemed more like a stranger than in this moment.

"If we stopped the games, then what are we doing?"

He props one forearm up on the doorframe, giving it his weight as he drops his head to look at the floor. Shoulders rising with a sharp inhale, he stares down at his bare feet as I stare at him. "We've never lied to each other." His head shifts just so, his temple pressing against his arm, so he can watch me instead of the threadbare carpet. "Eleven years, Holls. We were married for eleven years and not once in all that time did we ever lie to each other."

My fingers curl around my equipment at the ragged note in his voice. And my calm—whatever's left of it—vacates the premises. He looks at me like he's torn between dragging me into his hotel room or slamming the door in my face, and I . . . I breathe like I've run a marathon and reached the finish line, only to realize that I've still got another twenty-six miles to go and the first stint was nothing but my imagination.

In other words, I'm screwed.

We've done this dance. We've done it, and we haven't come out the other side intact.

"I've lied to you." His dark brows furrow together, and I plow on regardless. *We need space, humor, anything to break up this tension.* "I used to say that I forgot your peanut butter M&M's at the store when I went grocery shopping. I lied. I always caved and ate them all and had to throw the wrapper in the garbage before you saw the evidence."

"You could have bought two bags, one for you and one for me." His eyes narrow. "Or, better yet, a king-sized one for us to share."

"I could have, but—" I swallow the rest of the words before they can further incriminate me. The truth is, I *could* have done exactly that: buy multiple bags of the chocolate-covered peanuts and call it a day. But if I had, then I couldn't have played the *let me make it up to you* card, which involved me on my knees, Jackson's hands curved around the back of my skull, and the knowledge that he liked it best when I moaned around his dick.

None of that, however, is appropriate to mention in this moment.

You need to go. Now.

I step back, my gaze shooting to the right, toward the elevator at the far end of the hall.

"Holly."

My eyes screw shut at his deep baritone and the plaintive note that he can't quite hide.

"Your snack-stealing habits aside, can we agree that lying never had a seat at our table?"

Tipping my head back, I stare up at the ceiling. Suck in a harsh breath, even though my heart is pounding a mile a minute. "You were my best friend. Even if I'd wanted to keep something from you, my heart never let me—and my mouth, well, we both know that I say everything that sometimes *shouldn't* be said."

Jackson sets my backpack down inside the room, then makes a grab for my other gear. He puts those down too. He faces me, then, hands on the doorframe, his muscled torso all on delicious display.

"I don't want to lie to you." His dark eyes slip down my frame and then seem to drag, slowly, all the way back up to my face. Above his stubble, his cheeks are flushed. "I don't want to lie, and I feel like I've got to say this—to get it off my chest—but, fuck, I know you're not going to want to hear it."

Immediately, scenarios dart through my head and none of them are all sunshine and unicorns.

He's seeing someone else.

He's seeing someone else and he doesn't want me to find out the hard way.

He's seeing someone else and it's serious, and oh my God, I think I'm going to vomit. Or cry. Or maybe a mixture of both.

I thought I'd be ready for this moment. Hell, I've spent months preparing for a time when Jackson moved on and then I forced myself to move on, and I don't think I'm breathing.

In and out, girl. In. And. Out.

153

My hands go to my chest, tugging on my cotton T-shirt. I pull it away from my clammy skin, desperately needing air because my head feels like it's going to pop clear off my neck. I'm Holly Belliveaux Fucking Carter.

Carter.

I'll need to go back to my maiden name because no new girlfriend or future wife is going to appreciate the *ex*-wife still sporting her ex-husband's surname. And maybe I should have changed it by now, but—confessional—I'm rather attached to it.

I don't feel like a Belliveaux, I feel like a *Carter*.

"Holls."

In. And. Out.

In and out.

Inandout.

"Sweetheart, you've got to breathe."

I'm trying. Doesn't he see that I'm trying?

"Fuck it."

Muscular arms swoop around me, hauling me up into the air before I can protest. His name leaves my lips when he sweeps a palm over the back of my head, tucking me in like precious cargo so I don't bang my skull on the doorframe.

The door creaks shut behind us. The light flickers on with a flip of a switch. And then Jackson moves smoothly toward the full-sized bed in the center of the room. He sets me down with ease, on the edge so my feet come in contact with the floor. As though they've betrayed me—like they remember a time all on their own when Jackson used to fit himself between them—my legs spread, leaving enough room for him to settle in the V of my open thighs.

Jackson takes advantage.

He sinks to his knees before me, but he's so tall and I'm so short that we're almost at eye level. And then he settles his palms over the curve of my hips.

Like he has every right to do so.

I don't tell him to back off.

"You need to breathe," he husks out, gently squeezing my flesh until I meet his steady gaze. "You need to breathe for me, Holls. You're having one of your panic attacks."

I've had them for years, ever since I was a little girl and wondering if my parents would ever return for me and Sam. They never did.

Back then, my grandmother used to awkwardly pat my head and encourage me to be brave. It was as close to affection as she had to give, not because she didn't love me or Sam, but because she belonged to a different generation. She was a woman who felt no regret over shooting a man in the ass when he dared threaten her business, and then there was me . . . always remembering how Momma was dressed when she walked out the front door and never came back. My grandmother said I loved too hard back then, and she said the same thing about my relationship with Jackson right before she died.

"You don't need that man," she told me over the phone, "you divorced him. Do you see him banging on your door because he thinks y'all made a mistake? No, you don't. You love too hard, Holly-bear. You love too dang hard and they never deserve it *or* you."

The anxiety has been with me for as long as I can remember, crawling into my heart when my emotions threaten to get the best of me. But Jackson always knew, somehow intrinsically, how to bring me back from that panicked rush that seeps into my bones and lingers.

His fingers leave my hips to trail down my thighs, up and down, up and down, until I'm more focused on his mesmerizing touch than the shuddered breaths heaving out of my chest.

"That's it, sweetheart." The gentleness in the way he touches me is completely opposite to his gravel-pitched tone.

"Focus on me. You're good, you hear? Take all the time you need. I'm not going anywhere."

I want to ask if the new girl he's seeing is problem-free, unlike me. If she has a supportive family and parents who care. If she's laid-back and easygoing, and not a control freak the way I am. Does she make him laugh the way I used to?

"Does *who* make me laugh?"

I blink.

Oh. Oh, crap, that was said out loud.

My gaze lands on his hands, which rest on my knees. I want them to move up, up, up, until his thumbs linger near where I want him most. *Don't go there.* "No one. I just—"

His hold on me tightens. "I'm not seeing anyone, Holls."

The panic swiftly kicks me straight in the gut, and I swallow it down. "You can do whatever you want." My fingers tangle in the comforter, twining and squeezing the way my heart does at the prospect of Jackson loving someone else, *making* love to someone else, of being their best friend. "I'm not that crazy ex who'll hover over your shoulder and watch your every move. I'm the cool ex." *Oh, my God. Please stop talking.* "You know how they say if you're a cool mom or whatever? I'm that, without the kids. The cool ex-wife."

"The cool—" Jackson breaks off, his hand lifting from my leg to pinch the broken bridge of his nose. "I'm going to be straight with you, that's the stupidest shit I've ever heard."

"Is it, though? All I'm trying to say is that I support you living your best life. Whatever you want to do, I'm—"

"There isn't anything I want to do besides *this*."

And then Jackson, my ex-husband, crashes his mouth down over mine and steals every last breath from my lungs.

CHAPTER 16
JACKSON

She tastes exactly the same.

Sweet. Bold. *Mine.*

I'm crossing so many boundaries here, knocking each one down like a child chasing after his favorite toy. But there's *nothing* childlike about the way I mold my mouth over Holly's, nor the way I drag her down off the bed so that she straddles my thighs. Her weight is slight, her hips and curves slender but mine for the taking.

And I take.

Fuck, do I take.

I flick my tongue along the cushion of her bottom lip, demanding entrance. When she gives it with a familiar whimper that goes straight to my cock, I echo her small, feminine noises with a guttural groan that reverberates in my chest.

As though she's desperate to find the source of the sound, she touches my chest, her short, blunt fingernails dragging down over my skin, marking me in a way that feels at once familiar and foreign.

There's been no one since her.

No one could ever compare, not when we met at Cornell,

not when I drank myself into a stupor after the divorce was finalized—and I spent days, weeks, trying to lose myself in hockey and games and practice.

Losing Holly broke me—even if I was the reason we were broken in the first place—and only now, under her touch, do I feel as though I'm coming alive again.

I pin her to the side of the bed, bracketing her body with mine. My palms clamping down on the edge of the mattress, her spine arching as she nips at my top lip, her core circling down on my hard-as-nails erection. God, she feels so damn good.

Wrapping a hand around the back of my neck, Holly yanks me closer to deepen the kiss. It's messy, all clashing teeth and dueling tongues, and I'd be lying if I say that it doesn't send my pulse roaring. She's the rush in my veins, and nothing has ever felt so right or perfect. Desperate for her, I dig my fingers into her hips and grind her down on me, a slow, sensuous back and forth that leaves no doubt as to how hard I am.

How much I crave her.

Her lips tear from mine as she gasps my name, her sweet, Southern accent breaking on the second syllable.

Yes, sweetheart. Don't hold back.

"Say it again."

"Oh, my God," she whimpers, her blond hair a chaotic mess as she moves her hips in the agonizingly slow rhythm I've set in place, "Jackson, *please*."

I glance down at her jeans and my sweatpants, and oh, Christ, but I feel like I'm going to come with nothing but Holly dry-humping my dick like we're back in grade school. Each time she slides down, she kills me a little more. Because with that downward glide, she pulls at the waistband of my sweats, revealing the tip of my cock.

I'm leaking pre-cum, my cock desperate for what's between her legs, the same way my heart beats that much faster for the expression on her face. Cheeks flushed, pink lips parted, eyes half-shut.

Beautiful, fucking beautiful.

My mouth finds the sensitive skin behind her ear, that sweet spot of hers that's always felt like my secret weapon. If she's mad? Kiss her there. If she's sleeping and I want to wake her up? Kiss her there. If she's determined to hold the upper reign and I want to tumble her off the throne and regain control? Kiss. Her. There.

A wicked grin spreads across my face when her fingers scrabble for purchase on my body and her hips swivel a little off rhythm. I break from the "torture" long enough to roughly whisper in her ear, "Do you think I can make you come just like this?"

Her slick movements slow, and then her left hand is on my shoulder, the other folded over her heart. I see the crown of her blond head as she looks down, and I have no doubt as to what she's seeing: her legs spread wide; my cock pulling an X-rated peep show out of my sweats; my stomach and chest flushed with need.

I lean into her, fully prepared to take her mouth with mine, when the hand on her heart flattens over my own and applies pressure.

Like ice water has been doused over my head, everything freezes—my skin, my muscles, my heart.

"*Holls.*"

The pressure on my heart eases, her hand going momentarily slack, before strengthening again. "We can't."

Fuck that. "We *are*, right now. You don't think I don't want you? You don't think I haven't spent every day of the last year thinking of you, missing—"

She shakes her head, effectively killing the words on my tongue. "Our problem was never about wanting each other, Jackson. It was about everything else. The distance, the way we ended up coexisting like we were nothing more than friends who had sex, and then not even that." Her blue eyes, always so luminous and excited about life, appear dull and worn in her heart-shaped face, like sea glass that's been buried in the sand for centuries. "Having sex won't fix any of our issues. It'll feel good right now and then we'll regret it in the morning."

When she makes a move to climb off my lap, I instinctively curl my arms around her frame to keep her from leaving. It's a desperate attempt, a last move to remind her that I'm the same man she met and fell in love with at Cornell.

"Do you ever wonder?" I ask. My hands smooth over her shoulders and down her spine, and I don't miss the way she shivers under my touch. "Do you ever wonder where we'd be now if we'd fixed what was broken between us?"

Her hot breath skims my chest, and it's my turn to fight back a shiver. A soft, barely there kiss lands at the crook of my neck. It feels like good-bye and I squeeze her to me that much tighter.

And then she's speaking and there's nothing but a lingering chill all over again: "There was never going to be any fixing when we weren't willing to compromise. We wouldn't change—that was our downfall."

I open my mouth, fully prepared to say *something* to salvage what little relationship we have left but break off when I hear the door swinging open.

I turn just in time to see Cain burst through the door that should be *locked* right now, phone in one hand and his gaze trapped down on it. Shit, shit, shit.

"Carter! You got a sec for—" He glances up, jaw visibly dropping as he takes in the scene before him. "Oh, fuck."

Actually, fucking is definitely *not* what happened here.

I wind one arm around Holly, trying to shield her from his view as much as possible. "Can you give us a minute?"

"Yeah! Yeah, sure, you got it, man."

He doesn't move. Instead, he drops his gaze down to my

lap and his brows shoot up. Coughing into one balled fist, he mutters, "The beast is out, Cap."

The beast? I glance down, only to see the tip of my still-hard dick peeking out past the waistband of my pants.

Someone just kill me.

Dainty fingers that aren't mine snap my waistband back into place, and I don't know whether to hug Holly for doing me the favor or beg her to end my misery. In the end, I find myself going mute as she awkwardly clambers off my lap and lands on her hands and knees in a hasty attempt to flee the scene of the crime.

In other words, us losing control and nearly hooking up.

I look to Cain, who's now posted up against the door-frame, arms crossed over his chest as he assesses us. "Dude," I grunt, yanking on the fabric of my sweats as I climb to my feet. "What are you still standing there for? And how the hell did you get in here?"

It seems like a slice of poetic fate that I'm supposed to be the man in charge of a team of hockey players, the guy who's always in control, and I can't even make my erection submit.

No more hockey.

The Bachelor re-runs.

IRS auditing.

The damn thing swells in my pants, taunting me with the very clear point that I've got a *very* massive problem.

"Don't 'dude' me, man, the door was slightly ajar. Guess you didn't notice," Cain says, a smug smile all up on his mug. He points at my crotch. "Stand down, good sir."

Deep, even breaths, that's what I need. Maybe some Jim Beam, if I drank alcohol anymore. To the Blades defenseman, I do my best to look completely at ease when I mutter, "Please don't talk directly to my dick."

"Who should I be talking to?" He looks to Holly. "You up for conversation, Ms. Carter?"

Her cheeks burn a muted pink as she snags her backpack

and other equipment from the floor and tries to edge around him and out into the hallway. "Not particularly, Weston, no."

"Perfect!" His gaze flicks over to me again. Or, more accurately, to my dick, which has yet to get the memo that sex with Holly is most definitely *off* the table. Cain gives me a shit-eating grin. "Where were we again? Oh yeah, I was just—"

"Cain."

"Yeah, Cap?"

"Get the fuck out of here before I personally cut your laces."

He sucks in a harsh breath. "Low blow, man, low blow. But like I was saying . . ."

Holly glances back at me, her teeth digging into her bottom lip. I can read the hesitance in her expression. Though we've got a shit ton to talk about—starting with the fact that she rode my hard-on like a champ—it doesn't look like my teammate is going anywhere anytime soon.

I give her a curt nod, and she subsequently ducks under Cain's arm to sneak out into the hallway.

"So, yeah," Cain goes on, the bastard, "if I learned anything from my grandfather, it's that taking double the dosage of the little blue pill will do some serious damage. Doesn't matter how desperate you are to get it up, *don't* do it. Not unless you want your dick to fall off."

My hands land on my squared-off hips. "You realize I have to kill you now, right? There's no other option."

"There are *always* other options." Holding up a single finger, like he's checking the direction of the wind, his eyes go comically wide. "Oops, hold on a minute, I hear someone calling my name."

"*Cain*—"

I step forward as he leans his head out of the hotel room and shouts, "Having a laid-back night, Harrison! Yep, yep, super easy. Just having a little talk with Cap's dick and laying out all the ins and outs of over-abusing Viagra at his old age."

Old age?

Hooking my arm around Cain's shoulders, I forcefully drag him out into the hallway where I fully plan to dump his ass. When he comes up spluttering, I narrow my eyes on him. "Whatever you came in my room looking for, you can get it tomorrow."

He plucks at his old-as-heck T-shirt, righting it over his pecs like I've done it major harm. "Don't worry, I got what I needed."

And what the hell does *that* mean? My core muscles bunch together as I twist to face him. "What did you say?"

"What did I say or what did I mean?" He throws me an overly dramatic wink, and I have the sudden urge to bench him tomorrow, just for being a prick. "I *said* exactly what I said, but what I *meant* is, the team loves Holly, Carter. She's a good egg and you're a good guy, but most of us remember how miserable the two of you were by the end of things. Your game was off, and it cost us the Cup." His hands land on my shoulders, squeezing once. "So, we think that it's best if you took a little taste of your own medicine . . . focus on the game, Cap, and *only* on the game. We want to win. We don't want Holly to cry. And even though you can be a major asshole sometimes, we don't want you looking like some extra out of *The Walking Dead* anymore."

I can't deny it; my first inclination is to drive his body face first into the decrepit carpet beneath our feet. But my second . . . Hell, my second acknowledges that what he says has some truth to it.

I was miserable.

Holly was miserable.

And, yes, my preoccupation last season cost us our run at the Cup when I couldn't get my personal life separated from my life on the ice. I let emotion control me, the way I've constantly warned rookies like Kammer not to let happen.

Tonight, though, showed me everything that I need to know: I want my ex-wife with everything that I am. And I mean that I want all of her, both the seductress when she's grinding on top of me and the vulnerable side that she shows to no one but me.

I can win the Stanley Cup *and* earn back my place at Holly's side.

There's no way I can't.

I clap my hand down on Cain's shoulder and offer him a blasé grin. "Got it. No more trying out for *The Walking Dead*. That I can handle."

His blond brows knit together. "And eye on the prize, right? No fucking around with Holly when the two of you are finally getting your shit together and acting like normal, non-lovesick people."

"Oh yeah." Lie, lie, and lie some more—pretty sure I picked that up from a former teammate. "We lost our heads. Sometimes shit happens, y'know? Anyway, it won't be happenin' again. My dick can promise that."

Cain's expression relaxes. "Your dick's making promises now? Should I ask it—"

"No."

"But the Beast has got to have a say in—"

I give his shoulder a shove. "My dick would like to be left out of this narrative, thanks."

The door to my right opens and Beaumont's head pops out. "What's this about Cap's dick?"

Jesus Christ, they're like goddamn grandmothers on this team, always nosily eavesdropping. The least they could do is bring me snacks before breaking out the claws. Pointing at Andre, I grind out, "Shut it. We've reached the end of this talk and I'm going to bed."

From down the hall, I hear, "Carter's dick is making promises nowadays!"

Harrison.

And I thought we were friends.

I inch back toward my hotel room, thankful, at least, that us veterans are given our own rooms during away games. If I had to put up with any of these pricks for the next eight to nine hours, I'd smother them in their sleep and then send their families a gift card to the Olive Garden.

I'm a kind person like that.

"Jackson Carter, owner of the Genie Penis," Beaumont muses, rubbing his stubbled chin. "I'm thinking ahead . . . merchandise. T-shirts, mugs, bookmarks for our literary fans. I'm a genius."

"You're an asshole," I mutter, disgruntled, "and Zoe should have run from you at the altar."

He steps into the hallway. "I may have to make a wish for that to never happen." His big hands drop, and I see my life flash before my eyes before I'm smacking the two offenders away before they have the chance to grope me.

The problem with hockey players?

There's no boundary that won't be crossed in the name of screwing with your teammates, and not a single one of us has any shame.

Even so, the next person to touch my junk isn't gonna be Andre Beaumont.

No, Holly is the only one who'll have that opportunity—even if that means pulling out the big stops to show her how much fight we still have left to give when it comes to saving our relationship.

I flash Beaumont the bird, do the same for Cain, and then close my door in their faces, a grin on my face. They might be annoying as all get out, but after so many seasons together, they're also family.

Moving to the small desk by the window, I pick up my cell

from where I left it earlier. I'm not comfortable with the way things ended with Holly tonight, and though she probably won't see my text till the morning, my gut is urging me to send something to her now, to smooth any troubled waters.

Only, when I tap the screen awake, I find a text from her already waiting for me. I'll be damned if my heart doesn't take off like a sprinter at the starting line.

HOLLY:

> You asked me if I ever wonder about us . . .
> Only every day since we signed the papers.
>
> Sometimes I think you've ruined me for anyone else.

I run my thumb over the glass screen encasing her words, imagining them being whispered in my ear, her hot breath warming my skin. Opening the messaging app, I type back my response and lay it all out on the line:

ME:

> Tonight, I took my first breath of air in over a year. This thing between us . . . it's not over, sweetheart. If you think I've ruined you for anyone else, just know that for me there's been no one else. Full stop. Period. I'm ready to breathe again, Holls, and I only do that with you.

I set my alarm and leave my phone on the desk.

And when I climb under the covers and slip between the sheets, I do what I've done for months . . . I wrap my hand around my hard cock and jerk off to the vivid memories of my ex-wife. Only now, it's not to memories gathered from our marriage, but of tonight when I finally had the chance to taste her again.

Sweet. Bold. *Mine.*

I'm an addict, hooked on the feeling of her body rubbing

against mine. I imagine it's her hand gripping me. Her hand twisting at the crown before slicking all the way down to the base. Her palm cupping my balls and gently squeezing.

My knees rise up, tenting the sheets, my closed fist moving faster and faster over my dick as I recall her half-shut lids as I rocked her over me. The way her hips rolled seductively. How her hands fluttered over my shoulders as she clung to me and rode my body with everything she had to give. My name was a prayer on her lips. A prayer of sin, maybe, but I've never been the most penitent of men.

Until now.

Sometimes I think you've ruined me for anyone else.

As hot ropes of cum jet onto my stomach, I pray that there will only be me in her future. That she's as ruined as I am.

I've never been a religious man . . . but that's never stopped me from kneeling at the altar of Holly.

CHAPTER 17
HOLLY

I swallow a delicious mouthful of pasta, then dash a napkin across my lips. "Thanks for letting us crash Sunday dinner," I tell the Cain family, who are seated at the table around me.

Earlier in the day, Carmen, Adam, and I made the short drive south to Connecticut to visit Weston and his immediate family. We'd needed progress on his storyline for the show, something outside of therapy rooms and hotels, and Weston suggested family dinner at his parent's place.

It's the first family dinner I've been invited to in ages. In all the years that I've lived in New England, my grandmother visited only once. She was a creature of comfort, hated leaving her bubble of small-town Louisiana, and Lord knows her eyebrows might as well have been stitched to her hairline when we visited Sal's and she discovered that the restaurant only offered *un*sweet tea. Take away a Southern woman's sweet tea and there will be hell to pay, I assure you.

As for Sam, my brother is firmly planted on the West Coast. If your name isn't High Tech, then you simply aren't on his radar. I love him, but he's always been more interested in computer software than doing the whole sibling thing. Or, really, relationship *anything* with anyone. Case in point: he's never had a girlfriend or a boyfriend or a "friend" of any sort that involves him spending any amount of time away from his computers.

Jackson was my family in every way that mattered.

Jackson, who I humped rather shamelessly just last week in Chicago. *Nothing like eradicating boundaries one dry-humping session at a time.* If there was a competition for who could almost make oneself come just by grinding, I'd take first place.

At the kick to my ankle, my back shoots straight and I trade a quick glance with Carmen. "And," I rush out, making eye contact with the very blonde Mrs. Cain, "thank you for letting us film it all for *Getting Pucked.* Not every family would agree to do this for us."

The Cain matriarch's eyes twinkle as she spoons another helping of mashed sweet potatoes onto her plate. "We're not exactly like every family out there, Holly. Has Weston ever told you all about his very first hockey game?"

Weston, playing the part of embarrassed son, rolls his eyes and takes a long pull from his beer. "No, Ma, I didn't because they don't care about any of that."

"Sure we do." Adam mimics Weston and drinks from his beer bottle. "We're pretty much here for all of Weston's dirty secrets."

If my sound mixer wasn't seated across the table, I'd slap him upside the head. As it is, I grit out a smile and shoot metaphorical daggers at him with my eyes. "We're totally *not* here for the dirty secrets." I glance over at one of the four cameras we positioned in every corner of the room upon first arriving earlier in the evening. "If anything, we're interested in learning what it's like for all of you to have an NHL player in the house. What are the pro's, the con's? All that comes with being related to someone famous and in the public eye."

Until we'd arrived in Hartford, I'd had no idea that the

Cain family was ridiculously wealthy *or* that Weston was part of a dynamic-twin duo. Maybe I should have done more research or maybe it's because the Blades defenseman is notoriously tight-lipped about his private life.

Tory, the not-so-infamous twin, leans forward to prop his arms on the table. His blond hair is cut like Weston's, shorter on the sides and a little longer up front. If it weren't for the difference in their noses—Weston's has clearly been broken multiple times—I'd have no idea who is who.

Tory offers a slow, curling grin when he glances from his brother to me. "Pro," he murmurs in a silky voice that's cultured and refined, just like the slacks and pressed shirt he's wearing, "Weston's doing what he loves, even if it's not what our parents would want from him."

"No?" Carmen hums her interest beside me. "What would he be doing instead?"

"Real estate." Mr. Cain shrugs, then rakes his fingers through his hair, which is more white than blond, like his sons'. "It's been a family business since the turn of the century."

Weston clears his throat. "He's talking about the twentieth century not the twenty-first . . . in case that was in question. Regardless, the business will still be there when I retire from the NHL. I'm not worried about the commercial real estate market drying up anytime soon."

I don't want to ask the question and throw a wrench in the easygoing conversation, but I can't get Steven Fairfax's comment out of my head about Weston retiring after this season. Forcing a casual note, I ask, "And when do you think that'll be? Any concerns about the injuries you've suffered over the last few seasons?"

Laid-back or not, Weston's gaze hardens as he studies me. "On the record or off?"

I kick my chin in the direction of the camera. "Technically

on, but it's whatever you feel comfortable with. None of us will ever air anything that you don't want to be seen."

He's silent for a moment, staring directly at the camera like he's determined to discover if it'll spill his secrets or not. Swirling the beer bottle, he says, "*On* the record, then." He sets the bottle down and clasps his hands together on the table. "The thing about hockey is that it thrives in my veins. I want my career more than I want a position in the family business"—he glances at his father with a shrug—"sorry, Dad."

Mr. Cain shakes his head with a rueful smile. "It's not anything I don't already know, West."

Weston's answering smile is fleeting. "Like I was saying, I've never craved anything more than I crave being on the ice. Not a woman, not a job, not the need to keep up with friendships from outside the hockey world. I've got my team. The game comes first, and I'll continue to play for as long as the Blades will have me."

Carmen beats me to the punch, asking, "What about if the Blades won't have you any longer? Will you go somewhere else?"

"No."

It's not Weston who answers but Tory, and we all look to him. Unlike his twin, who practically exudes bullish testosterone, Tory is all cool elegance. That's not to say that he's any less masculine, but whereas Weston is fierce and bright colors, Tory is more remote, more . . . gray, as though he's struggled with something far deeper than being pummeled on the ice and has sunk back into his shell in response.

He's here but not fully present.

And he reminds you of you.

I swallow hard and sit back as Tory plows onward. "West is loyal to a fault, and that's the con of having him play in the NHL. He's the Tedy Bruschi of the NHL—he signed with the Blades at the start of his career and when they decide his time is up, whenever that is, he'll retire." He trades a glance with his brother. "It's been his plan from day one, and he's not someone who changes his mind once it's made up."

Well, then.

If *Getting Pucked* chooses to air this clip, the Blades are either going to love Weston for being so open and vulnerable or they're going to . . . well, I don't really know *what* they'd do. Coach Hall values guys like Weston.

Guys like my ex-husband, who have always put the sport first.

Weston picks up the beer bottle again. "The good news is that the Blades need a guy like me around. I'm younger than Beaumont and just as tough. While King Sin Bin ships off to the world of marriage and children and white picket fences, I'll still be here getting the job done. We're all replaceable at some point, but for now, I'm still dealing the cards and I'm not going anywhere."

THE CAINS HAVE a garden that could rival an English estate's.

After dinner, Carmen and Adam sit down with Weston and his parents for a more exclusive interview. They adjourn to the blue parlor—there are *three* parlors, as you do when you're filthy rich—with tea and sweets.

I bring Tory, Weston's twin, out to the gardens.

He's quiet as we walk, reminding me a little of Jackson, in that both men exude confidence without having to voice everything in their head.

My shoulders twitch at the thought of my ex-husband. Our hot-as-heck kiss. My red-eye flight out of Chicago when the panic hit me hard after receiving his heart-stopping, earth-shattering text.

The message both terrified and thrilled me all at once, eliciting a cacophony of emotions that simulated the sensation of balancing on a tightrope suspended twenty feet in the air . . .

with Jackson waiting for me down below, arms opened wide, silently daring me to take a leap of faith.

Most terrifying of all? How very much I wanted to jump and let him catch me, even knowing that we could end up as we already have: divorced, single, and *not* ready to mingle with anyone not in possession of the surname Carter.

Incredibly specific, I know.

I'm not proud of the way I flew out of Chicago, like a thief stealing away in the night, as my grandmother's words snuck their way back into my head while I hastily packed.

You love too hard, Holly-bear.

Do you see him banging on that door?

Is it wrong to love too hard? Is it some sort of defect in my wiring?

Is there something wrong with me for wanting Jackson back? Society would tell me yes. Statistics of divorced couples reuniting would tell me *hell* yes. My emotions, unlike the perfectly manicured garden before me, are a hot mess.

"Maybe I should be interviewing you?" murmurs Tory as we settle in at a rotund iron-cast table on the patio. "Looks like you've got a lot on your mind."

Nope, just trying to cling to the solitary sensation of being in a marriage and feeling so alone before I do something insane, like throw myself at my ex-husband and beg him to make the hurt go away.

It's times like these that make me feel grateful that my job is behind the camera and not in front of it.

I prop my tripod on the table, lowering it to its smallest height, and attach my camera to it. "Just running through some of the questions I've got for you, that's all."

Tory brings one leg over the other, hooking his hands over his shin as he fixes his attention on the equipment. "Can we retake anything if it sounds bad? I'm not . . . I'm not Weston. By that I mean, I'm no good in front of people."

"What's your role with the family business?" I ask,

genuinely curious. "I mean, I'm assuming you work with your dad?"

Weston's twin nods. "I'm on the backend. We don't only sell properties. We build them, design them. I suppose you could say that I'm the mastermind behind the scenes." He scratches the back of his head. Shrugs loosely. "I handle the software the architects use to create the plans."

"So you're a designer?"

His laugh rings out, shy and reserved. "No, *definitely* not. I create the software, troubleshoot any and all website bugs, that sort of thing. At company meetings, I don't think I ever say a word."

"Hey," I say, patting my tripod as I take a seat, "not all superheroes wear capes, am I right? The world needs us behind-the-scenes folks, too."

Tory grins. It's not flirtatious, which I'm thankful for, but the kind of smile you only give another person when they get you. "I'd need a black cape," he finally murmurs. "There's got to be some sort of contrast with all the angel-blondness I've got going on." He points at my head. "Same for you."

The interview moves smoothly after that, the ice already having been broken by our superhero-cape conversation. Tory is funny in a British-humor sort of way, and it's obvious within minutes that he's the very antithesis of his twin.

"Did you play hockey?" I ask.

"I did for a day." Tory laughs, probably at whatever memory is skirting through his head. "I played for a whopping two hours before I begged my mom to put me in something else."

"Did she?"

"Well, she tried—I guess that's what matters." He tips his blond head back, gaze lifting to the darkening sky above us. "Weston had this . . . hell, it was like a fire, you know? You saw him at dinner. The guy knows what he wants and goes for it with no reservations."

"Was it intimidating?" Even though I know I shouldn't, I can't help but let my brain flit to Jackson. He's ignited by that same fire as Weston, both men so driven, so focused, that standing beside them often feels like you're still in the outer periphery, looking in, wondering how the hell you can create some of that fire for yourself. I wipe my palms over my jeans, ridding my skin of the clamminess. "I mean, did you ever feel like—"

"Like I was an extra in the Weston Cain Show?" Tory meets my gaze. "Who wouldn't? We're twins, which I'm sure made it more difficult during my teenage years. I tried football and baseball and, hell, I even took up archery at some point."

My eyes go wide. "How'd that go?"

"Besides the fact that I nearly skewered another kid when I misfired on my first day? Not so bad. Granted, they didn't ask me to come back, but still, could have been worse."

Laughter bubbles in my chest at the visual he's created. I lean back in my chair, arms over my chest as I study Tory Cain. "So, despite the fact that you stumbled from sport to sport while Weston kept on with hockey, you finally found some of that fire of your own with computer programming?"

He glances at the camera. "I felt lost. I went to UConn with West and he was a powerhouse. Me, on the other hand? Bouncing from major to major until I accidentally signed up for a computer class. It was love from there on."

I'm so wrapped up in the conversation that I forget we're filming until Tory lifts a fair brow and I jump back into action. *Stop comparing yourself to Tory Cain*, I yell at myself, *there is no comparison.* Out loud, I'm all laid-back while I wrap up the interview.

"Anything else you want to add about growing up with Weston?"

Tory sucks in his bottom lip, deliberation written all over his face. Then, finally, "I learned a lot from West. I'm older, even if it's only by three minutes, but I spent our younger years looking up to him. He's . . . magnetic, I think is a word a magazine used once. And when someone is magnetic like he is, it's easy to lose yourself in that forcefield. But the way he is —the way he doesn't see obstacles as more than a speedbump in the road—that's something you can't help but admire. He's loyal, driven, quick on his feet. All that makes for an excellent hockey player." He shrugs, fingers moving to the table to drum lightly. "Off the ice, it just makes him *him.* You can take it, you can walk away, but at the end of the day, West is who he is. He won't change for anyone and I wouldn't want him to."

Do I want Jackson to change who he is?

Loyal, driven, quick on his feet.

Tory is talking about Weston, *girl, not your ex.*

My brain doesn't separate the difference, and I spend the entire drive back to Boston analyzing every word that Tory said and applying it to my own life. Do I carry the same passion for photography that Jackson does with hockey? I love my business, I love my employees . . . but am I fired up about it? Did I simply latch onto the very first thing I seemed good at when faced with Jackson's magnetism on the ice? Just how Tory fell into computer programming by accident?

By the time I climb into bed around one in the morning, I'm no closer to figuring it out. Confusion roils through me, pulling me apart at the seams and making me question everything. I toss and turn the whole night until sometime around four, I reach for my phone and type my name into Google.

I study every image of myself that I come across—noting my smiles and excitement over whatever award I'm being given—and when I've seen as much as I can handle, I look up old photos of Jackson and me together.

The way I'm positively glowing in the first picture, taken after his first game with the Dallas Stars, tells me all that I need to know. Photography fills me with pride for all I've accomplished.

But photography, and all of its accompanying material and financial successes, has never made me smile the way I am in this picture with Jackson, with my hand on his chest and my head thrown back in laughter. I want *that* again—the love, the knowledge that I'm standing next to my best friend, my other half. I just don't know if it's possible to reclaim what's been lost . . . or if it's even worth the possible risk of failing all over again.

I fall asleep with my nose kissing the glass screen, my arm thrown out to the left side of the bed, reaching for a man who isn't there.

CHAPTER 18
JACKSON

I t's not every day that I feel ancient, but today . . . today I
feel two steps from the grave.

Tightening my core, I bring the heavy-as-shit bar
down to my chest. Push the weight back up in the air. Once.
Twice. Thrice. With each press, my pecs and biceps protest
vehemently. My head, jam-packed with tunes from System of
a Down, throbs with an unyielding ache that hasn't eased
since our away-game stretch two weeks ago.

Fucking Fitzgerald.

Both ESPN and Sports 24/7 have yet to stop replaying
that clip of my helmet colliding with the Plexiglas, and each
time I see it on TV, it feels like I'm getting pummeled all over
again.

Sweat beads on my brow as I heft the bar back onto the
rack. I focus on my breathing as I stare up at the training facility's ceiling.

Captain or not, veteran or not, I'm not the same NHL
rookie that took to the ice a decade ago. I can admit that, even
if only in my head, but I'll be damned if I allow myself to skip
this season and retire too soon, too early, when I know we're

in a prime position to take what I want most. There's an instinctive feeling in my gut that this is our year to take the Cup home—a first for the Boston Blades.

What will undoubtedly be my last run for hockey's holy grail.

I'm thirty-four.

That's 238 years old in dog years.

At least four-hundred in hockey years.

The muscles in my neck relax as I sink into the bench's padding, then throw my legs over the side so I can sit up. My head swirls like I've put the damn thing in a blender and flipped the switch just for shits and giggles.

Makes sense, since the team doctor told me that Fitzgerald bulldozed me hard enough to hand-deliver a concussion like I haven't felt in years.

As I lift my weight off the bench, the heavy metal blasting in my ears drowns out the dull thudding in my skull. I'm the only one in the training facility—have been since I arrived earlier for an extra workout before our next stretch of games —and I'm thankful for the solitude when I step forward and my body sways with nausea.

Fuck. *Not again.*

I've pushed myself too hard the last two weeks, refusing to take it easy with so much at stake. The guys look up to me. To them, I'm damn-near invincible. Seeing me as I am now would be more than cause for concern—swaying like a drunk, blinking rapidly against the bright lights as though I'm taking a turn in the next *Twilight* movie, right hand tingling with pins and needles as it always does when the headaches return.

And they always return, more frequently than not in the last year.

With slow, even steps, I gather my car keys and energy drink where I left them, and then head for the parking lot. It's dark out already, the time eclipsing somewhere past eight, and not a single office door is open as I pass them.

That's because most people have a life outside of hockey.

I used to.

Back when Holly and I were married, I had that life. Fuck, I had the wife, the beautiful house, and a body that didn't feel like it might crash and burn at any moment. Although it ended up crashing and burning anyway—my marriage, I mean.

On a normal night, I'd give myself a healthy dose of a reality check. Tonight, I feel weak at the knees, literally and figuratively. Tonight, if I were the kind of guy who slept with one woman while dreaming of another, I'd head downtown and meet up with the guys at The Box, our regular hangout, and flirt with a woman who isn't Holly for the first time since I was twenty years old.

Wedding ring or not, though, my ex-wife has me by the balls and no one will do but her.

The soles of my tennis shoes scrape along the uneven concrete as I step out into the cool, October night. Removing the earbuds, I turn off the heavy metal and tuck my phone and headset into the pocket of my nondescript basketball shorts.

Lift my head as I pull out my car keys and then stop dead.

There's enough ambient light from the arena's security lights to spot the lone figure leaning against my driver's side door, arms folded over her chest and her blond hair pulled up in one of her usual messy buns.

My heart rate kicks back into gear around the same time that my gait resumes, and I gruffly ask, "You need to get into the building or somethin'?" At this time of night, security is long gone. Most of the permanent staff and players have a key card to access the practice arena during off-times, but Holly has always been a contracted employee via Carter Photography.

No access key card to slip into her wallet and use whenever she wants.

My ex-wife's arms fall to her sides, her fingers diving into the front pocket of her pants—jeans, I think. Dark-washed, if I'm not mistaken, and tight enough to make a man lose all blood in the head on his shoulders.

"Or something," she says after a beat, not moving or stepping aside when I stop before her.

The last time we were together, I had my tongue down her throat and she was grinding on me like she'd taken up mechanical bull-riding and was determined to ride until her minutes were up. She'd put on a hell of a performance that night, and then proceeded to ignore my calls following our return to Boston.

In a text that I've read more times than I'll ever admit out loud, she claimed that I've ruined her for other men.

Well, in the last two weeks, she's ruined my goddamn peace of mind.

Add that to a concussion and I'm lucky I'm still upright and walking.

"Not interested in *somethings*." I reach beyond her right shoulder to set my energy drink on the roof of my car, a little more forcefully than the car deserves. "Unless you've got something important to say, I've got a hot date with my shower and my TV—"

"The guys are worried about you."

My arm pauses in its downward trajectory, back to my side, as I dip my chin to look down, down, down at Holly blocking my entrance to my car. "The guys need to stay in their own lane."

In response, she only latches onto my forearm, the soft pads of her fingers digging into my bare skin. "Don't be a dick, Jackson. They've been concerned since the hit with Fitzgerald. You've been short-tempered, moody, and definitely not the patient captain everyone knows and loves."

My exhaustion is at its peak tonight, dragging me down, making me into the prick I reserve exclusively for the ice.

I tell myself that it's the only reason I do what I do next: dropping my hands onto the car on either side of Holly's beautiful head, leaning into her body so that her small but pert breasts press into my sternum, my already hard dick making its presence known against her tight stomach.

I drop my mouth to her ear, needing to hunch my shoulders and curl myself around her petite frame to get her exactly where I want her. "Is that the captain *you* know and love?" My nose rasps along the delicate line of her neck, my tongue coming out to flick the exposed shell of her ear. "The patient man?" Another flick of my tongue, another pulse of my headache forging a stampede in my skull. "The man who walked onto that flight the day after you and him kissed, fully prepared to do what it took to make shit right . . . only to find out you turned into a coward overnight and took a red-eye instead."

Her sweet voice is reedy thin when she speaks. "Jackson—"

"No." Stomach twisting, I ball my hands into fists and avert my face. The pulsing in my temples won't stop, narrowing my vision, making a sheen of sweat break out over my skin, only matched by the throbbing of my cock as I wrestle for control. "If I'm being a moody asshole, it's got little to do with Fitzgerald."

I was given the okay by the doc within days of that hit.

That's how it works in the NHL, how it's *always* worked. You get hit. You go down. You get your ass right back up again and give the game everything you've got the next time you step out onto the ice.

The NHL doesn't breed pussies—and we've all had our marbles rattled a time or two.

I'm no different.

No, as much as I've tried not to let her silence needle me,

Holly's the reason I've spent more hours than I can count in the gym. She's the reason sleep has eluded me. She's the fucking reason why my bark is definitely as bad as my bite these days.

There's nothing quite like putting yourself out there—to the woman who has always had your heart in a vice, divorce or not—and being slammed with the bat of rejection after reaching out.

Her small hand folds itself in the loose fabric of my over-sized Cornell T-shirt, and I'm not immune to the ironic twist of fate that the day I wear my alma mater's gear is the same day I run into the girl who's had me all twisted up since we first met at college.

"Jackson," she tries again, voice soft but dredged up by steel, "that kiss . . . I'm not denying that it felt good. God, did it." Her hold on my T tightens, twists a little harder, just like my heart. "I needed to collect my thoughts after what happened. I needed to remember every reason why we didn't work. I needed space because if I didn't have that then I knew—" She breaks off with a broken laugh, the sound so completely unlike her that I almost cave, almost cup the back of her head and bring her in for a hug and a promise that it'll all be fine.

That we can go on pretending that the kiss meant nothing two weeks ago and means nothing still.

I can't do that, though.

Not when I'm coiled so tight that I'm on the verge of snapping.

Of *begging* her to reconsider and give us another chance.

"Answer me this." I sound gruff, voice cut from stone. The tip of my finger goes to her chin, lifting gently so that I can look into her blue eyes. Get a read on her—on everything she's thinking but won't allow herself to say out loud because that's who Holly is, who she's always been.

I was the first to bring the L-word into the conversation.

The first to mention forever.

And then the one who looked into her gorgeous blue eyes and read what I knew she wouldn't say out loud: she wanted a divorce.

Fuck that.

"Answer me this," I hear myself repeat, no less gruffly, "how many times have you thought about what happened in that hotel room?"

Her lids fall shut, severing our connection as though it's too much for her to take.

Not happening, sweetheart.

I grip her chin, then slip my hand to curl around the nape of her neck. My thumb glosses down the smooth column, the shadows of the night kissing the very same skin that I touch. "Don't you dare retreat."

At my low command, her eyes spring open and her fingers yank hard on my T-shirt. "Please, Jackson."

Dropping my mouth to the fragile skin I'm caressing, I kiss her neck. A gentle nip. A soft tug on her ear. A scrape of my teeth that has her breath rattling loudly in my ears like a white flag of surrender.

Her free hand jumps to my bicep, her nails digging into my muscles as her head falls back, a sultry moan slipping from her lush lips. "Oh, God."

Not God.

Just me.

The patient man who knows exactly what she needs to drop her steel armor and let him inside.

Let *me* inside.

"Answer the question, Holls." My thumb swoops low, along the underside of her jaw to tilt her head just the way I want it—at the perfect angle to catch my kiss. I hover my lips over hers, refusing to eliminate those final few inches to heaven on earth until she answers. My control slips, the rapid tempo of my breathing slipping into a tight race with the thunderous roar in my head. "Answer. The. Question."

Her warm breath washes over my lips. "Every day," she whispers, "I've thought about that kiss every damn day."

"Good. Now you can think about this one, too."

CHAPTER 19
HOLLY

Jackson's kiss is seduction in its purest form.

And the irony isn't lost on me: the man kissing me now is the warrior who plays on the ice, the man who elicits fear from his opponents, the man who commands a room simply by existing in it.

He tempts me like no one else ever has.

Slays me with nothing but his dark eyes on mine.

Sabotages my plan to keep things platonic and easy and uncomplicated by backing me up against the side of his car and devouring my mouth with his.

I want to hate him for it.

Instead, I cup his face with my hands, thumbs tracing his stubbled jawline, and sweep my tongue along the seam of his lips.

He growls his approval against my mouth. This kiss, not unlike the one in that hotel room, isn't sweet. It's definitely not subtle. Not when he hooks my left leg around his hip and drags his still-clothed hard-on along the seam of my jeans. Not when his other hand gently pulls at my messy bun, releasing the strands, throwing the elastic band away into the darkness. Not when he fists my now loosened hair, breaks from the kiss, and grits out, "I've dreamt of this. Your hair tangled between my fingers. Spread across my pillow. Wrapped around my fist as I fit myself into you from behind."

His mouth lands on my throat, just like it was only minutes ago.

And just like then, words flee my brain on contact.

Not for him, though.

No, he only winds that spell tighter around me, winding me up with nothing but the softness of his lips on my flesh and the dirty words spilling from his mouth, tightening the need between my legs until I'm rubbing shamelessly against his crotch.

"I'd take you just how you like it," he mutters shamelessly, fingers twining in my hair, mouth slipping down to the crook of my neck and shoulder, "you bent over the bed, your sweet ass in the air, your hands fisting the sheets as you scream my name."

Jackson Carter.

Captain of the Boston Blades.

The only man to know exactly where I need to be touched, the precise pressure that I need to tip over the edge.

But I know how to touch him, too, how to make him lose control.

If we're going down in this downward spiral of ecstasy and bad decisions, I refuse to go alone.

My hands move from his rugged face, the latter half-eclipsed by the shadows of the parking lot, to the waistband of his mesh shorts. I don't give him any opportunity to steal back control before I'm slipping the material down over his narrow hips to his thick, muscular thighs.

Right under his balls.

"Holls—"

I hear the panic in his voice—the almighty Jackson worrying about having his throne of control usurped—and drop my lifted leg back onto the concrete.

Then I drop to my knees completely.

We're in clear sight of the practice arena, but the security guards are gone for the night, no other cars around but mine and Jackson's. The practice rink, unlike TD Garden which sits on the cusp of Boston's touristy North End, is in the suburb of Waltham, tucked away in a thicket of trees and shrubbery, away from prying eyes and reporters and crazy fans.

Our witnesses are the darkened sky, the twinkling stars, the thin slice of the moon peeking out from behind a cluster of clouds.

And not a one of them utters a single protest as I wrap my hand around my ex-husband's cock and slip my mouth over the crown.

"Oh, *fuck*."

Jackson's weight shifts forward, and I hear his palms land on the roof of the car as though he's desperate to find stability.

My fist arcs up his thick length, my mouth dropping simultaneously as I suck him deep and meet my hand in the middle.

"*Holly*," he works out, his voice nothing more than a guttural groan above me.

I don't stop. I don't slow down, my fist twisting steady and fast as I swallow him again and again. My free hand lifts from his thigh to cup his balls, squeezing, gently tugging the way he's always loved.

My reward is another string of incomprehensible words: "Oh, fuck. Fuck. Christ, you have to stop. I can't . . . It feels . . . you feel so—oh, *fuck*."

It's not a fair fight. I know what makes him tick. I know what makes him lose control. But in that space where my insecurities live—where I wonder, constantly—if I know him at all anymore, I still give him my everything and hope it's enough.

Opening my eyes, I pray for a splice of light across his face when I glance up past his Cornell T-shirt, which makes my heart squeeze with the memories.

Wish granted.

He's watching me, chest heaving with big, uneven breaths, his hands gripping the smooth curve of the car's roof. He stares at me like I'm a gift he doesn't deserve, cheeks hollowing with those uneven breaths of his, bulky arms straining with effort.

I make sure he's watching as I bob my head and take him deep, to the back of my throat.

His rugged features fracture, my name crossing his lips on an exhale, and then he yanks me up off my knees. He pulls open the driver's side door, his energy drink falling from the roof to the cement, and ducks his big body inside.

There's a *snap!* of what sounds like the glovebox closing.

A relieved, masculine sigh.

And then those arms are banded under my butt as he hikes me up into the air and rounds the front of the car. He deposits me gently on the hood, his hand circling mine until I feel something square press into my palm.

A condom.

My heart sinks at the realization that he has one in his car.

Have there been other women? Has there been anyone but me? He said there isn't anyone in the picture before he kissed me in Chicago, but that doesn't mean there hasn't been anyone else since our breakup. I can't blame him if there was —we're divorced—but it feels like knives are diving into my heart at the thought alone of Jackson being with someone else.

Maybe even *many* someone else's.

His smoky Texan accent pulls me out of my head. "Don't go there," he demands, framing my face with his hands and crushing my mouth with his before coming up for air. "No one. There's been no one since you. Fuck if I know, but those condoms might already be expired."

I crack a grin. "Don't romanticize this with talk about the pull-out method."

His brown eyes stare down at me, his mouth curving in a wicked grin. "It worked when you were eighteen."

"You think so?" My fingers dance up his chest, over the C in Cornell, as I marvel at the sinews in his biceps, exposed by the sliced-off sleeves of his T-shirt. "I specifically remember having to put the condom on you for our first time." I lean in. Kiss his chest, right over his heart. "You were so damn nervous, fingers all a-tremble."

His familiar boom of laughter settles the frayed nerves of my soul, the worried edges that we're doing something wrong here, even though the only people we'll be hurting with this mistake are ourselves. If it is a mistake at all. I'd prefer to think of it as . . . destiny.

"Let me tell you a little secret," Jackson murmurs against my ear, his nimble, *un*-trembling fingers undoing the buttons of my jeans with practiced ease. "You had me so worked up, I would have died without you touching me. Yeah, I was shaky. I had the girl of my dreams alone in her dorm room, laid out on a twin-sized bed with pictures of her grandparents and brother staring down at me from the wall."

I gasp as he tugs my jeans and underwear down the length of my legs, leaving my butt naked on the cold hood of the car. Probably unsanitary—but nothing about this night is classy or white-poster-bed-worthy.

It's dirty and a little wrong and so many degrees of catch-your-hair-on-fire hot.

I *love* it.

"Don't forget the picture of my childhood dog," I say, still clutching the condom as I lean back to stare at Jackson. His cock bobs confidently, long and thick, against the loose fabric of his T-shirt. "Rex was watching and judging the whole time."

"Little furry bastard," Jackson teases, his fingers now

dancing along my upper thighs. "He was the worst. First and last time any of them watched us get it on."

He'd taken the pictures down and bought me proper picture frames, which he never failed to turn facedown whenever he got me naked.

And he'd gotten me naked a hell of a lot back then.

"No one is watching us now." My voice is huskier than normal, even to my own ears.

"No," Jackson returns a moment later, his thumbs sliding along the crease of my hip and pelvis, "no one is here to watch us."

Those dancing fingers of his swoop inward as he leans forward, one hand lifting to grasp the back of my neck and pull me in for a heated kiss that curls my toes. I wait for reason to burst into my brain, all sorts of yellow caution tapes and red stop signs to send my full throttle to a sudden standstill.

It never does.

My brain goes virtually empty when Jackson nips at my bottom lip, chuckling low at my needy whimper. And when he finally gives me what I need, his thumb dragging over my clit—circling so slowly with barely any pressure that I nearly go mad, a glint of naughty playfulness in his dark eyes—all rationale flees the vicinity.

I arch my back at his electric touch.

Grip his forearm in a silent demand for *more, more, more*.

Open my mouth and beg out loud, "Yes, there. Right there—"

The hand at my neck goes to my left leg and he pushes it wide, hiking my thigh up onto the car. "I wanna see you, sweetheart," he growls. "*All* of you."

With a finger to my collarbone, he gently tips me backward like a set of Dominos teetering over in submission. My stomach goes concave when I land on my elbows, one leg dangling over the car's grill, the other bent at a ninety-degree angle on the hood. I'm exposed—or as exposed as one can be in the dark of night—and that's when he makes his move.

Two of his fingers dragging through my wetness, circling at my entrance, pushing inside on a slow, easy glide.

I'm not sure which one of us is louder: my satisfied moan or his guttural groan.

In this moment, I exist on every thrust of those fingers, drawing life when they curl just so and have me seeing stars. *Probably literal stars, given the time of day.*

Probably.

Maybe also some fake ones.

"Christ, you're so damn tight, Holls."

I *feel* impossibly tight. But the friction of his big body leveraging over mine as he bolsters his weight on the hand planted by my head, his feet still planted on the concrete, his hard-on grazing my belly . . . God, when was the last time I felt so full? So absolutely complete?

Tears prick my eyes at the thought.

It's more than just the sex or the good feels. I've missed *this*. Jackson. The way we read each other's wants and needs before we even voice them out loud. How he knows exactly how to curl his fingers to have me shuddering before him. How, when he knows I'm close, there's nothing I love more than for him to slip in that third finger, just so I can feel that added pressure—that acute line between pleasure and pain—that thrusts me over the edge into completion.

He teases me with that possibility now, and I beg shamelessly for it.

I wriggle my hips, popping them up off the hood of the car. "Now, Jackson," I whimper, "please."

"Not happening." He removes his hand completely from between my legs, palm pressing down on my pelvis to keep me in place. Then he leans in close, our noses grazing, his eyes locked on mine when he grinds out, "You're not comin' on my fingers, not after all this time."

"If you leave me hanging like this, I'll seriously—"

"Who said anything about leaving you hanging?" He plucks the condom from my hand, tearing open the foil with his teeth. Rolling the latex over his length down to the base, he hooks his hands under my ass and lifts me farther up the car. His cock lines up with my opening, the thick crown taunting me with all the possibilities of what's to come—of what I've missed with this man over the last year. "No, sweetheart," he whispers against my ear, voice rough, breath warm, "you're goin' to come all over my cock. Any objections?"

I swallow. Lick my dry lips. "Not a one."

"There's my girl."

He grins, wickedly, and then delivers on his promise: he thrusts home.

And, God, that's *exactly* how it feels in this moment. Like he's come home. Like we were always meant to be despite the divorce and the heartache and the coexisting like strangers. My heart wrenches with each drive of his hips, my breath shaky on each exhalation.

Don't hurt me, my heart whispers when he cradles the back of my head to protect it from bouncing against the car.

Hold me tighter, my heart yearns when he slicks his free hand over the crease of my hip bone to keep me in position.

I've missed you so much.

That last thought takes hold of my brain as I cling to his arms while he powers into me. I hold onto this man as he changes his angle, hitting me just right, the ambient moon casting his face in shadows and light, illuminating his narrowed eyes and parted mouth and the thin, white scar on his cheekbone where he had reconstructive surgery.

I've missed you.

He snakes a hand between our slick bodies to find my clit.

I've missed you.

He applies pressure, circling in quick, rapid circles that

wind me tight, tight, tight until my back bows and my hold on his arms turns into nails scraping down his broad back.

I've missed you.

"You're beautiful to me," he growls, "so damn beautiful."

The pleasure coils tighter, and with a gasp, I come just like that.

On my back, sprawled across the hood of a car.

Exposed to the dark, to my ex-husband.

Limbs shuddering and shaking.

Jackson follows a heartbeat later, elbows on either side of my face, hips churning fast and uneven as he erupts with his own orgasm, and—

"Shit, sweetheart," he breathes roughly into my hairline, "holy shit."

My head falls back, lax. Lungs heaving, I manage to work out, "Good news."

"Yeah?"

"You didn't need me to put the condom on you this time. A-plus work, Captain."

He laughs low at that, lifting his head far enough to press a soft kiss to my cheek. Another to the corner of my mouth. One last one over my lips, tugging gently on my lower lip before he mutters, "I'm gonna be honest with you. I'm tryin' real hard to think of something witty to say back to that, but all I've got is . . . how do you feel about pancakes?"

CHAPTER 20
HOLLY

Jackson takes me to a hole-in-the-wall diner across from Boston's South Station, and when he said pancakes . . . he really meant pancakes.

I blanch when the waitress sets down a stack in front of me.

They've got to be the size of my face, at least.

And that's saying nothing about the size of Jackson's late-night dinner: a stack of blueberry pancakes, three eggs done over easy, wheat toast slathered with butter, a bowl of fruit, and a side of bacon.

Eyes bulging at the amount of food that's covering the small table, I delicately unwrap the silverware from its paper napkin binding and clutch my fork and knife in opposite hands, caveman-style.

"You should be glad you got me naked before this feast. You're going to have to roll me out of here."

Jackson takes a pull of his milk, then winks at me. "I have complete faith in you."

"Sure, maybe *you* do but my jeans are already crying out for help."

"So pop the button," he tells me with a nonchalant shrug

before tossing a grape into his mouth like some sort of Greek god reclining on a chaise lounge.

Except, instead of a chaise lounge, we're currently seated on red plastic cushions that look like they haven't been updated since the seventies.

"I'm so *not* popping the button." I cut my first sliver of the pancake, reach for the syrup bottle, and completely drown my plate with it. If my pancakes aren't begging for air, then the syrup hasn't done its job—morbid, sure, but totally necessary in my book. I kick my chin in the direction of his plates. "Are you sure you won't be regretting all that food tomorrow when you play against Buffalo? Or, you know . . ." I swallow the bite of pancake and subsequently swallow a moan. God, that is *delicious*. Dingy-looking diners never fail to do my taste buds right. Wiping my chin with my napkin, I continue, ". . . regret staying up so late tonight?"

Jackson's dark eyes rove over my face, seeking, probing, and I feel my cheeks heat under his acute scrutiny. Finally, he murmurs, "There wasn't a shot in hell that I was about to go to bed without talking about what happened tonight." He pauses, full lips turning up. "You defiled my virgin car."

My jaw drops open unceremoniously. "Defiled your virgin —" Breaking off, I cough into my fist so as not to give him the satisfaction of combusting with laughter. But the coughing does nothing to hide my growing grin. "You've got to be kidding me."

"No kidding here." He holds up his big hands, a slice of crispy bacon thrusting upward with his right hand. "You didn't hear it protesting when I stripped you naked? *Oh no!* it screamed. *My eyes—they burn!*"

Oh, God. Trust Jackson to turn on the charm-o-meter when we're in public.

For that comment, I steal his bacon.

Leaning over the laminate table, I pluck the crispy deliciousness out of his hand, secretly delighting in the way his brows shoot up at my boldness.

Take that, Captain.

"First," I say, around a mouthful of bacon, "I was *half*-naked."

"Minor, inconsequential detail. You were naked where it mattered."

I roll my eyes at his smooth baritone. "And *second*, what happened tonight is . . . was . . ."

When words fail me, Jackson's dark eyes soften. He ducks his head to dunk his toast through the egg yolk. "The stars aligned."

Swoon.

Seriously, that shouldn't sound as romantic as it does, but there you go. Jackson Carter is clearly determined to steal my breath away tonight, by orgasm or by other, no-less-panty-melting measures.

Focusing on my food, I soak the fluffy pancake in the maple syrup and do my best to maintain my composure. But boy, is that hard to do when you're post-orgasmically blissful, the way I am right now.

"I didn't realize you believed in stars aligning or any of that."

His white teeth sink into a juicy, red strawberry. Chewing, swallowing, he then shrugs. "Truth is, I don't."

"Then why would you bring them up now?"

He meets my gaze head-on, his brown eyes unflinching. "It's nearly impossible to believe in that sort of thing when your life is falling apart. Same goes with fate." His thumb caresses the spine of the knife he's holding. "We were break-ing, Holls, and I was spending nights on our damn balcony making futile wishes on shooting stars."

My heart splinters at the visual of him standing out there, loose sweatpants hanging from his hips and one of his hoodies pulled on but unzipped, revealing his strong chest and cut abdomen—his usual attire when we were home together. "I don't remember any of this."

"Nah, you wouldn't." His smile is blasé but frayed. "Most nights, you fell asleep at the office after a long day."

At his words, guilt threads through my veins. "I'm sorry."

He shrugs, another casual offer of acceptance or forgiveness or *something*. "It's in the past. It happened." Another shrug, this one followed by a mouthful of egg and a swallow once he finishes chewing. "I was no boy scout either. We both fucked up, Holls. I know that."

"We both prioritized our professions over each other. We accepted the divorce the same way we lived our marriage at the end—quietly without digging deep and fighting for *us*. Counseling felt like a useless endeavor when we never made a change. What did we really change? Nothing. You shut down after that last night at Sal's and I . . ." The truth clogs my throat, clawing its way up. And then it spills forward in all of its ugly glory: "I grew to despise everything about hockey." His eyes go wide, but my confession isn't over yet. Palms tightly wrapped around my utensils, I continue. "I hated that I felt like I had to choose between supporting your career or growing something for myself. I hated that hardly anyone knew *me*. I was 'Jackson Carter's wife' or 'the captain's girl' or 'that chick who's always at the games.'"

Something in his rugged features splinters. He shoots a covert gaze at the packed diner—one of the few twenty-four-seven restaurants in the city, and thus a hot spot—and combs his fingers through his hair, still messy from my hold on it just an hour ago.

"You meant more to me than all of that," he vows, voice low.

Appetite dwindling, I set my fork down. "I know that I did. You meant . . . hell, there wasn't anything I *wouldn't* do for you. Except, I guess, that the bigger you got in the NHL, the more my own identity was just"—I drop my gaze— "squashed."

"By *me*?"

My hands turn clammy. When I reach for my short glass of orange juice, I can't help but note the tremor in my hands. An hour ago, I gave myself to Jackson fully, holding nothing back. I opened my body, bared my soul—gave him every ounce of control and power to do with me as he wanted—and yet this conversation is so much harder than sex. Harder than sex in public, no less.

As though he's read something in my expression, Jackson drops his fork and stretches his arm across the narrow table. He cups my cheek, eviscerating my heart with that one touch, and draws in a sharp breath before he speaks. "Don't do that." His thumb brushes over the crest of my cheekbone. "Don't run from me. Tell me what you need to say—I can take it, I promise."

A weak smile pulls at my lips.

He knows me so well.

Running is my M.O. and has been since childhood. I guess that's sort of what happens when you're constantly trying to box up your emotions and remove the perpetual hurt from your heart. You become way too good at putting on a happy-go-lucky front, even with those who matter most to you.

How many times did I lie to friends at school that my parents had been killed in some sort of horrific accident? Better that than the bitter truth, which was that my parents were cocaine addicts. By the time I was six and my brother four, they'd packed up their things and dropped us—their only children—off at my grandmother's house with our meager belongings.

They never came back.

No postcards.

No letters.

No phone calls to let us know how much they loved us.

In the end, my childish lies came to fruition. In a letter that my grandmother wrote to accompany her will, she finally revealed what happened to my parents. Momma had died years earlier—drug overdose. Daddy was locked in prison on a life sentence—he'd murdered someone after a drug deal gone wrong. I know that my grandmother was only trying to shield us from any more hurt. In the end, it seems I'd only loved the vision I had of my parents a little too hard. The reality, as realities tend to be, wasn't anything to write home about.

Against my better judgment, I cradle Jackson's hand with my own. Soak up that slice of affection as though it's the only batch I'll be given for the rest of my life.

His touch feels like home.

"I didn't know who I was anymore," I whisper after a drawn-out moment. "Not Holly Belliveaux anymore—not that girl who showed up at Cornell, ready to conquer the world and enter the world of sports medicine." Pulling Jackson's hand away from my face, I stare down at his calloused fingers, his roughened palm, the swollen knuckles that have been broken countless times after years of battling it out in the rink. "Hockey was your dream, and then you became mine. And, before you say anything to that, I'm fully aware that it was my decision to leave Cornell and follow you to Boston, to follow you everywhere you went." I release his hand. Fold mine in my lap and squeeze them together to stop the tremors. "But you can't make a life out of relying on someone else's happiness to fuel your own and make you feel complete, even if that happiness is your husband's."

Jackson slouches in his seat, food abandoned. His arms stretch across the back of the booth, and though he looks totally casual and at ease, I know it's for the sake of any onlookers.

His dark eyes reveal the depth of his emotional turmoil,

and what I see there breaks my heart—and the damn thing has already been lifeless for so very long.

"You started Carter Photography," he murmurs, his features tense, his voice tight. "That was all you."

"Was it, really?" I swallow past the hard lump in my throat. "In the beginning, it existed only because of your connections."

"Everyone needs a little help, Holls." Shaking his head, his lips flatline. "I gave you the stepping stool—you did the rest."

"And as soon as I did, you pretty much ceased to exist."

His lips twist, and I watch as his loose hands clench—though he remains otherwise physically unmoved. "What the hell does that mean?"

"Exactly what it sounds like." Reaching forward for the OJ, I down the rest like it's something a lot stiffer than one-hundred percent juice. It does nothing to quiet the riotous nerves in my belly, not that I expected it to. I keep the glass clasped in my hand, just to have something to hold. "You were all too happy to have me chasing you around the country like some sort of obsessed puck bunny."

"You were my *wife*."

"It didn't feel that way once my business became something more than a hobby. I had shows and yet you never came to one. Hockey was always number one. I get it, hockey is your job. But I invited you to photo shoots when you weren't at practice or at a game, and you chose the guys over me. Every. Single. Time." A bitter laugh falls from my mouth. "I spent years at your beck and call, Jackson. I was the perfect wife, boosting you up when your confidence was threatened; watching more hours of clips than I even knew what to do with because you needed to be on your A-game and I wanted nothing less for you; attending every game, away or at home, except for that one time I caught pneumonia and even *then*, I was glued to the TV on our couch."

Wrapping my arms around my middle, I struggle to keep the tears from resurfacing. I haven't cried in months and I won't start again now. But they threaten to spill over anyway, and I bite my bottom lip and fight for strength.

"I was your wife." I meet Jackson's turbulent, dark gaze, struggling to find the right words that pinpoint my emotions but don't tear at his soul. Because I still don't, after all this time, want to see him hurt. It's never been my intention—hurting him is like a knife to my own heart, and time and distance hasn't changed that. Ultimately, I lift my chin and force the words out into the open, for better or worse: "But when I finally had something of my own to show, I may as well have been married to a ghost."

CHAPTER 21
JACKSON

I n the span of a breath, Holly cuts me at the knees.

With my arms spread over the back of the booth and my legs spread wide under the miniscule table, I feel every muscle string tight like I've been delivered a physical blow to every inch of my body—starting with my balls.

All words die on my tongue as I struggle to find something to say in return.

Nothing in my defense—because what sort of defense do I have if the most important person in my life felt for *years* as though she didn't have my full support and all of my pride for what she's accomplished?

I knew Holly had been unhappy. It'd been all over her face for anyone to see. And maybe there's something to be said about growing complacent in the years that we were together: she expected me to read her mind and I assumed she'd always be there, the way she'd been for years.

We're both at fault.

If our marriage was a hockey game, then our stick play was sloppy. We failed to read each other's signs or anticipate where we'd be on the ice; didn't listen to our coach when he warned us that if we didn't open communication lines, we'd walk away with an L flashing on the Jumbotron.

And the worst part of it all: we gave up while there was still another period to fight for the win.

The past can't be reversed, not in hockey, not in life outside the rink.

But we can sure-as-hell learn from our mistakes and do better next time.

Because I *need* there to be a next time with Holly. The last month has shown me that my feelings for her are unchanged, no matter how much I've tried in the last year to stop loving her. And, to be straight-up honest, I don't think I tried at all.

I meant what I said in that text that I sent her: I'm ready to start breathing again, and I only do that with her, my ex-wife.

Only, I'm damn well ready to get rid of the *ex*-part of the equation—if she'll have me.

With stiff motions, I gesture at her half-eaten pancake. Gruffly I ask, "You want them to box that up for you?"

She blinks down at her plate, her cheeks blooming with color. "Ah . . . Um, no, thanks. I think I'm . . . yeah, I think I'm good."

I slide out from the booth.

Blindly feel for my wallet in the pocket of my mesh shorts.

My heart beats in time with my footfalls as I find our waitress and pay for our meal.

"How was the food? Everything all right?" *It was perfect.*

"Need a box?" *Nah, no boxes.*

"'Kay, you and your wife have a great night now." *Thanks . . . we'll do that.*

I return my card to my billfold and stuff it back into my pocket.

Shove my fingers through my hair and quickly deliberate how I broach the topic of dating with Holly. I fully believe that we can come back from our past to build something new

—based on the sex we had on my car, that area of our relationship doesn't need mending.

Our hearts do, and I'm fully prepared to do whatever it takes to earn back Holly's.

Holly Belliveaux Carter.

Carter. I shake my head, blowing out a heavy breath. Keeping my name alone leaves the impression that she's not over us, not completely, which definitely works in my favor. And God knows I'm not over her.

When I near our table, she's already picking up her purse and sliding the strap over her shoulder. Her blond hair is in disarray, completely disheveled from my fingers spearing through the silky strands. She pauses when she spots me, spine snapping straight. Blue eyes stare back at me, wide and hurt and—

I stick my hand out, palm up.

Her gaze drops to the offering. "What am I supposed to do with that?"

She doesn't say the words with a single trace of heat, only genuine perplexity.

I step in close, so that she's got to lift her chin to maintain eye contact. "Take my hand, Holly."

Nose scrunching, her cheeks flush even brighter. "I'm sorry, but why should I? You demanded a confession and then you *walked away*. Holding hands is all about trust, and right now I'm thinking I'd trust a random person on the street more than—"

I take her hand anyway, cutting off her rant by sliding my palm against hers.

Our fingers tangle, palms kiss.

Her chin kicks up defiantly, and I'm tempted to lean down and brush my mouth over hers. Instead, I wind my way to the front door of the diner, pulling her along behind me. She splutters at my back but follows anyway.

South Street is eerily quiet at this time of night when we

step out of the diner. A lone cabbie meanders down the road, and I can hear the distant sound of laughter and music from nearby Chinatown.

I cut a right at the intersection, and then duck into a narrow alleyway between two large buildings. Pressing my back to the dirty, stone façade, so that Holly isn't resting against it herself, I bring her body in close. Cup my hands around her biceps, then slip them up to rest on her slim shoulders.

"I'm sorry," I tell her, "I'm so fuckin' sorry for making you feel like I didn't care. That I wasn't proud of you and everything you've done. That you felt, even for one damn second, that you were taken for granted . . . and that when you were no longer there in reach every moment of the day, you weren't worth my time anymore."

I watch her swallow roughly, her face twisting to the side to stare at the busier stretch of road off to our right. In this alley, though, it's just us.

No outside world.

No interruptions.

Just us and all the hurt and heartache and the goddamn love for her that once consumed me—that *still* consumes me.

"That's on me." I duck my head, putting myself squarely in her line of sight. "I take full responsibility for letting you go when I didn't want to do so in the first place. You needed more—you needed our relationship to change—and I retreated to the familiar instead of giving you every ounce of the support and dedication that you gave me so freely for years." Squeezing her shoulders lightly, I go on, "I own that. *All* of it. Nothing I can say now can change any of those decisions, but I want to try again, Holls." The pressure beats at my temples and this time has nothing to do with my headaches and concussions and everything to do with the fear of the woman in front of me telling me no. "Shit, I don't even want to *try*. I'll do whatever it takes for you to see that we belong together."

"I . . . I feel like I need to breathe." Her hands flutter upward, pulling out of my grasp to shove her hair behind her ears. "Tonight was—well, honestly, it was sort of dreamlike. I need to process it all."

It's on the tip of my tongue to prove to her that all this is very much real.

The fact that she got down on her knees? Real.

The fact that she came in my arms? Real as fuck.

Through self-control alone, I only give a curt nod. Settling my hands on my hips, I stare down at her. "One week."

She blinks once, twice. "What?"

Screw it.

Caving to my need to touch her, I brush her lips with the pad of my thumb. "One week, Holls. Think about everything you need to—work it all out in your head and figure out if you want more from me than just tonight's hookup. If you do, next weekend . . . next weekend, I've got a three-day stretch with nothing but me, my couch and TV in sight, and I'd rather spend that time with you. We'll go somewhere."

"*Go* somewhere?" She laughs at that, the sound feminine and light. "Jackson, we can't just . . . we can't just leave the state."

Wanting to keep that half-smile curling her lips, I blatantly tease her. "Why not? You on house arrest or something?" I glance down at her feet. "No ankle monitor that I can see. Unless you got the invisible kind?"

She laughs again, and my heart warms right up. "You're ridiculous."

"I'm a realist."

"Says the guy who was allegedly wishing on shooting stars."

I grin. "What? Not manly enough for you?"

"No," she says, shaking her head, "I'm not saying

anything about manly. I just mean that realists don't normally wish on shooting stars. It's not in their DNA. Way too frivolous."

"There's a first time for everything, sweetheart." I tip my head back to squint up at the dark sky sandwiched between the two towering buildings on either side of the alleyway. Dramatically, I thicken my accent and drawl, "Lookie there, Ms. Carter, a shooting star!" For effect, I clamp my hand over my chest and give a fake *yee-haw* of joy.

She huffs out my name through peals of laughter. "I can't. I can't—please, Jackson—"

Unfortunately for her, I'm not done.

I draw her up against my side, her small frame tiny against mine, and tap her chin to encourage her to look up toward the sky, too. "There she is," I say, boisterous enough for her to hold her belly and continue to laugh. "Hold on, hold, gotta think about the right wish. Maybe somethin' about my car forgetting about her defilement? Nah, she'll have to learn about the birds and bees at some point."

"To winning against Buffalo tomorrow?" Holly pipes up, getting into the spirit.

"No, ma'am." I curl my arm around her shoulders, keeping her close. "Only one wish will do, but you have to go first."

"I thought it was age before beauty?"

I laugh softly. "Cute, Holls, real cute."

"Okay, okay." She shifts her weight, feet squaring off with her hips, which brush up against mine. "If I had to wish upon a fake shooting star, I'd . . ." She taps her chin, leaning her head back to get a real good look at the midnight sky. "I'd hope that if I *were* to go on this weekend away, then I'd maybe have the chance to convince the organizer that we should visit somewhere along the coast, WiFi not needed—so we could, you know . . . talk or what not—and pancakes may be necessary."

My heart squeezes and I do the same as her, lifting my face to the sky.

Wishing on a goddamn fake shooting star.

"I'd wish for us to go in with an open mind. No promises, no guarantees. Just leaving the past at the door for seventy-two hours and just . . . breathe."

I hear the sharp way she sucks in a breath, and then the quieter murmur, "It sounds like paradise."

CHAPTER 22
JACKSON

As a professional hockey player, I'm used to the limelight, the puck bunnies, the hardcore fans who will drop anything and everything when they see me walk out of the tunnel and onto the ice. In the hockey world, I'm a god among men.

But let it be said—I'm no Tom Brady, no LeBron James, no whoever-the-fuck is playing golf and ripping up the scoreboards these days.

Simply put, even after all these years in the NHL, I've always maintained some level of anonymity when I take to the streets.

Not anymore.

Fuckin' Getting Pucked.

As I bulldoze my way toward Mass General, its blue hospital signs beckoning me like a beacon of hope, there's no less than ten people who stop and ask me for an autograph.

And not a one of them is mentioning a damn thing about my stick play—at least, not the stick play that's routinely talked about by analysts on ESPN or Sports 24/7.

"Oh, my God, Jackson! Jackson, you're so hot. Isn't he hot, Sammy? Jackson, I've seen you on TV!"

"Hi! Holy crap, you're big. I didn't realize how big you are from TV, but you're just . . . please tell me you're that big in other places?! Like in your pants?"

Put your head down and just keep trucking.

Readjusting my sunglasses over the crooked bridge of my nose, I skim my gaze over the various entrances into Boston's largest hospital, hastily deliberating on the best course of entry.

"Mr. Carter, the ladies of America want to know . . . are you single?"

The last comment comes at me from a dude decked out in all black, a microphone being shoved in my direction, and a camera crew tailing him like a pack of lemmings. Unlike the women, this guy isn't here with a starry-eyed expression. Cold, calculated blue eyes blink back at me while he waits for my answer as though I'm standing on the red carpet and answering about what threads I'm wearing and what designer stitched them together.

"Mr. Carter," he says again, this time a little louder, "are you single?"

I say the first thing that comes to mind: "Who the fuck are you?"

Admittedly, it's not the most poised response, and it's a good thing I never hired another publicist after my last left to be a full-time mom because I can only imagine good ol' Miranda having a goddamn heart attack at my eloquence.

"I'm with TMZ and—"

I let the hospital door swing shut behind me, cutting him off.

"Fuckin' TMZ." I scrub my palm over my face. *Christ.*

Pulling the shades from my face, I tuck them over the neck of my white T-shirt and pull out my phone. Bringing up the Safe Space thread, I text the guys as I head for the wing where my appointment is.

ME:

Almost got mauled by TMZ just now.

HUNT:

Harvey was there?

ME:

Who the hell is Harvey?

HUNT:

Levin. Harvey Levin. Dude's in charge of the site/show/celebrity soul stealer.

BEAUMONT:

Fuck TMZ. Do you know how many times they showed my bare ass a few years back? On TV, on their website, on fucking Twitter. My ass had more hits than a Kardashian Instagram post.

CAIN:

Mistake on their part. No one wants to see all the hair on those sweet cheeks of yours, Sin.

Also, should I be asking which Kardashian you follow on IG? Or do you just want to take that one to the grave?

ME:

Please tell me you did not just tell Beaumont he's got sweet cheeks.

BEAUMONT:

First of all, sir, my ass is smooth. No hair.

Second, I have the best ass out of all you assholes. Setting the record straight, right here, right now.

HARRISON:

All I hear are lies.

ME:

> I've seen better asses. Beaumont's isn't even in the top 20.

HOLLY:

> I'm willing to bet that I have the best ass in this entire group thread.

And just like that, my cock stiffens against the seam of my zipper at the mere mention of Holly's heart-shaped backside.

Well, at the mention and the accompanying visual.

Sweet-fucking-cheeks doesn't even cover it.

Swallowing roughly, I hit the keypad on my phone, prepared to text her directly *exactly* what I think about her ass—only to note that the service bars at the top of the screen have dropped to nil.

I type out the text anyway. Hit send.

My phone *pings!* with ERROR scrawled across the screen in red font.

Stepping back, to where I had service a moment ago, I try another time.

Ping!

Error.

I move to the right, a single step that has my shoulder brushing up against the wall as I hold my phone up toward the ceiling. *C'mon, c'mon, c'mon.*

Ping!

Error.

"Fuck me."

"Mr. Carter," murmurs a masculine voice, "I'm not sure if I should be more startled by your language or the fact that you're attempting to tango—poorly, I might add—right in front of my office."

My head snaps up.

"I was just—" I wave my phone a little desperately. "No service, Dr. Mebowitz."

The corners of his brown eyes crinkle with humor. "An important missive?"

Just trying to tell my ex-wife how her ass is pure perfection.

I smile weakly. "Nothing that can't wait another hour."

"Perfect." Swooping an arm before him, he gestures for me to enter his office. "Let's get to it, shall we?"

I'd rather we not, but I step past the elderly doctor anyway and do my best to fight down the nerves while I take a seat.

The office is decorated in muted colors, pastel yellow on the walls and beige laminate flooring. Bookshelves line the wall to my right, and the one to my left is completely covered in framed awards and certificates and licenses. The grand window behind Dr. Mebowitz's desk, however, makes up for everything else with its view of the Museum of Science and the Charles River.

It's a specific view I've seen only once before.

Something that the good doctor makes note of when he rounds his desk to sit in his plush leather office chair. "I'll be frank with you, Mr. Carter. I didn't expect to see you here again—not after how our first meeting transpired."

Another hard swallow, and my gaze flicks from the man's face to his blank-screened computer and then back again. "It's been a wild year."

Propping his elbow on the armrest, he rests his chin on his upturned fist. "I hear the hockey season is officially underway."

I nod, once. "It is."

"Any chance the Blades will pull through for the Cup?"

The dry way he says it puts me slightly more at ease, especially when paired with the framed photo he's set facedown next to his computer. I indicate it with a tilt of my head. "Don't tell me you've finally switched loyalties? We both know you're a Bruins fan, Doc, unless you've traded out that photo of you and Cam Neely for one of me and you?"

225

He doesn't blush or pussyfoot around the issue, only casually shrugs his bony shoulders. "Well, what can I say? I've been alive six times longer than the Blades have even existed. When you're pushing eighty, you'll be wary of any new franchises who think they are God's gift to hockey too." His smile turns sly. "I'm sure my opinions are similar to yours regarding the new Vegas franchise. Or are you harboring a deep-seated love for the Knights?"

A touch sarcastically, I salute him with two fingers at my temple. "Touché, Dr. Mebowitz, touché."

He grins, no doubt having ticked off a point in his favor.

"Now, let's see where we left off." Reaching for a pair of thin-framed glasses, he slides them onto his nose and thumbs open the manila file before him. The shuffling of the papers is loud in my ears, like phonetic paper cuts slicing through the air and drawing droplets of blood with their mere existence. "Ah, here we go. Shall I do an entire recap of all our prior testing or would you prefer I rip the bandage off and spare you the punishment of listening to me ramble?"

In my tennis shoes, my toes curl, seeking firm grounding.

"The latter," I rasp, voice hoarse.

"Very well, then. Last year, you came here on a referral basis. You were experiencing headaches and that you, and I quote, 'felt as though you were living in a fog.'" He slides his frames off and taps the tip of one plastic arm to his mouth. "May I assume that you feel roundabout the same?"

My stomach clenches with unease. I shift my weight, bringing one ankle to rest on my opposite knee. Clasping my hands over my shin, I hope that Dr. Mebowitz can't tell that I'm doing my damn best not to show the tremors in my hands.

I'm nervous.

I'm so fucking nervous.

And, if I want to really dig deep and unravel my emotions, I know that I'd find fear is what's driving the nerves, nothing else. If I can't play hockey . . . if I'm forced to retire early, who even am I?

"Mr. Carter?"

At his inquisitive tone, I part my lips and force the words of self-damnation out. "Yeah." I clear my throat, fist to my mouth. Try again. "It's been . . . it's been worse, to be honest. The headaches, I mean. The fog, too, but mostly it's the headaches. Sometimes . . . sometimes I can't deal with the light at all."

He inclines his head slightly and slips his glasses back on his face. Grabbing a pen from a metal container, he clicks it open and puts ball tip to paper, waiting for me to continue, the pen ink leaving a mark on the written report.

I slam my eyes shut, drudging up the sensations after Fitzgerald slammed me into the boards.

"The nausea's bad. Food tastes bland. Sometimes I could eat an entire restaurant; others I can't even finish what's on my plate."

"Anxiety?" Dr. Mebowitz muses to himself as he glances down at my files. "Depression. Could be both."

"I've never been diagnosed with either, but . . ." I dig my nails into my jean-clad shin, welcoming the minute sting of pain to the more thunderous roar in my head that's only just begun to settle in the last few days. "Maybe, yeah, it could be"—I cough into one closed fist—"be something like that. When it's real bad, I feel like I'm on a boat. My legs don't feel steady. My right hand . . . it, uh, it tingles some—like it's fallen asleep."

Dr. Mebowitz's mouth tightens in a frown, his scrawl across the page slowing to a stop. "And you've seen the team's physical therapist about a possible spinal injury?" When I shake my head, he sets down the pen and leans back, hands linking over his stomach. "The issue, Mr. Carter, is that CTE isn't something I can diagnose while you're . . . let us say, while you're *breathing*, yes? Confirmation of the disease only occurs by studying the brain tissue after you've died. Now, taking that into account, your scans a year ago indicated—or, at least, suggested that TBI was a matter of concern. It made sense, of course, given your age and the longevity of your career. You've been playing for how long now?"

"Since I was four, maybe five."

"And now you are . . .?"

He leans forward, his index finger trailing along my report, and I do him a solid of telling him the answer: "Thirty-four."

"Ah, yes." He gives me a brief, noncommittal smile. "Thirty-four. That's thirty years of being in that rink, day in and day out. Studies have shown that children who play heavy contact sports, and who have suffered head injuries prior to the age of twelve, will run higher risks of brain trauma later on in life."

By the time I was twelve, I'd already caught more gloves to the head, more helmets to the Plexiglas, than I would ever like to admit.

My breath leaves me on a shaky exhale. "So, what you're saying is . . ."

"We need more testing, of course. Perhaps some time for you to sit with a cognitive therapist and reevaluate your moods. Tell me, do you ever experience out-of-character, impulsive behavior? Something that you yourself don't recognize but that friends, family, have mentioned in passing that doesn't seem very . . . *you*?"

"Never." In this, my voice doesn't waver. Aside from lifting Holly onto the hood of my car and taking her there, in the middle of a parking lot where anyone might see, I've never acted rashly a day in my life. Just as controlled as I am on the ice, the same can be said about my temper off it.

"That's good news, at least." Dr. Mebowitz scribbles

something down on my file, barely casting me a glance as he does so. "Listen, Mr. Carter, brain injuries are not to be taken lightly. When you were last here, I suggested that you step back from the game and give your body the chance to breathe without the added, unrelenting physical stress of body checks or fights, or any other potential causes to all those headaches you're experiencing."

The thought of leaving hockey, even for a short-term stint, has my chest tightening with pure panic. *Who am I?* The question won't stop spiraling through my head. *Without hockey, who am I? Without hockey, Who. Am. I?*

"Can't do that, Doc." I drop my raised foot to the floor and set my elbows on the desk. "The season's just beginning. My guys need me. The *team* needs me."

"Do they?" He only closes my file and then matches my pose, his forearms using my file as a prop. "The unfortunate truth is that everyone is replaceable, Captain. It's how the game progresses, how the team grows into its next entity, whatever that might look like. Your brain, alternatively, is *not* replaceable. You break a leg, and a doctor will reset the bone. If there are any levels of Tau in your brain, a neuropathologist like myself will never even discover it until you're dead and you've given your brain to science. *That* is the outcome of Chronic Traumatic Encephalopathy."

Christ.

I work my thumbs into my eye sockets, relieving the mounting pressure behind my lids. "It might be something else."

"It might be, yes. As they say, we'll hope for the best and prepare for the worst."

"And how, exactly, do you prepare for something you can't fully diagnose without me being a corpse?"

"Various tests. None are conclusive, but in ruling out factors like post-concussion syndrome or a possible spinal injury, we can narrow our accuracy and determine if you are indeed displaying symptoms of CTE." He watches me, eyes narrowed and certain. "I could give you a list of players more famous than you, Mr. Carter, who have walked through your shoes. They survived the transition from pro-athlete to civilian just fine. Not to mention, there's a reason why when CTE was first introduced, it was known as the 'punch-drunk syndrome.' I assume you can put two and two together to determine why a disease like this one might gain a nickname like that."

"I reckon I can."

"Good. We'll get you set up for a bone scan, just to rule out any possible spinal damage that's gone undetected."

"And the game?"

Dr. Mebowitz's glasses slip down the bridge of his nose, and he stops their descent with a single finger. "My professional opinion goes unchanged. You have less to fear from full-fledged concussions than you do from smaller, more repetitive impacts to the head. When it comes to matters of the brain, I advise to quit any sport that's putting you here in my office." He pauses, then adds, "With that said, I'm fully aware that you pulled a complete disappearing act on me a year ago. Considering the timing of Fitzgerald nailing you two weeks ago and your sudden arrival for the appointment you stood me up for, I can only guess that should I lay down the law, you'll do as you please anyway."

For whatever reason, the disgruntled note in his voice makes me grin—despite all the sobering news that's come my way in the last thirty minutes. I lean back in my chair. "Don't tell me that you've been following my career now, Doc. It'll go to my head. Next thing you'll know you'll be replacing that photo of Neely with one of my face. Just think of it now."

"Your head," he drawls with absolutely no humor in his expression, "is big enough on its own. I'll have my receptionist call you tomorrow with your appointment schedule—bone scans, cognitive therapy, a SCAT3 . . . You'll be a busy man, but I assume you don't know what to do with down-time at any rate."

Taking that as a dismissal, I haul ass off the chair and head for the door.

Ping!

Ping!

Ping-ping-ping!

"Did that missive of yours go through?" Dr. Mebowitz asks at my back.

"Whoever it is can wait. I just want to . . ." I glance back, meeting the doctor's dark eyes. "I would prefer that none of this be related to the Blades yet." I don't bring up *Getting Pucked*, even though this has been my biggest fear with the show from day one. If the media finds out—if the hockey world discovers that the Beast of the Northeast might be taking a permanent hit—then my career might as well be over. And I'm not ready to hang up my skates, not yet.

"At least not until we know—well, not until we rule every possibility out," I continue roughly. "This year is our year for the Cup, and headaches aside, I've never felt better." He doesn't look like he believes me, and my spine hardens. "We're taking home the Cup, and I'm going to be on that ice with the rest of my team."

Dr. Mebowitz only huffs softly. "Athletes and their God complexes." He nods with a quick wave of his hand. "I'll be in touch with the specifics, Mr. Carter. Shut the door on your way out."

I do as he says, clicking the door shut behind me.

As I head for the elevators to bring me back to the outside world where topics like TBI and CTE and head trauma aren't discussed like who's-having-what-for-dinner, I pull my phone out of my pocket and steal a quick glance at the glass screen.

Oh, fuck.

ME:

> Sweetheart, there's nothing I love more than cupping your tight ass and pressing you up against me.

> Sweetheart, there's nothing I love more than cupping your tight ass and pressing you up against me.

> Sweetheart, there's nothing I love more than cupping your tight ass and pressing you up against me.

BEAUMONT:

Did Carter just say he wants to cup my tight ass?

CAIN:

eating popcorn GIF

HARRISON:

Please tell me he was talking about Holly.

HUNT:

He's not answering.

He's guilty. Totally was talking about Sin.

CAIN:

100% ^^^

HARRISON:

I'm screenshotting this shit right now. Blackmail, y'know?

HOLLY:

Jackson does like a smooth ass . . . No wonder he left me. Clearly, he was thinking about Andre—only then Andre married somebody else. #plottwist

BEAUMONT:

He lost his chance. I'm a one-woman kinda man. He'll never have the opportunity to get between my sweet cheeks now.

HUNT:

Guys, Carter's on TV. Channel 4. TMZ.

BEAUMONT:

Is he talking about my delicious rump?

HUNT:

1) Don't ever say that again. 2) TMZ is reporting that Carter went to Mass General for penis reconstructive surgery.

CAIN:

. . .

HARRISON:

Holy shit. For real? I'm turning it on now.

HUNT:

No, not for real. But can you imagine his face when he reads this thread?

ME:

I hate all of you.

Except you, Holly. The next time I see you, be prepared to have your world rocked.

CAIN:

Will this rocking take place post penis surgery? Asking on Holly's behalf.

In the middle of Mass General with nurses and doctors and patients roaming around me, I burst out laughing. It can't be helped.

For me, my place on the team roster isn't just because of the level of stick play. It's because of *this*—my guys, my friends. My family. *Holly*.

Dr. Mebowitz may want me to quit the game, but the game is *me*. And I don't know how likely it is that I'll be able to strip this part of my identity from my soul.

Without hockey, who am I?

I hate that I don't know.

CHAPTER 23
HOLLY

"**C**an we get that again, Holls?" Adam asks as he readjusts the mic on Duke Harrison's lapel. "All I'm picking up are hockey players shouting about—"

The plane dips, bouncing along a bump of turbulence, and Adam braces his weight by setting a hand on the Mountain's shoulder. "Woops! Sorry there." A grimace pulls at his features before he tugs away sharply. He squints at me, head turned to where I'm standing a row behind with my camera at chest-level, ready to capture the interview. "I just had a moment," he says.

I lift a brow and wait.

"Yup." Nodding vigorously, he reaches out to squeeze Harrison's arm again. "Muscular. Maybe even a little veiny. Now I know why my wife secretly has you as the screensaver on her cell phone."

Harrison's eyes go wide as he splutters with laughter. "I'm sorry . . . *what*?"

"It's true." Adam goes about fixing Harrison's mic, then steps back to pick up his gear. "There she was giving birth to our firstborn child and her phone starts ringing. I pick it up, obviously, because whoever's calling clearly wants to know the status of the delivery. I get off the phone and then *bam*! There you are in all of your shirtless glory. And ass—it was a side shot."

My gaze cuts from my sound mixer to the Blades' goalie. At times like these, I generally pride myself on always having something worthwhile to say. But, holy cow, I've got *nothing*.

Interview. Think of the interview!

"So," I drawl out, unease coating my tone like thick honey, "about those Blades . . ."

But Adam isn't done yet. He flicks his gaze over Carmen, who's standing to his left, wide-eyed, video camera hoisted on her shoulder as she props one knee on the cushion of a seat. She looks to me and, to be quite honest, all I do is stare right back.

Is this the moment where I'll have to fire one of my favorite employees because he went crazy on a plane with America's most beloved goalie?

The plane dips again, almost as though it's preparing me for the worst that's yet to come, and I widen my stance and straighten my hips. I readjust my grip on my camera, fully prepared to turn it into a weapon if I have to bop Adam on the head to shut him up and not make us lose the Blades as a client.

Duke Harrison is nice, but there's only so much the man will take before he snaps.

"*Anyway*," Adam says, "I'm only bringing it up because she photoshopped my face over yours. Not that she could figure out how to get rid of your tattoos, so it was a bit of a dead giveaway since I don't have any myself." Offering a shrug, he grins big and pats his belly with his free hand. "It was hilarious, though. I don't think I've looked like you a single day in my life." Another squeeze of Harrison's shoulder. "Yeah, I don't have *that* so it's wicked nice to pretend I do whenever I look at her phone now. So, thank you. It's great for the ego to look like a hockey god in your wife's eyes."

I swallow down the laugh, and then I'm not even holding it in anymore.

I collapse in the closest seat and bring my camera up so I can grab a picture of Adam's smug smile and Harrison's shocked—maybe even creeped-out—expression with Carmen behind them looking, as usual, cool as a cucumber.

Click.

Click.

I choke out Adam's name between guffaws of laughter. "Oh, my God, Adam, *please* tell me that story wasn't in response to my question about the craziest things fans have done in Harrison's honor."

He holds up a hand, palm toward me. Solemnly, he murmurs, "Guilty as hell."

I'm still laughing at his ridiculous (and hilarious) antics as we clamber our way to the back of the team jet twenty minutes later, looking for our next victim—I mean, participant. Most of the team has gathered together to play poker. We'd caught Duke up front while he reviewed tapes of the goalie from the Washington Capitals, who we're playing tomorrow evening.

The only game separating me from a weekend away with Jackson.

I bite my lip at the thought, my gaze immediately seeking him out among the rows of Blades players. Logic tells me that it should take me a moment to find him. After all, there's got to be at least twenty players all seated around and shouting at Josh Kammer, the rookie, who apparently pulled a bullshit move.

And yet, it's like I've got a homing beacon on Jackson after all these years.

It takes me a single breath to locate him seated alone in the back row.

Another full second in which I do nothing but appreciate him and all of his rugged masculinity.

With his forearms propped up on the seat back in front of him, it's easy to see that he's holding a full hand of cards, just like everyone else. And, like the others, he's wearing a fancy suit for our late-night flight to the country's capital. The suit might be Armani or Tom Ford or any of the designers that have percolated in his closest for years, always worn over and over again. At the end of the day, million-dollar contracts and fame have not altered Jackson at the most intrinsic level: he's still the same Texan who'll prefer jeans and a T-shirt over dolling up in whatever designer suit he's been instructed to wear that day.

But *this* suit that he's wearing is one I've never seen before. It hugs the breadth of his shoulders, the navy-blue fabric a perfect contrast to the olive undertone of his skin. Underneath the jacket, sans tie, he's donned a crisp, white dress shirt and done the entire female population a service by leaving the top two buttons undone.

He looks casual, relaxed. Like a man who can have anything he wants if only he were to snap his fingers and request it.

As though sensing my stare, he glances up and catches me studying him.

His dark gaze warms. My heart skips a beat.

"Hey," he mouths.

Cue: the sensation of a rocket bursting in my belly, pink confetti going every which way.

I smile. Mouth back, "Hey."

Thanks to his schedule, and my own, it's the first time we're seeing each other since our night together at the diner and, earlier, on his car. Thankfully, Carmen makes it easy for all of us by exclaiming, "We need stories for a clip that *Getting Pucked* is using during commercial breaks."

Kammer's head pops up from two rows ahead of me. "What kind of stories?"

"Horror stories," Adam says with dramatic flair. "In particular, what's the craziest thing a fan has done? My wife juxtaposed my face on Harrison's body—well, on his face but you know what I mean—and I found out while she was giving birth."

"The Mountain? Tell her she got lucky with you."

"Shit, man! You ever want to work out with us, we'll have you looking like a Duke Harrison clone in no time!"

I hold up my hands, camera still clutched in my right. "Jokes aside, we need a few volunteers. We haven't decided if we'd rather shoot one interview per commercial break—we're looking at four or five of you then—or if we'd rather make an exposé with all of you and stitch them together."

Cain leans an elbow on the back of one seat. "My vote's for all of us. It'll be funnier that way."

I glance at the cards clasped in their hands and then over to my team. "We'll do it by suit. Everyone will get . . ." I count the number of rows that the players are filling up, then quickly do the math in my head. "Three cards a pop. It'll work toward three commercial breaks, and that way Fillmore won't have my head when I tell him we made sure to get every player."

"Aw, does he have a favorite?" asks Sylas Trent, a D-man on the second line. He flutters his long lashes and twirls a hand in the air. "No, don't answer that. I know it's me."

His right-wing partner, Quinton Dennis, slaps him on the back of the head. "Bro, you weren't even your momma's favorite."

The guys roar with laughter at what is clearly some sort of inside joke that I'm not privy to, while Trent's cheeks flush a brilliant shade of red.

After asking Cain to count out the cards and pass them all out, I confer briefly with Carmen and Adam about what it is we'll need before angling my body to pick my way to the back of the plane.

Thank you, turbulence, for easing up so I don't lose my breakfast.

I move quickly, careful not to elbow any of the guys in the back of the head, until I'm standing in the aisle at the very last row and breathing the same air as Jackson.

Up close, his suit is even more spectacular.

Or maybe it's just that *he* looks even more spectacular now that I'm inches away.

His rugged face tips up to stare at me, even as he tugs his new hand of cards close to his chest. "No cheatin', Holls," he murmurs in that husky Texas drawl of his, "I see what you're up to."

When he flashes me a grin, I can't help but shift my weight and steady myself on the seat opposite his, which is blessedly empty. "Your cards are safe with me." My tone, despite an attempt for dry and witty, comes out breathy instead.

Any lingering hope that he won't notice that I sound like I've inhaled helium goes out the window when he lowers his lids, giving my basic yoga pants and even blander white top a slow onceover. In that classic Jackson way of his, he draws his thumb over his bottom lip and simultaneously makes my knees clack together.

"But am *I* safe with you?"

It's not an innocent question. Does he mean his heart? His happiness?

I'm not given time to answer.

"Holly!" Carmen calls out, about seven rows separating us. "You want to get us started?"

Right. Yes.

I nod, then swallow down that airy, breathy voice that's a total giveaway as to how much I want Jackson right here, right now. "Everyone with diamonds, you're up first. We'll go around a few times to make sure no one's left out, so if you're still thinking on your answer feel free to sit this round out."

The guys jostle each other as they all decide who's up first.

Ultimately, it's Sylas, Cain, and the rookie, Kammer, who rise from their seats and sort of slouch in place to avoid hitting their heads on the overhead bins.

I try to hold back a snort and end up hacking out a cough. "Y'all, this isn't the classroom. You don't have to stand when spoken to." I wave a free hand toward my team. "Carmen and Adam will take care of making sure you're within the frame. Take a seat, gentlemen."

They all sit as one, and then the fun begins.

CHAPTER 24
JACKSON

"I once had this fan who tattooed my face on her tits. We're talking full on hairy 'stache inked over a left nipple—hold on, can I say nipple on TV?"

Laughter rumbles in my throat as Tommy Kase, Harrison's backup, looks to Holly for guidance, his brows drawn together in consternation.

For her part, Holly only throws her head back with a feminine laugh that goes straight to my dick. Her hair is up in its customary messy bun, and while the rest of us goons are rocking suits for the short flight to D.C., as is team protocol, Holls is dressed for pure comfort.

White, billowy T-shirt.

Black leggings that cut off right below the knee.

A pair of sensible tennis shoes that are such a neon pink they're almost blinding.

I want to pull her into the tiny-as-hell bathroom two feet behind me and strip her bare.

Then again, I can barely fit my own frame into the restroom—add Holly into the mix and I'd be unlikely to even lock the door behind us.

I eye the sweet curve of her ass again, which is inches away from my face, and swallow a groan.

Yeah, joining the Mile-High Club is not much of an option when you're topping six-four, weigh in at close to two-fifty, and are nicknamed the Beast of the Northeast.

Damn airlines and their inclusive propaganda—I call bullshit.

"On *that* note," Holly says now, her fingers fluttering over the buttons on her camera as she catches a picture of what I'm assuming is Kase's embarrassed expression, "we're moving on. Hearts are up for our final round. Any takers?"

I glance down at my hand.

Three of Hearts.

Seven of Hearts.

Nine of Hearts.

Clearly, the card gods are trying to tell me something.

Up ahead, Henri Bordeaux, Beaumont, and left-wing Chandler Eden raise their respective cards in the air.

Holly lifts her camera again. "Bordeaux, want to go first?"

"*Oui.*" Nodding, he smiles at Carmen and waves to the camera like he's the goddamn Queen of England. He ruffles his dark hair, then tugs sharply on the lapel of his black suit. "I was once fucked by a puck."

Pure.

Unforgiving.

Silence.

Blinking slowly, I lean my weight forward and lift one finger in the air. My mouth opens. Closes. Parts halfway. I mean, really, I've got no words here. "Henri, man, I—" My fingers curl in a fist that I bounce on my knee, once, twice. "I'm sorry, did you say that you were *fucked* by a puck?"

"And here I thought I couldn't bring up nipples on TV," Kase snickers loudly. "Keep going, Bordeaux. You're making me look like a boy scout and I'm over here living my best life."

I hold up a hand, silencing the rumble of laughter. "No, but, really. Henri, dude, that can't be—"

"To the *face*!" Bordeaux thrusts a finger at his chin. "A puck to the face, *épais. Osti de tabarnak de câlice*."

I might not know French, Canadian or otherwise, but playing with French Canadians for as long as I have? Yeah, I'm fully aware of what words like "*tabarnak*" mean. And they aren't all rainbows and unicorns. God knows what the rest of it all translates to.

We'll chalk this experience up to Lost in Translation, Hockey Edition, and call it a day.

"Holls?"

"Yeah, Captain?" She swings her blue eyes my way, humor making them appear that much brighter.

"Let's move on from the puck fucks, yeah?"

She ducks her face, but I don't miss the shit-eating grin that's about as subtle as Bordeaux's English faux pas.

"Sure, yeah, we'll move on."

Beaumont goes next, spouting off about some guy who once broke into his house during his rookie year with the Detroit Red Wings. "You think you've seen it all, honestly, until you come home one day to find a dude in a metal bathtub, fish heads all around him, holding up a sign that says, 'You don't deserve the 'pus.' And by pus, he was referring to octopuses . . . octopi?" Beaumont shakes his head, big shoulders lifting. "Whatever. Either way, he was pissed that we lost and he was naked, and *that* is a sight I'll never be able to unsee. Now all of you have to suffer with me—you're welcome."

Collective groaning ensues, just as Holly asks, "Anyone else wondering how all those fish scales feel against a man's . . . sensitive bits?"

"Oh, *c'mon*, Mrs. Carter!"

"My balls are itchy just thinking about it."

"Honestly, could be like a massage. I bet it's a luxury in

some parts of the world. Give a man a fish, and he'll find some way to masturbate with it."

The last one comes from Russell Allen, a right wing on our second line, and we all erupt in boos—and, if I'm not hearing shit, at least one fake-vomiting sprint.

"Gentlemen!" says Matt the Hard-Ass over the speaker system. "And two women—sorry, Carmen, Holly. *Any*way, we'll be starting our descent in approximately three minutes. One last answer for that commercial of yours, Ms. Carter. Perhaps the good Captain might do us the honor of responding to the question?"

As though *that* was subtle, by any means.

Matt, as his nickname suggests, is anything but subtle. Since my divorce from Holly, he's been a routine figure on the sidelines, questioning what I did wrong that made a "good woman like her" leave me.

He's not wrong in his assumption.

Good news, I'm on a mission to rectify the leaving bit.

Thwapping the cards along the center of my thigh, I drawl, "Just one story? Y'all are making this difficult for me to choose."

Carmen and Adam inch down the aisle toward me, no doubt trying to keep me in frame and within earshot, considering that I sat myself in the very last row of the plane. Holly sits down opposite me, her petite body twisting so that she can keep me in her visual line.

Caving to the need to touch her, I stretch out my right leg —and softly touch her pink sneaker with my brown leather loafer. When she doesn't pull back immediately, I stifle a satisfied grin.

"I'm gonna break protocol here—go for a story from my Cornell days, way before I was drafted to the NHL."

Across the aisle, I catch Holly's narrowing gaze, and I flash her a slow, shit-eating grin.

I loop one arm around the seat back in front of me, fingers

tapping the side of the cushion. "I had this shitty car back then. A Chevy Silverado with the paint damn-near chipped off completely. We'd lost a game that day, not that I hadn't done my best." I pause, then jut my chin toward my teammates. "Hunt's not the only one around here who knows how to score a hat trick. I've been dangling pucks since he still had acne."

Amid my guys' catcalls of "*ooh, feel the burn!*" and raucous laughter, I finger-salute our center, where he's sitting three rows up. "Love ya, Marshey!"

He flashes me the middle finger.

I make a point of catching it like he's blown me a kiss instead, then mime putting it in a slingshot and sending it into the crowd.

"Anyway," I go on, "I'm beat, right? I've had my marbles rattled—especially since I subbed for a guy on the D-line during the third period—and I skipped out on all the parties to head back to the house and hit the sack. Only—"

"Jackson." I feel Holly's fingers prod me in the side. She's moved in close, eclipsing any space between us, and I'd put good money on the fact that she's *this* close from clapping a hand over my mouth to keep me from talking. She pokes me again, her body shielding the movement from view.

I one-up her, leveraging my size so that she's standing in front of me. My palm skims the indent of the back of her knee, and I don't miss the way she twitches at the contact.

And then sinks back into my touch.

God, I love how responsive she is.

"Only," I repeat, my hand now on her quads, "there was this girl standing near my shitty-ass car, and she was standing there with a paintbrush. White paint, too, against the chipped blue of my car. 'You S-U-C' was written on my windshield in bold, block letters. I busted her before she managed to work the *K* on there too." I squeeze the back of Holly's thigh, and she releases the softest moan I've ever heard in my life.

So sexy, the sound is barely leashed as she looks back at me.

Her expression is set like she'd enjoy nothing more than to bash her camera over my head.

Her blue eyes, on the other hand, are pure liquid fire, molten and hot and eyeing me up like she's considering the miniscule bathroom behind us.

I tear my gaze from hers. "Turns out, Holly here thought my car belonged to the team's goalie, who gave up four shots on the net. She's always been passionate about hockey, and *that's* officially the craziest thing a fan has ever done."

"I wasn't a fan," she quips, her ass now in my palm and her fingers digging into the seat in front of mine.

"Nah, you weren't." I feather my touch down the back seam of her yoga pants. "*Yet.*"

Shaking her head, she chokes out a raspy laugh. "You're trouble."

"Always have been," I husk. "Now take a seat before Matt has something to say about you holding up the plane from landing." Folding up the aisle-side arm rest, I stretch my long legs out so that Holly can scoot past me. "I promise I won't bite."

A snort greets my ears as she bats my legs out of the way, calls out a quick, "Carmen, Adam, take a seat!" before settling into the window seat beside me. I don't even have the opportunity to appreciate her close proximity before she's whipping toward me, index finger stiff and at the ready to do some serious damage to my bicep.

"*You,*" she growls, and it's such a cute attempt at being all aggressive and feisty that I grab her hand in mine and press a kiss to her palm. Then murmur, "On a scale of one to ten, how much do you want to throw me out of the plane right now?"

Her nose scrunches in deliberation. "Twelve." She tugs on her captured hand to no avail. "I'm at a twelve, which is the equivalent of someone's mood after being force-fed anything you've cooked for at least three days in a row."

Amusement spreads like wildfire through my veins. I love it when she's all about the quick comebacks. Gently, I wrap my hand around the back of her neck and touch our foreheads together. "Low blow," I mutter, "but well-deserved. Payback officially has been served."

Her blue eyes dart from my gaze down to my lips and then back again.

Christ.

My grasp tightens ever so slightly, and my slacks feel incrementally tighter in the crotch than they did two minutes earlier. I open my mouth, voice rumbling out, "No crime in these guys knowing how we met. They're family and you're . . ."

She tilts her head to the side, as though silently daring me to finish that thought. "I'm what?"

Beautiful. Funny.

Mine.

"You're the kickass queen of Carter Photography, wielder of cameras and the sole heiress to—"

Her small fist collides with my bicep.

It barely registers.

"What?" I fold up the armrest between us, eliminating the remaining barrier. "I thought you'd appreciate that more than what I was going to say, considering that you're still in your *thinking about us* phase. Plus, I know how much you secretly love your fantasy books."

The pressure in the plane increases as we make our final descent into Washington. I've tried to avoid thinking about what Dr. Mebowitz said earlier this week in the lead up to tomorrow's game. Today, I feel like Beast of the Northeast—the relentless pounding in my head has eased, and my muscles feel limber and ready to put the Capitals into an early, hockey-induced grave.

And then there's Holly, leaning back against the drawn-shut oval window, one knee raised so that it rests lazily against my left thigh. She watches me like I'm the man she's always known: the hockey player who can make magic happen out of nothing; a team captain who's at the height of his game and shows no sign of slowing down; a guy who, once upon a time, she loved more than anyone else.

She watches me like I'm capable of anything, and sees nothing of the fears, the pain, the increasing worry that fate might have other plans for me aside from taking the Cup and memorializing my name one more time in hockey history.

The heat and familiarity in her blue eyes gives me a more addicting high than any win on the ice ever has.

The seat belt signs *ping!* and Matt's voice echoes through the cabin. "Looks like we're about to land, ladies and gents. I hope you're ready to take on the Capitals—between us, I can't wait to see their smug faces go slack the minute you guys step on the ice."

I clap and shout, along with the rest of my teammates, only to feel Holly's fingers dig into my thigh. At the slight pinch of her nails, my hands land on the seat back and I raise a brow in question.

She licks her lips. "What were you going to say? A minute ago, before Matt . . . you were going to say something."

My gaze flicks between hers. In the last week, I've tried to give her time to think, more for her sake than mine—because that's what she wanted. I know that we can't jump into things and expect them to go back to the way they were before we went our separate ways—nor would I want them to.

A year ago, I divorced a woman who I loved but who felt like a stranger all the same.

No, I wouldn't want a repeat of what used to be. But I sure as hell want the chance to reconnect and build something new. Something better.

Giving her the time to say no if she's opposed to it, I

slowly fold my hand over her knee, my thumb flirting along the hem of her yoga pants. Her skin is hot to the touch, despite the chill from the overhead vents.

"I was going to say that they're family"—I slip my thumb under the fabric of her pants, drawing small circles over the smooth skin—"and you're Holly. Beautiful, live-life-to-the-fullest, Holly." I squeeze her leg and meet her gaze. "The rest of what I wanted to say can wait for our weekend away . . . if you'll want to hear it."

She visibly swallows, and I catch the sight of her bright pink shoe flexing like she's enjoying my touch more than she'll ever admit.

Then she's leaning forward, her fingers curling under my chin—her quiet, gentle way of making me look at her. Her blue eyes are large in her face when she sets my heart on fire with six little words.

"Don't leave out a single word."

CHAPTER 25
HOLLY

There's no other way to put it: the fans are *pissed*.

In a sea of red, Carmen, Adam, and I are a solitary navy-blue blip on the Jumbotron whenever the camera swerves past us. The legendary Kiss Cam is being met with blank stares; poster boards with enthusiastic, pun-tastic catchphrases are inching farther and farther down with each blow-out period that trickles past; and if all that wasn't enough to prove that the D.C. fans are sore losers tonight, then the jerk duo seated behind us are doing a good enough job proving it for the rest of the arena.

"Fucking Carter!" shouts one of the jerks as Jackson dekes a Caps player.

My breath lodges in my throat as Jackson slips the puck between his legs, out of position to be stolen away, and then cuts its trajectory toward the boards short with the blade of his stick. My camera hangs loosely around my neck, forgotten, my fists jutting up into the air as I stand on my tiptoes to see around the guy in front of me.

"Go, baby, go!" The words are out before I can put a lid on them.

I've never been so thankful that hockey fans are a rowdy

bunch because no one hears me—and, if they do, no one gives me a second look, mistaking me for just another rabid Blades groupie.

Cutting short on his skates, Jackson swivels his massive weight like he's nothing heavier than a feather.

I look from the ice rows below me to the Jumbotron, where the camera is locked on my ex-husband's face. He's sweating profusely. His dark eyes are sharp as he tracks the ice, looking for his chance, and I know the minute he's found what he's searching for.

His lips curve in that same wicked grin he always wears seconds before he strips off my panties and hunkers down between my thighs.

The irony isn't lost on me—giving me pleasure has always existed in the same playing field as the joy he reaps from outsmarting the enemy on the ice.

The puck shoots like a dart from Jackson to Marshall Hunt, who's waiting in the slot.

"Shit!" one guy hollers at my back. "C'mon, miss, you motherfucker! Miss the shot!"

Hunt doesn't miss.

He aims.

He shoots.

He scores.

The lamp lights, and I can just imagine the long-time Sports 24/7 announcer, Justin Daily, chuckling into the microphone as the TV cameras cut his way. "And wouldya look at that? The Blades are on fire tonight."

Fire doesn't even begin to cover it.

By the time the buzzer echoes in Capital One Arena, signaling the end of the game, the Blades take the W with a final score of 4-1.

Adam cups his hand around his mouth to be overheard over the din, "What's the game plan, Holls?"

Inching my backpack toward my front, like a kangaroo

pouch, I slide the camera strap from around my neck. My hair falls forward as I unzip the bag and tuck my camera safely inside.

For the first time in years, I didn't take a single picture while being technically on the clock. At every game in the last month, I've used the time in the stands to snap photos of fans cheering on their favorite players or children perched on their parents' shoulders as they watch their heroes fight for the win.

Some of those photos have gone on a dedicated Fans Only page on the Blades website—the team's way of showing how much all the support means. Others went on the Instagram page for Carter Photography, racking up thousands of likes while local fans tried to find themselves in the posted photos.

If they did, I sent them the picture free of charge—and included a card for a discounted photo session should they ever be interested.

Hey, business is business.

"Holly?" Carmen's fingers circle my wrist and give a sharp pull. "Earth to Holly."

I sling my backpack over my shoulder. "We're taking the night off."

Carmen and Adam exchange a glance.

"We are?" they ask in unison, each looking respectively bewildered.

"Yup!" When was the last time the three of us relaxed? When we're not with the Blades and trailing them all over the eastern seaboard like a pack of desperate puppies, we've been at the office holding down the fort. Hell, even Adam's wife has visited him at the office with his newborn after a long night of editing sound clips—*twice*. They need some time to let loose, and I . . . I glance back up at the Jumbotron, where they're replaying the clip of Jackson's amazing fake out.

Truth is, I need this too.

"Y'all are free to go," I tell them with a genuine pep to my tone. "We're in D.C.—or, I mean, we're *right* next to D.C. Adam, haven't you said that you've always wanted to see the Georgetown area?"

He stares at me, brows pulled together. "Well, yeah."

"Now's the chance! Or I'm sure the guys will all go to a local pub, if that's more your flavor."

"I'm going to sleep."

Adam and I both look to Carmen.

Sheepishly, she shrugs. "I love working for you, Holls, but you've got endless energy and I feel old."

That makes me laugh. "You do realize I'm older than you are, right?"

"Semantics." She waves me off with an exaggerated yawn. "Either way, if you're giving us the night off, that means my three-day weekend just turned into a *four*-day weekend, and you'd be crazy if you think I won't take full advantage of a hotel stay where I don't even have to wash the sheets or towels after I use them."

Adam nudges me in the arm. "I'm going for a beer with the team. Maybe the Mountain can give me fitness tips."

I think of Adam's wife photoshopping his face onto Duke Harrison's body, and barely leash in my laughter. "I think . . ." I clap Adam on the shoulder, squeezing briefly. "I'm sure Harrison will have a specific fitness regimen for you to follow. How do you feel about hard-boiled eggs?"

"Hate 'em."

I hoist my backpack higher on my shoulder, evenly distributing its heavy weight. "Sit-ups?"

Adam shakes his head. "It's the devil's work."

"Eh, well, maybe if you go to bed wishing you were Harrison every night, one day you'll wake up and find out dreams really do come true."

My sound guy grins, his slightly crooked teeth making an appearance. "Now *that's* the kind of workout I'm talking about."

Funny, because after watching Jackson play with his heart on his sleeve tonight, I'm thinking of a different workout entirely. I pull out my phone, thumb my way to his contact number, and send a single text.

ME:

> Interested in meeting at the hotel bar for cocktails? It's on me.

We're nearing the team bus when I finally feel my phone vibrate with what I'm hoping is a reply from Jackson. Slipping the smooth case out from my pocket, I glance down at the glass screen and feel the happy *thud-thud, thud-thud* of my heart go into overdrive.

JACKSON:

> You know I never did do well with rejecting propositions like that.

> First round's on you. But the rest of the night . . . that's all on me, sweetheart. All. On. Me.

My gaze shoots from my phone to the rows of seats behind the driver as I step onto the bus.

Most of the guys are already seated—and Jackson is front and center, long legs spilling into the aisle, so that I'm forced to step over him or trip and fall flat on my face. Next to him, in the window seat, is Coach Hall.

Their heads are tilted towards one another, like they're in deep discussion, probably regarding the game, and I duck my head to skirt past them for the empty row three behind theirs.

Familiar, blunt-tipped fingers tangle with mine as I step past.

The touch is so brief, so lighting fast, that my head whips to the right to stare at Jackson.

He's still facing forward, big shoulders hunched as he discusses who-knows-what with Hall. My gaze skims down his broad, muscular form, over his shoulders and the heavy, corded muscles of his arms, to his right hand which is held straight down at his side.

It's balled in a fist, his thumb rubbing slowly against his other fingers.

And I grin.

I grin so hard as I fall into an empty seat and plop my backpack down in my lap.

To the world, Jackson Carter is an enigma. A stone-faced enigma who sees what he wants and conquers it all in the same breath. He's ice and confidence, cool reserve, and domineering in the face of adversity.

But long before we fell apart, he was something else to me entirely: a man who sought affection and gave it in return with no barriers held, a man who held my hand without worry as to who might question his masculinity or "toughness," and a man who, when we went our separate ways for the day, would touch me and then ball his hand in a fist as he did just now. Only to make a joke about needing to keep me with him.

We had our own language, then.

My grin widens as I rest my head on the seat cushion, then bring my hand to my mouth, curled in a fist. I kiss my first knuckle, as I always used to do.

On our drive back to the hotel, for the first time in months, I allow myself to dream.

CHAPTER 26
JACKSON

"**W**hat can I get you to drink, my man?"

Giving a quick, cursory glance over my shoulder, I turn back around and make a move to grab my wallet before popping my credit card on the bar. "Just some soda—Coke, Pepsi. Whatever y'all got on hand. You can open a tab for me."

If the bartender thinks it's a little odd that I'm seated at the hotel bar and ordering a soda, he doesn't say a word. After picking up my black Amex, he turns on his heel and takes another order from a guy a few barstools down who looks like the love child of Will Ferrell and Mark Wahlberg.

If Will and Marky Mark were to ever beat the odds and procreate together, that is.

As though sensing my stare, he swivels on his stool and meets my gaze. "You lookin' at something?"

I go for broke. "You ever get told you look like—"

"Chris Hemsworth?" He shakes his curly brown hair, giving it some added fluff in the back. "Only *every day*."

My mouth opens, and I'm seconds away from asking in what universe does he think he would ever look like Chris-Thor-Hemsworth when a blur of blue sinks down onto the stool next to mine, effectively blocking my view of Mr. I'm-Almost-Famous.

"Did I miss anything?" Holly asks, her elbows landing on the bar as she settles herself on the stool.

I blink.

Then blink again.

No, I'm seeing things right. She's *definitely* changed out of the clothes she wore to the game tonight. Gone are the light denim jeans and black top. She's in blue now, the same hue as her beautiful eyes. A dress, not jeans. It hugs her slim frame, cupping her small breasts and gliding over the curve of her hips and ass.

When she places her high heels on the stool's metal rung, the dress's hem drags up her thighs.

My mouth turns as dry as the Sahara.

The bartender chooses that moment to return with my drink, just in time to hear the groan that steals into my throat and escapes on a heavy exhale. He quirks a single eyebrow, then slides his gaze over to Holly. "What's your poison, beautiful?"

Almost immediately, she wraps an arm across her chest, her nails biting into the shoulder closest to me. "Um . . . hot tea, if you have it?"

The bartender glances between us, shakes his head, and heads down the length of the bar again.

Her slender fingers touch my bare forearm. "What are you having?"

"Vodka."

At my deadpan tone, her gaze snaps up to meet mine. "Liar." A smile widens her mouth, and she wraps a hand around my cup to peer dramatically inside it. Soft, feminine laughter greets my ears like a lover's caress. "Coke, huh? What's happening to us?"

I pluck my soda out of her hand and take a long pull. "Old age, Holls. We hit thirty and it went downhill straight from there."

"Pretty sure they call it the 'dirty thirties' for a reason."

Setting the glass back down, I take her all in. The loose, blond hair blown out in soft waves. The smoky eye that's smudged to perfection. The damn-near-killed-me blue dress that keeps hiking up the length of her thighs to the promised land.

"If that's what they're callin' it," I drawl, "then you're doing it right." With a little gesture at her getup, I add, "I'm only sorry I didn't get the memo that this was a no-basket-ball-shorts kinda night."

She squirms on her stool. "No, you look good. I mean . . ." All her squirming is doing nothing to halt the slow climb of her dress, and she must know because her fingers yank relentlessly at the fabric. It doesn't help. If anything, each sharp pull only manages to have the opposite effect. *Not that I'm complaining.* "I don't ever dress up anymore, honestly," she tacks on and then snaps the hem back into place with a soft, barely audible curse.

"And you just happened to have this dress on hand?" Propping one forearm on the bar, I lower my voice and lean in close to her. "No complaints over here. You look . . . stunning."

More squirming. The corners of her lips turn up in thanks when the bartender drops off her tea and heads back down to Mr. I-Look-Like-Thor. Finally, she murmurs, "I put it in my suitcase at the start of preseason. I had no idea where we'd be asked to go." She offers a delicate shrug. "Figured it was better safe than sorry. Thank God for hotel rooms having irons nowadays."

I'm not sorry at all.

I swallow down a mouthful of soda, trying to get my brain back in working gear. But it's almost impossible to scrub her in that dress from my retina. In a raspy voice, I grind out, "No bra?"

She visibly swallows, and I almost die right then and there. It doesn't take a lot of imagination to see the hard peaks of her nipples through the fabric of the dress.

Resolutely, I keep my eyes on her face. "You're not denying it."

With her cheeks awash with color, she spoons some sugar into her tea. "Seems I forgot one of those when I was packing yesterday." Her blues flick to mine. "Oops."

She.

Is.

Killing.

Me.

I hook a finger over the collar of my T-shirt, needing cool air on my hot skin. *Or cubes of ice down the front of my shorts.* I'm not wearing briefs, so that'd be self-torture at its finest. Then again, there's something about feeling this on edge, without us having even stripped off our clothes, that's a turn-on in and of itself.

Shock slicks through my system when Holly nabs a napkin from the bar, sets one hand on my upper thigh, her fingers dancing mighty damn close to my erection, and drops the black linen over my lap.

Then, porcelain mug to her mouth, she blows away the curling steam and takes a long, purposeful sip. "Rookie move there, Captain." She juts her chin toward my crotch. "Never wear white to a bar."

I feel my brows shoot up in question, even as my fingers are already wrapping around the edge of the linen—

"I wouldn't."

My hand locks in place. "No?"

Another slow sip of her tea—and maybe I'm losing my mind, but she *really* shouldn't look as hot as she does while doing so—before she shrugs all blasé and murmurs, "Maybe that particular wet spot is spilled soda . . . or maybe you're just that turned on? Either way, this is for your own good."

Her blue eyes drop to my crotch, then linger long enough that my cock takes it as a sign to swell some more.

Christ.

I hunch my shoulders, dropping one elbow to my right knee to shield the tented napkin in my lap from plain view. Nobody, especially one of my teammates, needs to know how hard I am right now. When I've regained enough of my I'm-in-public-and-trying-to-behave composure, I look back up and catch Holly trying to wipe the huge grin off her face.

I rake my fingers through my hair, pulling on the strands. Heave a big, dramatic sigh as I ask, "Pleased with yourself, Mrs. Carter?"

The *Mrs.* slips out on habit alone, but Holly merely sends a wink in my direction. "Aw, does the big, bad captain not like having the tables turned?" She skips a finger from the bend of my knee up, up, up, until she's reached the linen. "It didn't seem fair that I be the only one with hard . . . peaks, if you know what I mean."

When she drops her chin to stare briefly at her nipples, my cock jumps right back to attention again because he's nothing if not a mutineer.

"Holly." Her name rolls off my tongue, thick, with heavy emphasis on the first syllable. I say it again because I like the way *her* tongue comes out to flick across her bottom lip when I speak. My hand goes to her naked shoulder, my thumb caressing the jut of her collarbone. Just like that, I have her in the palm of my hands, her blue eyes dark with arousal, knees bouncing up and down with pent-up energy.

"Tell me, Holls . . . did you wear this dress because you wanted me to spend the next hour admiring you in it?" I finger the thin strap that encircles her neck and dips down to her back, not missing the sharp lift of her shoulders as I play. "Or did you wear it because you wanted me to strip you naked?"

"Neither."

Just like that, my limbs lock in place. I want what she wants, and I would never, ever push her past that. This woman . . . fuck, she means so much to me—more than she'll probably ever realize—and I could never, in good conscious, take what she's not offering.

Even if it feels as though she's just made a slapshot to my groin.

Slowly, as not to spook her, I pull away.

Keep it together, man. Don't let her see how much you want this.

Her small fingers wrapping around my wrist keep me in place, and her breathy voice damn-near makes me lose my mind.

"I said neither, Jackson, because I don't want to sit here and objectively be admired." She tugs my hand until it's gripping her hip, my fingers splayed along the upper curve of her ass. I suck in a deep breath.

She smiles, then, and it's pure seduction.

It slays me with its flirtatiousness.

Sabotages every hope that I've got still kicking around to do the gentlemanly thing and leave her be—to not drudge up all our old wounds and heartaches and all the damn love, simply so I can feel her against me again.

When she speaks, it's nothing but a purr that sets my skin aflame. "I didn't wear it because I wanted to see it slung across the room either." The smallest pause. "I wore it because I want it yanked around my hips while you make me come all over your dick. After all, you promised that every other round would be on *you*."

Glass shatters.

My jaw drops.

"Ho*ly* shit."

The last bit didn't come from me—neither did the glass breaking—although I'm sure as hell two seconds away from doing both.

I swing my gaze toward the bartender, who's standing there with a slack jaw, wide eyes, and a tent in his jeans that's got nothing to do with me and everything to do with Holly.

Not happening.

"We'll take the check."

"Please," Holly supplies for me, a quick smile in my direction. She glances back over at the bartender, who's yet to move an inch. "But thank you for that tea. Whatever it was" —she fans her face, whistling low—"has me *so* worked up right now."

It takes another round of prodding on my part for the bartender to come back with the check. As soon as he does, I slip a hand around Holly's elbow and pull her close enough that I can touch my nose to her ear and mutter, "You're trouble."

She presses a kiss to my cheek. "There's nothing I like more than seeing you come undone."

Then she's in luck.

Because tonight, I plan to return the favor until the only thing she's begging for me to do is make her come again.

CHAPTER 27
JACKSON

Everything is hard.

My cock, my body, the rough way that I crush my mouth over Holly's. I've got her hands tangled with mine, lifted to the wall above her head. The hotel hallway is empty, save for us, and even if it weren't, I don't think I'd find the strength to stop and step away.

The night that we were together outside of the practice arena, there'd been a measure of hesitance in my touch. Would she tell me to stop? Would she turn away and leave me standing there, my dick out of my pants and my heart bleeding on the concrete?

There's none of that hesitance tonight.

I kiss her like I own her.

She mewls into my mouth like I've always been hers and hers alone.

I lean into her body, my hands palming hers flat on the wall as I nip at her mouth and growl, "Legs around my hips. Now."

A shiver wracks her shoulders as she throws her head back. "Give a girl a boost."

Never let it be said that I don't know how to take an order.

I give her the boost.

My hands under her ass. Her hands locked on my shoulders as her feet come off the floor. I hoist her up until her muscled thighs are clamped around my hips and I've got her back pressed to the tiled wall. She moans when my hard-on brushes the apex of her thighs, one hand clinging to the nape of my neck.

Nose brushing the underside of her chin, I mutter, "Hands on the wall, sweetheart."

"Tell me why."

A husky laugh rips from my throat. "What do you mean, why?"

She lowers her weight ever so slightly, taunting me with the very real possibility of her riding my cock once we get in the hotel room. *Fuck*, even that slightest graze of her panties on me . . . My forehead falls to her shoulder.

Like a temptress, she uses her hold on my neck—her fingers splayed over my traps—for balance as she grinds down on me. She swivels her hips to a rhythm she only hears, but that doesn't mean I don't lose my mind all the same.

Her blue eyes flick up to meet mine, pupils dilated with desire. "You think you're the only one who can have control around here?" she taunts playfully. "I don't think so, Captain. I don't think so."

She punctures each word with another roll of her hips, using my frame like a pole as she undulates like rippling water. A groan works its way up my throat and I don't bother to silence it. Holly does this to me: strips my control and leaves me a panting, hot mess.

My forearms fold in on either side of her head, my legs planted evenly as she fucks with my mind, my body.

Teeth nip at the juncture of my shoulder and throat. "You're not the only athlete in this hallway, Jackson." The words are whispered against my heated skin. Her nails bite into my shoulders as her rocking turns dirtier, more pointed in the way she hovers and dips over my dick. "Do you remember coming to see me dance at Cornell?"

Dance, as in Jazz, Hip Hop, mixed in with a season-long stint on Cornell's gymnastics team before an injury sat her out for good. She'd been music in motion, twirling on her toes and leaping through the air. So different to what I did for the school—bulldozing guys into the boards, dropping mitts and going to bat, fists snapping out to connect with jaws and skulls and noses.

Holly was poetry, all lean muscles and elegant lines.

I was a beatbox rhythm, fast counts and broken expectations.

"What do you want?" I rasp against her skin.

Her lips skim the underside of my jaw. "To bring you to your knees."

Famous last words, right there.

Without giving her the chance to protest, I readjust her weight in my arms and stride down the hall to my room. There's nothing but the sound of my soles brushing over the thin carpet and our heavy breathing as I close that final distance.

Ten feet.

Six feet.

Three feet.

"Reach into my front pocket, sweetheart. Get me the key."

She doesn't need to be told twice. Her fingers delve into my shorts, pulling out the flat key card that she promptly swipes over the lock. We're inside the room within a heartbeat, my foot kicking the door firmly shut. I waste no time in getting her exactly where I want her: her back up against the closed door, her pretty blue dress tugged up around her hips.

I fall to my knees before her.

"Jackson?"

I only tap her ankle in silent encouragement to lift it. Up, up, up it goes until her trembling thigh is on my shoulder and her fingers are sifting through my hair. I kiss the soft skin near her knee. Press another one to her inner thigh, no longer as tight and as muscled as back in her dancing days.

She's no less beautiful in my eyes, no less enticing.

My hand wraps around her leg and I squeeze the supple flesh, bringing my gaze to her face. I make sure to hold eye contact when my lips move farther north, so close to the line of her panties and the road to my idea of bliss.

"You have me on my knees." Another kiss, this one a mere inch from paradise. Her chest heaves with a sharp breath. One last kiss, this one over the fabric of her underwear, directly on top of her clit. "Now do something about it."

Blue eyes burn down at me like the center of a candle's flame, so damn hot that I'm surprised I don't combust. And then I do, my cock straining in my shorts, my fucking heart ready to burst from my chest.

In a move that's smooth and seductive, Holly skims her palms up her chest to the strap of her halter dress. Her leg never moves from my shoulder, not as she unties the knot behind her neck and lets the fabric fall to her chest. Not when she cups the weight of one breast and flicks her thumb over a pebbled nipple.

My mouth dries at the sight, and I dig my fingers into her hips to keep from passing out.

"*Holls*."

She never cuts our eye contact, not once. Her fingers tug at her nipple, rolling the hard peak as her hips do the same. Air catches in my lungs when one hand leaves her breast to lay flat on her sternum and skim down past her ribcage, down past her once-pierced belly button, down past her pelvic bone. That finger teases the waistband of her underwear, dips briefly under the cotton, and steals what's left of my oxygen supply by running along the elastic and pulling her panties to the side.

Revealing herself to me completely.

Making me almost come in my shorts.

"I've brought you to your knees," she whispers, "now do something about it."

Challenge accepted.

Like a man possessed, I don't stand a chance in telling her no. I drag my hands from her hips to under her ass. Her clit is pink and swollen—and mine. At the first touch of my tongue, Holly shoots upward onto her toes, her calf muscle flexing like she's doing one of her old relevé moves. She doesn't get far; I lay a forearm across her lower stomach, keeping her locked in place.

She wanted me on my knees.

Now she has to suffer through the consequences.

And suffer she does. I fuck her with my tongue, swirling it over her clit in tight, little circles that has her crying out my name. Her hands fist in my hair, and I bite back a grin before seeking to push her right over the edge.

Tongue swirling, I drag my finger from the curve of her ass, through her wetness, until I'm gliding two fingers into her heat.

"Jackson," she whimpers, and I don't mistake the way her knee almost buckles.

I don't ease up on her. Instead, I alternate the timing between my thrusting fingers and when I heighten the pressure on her swollen clit. Her stomach clenches behind my forearm, her inner thigh shaking with the effort to stay standing upright on only one foot.

I'm doing something about it, sweetheart.

I work a third finger into her heat, then curl my fingers inward.

She splinters immediately, coming against my mouth as her nails bite into my skull with the force of her orgasm. I ride the wave out, slowing the thrusts of my fingers until she's no longer got me in a vice. Slowly, I pull my fingers from her pussy and, when I'm sure she's watching, I pop them into my mouth and lick off her juices.

"Oh, my God." Her blue eyes are wide and luminous as she struggles to catch her breath.

Reaching forward, I tweak her bare nipple with the fingers I had inside her. "Get on the bed, sweetheart."

She practically throws me to the side in her haste to climb onto the mattress.

Chuckling, I stay back and enjoy the view. Her dress hiked up around her waist, her naked breasts on full display. She reclines on her back, propped up on her elbows. Almost blindly, I move to my suitcase to grab the box of condoms I bought before our trip to D.C. Did I know that she'd hop in my bed? No.

Had I hoped she would?

Hell, fucking yeah.

Shucking my shorts, along with my T-shirt, I roll the latex down the length of my dick as I stride toward the bed. Holly's waiting for me, legs tipped open wide, and I grip the underside of her thighs and haul her butt toward the edge of the mattress.

I line up my cock with her pussy, then swing my gaze up to her face.

"I'm not going to last long," I tell her in a low voice. "You've got me so wound up that I feel like I'm going to—"

Holly's heels dig into my ass. "Now, Jackson."

I give her what she wants in a single thrust. The skin on my throat pinches as I throw my head back with a groan. Goddamn, she feels even better than the last time. Tighter. Wetter. Or maybe I'm so turned on that she could touch one finger to my dick and I'd be ready to come.

My ass flexes as I pull out and push back in.

I should slow down my pace. Make sure that it's as good for her as it is for me right now. But I can't stop the churning of my hips, the walls of her tight pussy clamping down on my cock every time I thrust deep. It feels like heaven. It feels like sin. It feels like love.

Dragging my eyes off where we're joined, I focus on Holly's sweet face.

Beautiful, so unbelievably beautiful.

I grip her legs, unwinding them from my back and straightening them so that her ankles are resting on my left shoulder, her inner thighs pressed together. The position creates a vice-like grip on my dick, and Holly's mouth parts in an *O*.

"I've missed you," I confess as I watch her small tits bounce with the force of my thrusts. "Maybe I shouldn't have, but I missed you every fucking day that you weren't mine to touch, mine to fuck, mine to *love*."

Her hands fall to the bed where she fists the sheets. "Jackson, Jackson I'm going to come."

My eyes on her flushed face, I split her legs and press them up toward her chest, until she's clutching her knees and my finger is circling her clit. Her neck stretches and everything about this moment is messy and raw, but I wouldn't a change thing.

Not when she comes, crying out my name as she twines her fingers in the hotel sheets.

Not when I let out a guttural groan as I empty everything that I am inside her.

When she smiles up at me, her fingers lazily moving to trace the slope of my broken nose, there's no denying that it's also perfect.

CHAPTER 28
HOLLY

I t sounds pitiful, but I think I've forgotten how to cuddle.

Is there even going to *be* any cuddling?

I hoist myself up in the queen-sized bed and stare at the remnants of our . . . lovemaking? Fuck-fest? Sex session? My eyes slam shut, the rest of the room disappearing behind my lids.

There should be a handbook for this sort of thing: *What to do When Your Ex-husband Makes You Come Three Times 101.* Followed up by the highly requested sequel: *Sleepover Protocol, The Divorcée Edition.*

Really, Jackson and I are both adults which means that we ought to be able to have this conversation easily.

Instead, the beats of The Clash's *Should I Stay or Should I Go?* ring in my ears, and I experience half a second of panic where I seriously consider stripping off all my clothes, standing outside the bathroom door, and announcing, "Do with me as you will."

Except that he sort of did that already, and I have the whisker burns between my thighs to prove it.

The toilet flushes in the adjoining bathroom and I leap into action. Stuff one lone boob back into her rightful place in my dress, then do the same with the other. Once the girls are back in order, I haul butt out of the bed. My blue dress resettles around my thighs, my bare toes curling against the thin carpet.

"If you were plannin' to leave, you should have thought to escape while I was getting rid of the condom."

At Jackson's slow, husky murmur, I glance his way and wish I hadn't.

Without the high-energy thrum of lust in my veins, I take a moment to appreciate Jackson's naked body in a way that I haven't in so long. His arms are powerful ropes of muscle, big and bulging as opposed to lean and sinuous—he's a Tom Hardy on the *How Muscular Is He?* scale, and not a Tom Hiddleston. Though I'd have to be dead to find fault with either. (And I'm definitely not dead.)

With every breath, his abdominal muscles flex, the obliques tightening and releasing. His thighs . . . I never really thought it was normal to fantasize about a man's thighs, but *Jackson's* thighs are utter perfection.

Particularly when he's holding me between them, my back to his hard front.

After a sharp breath of my own, I smooth my hands over the fabric of my dress. "I wasn't sure what the code was."

His brows furrow together. "Code?"

"Yeah, you know—" I wave one hand in the air, flicking it between us. "The *code*. Do I go upstairs to my room? Do I stay down here in yours? I mean, you'd think there'd be some sort of advice on the internet for this sort of thing, but I looked after the last time we were together, and for once the internet has failed me."

Jackson doesn't seem to care that he's not wearing a single stitch of clothing as he pushes away from the doorframe and ambles toward me, all loose limbs and long strides. "You know what I think?" His tone is sinful, a low rumble. "I think that you should do whatever *you* want to do, not what society thinks is healthy for you."

I laugh awkwardly at that, a *ha-ha-ha* that sounds stilted to even my own ears. "I think that ship has sailed. The internet has a firm stance on divorced couples hooking up again."

"Oh, yeah?" He slips behind me, his big hands going to my shoulders. I moan out loud when his thumbs dig into the tense muscles there, circling and circling and circling over the deep tissue. "What's the consensus?"

He asks the question near my ear, and I fight off a shiver. Everything Jackson does is sensual, a fact that he proves by gliding his hands down my spine and taking the zipper of my dress right along with them.

The dress parts, cool air hitting my skin. It feels heavenly, if heaven came in the form of a six-foot-four hockey player with magical hands and a smooth, honeyed drawl.

"Holls?"

"Generally frowned upon," I manage on a shuddered breath, "a big no-no."

"But not illegal?"

"What?" My brain empties when all that cool air hits my bare backside. "No, not illegal—"

"For the record, I'd sacrifice myself to a lifetime of bending over for soap if I got a little more time with you."

I'm not given any time to process *that* crazy statement before I'm flying—literally, *flying*—through the air and landing with a massive bounce on the mattress.

The coils shriek in protest.

"Jackson!"

In that moment, I'm a naked acrobat who should have been fired on my first day on the job.

My limbs flail this way and that, and really, I should have been less concerned about landing face-first on the floor and more worried about what my hundred-and-ten-pound frame has done to the bed frame.

On the second bounce, the bed *cracks!*

And on the third, it quite literally goes concave with me in the middle of the cavern.

Butt cheeks burning from the abrupt crash landing, I swing my gaze toward Jackson and glare accusingly. "You broke the bed!"

Only, the damn man is on his knees, hands on the ground, doubled over in laughter at my expense. "I can't—" His handsome head falls forward, his laughter eating away at any leftover awkwardness infiltrating the room. "Oh, God, Holls. I'm so sorry, but your face when you went down . . ."

"Jerk." I huff out a breath, but it lacks any true heat. Already I feel laughter bubbling to the surface. "I can't believe that just happened." I flap my arms at my side, tightening my core muscles as the mattress wobbles over the broken slats. So much for beautiful (and sturdy) antique furniture.

"It's a conspiracy," I mutter glumly. "We literally had hardcore sex on this thing and not even a whine! Then you throw me on it and it decides to break? How screwed up is that? If I didn't know any better, I'd say you were pranking me."

"Not a prank." He gasps out the words between fits of laugher, still on his hands and knees like he's praying to the Almighty Shitty Bed for making his night.

Newsflash, *I* made his night.

"Just so you know, you can stop laughing at any time now."

His only response is to keel over and laugh some more.

"*Any* time now." I drum my fingers on the mattress, staring at the "reserved" Blades captain losing his mind and all because I broke a bed. Funny, so funny. "Jackson. Really, you can stop."

The overhead light illuminates his big grin when he climbs to his feet and comes toward me, arms wide open. "C'mere, sweetheart. Your Knight in Naked Birthday Suit has arrived to save the day."

I roll my eyes at the cheesiness factor, but my heart swoons when he pulls me from the rubble—okay, the broken slats and crooked mattress—and hauls me close to his chest. He tucks my head under his chin, but our heights are so opposite that it's more like he folds his big body far enough over to put me in the desired spot.

"How's the butt?" he asks, reaching down to massage one butt cheek and then the other.

I snort into his hard chest. "Strong enough to crack a slat of wood in half."

"Imagine if it was an Olympic event—you'd place first."

"I've always wanted a gold medal."

"Now's your chance to take what's yours." He kisses the crown of my head, then loops his arms around the small of my back to lift me off my toes in a tight hug. "How about you go upstairs to your room and get ready for bed?" He sets me back down on my feet again, stealing away his body heat while heading for the room phone that's perched on the desk. "I'll take care of all"—he plucks up the phone from the receiver and gestures to the broken bed—"this."

"What are you going to tell them?"

"That you had your wicked way with me." He waggles his eyebrows. "Wouldn't let me come up for air because you were so desperate to have me sucking on your cli—oh, hey. *Cliff.* I was just about to say that I'll be climbing a cliff tomorrow." Jackson flashes me a thumbs up, mouthing, *go upstairs.* "No mountains in the area? Seriously? Damn, well there goes that idea. Way to kill a man's dreams, Joe."

When he gestures at me to get dressed, I swallow an ill-timed chuckle and begin pulling my clothes on again.

Jackson, on the other hand, remains fully nude, not a hint

of embarrassment straining his features while he apologizes to the front-desk receptionist about "the travesty done to the bed" and asks that all damages go on his personal credit card.

Picking up my purse from where I'd sent it sailing earlier in the evening, I hook the strap over my shoulder and move toward Jackson.

He hooks a hand around mine, eclipsing the final steps between us. Drops his mouth to my ear, away from the receiver, to ask, "What room are you in?"

Guess the cuddling thing is definitely going to happen.

I search around for a hint of worry, any slice of panic that I'm making the wrong step here, but I find nothing but excitement. "301. First door on your right out of the elevator."

He nods, once, and sends me off with another kiss to my temple.

I head up to my room with a bounce in my step.

Strip off my clothes and pull on a basic T-shirt and sleep shorts with a smile that can't be stopped.

Twenty minutes after I climbed into bed, with the TV's volume turned down to a gentle murmur, I hear the knock on the door.

And the grin comes right on back.

Once inside my room, Jackson wastes no time teasing me out of my clothes all over again, tugging my shirt up and over my head and my shorts and panties down the length of my legs. He eyes the full-sized bed with distrust, making a dramatic show of giving the mattress his weight in several increments.

He makes me smile.

He makes me throw my head back in laughter.

And when he wraps me up in his big arms, my chin resting on his chest, as he surfs the TV for something good to watch, he makes me crave something more than a hotel-room stay while I'm technically on the clock.

Love. Forever. Him.

I don't know if any of it is attainable—not in the long run, not if we allow all our past faults to come tumbling in between us again.

I squeeze him tight, inhaling his familiar sandalwood and fresh-breeze scent.

For tonight, I just breathe.

CHAPTER 29
HOLLY

Jackson's weekend getaway brings us to Newport, Rhode Island, home of Gilded Age mansions and beautiful oceanside views and picture-perfect little shops along the main strip in town.

I mean, even the Dunkin' Donuts that we stopped at for coffee looked like something out of a magazine. It had seating outside and cute little picnic benches, and the girl at the counter actually smiled when she took our order.

Smiled.

Boston has its charm, don't get me wrong, but the term "Masshole" is applicable because it's the undeniable truth. Having grown up in the South, the land of gentile hospitality, I'm fully aware that there's a difference.

Here in Newport, the only asshole we've come across is the Massachusetts driver who cut us off at the intersection in front of our bed and breakfast, and then proceeded to roll down his window and shout obscenities at us.

And maybe I've lived in the Northeast a little too long, the Dunkin's coffee thickening my blood and steeling my spine, because I rolled my window down and yelled right back at him.

"Can't take you anywhere," Jackson teased as he pulled into the small parking lot behind the B&B where we're staying. "Can't lie, though. It's a turn-on when you're all fired up like that."

Unfortunately for him, whatever lust heated his dark eyes died a quick death the moment the B&B innkeeper ushered us inside.

"You're here!" she exclaims, clapping her hands together before yanking us in for a hug, one after another. Her bony arms threaten to cut off my oxygen supply, and I swallow a fistful of air and hope for the best. She's somewhere between fifty and sixty, give or take any range of years on either side. "Oh, my goodness, this is brilliant. Just brilliant."

Her red hair is pulled back in a low ponytail, her face makeup free. Unable to contain her enthusiasm, she bounces on the balls of her ballet-slippered feet. "I have all sorts of people stay here at The Ruby Slipper, but I've never had a *hockey* player before."

Oh, God—a fan.

I don't know whether to laugh or hustle Jackson back out to the car and make the trek back up to Boston before anyone else notices that we've got a pro-athlete on our hands.

"I've been watching *Getting Pucked*," she goes on, all smiles and jabbing hands. "I'll be honest, I'm not the biggest sports fan. Unless we're talking about cricket, since I do love me some cricket. Oh! And I do love golf. But that hockey show is just"—she snaps her fingers in the air—"it grabs you, just like that! I was hooked from day one."

Jackson's smile is strained. "So glad you're enjoying it . . . I'm sorry, is it Ginger? I think we corresponded when I booked our stay?"

Now he's done it.

Ginger's face positively *blooms* with happiness. "Yes! Ginger, that's me. That's so kind of you to remember my name. And I *have* to tell you, you sound exactly the same as you do on the TV! So very manly." She gives Jackson a slow, appreciative onceover before glancing at me, her smile still evident on her face. "And you! I know you too."

It's been a long time since I was recognized in any capacity, and I grip the handle of my suitcase a little tighter, amusement curling through me. Maybe she's seen my face in passing on the show? I've been careful to stay out the way for the most part, but when you've got multiple camera crews all bustling around the same area, it's hard to be completely invisible. "That's so sweet of you, Ginger." I rock onto the back of my heels, then ask, "You've seen my work before, then?"

I bump Jackson's hip with mine. *She knows who I am!* I want to shout.

The tip of Ginger's nose bunches as her brows tug inward. "Your . . . work?" She shakes her head, and I feel my stomach drop with dread for the words that will inevitably come next. "No, I don't know anything about that, but I *do* know that the two of you were married! I saw you on Mr. Carter's Wikipedia page. How cool is that, by the way? I'd love to be on the Wikipedia although I'm sure I wouldn't have an interesting enough story to warrant anyone wanting to write about me."

My lungs seize as her words sink in.

She doesn't know me, not anything about my photography or my business or my work with *Getting Pucked*.

Though I shouldn't let it get to me, her easy dismissal that I could be anything more than Jackson's ex-wife feels like a punch to the gut.

So much for progress.

Ginger claps her hands again, completely oblivious to the slap of reality she's hand-delivered. "I promise I won't say a word to those newspapers, but are you two . . . are you getting back together? Oh, please, *please* say yes. You would make such adorable babies!"

Jackson's expression stiffens.

No doubt about it, he does *not* look charmed by the effervescent Ginger.

Well, that makes two of us.

Lifting his duffel bag off the floor and over one bulky shoulder, he stares down at the innkeeper with a look that would send any sane person running. "We'll take the room keys, Ginger."

Keys? As in plural?

I try to catch his eye, but he keeps his gaze resolutely on the woman in front of us.

She giggles at the steel in his voice. "I know you mentioned the two rooms, Mr. Carter, but this will be on me." Prancing behind the front desk, she plucks a key from an old, fancy-looking vault and thrusts it up in the air. "You'll have one, instead." At Jackson's protest, she cuts him off with a raised hand and an unsubtle wink. "No, no need to thank me. I'm just doing what anyone else in my position would do."

When I make a move to grab the key off the counter, she adds, "An invitation to the wedding wouldn't hurt either, of course."

"Jesus," Jackson breathes out next to me. He scrubs a hand over his face, his dark hair falling over his forehead. Louder, he says, "You got it, Ginger. Where are we?"

She drops a chin to an upturned hand and lets out a long sigh. "Second floor, second door to your left. There's a king-sized bed, too!"

The last bit is hollered at our backs because we're already halfway up the flight of stairs. Neither of us says a word until we're locked in the guestroom and taking in the "charm."

Four-poster, king-sized bed.

Floral decorations *everywhere*.

Creepy porcelain figures situated on every flat surface throughout the room.

An old TV that's the depth of my arm span, or close to it.

"The view's pretty, at least," I say, setting my camera bag down next to the door.

A low chuckle is my only answer before he mutters, "The curtains are clear plastic."

I point at the settee in the far corner of the room. "It looks like the seventies vomited all over." Striding forward, I whip open the plastic—who uses *plastic*?—curtains. There's nothing but ocean as far as I can see, a beautiful blue that I can't wait to photograph over the next two days. "But this view makes up for it." Throwing a glance over my shoulder at Jackson, I murmur, "Who knows what our other *two* rooms would have looked like had Ginger not given us this one?"

His heat warms my back as his hands rest on the glass doors that lead out to a tiny balcony. "I didn't want you to feel as though you were quarantined to the same room as me." I feel his heavy sigh skate along the nape of my neck, and I fight off a shiver. "Let's face it, Holls. Talking is gonna happen this weekend, and I'm sure most of it isn't going to be all sunshine and unicorns. I never wanted you . . . fuck, I . . . I need you with me on this, us taking these steps together, not me pulling you along behind me. I figured space would help with that. I figured it wouldn't make you panic."

Panic, just like I did that night in Chicago when we kissed for the first time in a year.

I get where he's coming from, I really do.

And, in a way, I want to hug him for thinking this out and doing what he can to make sure I have the space I need at all times. He's assuming that things will get bumpy and I'll want somewhere to lick my wounds in peace.

But space tore our relationship apart.

We were two boxers sitting in our own designated corners of the ring, never confronting each other with the issues that bubbled up between us.

He went to his teammates.

I stayed in my office.

Until our lives truly became a permanent separation.

Staring hard at the glass door, watching the whitecaps of the waves as they crash and tumble over each other, I lift my hands to settle them over his. "Sometimes love gets messy, babe. The way we were before didn't work, so if we're going to do this—you know, making Ginger a proud member of our future wedding—then we've got to change the game, flip the rules."

His big hand leaves mine to sweep my hair back from my neck. It's a gentle gesture, a familiar one, and so are the lips that claim that spot right behind my ear. The shiver I fought earlier returns, and this time there's no holding it off. Jackson knows how to touch me, how to make me pant with want.

"You've always been a rule follower, sweetheart," he says, his tone husky, "you sure that you know how to change the rules?"

"Weren't you just telling me two days ago how much trouble I am?" I rock my butt against his crotch, which is nestled up against my backside. "Don't doubt my trouble-making prowess, Mr. Carter."

He grips my hips, pulling them sharply backward. "To a weekend of trouble."

I ignore the fact that we don't have champagne to properly toast and instead twine my fingers with his and rest the back of my head on his hard chest. "To a weekend of messy love."

I feel his rumble of appreciation reverberate in his chest, and then again as he asks, "What's up first on the agenda?"

If I listen hard enough, I can hear the ocean waves crashing on the beach. It calls to me like no other, probably from having grown up in a middle of a state where muddy rivers were our only water source.

"To the Cliff Walk."

CHAPTER 30
JACKSON

Holly and I spend hours along Newport's famous Cliff Walk, a stony width of space that winds along the city's rocky coastline, offering views of the Atlantic Ocean on one side and Newport's infamously grandiose mansions on the other.

The farther we walk, the more natural our conversation becomes.

I tease her about being able to see her bright pink sneakers from outer space.

She leaps on my back, arms clinging to me like a hundred-pound-and-change monkey, just to throw me off guard when I stop and stare too long at a seagull attacking a poor woman down on the beach while he aims for her lunch.

I hold Holly like that, her arms hooked around my neck, her legs wrapped around my hips, for far longer than necessary.

She nips my left shoulder. "Put me down."

I readjust her weight and keep trudging along the elevated path. During team workouts, I bench-press double her weight. I could go miles like this and not even lose my breath. "Your view is better on my back. You can see over the stone wall now."

"Jerk," she mutters, but I can hear the smile in her voice, "I'm not *that* short."

Yeah, she is. "You're what? Five-two?"

"Subtract an inch, maybe."

"Like I said, short." The walls of the Cliff Walk come up to my waist, but Holly makes me feel like I'm a teenager on some mission to prove I'm as tough as the Hulk, sans the green body.

But just as Bruce Banner is stuck in the Hulk's body, my brain is locked inside my skull—whatever the hell that'll do for me if the migraines worsen and Dr. Mebowitz lays down the law. In coming to Newport this weekend, I knew right away that telling Holly about the possible CTE was a necessity.

You can't build a relationship without all the facts, and the fact of the matter is, I don't know where my future leads. All I know is that I need her in it.

I don't know what kind of life I can offer.

That's the kicker, isn't it?

I'm not some average Joe with a normal nine-to-five job that requires sitting at a desk, day in and day out. I'm no soldier, no cop or fireman, but every time I step out onto the ice, I risk another chunk of my soul to see the lamps light and to hear the crowds cheering us on—all at the expense of doing so much harm to my body that migraines might one day be the least of my worries.

The night I shared her bed in D.C., I spent hours on the internet after she fell asleep. Hours of reading account after account of NFL players and hockey players—some I personally knew—who experienced all the same symptoms that I do, only to have a brain aneurysm or a stroke or begin to lose their precious memories.

I watched a fellow NHL player sit in front of a camera,

tears coating his lashes, and announce to the world that if he'd ever been told how much his brain would suffer from the repetitive head trauma, he never would have picked up a pair of skates.

Behind my dark-tinted aviators, my lids slam shut. Slowing to a halt, I let Holly's body slide down the length of mine, until her feet touch the stone walkway. I can't un-hear the tremor in his voice. Can't un-see the anger in his gaze. I wish I could, but I can't.

I'm already itching to get back on the ice next Tuesday and win against the Tampa Bay Lightning on our home turf.

It's fucked up, all of it.

"I remember your very first game with the Bruins."

I blink my eyes open. Holly's leaning on the stone balustrade, her eyes on the ocean. She looks younger than thirty-two, dressed as she is now: knee-length shorts, those bright pink shoes of hers, a faded Cornell T-shirt that hugs her trim back and reveals the twin dimples at the base of her spine.

So damn beautiful.

Unable to stay away, I move in beside her and mimic her pose. "It was a shit show."

She laughs softly, the sound merging with the crashing waves and the squawking seagulls circling like ruthless scavengers above us. "Yeah, it was. Do you remember what you told me when we got home that night?"

I search through the memories, shifting through that time period like a slideshow of events, and come up blank. My first instinct is to lean into the panic that's sprouting to life in my chest before I shove the fear so far deep in my soul and clamp a heavy, wooden lid over it. Loads of people can't remember things from their past—and what's memorable to one person might not be so to someone else.

Easy. Simple as that.

It has nothing to do with TBI or CTE or whatever Dr. Mebowitz wants to call it.

At my silence, Holly clasps her hands together and lets them dangle over the stone wall. "You were barely given any ice time. You vomited in the locker room. And yet, we met in the parking lot at my car afterward, and you said, 'I've never felt such an adrenaline rush.' I teased you about turning into a junkie."

"That's exactly what I am."

Funny how I've thought the same thing for years but never really put it into exact words. A junkie. Hockey is my vice: the thrill of a goal, the high of faking out an opponent and nailing the puck to my teammate, the satisfaction that thrives in my veins with every good play that's made.

"Trust me," Holly says lightly, her shoulder bumping mine, "I'm *fully* aware."

The soles of my tennis shoes scrape along the stone as I turn to stare at her profile. "What's brought this on?"

Sunlight kisses her features. Already her nose is turning pink, despite the fact that we're now long into fall. She shields the top half of her face from the sun, which is directly over-head, and I miss the chance to get a full read on her now that I can't see her blue eyes. "I don't think I have that same rush with photography." She says it with no hint of frustration in her tone, and I'm struck momentarily speechless.

Which I guess works fine for her because she keeps talking anyway.

"Please don't take this in a creepy way or anything, but I couldn't help but watch you over the last month that *Getting Pucked* has been filming. I'm not even sure if you realize it or not, but you light up when you're on the ice." Her hand falls from its spot at her temple to gesture through the air in that Holly way of hers that I know so well. "You're always *on*. Even when you're not playing, you're talking with the team, keeping everything in line."

"It's my job, Holls. Everything you've just said . . . I mean, I'm paid to be that guy. As captain, I lead the pack."

She shakes her head. "You're not paid to go out of your way to sit at hotel bars to keep the rookies from partying too hard. You're not paid to stay so late at the rink that you're there past the security guards' clock out time. It isn't like I'm realizing any of this for the first time. I mean"—she sends me a quick, furtive smile—"we *were* married for eleven years. I guess that it's just . . . I love what I do, and I've always thought that it truly fulfills me. It does, to a certain degree. But I'm missing the high that hockey gives you." Almost shyly, she tucks her hair behind her ears. "I'm no junkie, I guess is what I'm trying to say, not when it comes to taking pictures."

It's on the tip of my tongue to tell her that my junkie days may be over soon enough. But she's opening up—baring her soul—and this moment is hers alone. The fact that she even trusts me enough to talk about it? Damn, but it feels so good.

So right.

"Do you trust me?"

The question comes at her from left field, but she doesn't waste a second in answering. "Yes."

I've seen enough signs along the Cliff Walk to know that this is against the rules, but I promised Holly that we would change the game this weekend. *No time like the present to make it happen.* My hands skim along her sides until they're tucked under her ass and I'm lifting her up onto the stone wall.

There's no guardrail behind her, nothing to stop her from tumbling down to the beach below.

Except for me.

I loop my arms around her back, one hand nestled between her shoulder blades and the other above the curve of her backside.

"Oh, sh—"

The rest of her sentence cuts off as I tighten my hold,

proving without words that I've got her back. I won't let her fall.

"There are different types of adrenaline highs," I tell her, raising my voice just enough to be heard over the gust of wind whipping through her blond strands. The tips smack me across the face, sticking on my mouth, and she's forced to shake her head in order to free me again.

A flirty smile on her lips, she urges, "Go on, O Captain my Captain."

I laugh hard at that.

Then I loosen my hold, just enough for her eyes to grow round in her face and her nails to claw into my biceps, holding on.

"There's the adrenaline that comes from tumblin' into the unknown." My fingers bite into her back as I lower her, inch by inch, until she's nearly reclining horizontal, her hair dancing wildly in the breeze. My hips press into her pelvis, her legs looped around my waist, as I hold her in place. Keeping her safe. "I could drop you, let you fall, but it feels freeing in that space where you're almost lettin' go but still holding on."

She lets her head drop back, the column of her neck completely elongated, and I know she's taking in the expanse of the ocean. It's bigger than her, it's bigger than us. "My heart is racing a mile a minute."

"No faster than mine." Slowly, I bring her back up until her weight is completely on the wall. Her cheeks are flushed pink, lips parted on a heavy breath. Beautiful. Cutting my gaze from hers, I take her hand and fold it over my heart. "I like to think of this as the *Titanic* Adrenaline High, where Leo's holding Rose on the bow of the ship."

"Jack."

"What?"

"It's Jack in the movie. That's his name. Leo's his *real*

name." She eyes me for a second, then laughs softly. "Never mind, continue."

Jack . . . Leonardo DiCaprio. Shit, right. Well, doesn't matter. Not like he'll be banging on my door anytime soon to get his comeuppance. Unlike our football counterparts, pro hockey players tend to stay out of Hollywood for the most apart.

Although if TMZ keeps up their elite-level of stalking, that might not be the case for long.

The thought alone makes my dick shrivel in dread.

"Babe?"

It's the second time she's used the endearment today, and it feels no less sweet than the first time around.

"Kiss me."

Holly visibly swallows at my soft demand. Her blue eyes skirt to the right, to the left, before zeroing in on my mouth. One slender hand smooths up to cradle the back of my head, while the other remains firmly planted on my chest over my heart.

"Never let it be said I wasn't a rule follower," she whispers, then closes the distance between us.

The first taste rocks me to my core. It teases more than it satisfies. I let her take the lead, willing to go where she blazes the trail she desires, knowing I'll still go up in flames no matter what pace she sets.

And the pace is slow.

Heart-wrenching, like she's trying to deliver some secret message only for me to find out she's used invisible ink. But I follow anyway, opening my mouth when she touches her tongue to my bottom lip, letting her wrestle all control from me.

With the sounds of the waves crashing over the shore and the wind whistling past us, I let Holly steal my breath and give me back some of the man I used to be. The man only she had access to.

I groan into her mouth.

Then pull away.

She protests with a whimper.

My hard-on protests just by existing when there's not a damn thing I can do to come.

I swallow, hard, and mutter, "The second type of adrenaline high." I sink one hand under the hem of her T-shirt solely so I can feel her naked skin. "A junkie who knows what's coming next. It's choreography that's been done before." For fourteen years, it's a choreography I've only ever known with Holly. My gaze latches on to the rise and fall of her chest. "The thrill isn't in the unknown but in the familiar, the sense that you're coming home."

Her fingers curl into the fabric of my shirt. "Is there a third?" she asks, voice raspy with need.

I nod. "Yes."

"Show me."

As gently as I can, I drag her off her perch atop the stone wall and let her slide down the length of my body. When my cock collides with the apex of her thighs, we both release a groan.

Not now, man. Not right now.

Once she's on the ground, I step back and unzip the backpack she's brought with her. The one I've seen hooked over her shoulder for so many years that, to see her without it, feels abnormal.

Fingers brushing over the white tab on the interior of the bag, my gaze lingers on the now faded black writing.

Dream big, sweetheart. Love, Jackson.

In the rink, I may as well be composed of ice. No one gets through me. No one breaks through my outer wall, not a heckler, not an asshole on the other team, no one.

Off it, Holly is my weakness.

Something that clearly rings true when my heart squeezes and my lungs feel too tight to breathe as it hits me: she still carries around the same backpack I bought for her when she first started Carter Photography.

Pushing away the emotion so I can slam my final point home, I cup the back of her prized camera and lift it from the bag. Straightening to my full height, I turn to Holly and lay it all out on the line.

"Sometimes the high doesn't feel like a rush of emotions." I slip the camera strap over her head. "Sometimes it feels like it's only job is to soothe you. It's the place where you go when you need to breathe. It's how you work out your stress and how you bring your own blend of creativity into the world. *That's* the high, sweetheart. It's not about the fear of the unknown or the warmth that comes from the familiar—it's all about fulfillment."

A single tear splashes onto her cheekbone.

She doesn't make a move to wipe it away.

Neither do I.

"Thank you."

The two words emerge as a hoarse whisper, but I hear the level of gratitude behind it. "Always." My voice is pure gravel, but she doesn't point it out.

Instead, she presses a button on the camera and the little beast whirs to life. She lifts it, holding it to her face, and I hear the telltale *click* of a picture being captured.

"You," she says after a moment, "you're my high."

CHAPTER 31
HOLLY

"**A**nymore wine, miss?"

I'm two glasses in already, which is honestly one glass past my usual limit.

That's what happens when you stop going out all the time and spend your evenings with Chip and Joanna Gaines on HGTV's *Fixer Upper*—the wine gets pushed aside for other, more delectable treats. Like ice cream.

Across the wooden table, Jackson meets my gaze, then jerks his chin toward the waiter. "Want another?"

Considering the fact that I'm drinking alone tonight, it's probably best that I don't end up the only drunk. See? Adulthood in its purest form—knowing when to stop imbibing before you end up belting out lyrics to a song no one else in the restaurant knows.

Off a quick assumption, as we walked through to our table, I'm harboring a guess that the clientele here wouldn't know a Rihanna song if it bit them in the butt.

"I think I'm okay for now, thank you."

The server's twin dimples appear briefly with a smile before he heads off to help guests at another table.

We're seated on a veranda, small tables situated

throughout the open floor plan. The ocean lies off to our right, as black as the evening sky. When we were first seated, I counted the number of boats I saw bobbing along the open waters: five, maybe six. Their lit windows do little to illuminate the sky, just as the trio of candles on the table offer a romantic feel but are hardly potent enough to stave off the nippy October night.

I nuzzle in the soft, warm fabric of my cardigan. "You never mentioned why you don't drink anymore."

Jackson is mid-soda sip when I speak.

He coughs—splutters, more like—into a balled fist before setting down his drink. "I, uh . . ." Drawing in a deep breath, he picks up his knife and twirls it over the backs of his knuckles—a nervous habit he's had since I've known him. Interesting. "Sorry, wasn't expecting that question."

I sip what's left of my wine. "Take your time."

In the last day, Jackson and I have taken to Newport like newlyweds on a honeymoon. For every touristy activity we do about town, we've hooked up back at The Ruby Slipper. We've gone toe-for-toe, have baptized every space of our guestroom, and other than our talk along the Cliff Walk, we've stuck to safe, surface-level conversation.

If we're going to really do this, I need more than sex.

And it should start with him opening up as to why he's ditched his preferred Beam and Coke when we go out for plain, old Coke.

Like me, Jackson took the time to dress up tonight. His hair is slicked back, his face completely smooth of any hint of stubble. He's wearing black from head to toe, and when I stepped out of the bathroom after curling my hair, I nearly demanded that we stay in and go right back to our competing tally of Outdoor Activities vs Sexy-times All Over Our Guestroom.

Only the fact that we caught Ginger creeping outside our door kept us from ordering in.

Not that I'm complaining.

The food, the ocean, even the nip in the air have made the evening out worth it.

If only Jackson would just—

"I'm old, Holls."

Is he kidding me right now? Rolling my eyes, I tease, "You're a real geriatric, all right." At his mute silence, I raise a brow. "You're pulling my leg, aren't you?"

Lips flatlining, he reaches up to run his fingers through his hair, only to stop halfway and drop his hand to the table. "Thirty-four in hockey years might as well put me in the prehistoric category," he mutters. His dark eyes narrow, but not on me—they lock on my hands, which are fiddling with the stem of my wineglass. "I gave up alcohol after we divorced. I had two important things in my life, and I'd just lost one."

His gaze snaps up to meet mine, pinning me in place with the complete intensity that I see swirling in the brown depths. "There wasn't a shot in hell that I'd lose hockey, too. Guys my age become victims to injuries," he says thickly, like even the thought of turning out like any one of them has him up at night, "the career-ending kind, though."

"I was going to say, you've had your own fair share of almost-career ending injuries." I gesture to his reconstructed cheek bone, which Andre Beaumont broke some years back when he still played for the Detroit Red Wings.

My attempt to lighten the mood falls on deaf ears.

Jackson's lips don't turn up in a smile. "I never want the team I play for to think they could do better without me." His bulky shoulders lift in a casual shrug. "I can't stop what happens on the ice. On any day I could go out there and come wheeling back out on a stretcher. But I can keep myself healthy—that's all in my power."

"So, no alcohol."

Now, his mouth curves ever-so-slightly, and my heart

thrums in triple time at the sight. "No fast food either," he corrects. "Although I can't help but make an exception for Coke."

I mock-smother my shock with a hand over my mouth. "How terrible for you. And here I was thinking about how many bags of chips I devour weekly. Here's a clue—way too many."

He's all masculine confidence when he pats his flat stomach and rests an arm on the walled barrier that separates us from the craggy rocks ten or fifteen feet below the veranda. "This body's a temple, sweetheart."

Laughter sticks in my throat. "Oh, my God, you did *not* just say that."

"What?" He holds out his arms, all the better for me to check him out, I'm sure. "These are the same arms that carried you over the Cliff Walk yesterday, when—"

"You nearly fed me to the seagulls by throwing me over the side?"

He slicks his thumb over his bottom lip, laughter finally easing his tense expression. "Better than the alternative, at least."

"Which is?"

Elbows on the table, he leans forward. "Pigeons."

I nearly cough on my own spit, he's caught me so off-guard. "I won't lie, I thought you were going to suggest alligators or, well, I don't know. Something less . . . horrid."

"Being thrown to the gators is less horrid?" He doesn't sound convinced. "Tell me more."

"You're out of your mind."

"With lust."

"With all that Coke you're drinking." I point at the offending drink. "Sugar's going to your head."

"What can I say?" he drawls, eyes bright with humor. "I like sweet things."

At his wink, I bring the sleeve of my cardigan up to hide

my growing grin. The soft fabric is warm against my face, and I burrow deeper in the cashmere. "You sure there's no liquor in that drink of yours?" Raising a brow, I watch him steadily. "You're acting . . . frisky."

"Frisky, huh?" He laughs low and hard at that, and my entire body heats with appreciation. God, he's so handsome. His blunt-tipped fingers wrap around his glass. "Tell me something that happened to you this year." He pauses, rotating his wrist so that the soda swirls in the glass. "Something that made you want to pick up the phone and call me."

I strive for a neutral expression despite the quickening of my heart. "You're assuming that something actually happened."

Glass to his mouth, he drains the rest of the soda in a single swallow. "It's been three-hundred-and-fifty-something days, Holls." Glancing at me over the rim of the glass, he murmurs, "That's a long time for nothing to happen."

I lean back in my chair.

No doubt he's expecting me to take the easy route. Maybe mention the time that I accidentally tumbled off the ladder when I changed a light bulb in my fourteen-foot-tall room. Or maybe that one time I ate so much pizza by myself that I didn't move from my couch for twenty-four hours except to pee and drink water.

I could go the easy way.

But the point of this weekend is to open up and let down our walls, and giving him BS anecdotes doesn't help either of us.

Clasping the wineglass between my hands, I opt to tell him the one time that I nearly did break down and reach out. I'd needed to hear his voice. I'd needed his comfort. It's been months since, but the ache hasn't left my heart.

I rip the proverbial bandage off with six little words: "I found out about my parents."

Jackson's easygoing smile flatlines, concern lining his features. "Tell me, sweetheart."

A breeze lifts my curled hair, and I wrap my fist around the chaotic strands to keep them under control. All around, diners laugh and drink and make merry. At our table, my information drop has thrown everything out of whack.

Too late to turn back now, though.

Swallowing roughly, I rub my hand along the underside of my jaw. "When my grandma died, she . . . uh—I should say thank you, first, for coming to her funeral. I'm not sure if I have before, but seeing you there, even though we didn't speak, it meant the world to me."

Jackson's hand reaches out to clasp mine. He gives my fingers a quick squeeze. "We're family, Holls. I told you that."

That's right, he did. A screwed-up family, I believe he'd written in that envelope last month, but a family nonetheless. It feels like ages ago that he sat down in the row opposite mine with all of his crazy gifts.

I squeeze his hand back, and then I don't let go.

"It's not like she had a lot to give away for an inheritance, you know? Maybe a few furniture pieces? Some clothes that she'd had for decades?" I can't help but laugh. My grandmother was nothing if not tidy and organized. If she didn't use something, it went in the trash—a life motto that could also be used to describe her personal relationships with friends and family.

Funny how I miss her so much at the most random times.

"Anyway, it wasn't like Sam or I were concerned about any of that. He hated her taste and I did, too, but we figured we'd split it all down the middle. Then we found out that she'd left us a letter."

"A letter?"

I nod. Turning over Jackson's hand, I run my fingers over the veins, tracing them until I hit his wrist. "A letter," I confirm. "Sam didn't care to read it because let's face it, that's how Sam is. But I was in a rut . . . everything with us and then her passing away . . . I guess I wanted something of the familiar, even if she was reprimanding me in that way of hers."

Jackson's gaze flicks from my face down to his hand and then back again. I can tell he's anxious to have me spill it all. Still, he waits in silence for me to go at my own pace.

I wait as the server brings me more wine—this time, I gladly say yes—and then down a sip for liquid encouragement. "Turns out, she'd lied. For years, she let us believe that my parents took off and chose to live a different life somewhere else." Another sip of wine that goes down as smoothly as the first. "I knew they were coke addicts. Grandpa used to mutter all sorts of crap whenever Sam or I brought them up. I may have not known what any of it meant until I was much older, but I still caught the general feeling: Momma and Daddy were not good people."

Jackson's silence breaks with the sound of his chair scraping back over the stone floor. He drags the damn thing to my side of the table, turning it toward me so that when he sits down, he's effectively straddling my chair.

He's shielding me from anyone who might be watching.

The thought alone makes me want to hug him.

"Keep goin'," he rasps, one hand coming to meet mine on the table again. He twines our fingers together. It feels so wrong to look at our clasped hands and see that our ring fingers are bare. "I'm here, sweetheart."

My throat pinches with a hard swallow. "In the letter, my grandmother wrote about how she'd kept tabs on them after they left me and Sam with her and Grandpa. She didn't trust them, she said, but she'd never thought her daughter would fall into the hell that she did." When tears prick at my eyes, I dot at them with the heel of my free hand. I've had *months* to come to terms with the news, but somehow, relaying them to someone other than Sam makes it all feel more real.

More depressing.

"Momma overdosed," comes my ragged whisper. "I think I was around thirteen, my grandmother noted. I don't know if anyone attended her funeral. I don't know if she *had* a funeral. Given what little I know about her, I'm guessing probably not. I might remember her smiles and hugs, but those are child's memories. Reality paints a much darker portrait."

With his hand still clasped to mine, Jackson asks, "And your dad?"

"He's in jail."

"*Damn*." Shaking his head, Jackson's jaw tenses with emotion. "What did he do?"

"Murder." I let that settle in before I continue. "A drug deal gone wrong, I guess. Or, at least, that's what my grandmother wrote. He's going to do life at Louisiana's Angola State Penitentiary."

"Will you visit him?"

"No."

His thumb skates across the top of my hand. "You're okay for feeling this way, Holls. They abandoned you and your brother. They chose drugs over their kids, their families. I can read the guilt all over your face." He tugs on my hand until I drag my gaze up to his face. Vehemently, he growls, "Do *not* feel guilty for putting up boundaries and doing what's best for you."

I want to believe him, I do. But . . .

"I should feel guilty."

"Tell me why. Right now, tell me why you should feel anything of the sort over a man who never bothered to contact his daughter after he *left her*."

"Because when I read my grandmother's letter all I could think about was *your* mom and your dad, and the fact that at least you knew that he loved you to his dying breath."

The words slip from my mouth, and I wish I could reel them back in and staple my lips shut.

Jackson's cheeks hollow with a harsh breath. Unsurprisingly, he pulls his hand from under mine, but it's only to scrub at his face in overt frustration. "I don't see the correlation," he grits out, voice unsteady. "There *is* no correlation. My dad died overseas while serving his country. He was a patriot."

"And he *loved* you."

I never met Jackson Carter, Sr., but I'd heard enough of Momma Martha's stories to know that Jackson's father was a one-in-a-million kind of man. He spent endless hours teaching Jackson how to skate, even when the hot Texas heat would have dissuaded an average man. He went to each of Jackson's games, always showing up with his military buddies to cheer on his young son.

Momma Martha's eyes always shimmered with tears when she relayed the stories. "My husband—he loved hard just like he lived hard. I couldn't have asked for a better father or husband."

My tongue feels swollen when I speak again, determined to make Jackson see where I'm coming from. "I read those letters and I thought of your family. *Yours* encouraged you to love hard, Jackson, no matter what it was you were loving— me, hockey, your friends. Even after your dad passed, your mother never warned you off from giving something your all."

I look at my hands, at the wineglass I've forgotten I'm still holding. "You were allowed to grow bright—that's what I'm saying."

"And you were what?" Jackson says the words low and stark.

I drain the rest of my wine. "I was told that I loved too hard, Jackson. That I loved too hard and that would ultimately hurt me. My grandmother grew up in a different generation, one in which nothing was ever handed to her. Your parents led by love, my grandparents by fear. And so I read that letter of hers and I realized why she'd always told me to be careful with my heart. She knew she'd disappoint me, that others would disappoint me, and she wanted me safe."

"She was wrong."

I blink. "What?"

Jackson leans forward, and for the first time ever, I feel like I'm about to be a recipient of one of his captain pep talks. "Yesterday, you asked me about finding that high. Fun fact, sweetheart, you can't be careful and love hard all at once." Gently, he touches one finger to my chest, giving it a little poke. "It's got to be all in or all out. When I step onto the ice, I don't worry about the *what-ifs*. They've got no room in my mind. I'm there to win; I'm there to make the other team piss their pants."

"I don't see what this has to do with—"

"The same goes for Carter Photography," he goes on, cutting me off without a hint of shame. "You've stuck to the Northeast. Why?"

"Um, because it makes sense logistically?"

"Wrong." Another poke to my chest. "It's because even considering a game plan that includes countrywide domination sends you into a panic attack. I'm reading you like I do my opponents on the ice, and what I'm reading is that you haven't been lovin' hard at all. You've been too scared to even try."

My jaw drops. "I'm sorry, but did you just say that I've been *scared*?"

Confidence lines every curve of his face, including the smug smile tipping his lips. "Your parents may have been assholes, Holls, and your grandmother may have cautioned you against giving yourself up to vulnerability, but you can't live life waiting for the other anvil to drop and crush you. You want the high, crave it more than anything . . . but you won't even take the initial hit."

Emotions tangle in my throat as I fight to keep my hands from gesturing wildly in the air. "So, what do you recommend, huh? Calling every hockey team west of the Mississippi River to hire me?"

"I recommend lovin' me as hard as you can."

I swear that I don't even blink as I stare Jackson down. "*That's* your suggestion?"

His answering grin is all wickedness. "Doctor's orders."

"There's no doctor," I grit out from behind clenched teeth.

His fingers brush the side of my face. Then, leaning forward, his mouth finding the shell of my ear to husk out, "I'm not goin' anywhere, Holly. You can love me as hard as you want, and I won't budge. I'm a safe bet."

My gaze finds his.

He looks so damn earnest, genuinely wanting to help me. It does something to my insides, stripping away the fear and all the remaining worries that we might not work.

I hope we will.

No, I *believe* we will.

"I'll take that bet, sir." I slip my hand over his thigh, squeezing once, and angle my face to catch his lips with mine in a gentle kiss. "Now about that no-sweets rule . . . is dessert off the menu? Or am I the only sweetness allowed in your daily diet?"

CHAPTER 32
HOLLY

"**G**uys? Have I ever mentioned how much wax figures creep me out?"

I stifle a snort as I prod Adam in the back and urge him to keep moving along the dimly lit hallway. Although it's been ages since I've visited The Box—the unofficial Blades bar in Cambridge—there's no forgetting the narrow hall that leads from the front of the establishment to the back, the latter which is reserved exclusively for the Blades and their guests. This hall is a shrine to the best hockey players the NHL has ever seen, like some sort of modern-day equivalent of a mummified Egyptian tomb with sarcophagi.

Except that the players who've been transformed into wax replicas aren't dead in real life. Well, I think all but one or two aren't, anyway.

"If it helps," Jackson drawls from behind me, "we're coming up on Duke Harrison's figure now. We all know he's your favorite."

"It's not helping, man." Adam's shoulders twitch with a shiver. "They've got some of the beadiest eyes I've ever seen. Seriously, have you guys ever been to one of Madame

Tussaud's exhibits? My wife loves going, mainly because I think she likes to see me cry."

When we pass Duke's lifelike wax figure, I tease, "Does that mean you don't want to confiscate this one right here? I bet Madeline would be *thrilled* for you to bring home her own Duke Harrison."

Adam snaps a horrified look at me over his shoulder. "First off," he says, flustered, "low blow, boss, low blow. Second, the only place that thing is going, if it left with me, is in a firepit. Have you ever smelled the scent of burning wax? It's *glorious*."

I feel Jackson's warm hand connect with the small of my back. "Pretty sure *glorious* is not a word anyone would use to describe burning wax."

"Pretty sure that whoever makes these creatures should be put in an asylum," Adam grumbles, turning his body sideways to avoid being stabbed by the legendary Bobby Orr's hockey stick. Adam's hands come up, stomach sucked in, as he inches his way past the wax figure like Bobby might come alive at any moment and launch at him.

I'm sure good ol' Bobby will be getting a lot of reactions like that tonight. It's the mid-season finale for *Getting Pucked*, and instead of watching the show at home like everyone's done for most of the season, Mark Fillmore suggested a massive watch-party with the team, the Blades' staff, and the crew from the show.

To everyone's surprise, Jackson was the one to suggest holding the party at The Box. Since the Blades franchise began, the bar has been a well-kept secret—unless you know someone who knows someone, there's not a single chance you'd ever receive an invite.

Tonight, the bar is packed.

The minute Jackson cracks open the door to usher us in, it's safe to assume that everyone and their mother is here. Not an exaggeration. I'm pretty sure that I spot Henri Bordeaux's mom eating a slice of pizza on one of the sofas on the far side of the room.

Trying to catch Jackson's attention, I hook one of my fingers through the belt loop of his slacks. Immediately, his pace slows and he ducks his head near mine to hear me. The gesture shouldn't be as swoon-worthy as it makes me feel. But that's been Jackson's M.O ever since we spent our time in Rhode Island a few weeks ago.

We've spent almost every waking moment together since our return to Boston. If I have a shoot to handle outside of my work for the Blades, Jackson's made a concerted effort to either meet me there or be waiting after for lunch or dinner or whatever our respective schedules can manage. Thanks to *Getting Pucked*, it's not like I've had the opportunity to miss any of his practices or games, but I'm already thinking of ways that I can show my support once filming for the season has ended.

Jackson may have promised that he's a safe bet, but I desperately want to show him that he can expect the same from me too. We're in this together, no matter how long it takes for us to feel out our footsteps and truly learn to trust again. I know that we've been through too much to expect things to go back to the way they were before. And, if I'm being honest with myself, I'm not interested in any re-runs of what used to be.

Not if it means living separate lives all over again.

My hand finds Jackson's forearm, which I use for balance as I lift onto the balls of my feet and touch my nose to his ear. "How much do you want to bet that Adam trails Duke like a lost puppy tonight?" I half shout, trying to be heard over the loud chatter in the room. "I'm sensing a bromance brewing."

Jackson binds an arm around my back, shoring me up against his hard frame. "If I take you up on this bet, do I get you in my bed tonight?"

"As if that's different than any other night?"

I got him there. Boyishly, he scratches behind his ear and flashes me an endearing smile. It's all innocence, which I don't believe for one hot second. I tap him on the chest, right over his heart. "Don't give me that look."

"What look?" he asks, giving me The Look, dialed up to a hundred.

A giggle escapes my mouth. "The one where you're thinking about getting me nak—"

"Carter!"

At the masculine voice behind me, I whirl around, only to find Mark Fillmore standing there with his arm wrapped around another man's lean frame. After two months of working with *Getting Pucked*'s director, I've never seen him out of his usual attire: slacks, dark shirt, leather loafers.

That's not the Mark Fillmore who showed up tonight.

He's rocking dark-washed jeans and a burgundy turtle neck, and holy crap, but is he wearing *cowboy boots*? Not an everyday sight here in Boston, that's for sure.

"Carter, I'm *so* excited that I ran into you." Fillmore sends me a quick hello and draws the other man forward. "Sorry for pulling the fanboy act over here, but my husband Carl has always been a fan of yours."

When I make a move to step back and give them some space to talk, Jackson's arm tightens around my back and stalls my flight. Given the circumstances, I'm not sure how Mark Fillmore might take my relationship with Jackson. Had he hoped for some drama like Steven Fairfax had? When he doesn't even bat an eye at seeing Jackson and I standing so close together, I decide that Mark Fillmore probably doesn't care at all.

"As soon as I told Carl that you'd be here tonight, he *had* to come," Fillmore is saying now, all bright smiles and twin-kling eyes. "From one queen fan to another, he couldn't pass up this opportunity."

Beside me, Jackson's body freezes.

Tossing him a quick, confused glance, I fix my attention on the Fillmore couple in front of me. "A Queen fan?" I ask, my hand looping around Jackson's back to slip into the front pocket of his slacks. "Like, *We Are the Champions* Queen?" I bump Jackson's hip with mine. "How appropriate, right? This season is totally reminding me of a scene from *The Mighty Ducks* when Emilio Estevez first met the team."

"Emilio Estevez?" Fillmore asks, brows drawn together.

"Coach Bombay? You know, now that I think about it, it'd be hilarious to do a round-table interview with the guys on which player they think they're most like from the movie." Slyly, I prop my chin on Jackson's arm and glance up at his face. "You'd be Charlie Conway, I think. Stoic, an over-achiever, the captain."

Jackson's throat works with a hard swallow, his Adam's apple dodging downward. "Fillmore's, ah, not talking about Queen."

"No?"

A flush crests over Jackson's cheekbones. "No, he, uh . . ." He hooks a finger over the starched collar of his button-down, pulling at the material in obvious discomfort. "He's talking about—"

"Celine Dion," says Fillmore's husband, Carl. "The *true* queen."

I think, maybe, a sound emerges from my throat. It's tough to tell when I'm choking on air and burying my face in Jackson's arm. *Celine Dion*? Not that there's anything wrong with her—she's got an *amazing* voice—but Jackson is more of a heavy metal or rock connoisseur. The more screaming, the happier he is. He wouldn't know a Celine Dion song if it bit him in the butt.

Jackson fidgets under my touch. "Listen, Carl, I think it's great that you're a fan but—"

"I asked the bartender if he could play us *My Heart Will Go On*."

Oh, oh this is *too* good.

Conspiratorially, I lean toward Carl. "You mean, like karaoke?"

I don't think I've ever seen a man smile the way Carl does now. He positively lights up at the mere thought of rocking it out to some Celine with his athlete crush, Jackson. "That would be lovely!" he exclaims, hands already forming a fake mic and a stand. In pure mime fashion, he dips the invisible stand like he's impersonating Elvis Presley, and even begins to tap one foot in beat to the rhythm playing in his head.

"I think I need to piss."

"You're fine," I tell the terrified man beside me as he eyes the bathroom over the sea of heads. "You play in front of thousands of fans weekly. What's one little song with a fan?"

His dark eyes narrow to slits. "I don't know, *sweetheart*," he grinds out, mouth next to my ear, "how about you find out with me?"

I jerk back. "No way am I singing with y'all. No effing way." Pointing at my chest, I feel my anxiety spark to life. "I'm the woman behind the camera, not the one in front of it."

Jackson quirks a brow. "Scared?"

"*Yes*. Are you kidding me? Of course I'm scared."

"Great, I am too. Let's go." Jackson wraps a hand around mine. "Carl, you comin'? I'm doing this one time and one time only. You're in or you're out."

CARL CHOSE TO BE IN, which is how the three of us end up belting out *My Heart Will Go On* before all of our peers while we wait for the *Getting Pucked* episode to begin at the start of the hour. Much to my chagrin, Carl doesn't take center stage, apparently more content to remain in the background and hum the melodies.

Unfortunately, both Jackson and I are completely tone-deaf and only know half of the words.

I try to make up for it by bringing in my old dance skills and prancing about the makeshift stage—we're standing on a rug, literally—while all eyes are glued on us. Jackson, for all of his skills on the ice, might as well be a tree. He sways a little, mic close to his mouth, and watches the ceiling like he keeps hoping it'll open up and drop down on him.

His teammates are beside themselves.

Beaumont throws dollar bills at us, hollering for Jackson to sing louder for the peeps in the back of the crowd.

Hunt has Gwen, his wife and my publicist, clutched to him as he twirls her around.

Even Coach Hall is laughing at his captain's expense.

"All for the fans," Jackson had muttered before Celine came blasting over the loudspeakers.

I dance up to him now, my free hand reaching out to clasp his. He stares at me, eyes round, no doubt trying to dissuade me from making this even more like hell for him.

Too late.

There's nothing I love more than to see Jackson Carter lose control.

"Love was when I love you," I sing into the microphone, not even bothering to wince when my voice cracks. I'm no Celine Dion, folks, but I *am* Holly Carter, and I'm ready to make Jackson come undone. "One true time I hold tooooo!"

The tense lines in his face break.

I coast my palm over his chest, swinging my hips. My gaze meets his, and this time, *I'm* the one issuing the dare, the challenge. "Your turn, Cap. Sing to me."

He looks at me like he wouldn't mind throwing me over his shoulder and tossing me out of The Box forever.

He looks at me like I'm all he's ever wanted, even when I'm hell-bent on driving him insane.

And then, in front of everyone and their mother (literally), Jackson sings to me.

It's *awful*, maybe even as bad as his cooking. His husky

pitch never climbs high enough to hit the notes and he stumbles his way through the chorus with red cheeks. When Weston Cain shouts at us to get a room, Jackson only flips him the bird and proceeds to throw his head back, one arm jabbing forward like he's playing a set of drums. The grand finale comes with a crack in his voice and a dramatic wiggle of his hips.

I laugh so hard that I have tears gathering in my eyes.

I laugh so hard that when the bartender takes mercy on us all and switches the music off mid-word, cutting Jackson off, I double over and breathe through my nose before I pass out from sheer joy overload.

A warm hand grazes my lower spine, flirting with the waistband of my skirt, and it doesn't take a genius to figure out which person those fingers belong to. Jackson touches me like he owns me, body and soul, and I can't deny anymore that he does.

He tangles our fingers together, and then he's bent over too and whispering in my ear, "Happy now?"

I kiss the corner of his mouth. Then whisper back, "Always you."

His hand tightens reflexively around mine. "Fuck, Holly. You have no idea how much that—"

"Carter!"

We jerk upright, and my gaze flicks over the crowd. At my ninety degrees, I watch as the Blades' on-hand doctor comes striding toward us.

Jackson breaks our connection and shoves his hand through his hair. He blows out a heavy breath that sounds rife with sudden tension. "John, man, hey." He reaches out a hand to shake the doctor's. "How's everything?"

"Good." John spares me a barely there glance. "Listen, you got a sec? I know the show's about to start, but I got your voicemail and wanted to catch you before I head out on vacation on Monday."

For as many years as Jackson's been with the Blades—or any NHL team—it's never been a secret that the team doctor is persona non grata for the players. On a personal level, I'm sure none of them have a problem with John. He's a good guy, has a great family whom I've met a few times, and who always wants the best for the team. Professionally, though, a meeting with John means that something is wrong.

Until now, I didn't realize that anything was wrong with Jackson, at all.

I politely excuse myself to give them privacy to talk about whatever it is that Jackson left the voicemail about. My ex-husband sends me a quick, beseeching look over his shoulder that I can't even begin to decipher. When John thumps a hand on Jackson's back, the look turns to stone and he twists away.

He's wearing his gameday face. That stony expression is the same one that filters over his face like a mask the minute he steps on the ice and decimates his opponents.

Unease slithers through my veins.

I should wait for Jackson to tell me whatever it is that he's keeping a secret. Eavesdropping on his conversation would hurt the trust we're so desperately trying to rebuild. My hands curl in at my sides, and I'm surprised how physically *torn* I feel between walking away or stepping in close to over-hear what's going on.

I'm a safe bet, he told me two weekends ago.

The truth is, I love Jackson. I don't think I've ever stopped loving him. And I won't stoop to listening in on his conversation to learn why his smile disappeared and he looked back at me like he was being led to the gallows.

In the end, I pay the bartender for a glass of wine and then find an empty seat to watch the mid-season finale. He'll tell me when he's ready—and, whatever it is that's troubling him, I'll prove to him that we'll face it together.

CHAPTER 33
JACKSON

I don't want to be alone.

It's the first thought that enters my mind when I pull into an empty spot at the Mass General parking lot on Monday morning. Quickly, I scan the digital clock on the dashboard.

11:14.

I have sixteen minutes until my appointment with Dr. Mebowitz.

I'm dreading the hell out of it, especially now that I know all the issues I've been having aren't related to any undiscovered spinal injuries. John, the team doctor, assured me that I looked in tip-top shape after reviewing all my scans.

"Excuse the corniness, but you're as healthy as an ox, Cap," he'd told me at the *Getting Pucked* mid-season finale watch-party. "There's nothing out of the ordinary. Some swelling in the joints, that fissure in your patella that's never really healed. But other than that? You're solid and looking great for the season."

You're solid and looking great for the season.

The words felt like a punch to the gut. Wasn't that the fucked-up truth? To the random onlooker, I don't *look* ill. I don't have any bones bursting through the skin or a lopsided gait thanks to a limp.

I look just fine.

If only my brain would get on the same playing field.

Dragging in a fistful of air, I drop my forehead to the top of my steering wheel.

For over a year, I've ignored the signs: the constant headaches, the regular fogginess, the sluggishness when I play hard on the ice, and the way my body has begun to feel like it's always one step behind my brain.

Without hockey, who am I?

I don't know. *I don't fucking know!*

Another glance at the clock reveals that time is ticking away from me.

11:21.

I need to go inside. I need to do something besides sit in my car and stress about factors that I can't change. I can't change that I've had concussions. I can't change that I fell in love with a sport that has done damage to my body, in a way that remains invisible to everyone but me. I can't change that I live for the sound of skates slashing over ice or the feeling of pride that I experience every time I pull on my Blades jersey.

I'm no idiot. I've played in The Show for longer than many other players will ever have the chance to do. I've left my mark on the sport, both through my own successes and the work I've done with the rookies each year.

Call me crazy but walking up to this appointment feels like I'm going through another divorce all over again.

11:27.

"Fuck."

Throwing the door open, I shoot out from the car and head for the entrance. My strides are quick, clipped, as I angle past doctors in white coats and patients as they're shuffled from one room to another. Some of them look sick: jaundiced skin, thin bodies.

Some, like myself, show no outward signs of having anything wrong.

The Badass of Hockey isn't feeling so badass today, I think, as I palm open a swinging door and wait for the elevator that'll bring me to Dr. Mebowitz's office. When it *pings!* I step inside, head down. Pull out my phone and check the time once more.

11:33.

I'm late. Well, at least I'm not a year late like the first time I showed up here.

The elevator doors swing open and I step out, feeling like I might vomit. My stomach twists unpleasantly—to say nothing of the pounding coming to life in my head. And then I finally admit to myself what I haven't wanted to for so long: I'm terrified. I've always been a man who takes what life throws at him with a grain of salt. I rule with confidence, strength, and control. But with this . . . with this, I'm scared fucking shitless.

I don't want to do this alone.

My heart thuds erratically in my chest as I fumble for my phone.

"Ah! You're here, Mr. Carter. I was beginning to think that you were going to stand me up for yet another year."

I thumb through my contacts, praying to the cell-phone-service gods, until I come across her name. Stepping back, I mutter something unintelligible to the doctor before I give him my back and eye my phone's screen for the little bars to shoot to full service.

"C'mon," I grind out, "c'mon, c'mon, you mother*fucker*—"

There! Right there.

I lock my feet in place, tap on Holly's name, and wait.

And wait.

And fucking wait some more until—

"Hello?" comes her sweet voice over the line, and my knees nearly collapse with relief. "Jackson?"

My voice emerges as a rasp, "I need you." I slam my lids

shut and tilt my face up like I'm going to wish on a fake shooting star in the middle of a damn hospital. "I'm at Mass General. Dr. Mebowitz—he's in neuropathology."

Her panicked gasp echoes in my ears, and I rush to add, "I'm okay. I mean, I'm *not*. But it's not . . . it's not an accident." I swallow thickly, the emotions tangling in my throat as the anxiety latches onto my lungs. "I need you here with me, Holls. Fuck, I—*I need you*."

"I'm coming. Whatever it is, I'm there, okay?" There's the sound of a door slamming shut and jangling keys. "I'll be there in fifteen—in the car now. I love you, Jackson. I love you so damn much."

There's the *click* of the line going dead.

And then I turn around and walk into Dr. Mebowitz's office, feeling like I'm walking into my execution.

I love you, Jackson.

My ass collides with the same chair I took last time, and I wait.

For whatever news Dr. Mebowitz is about to hand over.

For the woman I love more than life itself to get here and take my hand.

For my life as a hockey player—as captain of the Blades—to come crashing to an end.

CHAPTER 34
HOLLY

I don't remember the drive from my office to Mass General.

In full honesty, I don't remember much besides the tremble in my hands and Jackson's words on repeat in my head: *I need you here with me, Holls.*

He needs me.

He needs me.

He needs me.

It's on a constant loop, never lessening to anything else but a thunderous roar in my head.

By some twist of fate, I spot Jackson's car in the parking garage and pull my vehicle into the empty spot two down from his. I'd been on my way to a photo shoot with the Boston Celtics when he called, my backpack slung over one shoulder as I took the stairs down to my car.

I cancelled the photo shoot via email, my brain so wired on Jackson that I didn't even think to send my team there without me. No, my brain went to one thing only: Jackson was in trouble and nothing else mattered.

I leave my backpack on the passenger's seat where I tossed it haphazardly upon first getting in my car. If someone wants to be a jerk and steal it while I'm at a hospital, let them have it.

With lightning-quick steps, I hustle out of my car and toward the hospital with only one destination in mind.

I'm forced to ask for directions twice before I finally find Dr. Mebowitz's office. My fist hammers on the closed door, matching the beat of my heart, before I hear two masculine voices talking.

The door swings open.

"Ah, Mrs. Carter." The doctor staring down at me smiles widely. "I'm so pleased you could make it." He steps to the side, gesturing for me to slip past him. "Come in, come in. Jackson has been waiting for you."

Seated in a chair before a behemoth-sized desk, Jackson props an arm on the back of the seat and twists his torso. Meets my gaze silently.

We don't need words, not in this moment. To anyone else, I'd have no doubt that they'd take one look at him and see the Jackson Carter he's always portrayed to the world: formidable, unshakable, with confidence that borders the line of arrogance.

But I know him, and what I read in his dark eyes shatters me.

Oh, Jackson.

"Coffee or tea?" Dr. Mebowitz asks me. "If you'd like either, I'll have my secretary bring us some."

I shake my head. No, no coffee or tea.

Silently, I take the empty seat next to Jackson's. Without waiting for him to move first, I reach out and slip my hand through his. Squeeze his fingers once, just to let him know that I'm here and I'm not going anywhere.

We're a family. We're in this together, no matter what a slip of paper says.

He's utterly silent as he tugs our clasped hands up, up, up and presses a kiss to my knuckles. And then, so softly I almost don't hear it, "Always you, sweetheart. Always you."

Everything in me goes taut at the whispered words, meant for my ears only. I won't cry, not here in an office in front of a doctor I don't even know, but those are *definitely* pinpricks of tears blurring my vision right now.

With nothing to wipe them dry with, I settle for accepting that this is who I am right now: a woman so in love with a man that she'll drop everything, *everything*, to be *his* knight in shining armor. For the length of our marriage, Jackson was the one, out of the two of us, who remained completely unflappable. He rescued me, fed my high on him and on love.

It's my turn to return the favor—and I do.

As Dr. Mebowitz explains to me about traumatic brain injuries and CTE and his early suspicions as to Jackson's symptoms, I don't cry. I don't whimper, even when each word feels like a knife being dragged through my heart. I remain strong because Jackson needs me to be.

Never once do I let go of his hand.

"And these tests—when will they happen?" I ask.

Dr. Mebowitz fingers through a calendar planner. "Sooner rather than later. They've been set up by my team, now that we've ruled out any possible skeletal possibilities." As though realizing he's given us a lot to digest, he presses a flat palm to the calendar. "This is not . . . this is not a short case study, Jackson. I've had players just like yourself walk in here with no memory to speak of, others who've lost the ability to walk. The longevity of which you've been experiencing all of your symptoms leads me to make the assessment that you *do* have TBI. And, perhaps, maybe, CTE—although that remains to be seen."

"But?" I push, when he trails off.

"*But*, you are certainly an early case. That works in our benefit, to be sure."

"And hockey?"

"I'll need to quit."

My head jerks toward Jackson. "You don't know if it'll come to that. Tests first, right, Dr. Mebowitz? The season is—"

"A month in." Jackson tugs his hand from mine, elbows dropping to his thighs and his head falling into his upturned hands. He looks . . . broken. I don't think I've ever wanted to hug him more. "You heard what he said. I could—I could forget everything. What kinda life is that to live, Holls? Me and you, say we have kids in two, three years. You want me forgetting things that they've done? Parts of *our* life that I no longer remember to tell them?"

I don't know which part to reply to first, the fact that he's worried about memory loss or that he mentioned kids *with me*. A single glance at Dr. Mebowitz reveals that he's left the office, probably to give us some privacy.

Ex-husband.

Ex-wife.

And yet I've never loved him more.

I sink my hand into the soft, thick strands of his hair. Dig the pads of my fingers into his skull, gently massaging his head. "When we have kids," I tell him, my voice wavering with emotion, "they're going to know that their father was the biggest badass the NHL has ever seen. They'll know about the time your best friend busted your face so bad that he broke your cheekbone and that oh-so-pretty one you have now is straight metal." Pushing my chair back, I lower to my knees on the thin area rug and force Jackson to look at me. Tears cling to his dark lashes, and I lean up and kiss his closed lids. "They'll boast to all their friends about the time their dad won the Stanley Cup, broken *paella*—"

"Patella," he says on a choked laugh, "not *paella*."

"Just wanted to see if you were paying attention." I give him the smallest smile. "And when we tell them that Daddy finished his last season playing for the Blades, he did it with the Cup coming home one last time."

"Holly—"

"Not all superheroes wear capes, Jackson." I squeeze his hands and bring them to my chest. "Dig deep and find another way to make your dream a reality. Now let's wrap this up with Dr. Mebowitz so we can go home, and I can take care of you."

CHAPTER 35
HOLLY

"H ome" turns out to be Jackson's condo.
I'd like to pretend that we sit down and immediately dive into a conversation about everything we discussed with Dr. Mebowitz. Instead, the only conversation that's happening is the one between our bodies.

The door closes behind Jackson, and then I'm being yanked into his embrace. I go willingly, rising onto my toes to shorten the distance from my mouth to his. Our lips collide in a kiss that's raw and desperate.

It's exactly how I feel: desperate.

For him.

For us.

"I'm sorry," he rasps between kisses, his hands clutching my hips and keeping me close. "I'm so sorry for letting us fall apart. This year . . . these last *three* years." His kiss turns aggressive, nipping at my lips before sweeping his tongue into my mouth.

He kisses me like he plays hockey: with every last corner of his soul.

And I kiss him with every inch of my heart.

I hook an arm around the nape of his neck, tugging his

big frame down until we're as close to eye level as we'll ever be. Dark eyes stare into mine, the hue already so close to black that I can't even tell if his pupils have dilated with lust. "What we have . . . what we have doesn't stay between the lines. It's messy and beautiful and one-of-a-kind. It's *us*."

Jackson groans into my mouth, like the words are everything he needed to hear, and the sound is so guttural that it goes straight to my core and burns me up with lust. Wanting him naked, I flatten my hand and move it from his neck to his traps. I claw the cotton T-shirt into a fist, then drag the material over his head.

He releases me long enough for me to strip him half-naked.

"Turn around."

Biting down on my lip, I do as he says and present him with my back. My head drops as I wait for him to make his move.

He does, slowly.

My shirt, like his, is pulled up until I blink, and I see fabric, and then blink again and Jackson's living room comes back into place. Calloused fingers stroke down the pearls of my spine in light, feathery touches. The band of my bra tightens, making it momentarily hard to breathe—and then loosens when the cups fall from my breasts. I let the undergarment fall to the floor.

Masculine lips collide with my shoulder blades. The space behind my ear that never fails to make me quiver. Down they travel, covering the expanse of my back until Jackson pauses and I hear him lower to his knees.

"Grip the table, sweetheart."

My tongue feels swollen as I move into place, fingers finding the lip of the entryway table that's waist-high. When I feel Jackson at my back, kissing the base of my spine, there's no more hope of ever catching my breath. Particularly not when my skirt is inched down my legs, my boy shorts right along with it.

Jackson's palms cradle my butt, his thumbs pressing inward in small circles. "I don't know what I did to deserve you—other than being caught with the same truck as Cornell's goalie, that is."

It's not what I expected him to say, and laugher spills from my lips. Twisting at my waist, I peer down at him behind me. Reach forward and cup his face, and murmur, "Don't worry, yours is the only car I've ever vandalized."

"Better be," he grunts with male satisfaction. His hands graze my skin as he hooks them around my outer thighs. "I knew right then that no one would ever make me feel the way you do."

Breath catching when he inches my legs apart, I manage an uneven, "And how is that?"

"Like I'm home." His brown eyes zero in on my face, rooting me in place with the intensity that I see in them. "You walked into my life fourteen years ago, Holls, and you turned the whole damn thing upside down. And when things came tumbling, I had no idea how to stop it from shattering alto-gether. I let you down, sweetheart, and for that, I'll never forgive myself."

"Jackson, you can't—"

He kisses the back of one thigh, shutting me up. "Let me get this out."

My core clenches at the command in his voice. I can't force myself to look away, not yet. It hasn't escaped my notice that I'm naked—so very, very naked—while he's mostly clothed. "Go on, then."

His smile is fleeting but grateful. "I fucked up in letting you walk out of my life, but I think—in some weird, screwed-up way—I knew that signing on for *Getting Pucked* would mean having you back in my life . . . if I could only convince you to take on the job."

Just like that, realization hits me square in the face. "The interference," I whisper, "this is what you meant, isn't it, when you said that you were being selfish in asking me to take on the job with the show? You wanted to ensure that nothing about your headaches or visits with Dr. Mebowitz would make it on TV."

Dark lashes fall closed as he drops his gaze to the floor. His shoulders rise and fall with a deep-seated sigh, and this time I turn around completely, unable to keep my back to him when we have this conversation.

Voice ragged, he manages, "Everything I've been feeling . . . I've been feelin' it for a while. Enough that, after we divorced, I finally worked up the nerve to go to a doctor about all the migraines."

I furrow my brows, confusion slicking through me. "But Dr. Mebowitz, he said that you never showed up? Right?"

Jackson lifts his head, his expression revealing all of the pain he's kept locked down for so very long. "I showed up. Once." He laughs bitterly. "Everything he told me, though, had me running and never looking back. I'd lost you, Holly, and the idea of losing hockey, too . . . God, it felt like I'd stepped into my own version of hell." Shaking his head, he continues, "I'm stubborn, as we know, but I'm not stupid. Everything felt worse this year . . . more acute, more . . . debilitating, I guess you could say. I knew I'd have to go back at some point, and I knew that there was only one person I could ever trust to keep my secret."

"Me."

"You." Holding my gaze, he says, "You, the girl I knew I'd marry within weeks of meeting her." He gently spins me back around, one big palm landing on my lower back to apply pressure and tip my butt up into the air. My chest grazes the cool marble table. "You, the girl who gave me everything she was and loved me just right." The heat of his arm circles my leg, and I don't even have the chance to think about what's happening until his middle finger is already pressing down on my clit. A moan tears from my throat.

"You," Jackson goes on, as though he's not driving me mad, "the girl who I lost, the girl I love. I should have told you about Dr. Mebowitz earlier than now but admitting the pain to you would make it real. Permanent in a way I desperately wish it wasn't. And I didn't want to change the way you look at me. I didn't want you to see me as anyone but the man who loves you beyond reason. But I realized today . . . I can't do this without you by my side. I need your strength when I've got none left. I need your love when everything feels like it's going to hell. No one compares to you, Holly. Not for me. For me, it's always been you."

A cry bursts from my lungs when I feel his tongue dive between my legs, stroking along my seam. My hands turn to fists on the edge of the table as pleasure sinks into my limbs.

I arch my back and catch my gaze reflected back at me from the mirror above the table. I see nothing of Jackson from my vantage point, just the crown of his head, but I see *all* of me. My hard nipples and my tight stomach. My half-closed eyes and my open mouth. When Jackson sucks on my clit, I mewl like a satisfied kitten—and my shoulders roll with me as I stretch to give Jackson better reach.

It's erotic, watching myself as Jackson works me to abandon.

Two fingers sink into my heat, and colors blooms in my cheeks. I catch myself driving back against those fingers, against his circling tongue on my clit, and, for the first time, I see the woman Jackson must see.

A woman who loves just right; a woman who's fiercely loyal and will always, *always*, give every last bit of her soul; a woman who isn't afraid to get dirty if she believes in the cause.

Jackson may be the one on his knees, but *I'm* the one feeling as though I've been knocked on my butt and forced to wake up and see the world for what it is, disallowing my grandmother's revelations to dictate how I live.

"Another," I beg Jackson shamelessly.

He must know exactly what I mean because a third finger joins the first two. It only takes two more pumps of his fingers to send me teetering over into an orgasm. I come, not looking at myself in the mirror but twisted at the waist so I can stare down at the man between my legs. His dark eyes snap up to mine, and maybe it's that instant connection that does it, but the subsiding orgasm rocks into another one. My legs tremble under my weight, my inner walls locking tight on his fingers.

"Hell," he grunts, his breath hot on my swollen clit, "you're so damn gorgeous."

Jackson picks me up and carries my limp body to the bed. He lays me down with care, crawls over me, and brushes his lips with mine. "You up for the main course?"

"Since it's your body and not your cooking?" I slide my hands down his muscular spine. "Get naked, Mr. Carter."

I help him out of his jeans, unbuckling his belt and tugging down the zipper. He stands on the floor and I kneel on all fours on the bed. When I tug down his jeans and briefs, I take his hard-on in hand and give it a firm stroke. "One more appetizer," I mutter when he begins to pull away, "it's my favorite one."

Kissing the crown of his cock, I slide my tongue down the length of him.

"Oh, *shit*."

I reward his responsiveness with sucking him into my mouth. On each upward glide, I hollow my cheeks and apply the pressure at the root with my tight fist. I keep my eyes open, unwilling to miss anything, and there's no mistaking the way the veins in his thighs leap each time I squeeze him a little tighter. One glance up at his chest and it's so very clear that he's having a hard time regulating his breath.

"*Holly*." He spits out my name on a ragged breath, his hands coming to the back of my head to control my pace.

Not happening.

I promptly swallow as much of his length as I can handle, and his knees give out.

Just when I think he's about to go down for good, he swoops forward and throws me back on the bed. In jerky motions, he yanks open the dresser drawer and pulls out one of the condoms that we bought upon our return from Newport.

It's on the tip of my tongue to tell him to go without but I'm not on birth control and we have enough on our plates with the grand unknown in front of us. As he rips the foil and rolls the condom on, I cradle his face and kiss him hard.

"You're my high, Jackson Carter," I say against his mouth, my legs already spreading so he can fit between them. "You're my family. You called me today and I've never"—I swallow past the lump in my throat—"I've never been so scared in my life. You asked me once if I feel fulfilled from photography. I do, but I . . ." I kiss his cheek, his chin. "There's nothing in this world that makes me feel happier than you. And I know how ridiculous that sounds—how I've always wanted to build something of my own and be successful."

The head of his cock lines up with my entrance and in a single push, he thrusts home. We hiss simultaneously, his hands on either side of my head and mine clinging to his shoulders. "You can have both, sweetheart," he growls as he pulls out, then drives forward, filling me up to completion. "You're a superhero with a camera." Another slow glide out and inward push that curls my toes in the sheets. "You're a woman who's loved more than she'll ever know."

I gasp when he flicks his finger over my clit. "And you?" I ask on a throaty moan. "What are you?"

"I'm yours, however you'll have me. Now. Forever."

His thrusts pick up speed and I bow my back when he hits the most *delicious* spot. He does it again, and again, and yet again. I crane my neck against the mattress, relishing the way his always-so-carefully-constructed control splinters. Gripping my hips, he pushes my legs wide and powers into me.

My hands fist the bedsheets.

My gaze never leaves from his.

He changes his angle, leaning forward so that each thrust glides along my clit, the pressure there so acute that I come apart.

"Oh, God, Jackson!"

"I love you," he growls, "and I'm never letting you go again."

Dropping his hands to the flat of my belly, he drives into me, and this time, he follows me into oblivion with my name on his lips.

I welcome his bulky weight in my arms, and as he comes off the high of his own orgasm, he kisses the top of my breast. "You have something to tell me, Holls."

"Yes, I'll marry you again."

He props his chin on my chest. "That wasn't even a question. Now tell me that other thing."

"We're about to have company?"

Jackson stills in my arms. "We're *what*?"

"Company." I lift my hips and wriggle them side to side, just to mess with his head. "You might want to get up. I don't know what time it is, but I told them we'd need an hour."

"An *hour?*" Leaping from the bed, Jackson stares down at my naked body and then at his dick, which is still mostly hard. "Please tell me you didn't invite my mother."

I roll over on my side, bending one elbow so I can lay the side of my face on it. Not going to lie, there's something rather amazing about watching stoic, formidable Jackson Carter lose a little of that reserved edge of his. Just to see him flush, I singsong, "You might want to put on some clothes.

Momma Martha doesn't need to see any of *that*." I wave at his nakedness.

Jackson looks like there's nothing he'd love more than to jump out of the closest window.

"*Any* minute now." I roll over onto my back and do my best to kick the smile off my face. "I'll just stay here, if you don't mind."

"Hell no. Are you kidding?" He trips over a stray pair of shoes in his haste to pull on a pair of briefs, then half hobbles to the dresser. "You, ma'am, better get your pretty ass dressed. I'm not facing my mom alone after all of—"

Raising up onto my elbows, I stare him down. "All of what? *Sex*?" You'd think that after all these years of being married, the Beast of the Northeast, the *Badass* of Hockey, wouldn't be terrified to talk to his momma about the birds and the bees.

Luckily for him, Momma Martha isn't our visitor for today.

"*Caaarterrrrr!*" Ensue banging on the front door.

Right on time.

Jackson's handsome face turns toward the front of the condo. "Who was that?"

I roll my eyes. God, men. Sometimes you really do have to spell it all out for them. "It was the Ghost of Christmas Past." I pause, letting him soak up all of that brilliant sarcasm, and then add, "I called in the reinforcements."

"Carter! We're coming in and you better be dressed!"

"No naked dicks, either! Unless you really did get that penis reconstructive surgery—then I'm intrigued!"

Jackson pauses halfway in pulling up his jeans, understanding dawning in his expression. "You invited the guys."

I crawl to the edge of the mattress, then swing my feet to the floor. Naked as the day I was born, I amble over to Jackson and hop up on my tiptoes to press a kiss to the underside of his jaw. "Family doesn't come down to a piece of paper," I say, brushing my hand over his bare chest. "It doesn't matter if you have a hockey contract or a marriage license marking it as true and legal." Palm flat on his heart, I risk a glance up his face. "You need them just as you need me. Now go let them in before they break the door down."

"Christ, Holls." He wraps his arms around me, lifting me off the floor in one of his tight, familiar hugs. "I love you."

"I love you, too, Jackson." Pausing, I tap his chest with a finger. Once. Twice. Then, "Even if you did opt for penis reconstructive surgery."

I'm over his shoulder in the very next breath, my butt to the ceiling and his palm clamped down on it. "You're going to pay for that one, sweetheart."

"Yeah?" I stare at the tight globes of his ass. Honestly, this isn't a bad view. I could get used to it, gladly. "You're here-after banned from the kitchen."

"Fun-killer."

"CARTER! Goddamn, will you two stop hooking up and let us in?"

Eventually, Jackson puts me down.

Eventually, I dress before he lets his teammates inside.

I watch them like a military sergeant watches his platoon members, checking each one off my mental list as they come to talk with Jackson and offer him an ear from his peers, people who know the risks of the game.

Duke Harrison.

Andre Beaumont.

Marshall Hunt.

Henri Bordeaux.

Weston Cain.

Turns out, the immature one in the Safe Space group thread was the rookie, Josh Kammer, and he comes in too, bringing up the rear.

They crowd Jackson in the living room, threatening to sit on his face if he doesn't open up and tell them everything.

When I pause in the kitchen to gather plates and utensils for the food Duke brought, I grab my phone and scroll through the new group message I began on our separate drives back to Jackson's condo, appropriately titled, *The Best Group Thread To Ever Exist.*

ME:

Rules of this thread.

1) I'm in charge. 2) Repeat: I'm in charge. 3) No mention of sweet cheeks or you're out. 4) Are you in?

HARRISON:

At least I can listen to someone else be in charge. Jackson never shuts up.

CAIN:

The sweet cheeks are a thing of the past.

BEAUMONT:

You're killing my vibe but I'm in.

HUNT:

New rule—Beaumont can't text more than once an hour.

KAMMER:

Is it wrong that I'm just excited I was invited? #fullconfession

ME:

Jackson needs y'all. I can't give information without his okay, but I know that he'll feel better with you guys here. We're heading back to his condo now. If you could make the time . . . we'll be ready for you in an hour.

BORDEAUX:

I coming.

HUNT:

I'm on my way.

CAIN:

omw

BEAUMONT:

Is it creepy if I sit outside his door and wait?
Kidding, you never have to ask. Carter needs
us and I'm there.

KAMMER:

You got it!

HARRISON:

Carter has dropped everything for us for
years now. I'm heading there now. I'll pick up
pizza so we've got food.

Familiar arms pull me into an equally familiar embrace.
And then that voice . . . that same voice that has whispered in
my ear for nearly fourteen years, whispers the sweetest words
I've ever heard: "Always you, Holls. Always you."

CHAPTER 36
JACKSON

Six Months Later

"**N**ow *that* was a cliffhanger if we ever saw one, right? No kidding, I don't think I've felt so on the edge of my seat since the last *Game of Thrones* season."

The audience around me cheers on Dominic DaSilva, Sports 24/7's notorious analyst, as he moves across the stage with a microphone in hand. I've met the guy once before, back when I was a rookie with the Bruins and he was in his second season playing football for the Tampa Bay Buccaneers.

Fast forward a decade and we're both old geezers who had our seasons and careers ended prematurely. Six months ago, I wasn't quite ready to pack in the proverbial bag—and I didn't. Stubborn ass that I am, I straddled the fence for as long as I could hold out. I played hard on the ice and played hard off it, too, with doctor appointments and therapy, and *Getting Pucked* following me from one place to another.

I had my eye on the Cup, and I'd be damned if anything impeded that.

In March, Dr. Mebowitz got his wish. A hard hit from a

Canadiens D-man had me seeing stars for weeks. Stubborn or not, there was no coming back from a body check like that. I'd been sidelined by an asshole with a unibrow and a weird, idol-like obsession with Beaumont.

Holly told me it was fitting that Andre was the one to bust in my cheek, taking me out for half a season years ago, and the guy who wanted to *be* Andre was the one to end my pro-hockey career for good.

I don't think it was fitting so much as it was ironic, but there's life for you.

One fucked-up string of ironic event after ironic event.

"Well, I've got some news for all of you tonight," DaSilva goes on, looking like some sort of mafioso up on the stage. He's not wearing a single thread that's not black—and the ladies in the crowd love him for it, if their initial swooning when he got up on stage is anything to go by. "*Getting Pucked* has not only allowed us access to a clip of the exclusive interview between Jackson Carter and Holly Carter before it airs on primetime TV next week, but we'll be joined by Mr. Carter himself on stage following that."

Wild applause erupts in the massive hall.

I slide a glance over to Holly, who's seated next to me in the front row of the theater. She looks gorgeous with her blond hair down around her shoulders and wearing that same blue dress that I stripped her out of months ago. Reaching for her hand, feeling the cool gold of her wedding band on her third finger, I pull it onto my lap, needing her touch and support.

"You're going to be fine," she says for me only, cupping our clasped hands with her free one. "If you can sing *My Heart Will Go On* to a bunch of hockey players, you can go up there and talk to a crowd about the sport you love so much. Plus, you've got another few minutes before you have to leave this seat. I believe in you."

"The singing happened because you were up there with

me." I duck my head, brushing my lips across her temple. "You wanna come up on the stage with me?"

"Not a chance." She smooths my swollen knuckles with her thumb. "But I will *absolutely* come with you later, if you know what I mean."

My cock stiffens in my slacks. "Tease."

"Took your mind off the talk, didn't it?"

She's right, it did. At least, momentarily, until the lights in the theater dim and my face quite literally makes it on the big screen. It's jarring to see myself as everyone else does, and not for the first time do I think about the fact that I *look* normal. And, for the most part, I feel normal, too.

"Tell me your name," I hear Holly say over the surround-sound speakers, "and two facts about you that fans wouldn't know." She's not visible to the viewers, purposely seated behind the camera, so as to allow me to remain the sole focus of the episode.

Getting Pucked's season-one finale.

I watch as I fidget in the frame, this big-ass dude constantly fiddling with his Blades ball cap until he *thwacks* it against his thigh and leaves it dangling from his knee. "I'm Jackson Carter, and I love belting out Celine Dion lyrics with my wife, generally loud enough for our neighbors to come banging on our door at all hours of the night. I, uh, also love hockey."

It was Holly's idea to approach Mark Fillmore about the final interview. I'd been hesitant at first, unwilling to even consider the level of vulnerability necessary to do something like this—open my heart and my fears to the public.

I wouldn't have done it, either, except that my wife had one very good point: "You have a voice, Jackson. Fans adore you and players admire you, and I swear, you have enough trophies under your belt to fill an entire room. Lend that voice to someone who might not have it."

In the clip, Holly poses the next question: "Why do you love hockey?"

I smooth real-life Holly's hand flat on my thigh, playing with the same wedding ring I put on her finger almost twelve years ago now. We wed on a different day for the second time around but decided to keep our rings. To the utter surprise of no one, neither of us had thrown them out or sold them to a pawn shop.

It was fate, obviously.

A shooting star that took pity on me and made my wish happen.

"Hockey feeds my soul," I hear myself respond huskily, "it's my high. I don't drink, I don't do drugs, but for years, hockey has satisfied the adrenaline junkie in me. It was the thing that I did with my dad, who was a military intelligence officer in the Army. He deployed a lot, while I was growing up, but he'd come back home and ask how my skating was doing. The ice allowed me to thrive, it allowed me to grow up and discover the man I was meant to be."

There's a small pause in our interview and though the public will never know, thanks to the miracle that is video editing, it was in that moment where Holly held me while I broke. I didn't shed a single tear, but I broke all the same.

The very next morning, we dressed in the same clothes we'd worn the day before and continued filming like we'd never stopped.

Slowly but surely, the interview continues. Holly's questions grow more targeted until I'm admitting to what I now realize were the early signs of an addiction to painkillers: "You think you're invincible on the ice. Every injury can be reset, every lost game can be overturned by one that you win. But when the enemy is what you love, and it's slowly chipping away at your health, it's a battle not everyone will win."

"You won," Holly says on the screen.

"I only won because someone paved the way before me.

She showed me what mattered, what I could lose if I kept going. You don't mess with my wife when she's trying to make a point."

Beside me, Holly squeezes my hand. Almost two years ago, I saw Dr. Mebowitz and it took me an entire year to go back. It took me seeing a future again with Holly, knowing what was at stake, to lead me back to his office.

"Before we cut to a break, I want to ask . . . what are your plans going forward? Do you have any?"

Without TV-me answering, the massive screen goes dark and I heave out a big breath.

Here's to my five minutes of fame—I much prefer it while wearing hockey gear.

DaSilva comes back on the stage a moment later. He's ditched his suit jacket and unbuttoned the top two buttons on his shirt. I don't think it's my imagination when I hear feminine sighs throughout the room.

He doesn't pay any of it any attention when he says, "Sorry for cutting that clip short. Looks like you're just going to have to tune in next week when it airs on Sports 24/7! Shameless advertising? One-hundred-percent, folks. Anyway, we're going to welcome Jackson Carter to the stage now."

Just before I stand—and try not to vomit—Holly kisses my cheek. "Knock 'em dead, tiger. I love you."

I steal a deeper kiss from her mouth. "Love you, too."

The crowd roars with enthusiasm as I pick my way to the side stairwell and then up onto the stage. A microphone is waiting for me, and I pick it up on the way to meet DaSilva in the middle of the stage, as we rehearsed earlier today.

"Jackson Carter is a legend in the NHL," DaSilva starts, ambling across the stage as he speaks to the audience. "With one Stanley Cup under his belt from his time with the Boston Bruins, he's also been the recipient of the Art-Ross and Conn-Smythe awards. He's played with the Dallas Stars, the Bruins, and the Boston Blades. He comes in a *measly* fourth place in terms of most goals scored during a career with 745 to his name. Don't worry, no one would dare knock Wayne Gretsky out of the number one seed." DaSilva chuckles low, and a girl in the front actually presses her hand to her heart.

"Let's welcome the Badass of Hockey, shall we?"

DaSilva steps to the side, ushering me to take his spot on the X marked on the floor. I'd tried to memorize tonight's speech after Sports 24/7 told us that *Getting Pucked* was actually up for an award for best docuseries of the year.

Steven Fairfax did *actually* faint when the nomination email hit his inbox. Mark Fillmore took a picture and texted it to me right after.

Gripping the microphone tight, I allow my gaze to bounce along the unknown faces in the audience. "I had a speech prepared," I murmur, keeping my tone light, "but I have a feeling that it was somehow left on my kitchen table. Which means I'm gonna have to wing this for y'all, and it's going to have to be short because the Blades are down to game seven tomorrow, and if I miss my flight, I know who I'm comin' after."

The crowd applauds at that, and I mentally thank Holly for booking us a red-eye from L.A back to Boston. My wife knows how to plan ahead, and for that I'll always be thankful.

"See," I say once the clapping subsides, "I planned to come up here with a perfect speech about how I transitioned from hockey player to hockey coach in the quickest time in the history of the league. Hey, DaSilva"—I point the mic in the analyst's direction—"I got Gretsky on something. Man might be a god in my book, but he can't hog every top-place slot."

DaSilva offers a gallant, dramatic bow. "Touché, Carter, touché."

I give a little bow of my own, sending the audience into a

fit of laugher. Maybe I'm not *that* awful at this public-speaking business.

Pushing the thought away, I keep going. "The truth is, I was a wreck. Tell any pro-athlete—hell, ask *anyone* who has an extraordinary love for their craft, whatever it might be—that their time is up, and I promise you that it's not going to be a smooth process. It wasn't for me, as you've seen during the course of this season's *Getting Pucked*."

I step back, away from the stand, taking the detachable microphone with me. "There's nothing more terrifying than realizing that you're only hurting yourself if you keep up with what you're doing. For me, that was playin' hockey. Each time I stepped onto the ice, I risked injuring myself more. And I'll be honest, I didn't quit—against the advice of my very nice, very patient doctor. In my defense, I wasn't willing to stop until he traded a picture of Cam Neely on his desk for one of me, but that's another story for a different day.

"So, I kept going until I could go no more. There's something refreshing about waking up and thinkin', *well, shit can't get any worse from here.* I pushed my body to the brink and my body flipped me the bird. Don't worry, we're on speaking terms now." Scrubbing a hand over my jaw, I run through the words I'd rehearsed with Holly. All of them, now, come up blank.

Fuck it.

Time to go off the cuff and wrap this up.

"I've been asked multiple times what changed my bitter outlook, and I'll tell you that it was thanks to one person—the woman who interviewed me for the final episode of *Getting Pucked*. She was a constant on the show the entire season, working some of the most brilliant magic behind the scenes. My wife, Holly Carter."

Fruitlessly, my gaze searches for her in the crowd. When I don't see her, I push onward. "I once asked myself, without hockey, who am I . . . and I'll admit, I didn't have an answer six months ago. I was me, a man who loved hockey and a man who loved *her,* Holly. But then I thought about it, *really* thought about it, and I finally knew what I hadn't realized all along: hockey may feed my soul, but it's not because of the rush of the ice under my skates or the sting of my helmet hitting the Plexiglas. It's because of my guys on the team; the staff who work diligently to improve us, game after game. It's the fact that, when I was out for the count, my family came to me with pizza and trash talk and goddamn *Cards Against Humanity,* and me and them and Holly stayed up until four in the morning playing ridiculous board games."

"I love hockey because I'm part of a family." I shove my hand into the front pocket of my slacks. Draw in a deep breath before going for gold. "My brilliant wife then slapped me with a healthy dose of reality, and said, *Not all superheroes wear capes, Jackson.* So, I stand here before you, out of my usual Blades uniform and skates. I put down the hockey stick in favor of working together with doctors like Dr. Mebowitz and others who study TBI and CTE. We can't change what happened to me or what's happened to so many other athletes, but we can do something different for our children."

There's a commotion at the side of the stage, and it takes me a moment to register the fact that Holly, *my* Holly, is making her way up toward me. In her hands, she carries what looks like a navy-blue towel.

Only when she shakes it out do I realize that she's bought me an honest-to-God *cape* with the words ASSISTANT COACH emblazoned in silver.

"You didn't," I rasp, not even giving a shit that the entire theater can hear me.

I stand, rooted to the spot, as Holly gives the fabric an extra shake like a matador waiting for the bull. She steps in close. "Turn around, Coach."

Like any husband who knows the benefits of obeying his wife, I turn my ass around.

Her nimble fingers close the front around my neck, snapping the cape's button closed before lingering a tad longer than is socially appropriate. She skims her nails over my chest before snagging the microphone from my grasp.

Whirling around to the crowd, she sidles under my arm and rests her head against my chest. "Let it be a lesson learned," she says into the mic, "not all superheroes might wear capes, but when you're the Beast of the Northeast, the Badass of Hockey, there's no other option. Anyone think Jackson here should wear this cape tomorrow at the game? Maybe it'll bring him and the Blades a little luck?"

As the crowd freaks the hell out, I don't know whether to kiss or spank my wife.

But when Marshall Hunt scores the winning goal the following night, clinching the playoffs for us and bringing home the Cup, I opt to do both.

And I make sure to wear my cape for a little luck.

EPILOGUE

HOLLY

Five Years Later

"**M**ommy, can I eat cereal out of Stanley?"

Normally, the answer to that question, posed by my four-year-old son, would be a hard *hell no.* (Without the four-letter word additive, obviously.)

Usually, "Stanley" refers to our Great Dane who drools in my shoes and hogs up the entire bed until both Jackson and I are clinging to our respective edges. Even our king-sized bed is no match for our furry firstborn.

I glance down at Mikey, where he's clinging to Dog Stanley's leg. "Please?"

He makes the most pitiful face I've ever seen. I'm seconds from caving and he knows I'm in his four-year-old clutches. Casting a quick glance at the Stanley Cup, which is seated in the center of our living room, I briefly wonder if Josh Kammer decided to clean the damn thing down with antibacterial wipes before schlepping it over to our house.

For the third season in the last five years, Jackson has led the Blades to victory as their head coach after Coach Hall retired. Without waiting for the board's permission, Hall promoted Jackson because he refused to pass his team into anyone else's hands. If you ask any of the other teams in the league how they feel about the Blades' winning streak, there's sure to be a *host* of four-letter words being bandied about.

If you ask a Blades player or fan, Jackson is a god among men.

"Man just keeps getting better with age," Kammer told a journalist a few years back. "Let's get real here for a sec, he wears a goddamn *cape* during playoffs and no one—not a single person judges him for it. Instead, they're selling capes out of the gift shop. That, my friend, is the power of Jackson Carter."

It'd be funny if it weren't also true.

And, as I've told my husband during late nights while he watches clips and I edit footage for Carter Photography, it's also damn sexy.

"Mommy? Cereal?"

I spare the Cup one more glance. "Can you pull the Frosted Flakes out while I wake up Daddy?"

My words fall on deaf ears as Mikey all but sprints to *his* special cupboard. Stanley tosses me a look, then trots after his favorite person.

There's no loyalty in this house, I tell you. Since Mikey's birth, I might as well be chopped liver to the Dane. But as Stanley stands over my son, always watching his back the way he's done for four years, I merely fumble for my phone and snap another picture of the two of them together.

The picture isn't perfectly angled or aligned, but it's the content that matters to me most.

After settling in Mikey with a bowl that is *not* the Stanley Cup—Kammer's a player and, knowing him, I have no doubt that Lord Stanley has been through some debauchery during the twenty-four hours where Josh had the trophy—and propping him in front of the TV with one of his favorite shows, I head up our worn stairs to the second floor.

We sold Jackson's condo the month Mikey was born. Living in the city worked when it was just the two of us, but we wanted more space. We're on the South Shore now, just twenty minutes outside of Boston, but with a house on the oceanfront for Jackson and an outdoor mother-in-law suite that we converted into a studio for me.

The old Colonial shows its bones in the most beautiful ways, and as I ascend the circular stairwell, I run my hand along the oak balustrade.

On quiet feet, I head for our master bedroom at the end of the hall.

This season was harder on Jackson than the last few. The Blades finally overhauled their team, as Steven Fairfax had predicted ages ago, and it wore my husband down to the bone.

When I push open our door, it's to find him still tangled in the bed and shoved into one corner. My mouth turns up at the thought of Stanley from this morning, his ass near our faces and his giant paws shoving Jackson and I to the ends of the earth.

I leave the door ajar in case Mikey calls for me, then climb into the bed beside my husband.

He groans in his sleep and rolls over, his arms instinctively reaching for me. "Holls?"

The Texan drawl is softer now, like an age-old blanket that's been used down to the threads. When he's angry or excited or ready to tear my clothes off, the accent always makes a delicious comeback.

He's naked beneath the sheets and I sling one leg over his waist. "Time to wake up, Mr. I Am The Champion."

His erection brushes my core as he rolls on top of me. "Don't start quoting Queen at me this early in the morning." He nuzzles the crook of my neck; his stubbled jawline makes me shiver. "I already had to deal with Carl calling me yesterday. Wanted to know if I was interested in going to a Celine concert next month."

Laughter climbs my throat. "You'd think that after all these years he'd realize you can't stand Celine Dion."

He drops his forehead to my shoulder. "Our one night of karaoke together sealed the deal forever. Do you know how many concerts I've been to with him at this point?"

My hands skim down over his hard obliques to the firm curve of his butt. "Seven?"

"*Twelve*, Holls. Twelve. He keeps count."

Just to see his eyes narrow, I begin to hum the chorus to *My Heart Will Go On*.

Poor Jackson. It's like a needle in his skin now. The minute I start humming, he's singing the words right along with me. He breaks off with a pained groan. "I'm going to tell Carl I'd rather eat my own toenails than go to another of her concerts."

I pat his back in mock-sympathy. "You want me to go with you this time? Or am I off the hook?"

"You're *so* not off the hook."

Warm lips find my collarbone, pressing soft kisses there until Jackson is rolling my nipple between his fingers and my panties are being shoved to the side. He dips his fingers into my wet heat, then drags them to my clit, which he rubs in tight, little circles.

"Mikey—" He grinds out, looking over his shoulder at the door. "Is he watching TV?"

I nod, already wrapping my hand around Jackson's hard-on. "Are you sure you feel okay?"

"Never been better, sweetheart."

It's his standard answer when I ask about his headaches. They come and they go, as they always have, but the researchers at Boston University, along with Dr. Mebowitz, are convinced that it will be many years—maybe decades— before Jackson experiences anything worse than his current symptoms. It's not a perfect diagnosis and I'd be lying if I said there haven't been nights when the stress of those blasted *what-ifs* have worn my confidence down.

But Jackson is adamant that he's doing better than he ever has. When the season grows busier, it's easy for me to see that his anxiety rises along with it—and that anxiety, as we've learned, is another indicator of CTE. When the panic rises, I'm right there with him to ride out the storm.

And when he pulls off another win for his hockey family, like he did a month ago, I know that *he* believes that everything has worked out as it's fated to be.

Trust me to fall in love with a man who will tear a guy a new asshole on the ice and then, hours later, spend the evening with me on the balcony as we search for shooting stars.

My breath catches in my throat as Jackson eases me onto my stomach and fits an arm between me and the bed. He urges me up on my knees, tipping my butt in the air, and then his cock is pressing into me.

I moan his name into a pillow, my hands fisting the sheets.

His thrusts are slow, languid, like he has all the time in the world to make love to me. Big, masculine hands follow the line of my spine, and, God, it feels so good. Jackson reads me like I'm a language only he understands.

When he fists my hair, I arch my back and beg for more.

When the pump of his hips picks up speed, I sink downward and meet him thrust for thrust.

His damp chest connects with my damp back, and he returns his arm to fold over my belly. I feel every drag of his cock. Every drag, every pump, every time he can't help himself from kissing my shoulders as he brings us both to the edge.

"*Fuck,*" he groans behind me.

With every ounce of energy that I have, I lift onto my hands and twist to stare at him over one glistening shoulder.

He's every inch the man I fell in love with nineteen years ago, but so much more after everything we've been through together.

I flip my hand over, palm up.

Jackson's dark gaze drags off my face to my waiting hand, and he shifts his weight to settle a palm over mine. The angle changes, his hips pistoning faster and faster, and I burst apart the second he circles my hips and presses down on my clit.

He pumps once more, twice, and then his rugged face twists with pleasure as he empties himself inside me. "Damn," he breathes out, holding up his weight so he doesn't squash me. "I could go for some pancakes."

"Well, the Cup *is* in the house," I tease, wriggling my butt under him, "I suppose I could cook pancakes in celebration instead of heading to South Street and our favorite diner."

"You're a goddess."

"Damn right I am. Don't you forget it."

Jackson's mouth finds mine. The kiss is familiar now, a high that reminds me of home and safety and love but is no less exciting than the very first one he gave me so long ago. I pull back and brush my finger over the crooked slope of his nose and then trace the white scar on his left cheek.

"Do you have any regrets?" I ask softly.

"For the season?"

"For life."

"None," he says, rolling me onto my back so he can stretch out alongside me. "I love you, Holly Belliveaux Carter. I love Stanley, our firstborn, and I love Mikey. He reminds me so much of you—always so inquisitive."

"He's already in skates, Jackson. I'm pretty sure that he's got future hockey star written all over him."

Jackson's nose nuzzles mine. "I'm gonna make a change, sweetheart. I won't let what happened to me happen to our son."

"I know."

And I do.

Only, I don't have the chance to expand on that because my heart rips out of my chest when I hear Mikey scream.

Jackson and I are out of the bed in a heartbeat. I'm mostly dressed still, and as I sail down the steps—my husband hot on my tail—I think of *everything* that could have gone wrong. Did I leave the stove on? Was there a knife on the table? Did my baby fall and hurt himself?

"Mikey!" I call out. "Mikey, baby, Mommy is right—"

I skid to a halt.

Blink.

My son's sitting on the couch where I left him, eating his favorite Frosted Flakes, and staring at Stanley peeing on Stanley.

As in, my Great Dane *pissing* on the Stanley Cup.

I hear Jackson's arrival before I see him. "Well, shit," he mutters, "that's got to be blasphemous on *so* many different levels."

"Let's never speak of this moment again?" I ask.

"Lips are sealed, sweetheart. Lips. Are Sealed."

Unfortunately, it only takes the arrival of Beaumont, Harrison, Hunt, and their families later that afternoon for Mikey to spill the beans to anyone who'll listen to him retell the story of furry Stanley lifting his leg and going to town all over the greats of the NHL marked on the Stanley Cup— including Mikey's own father, Jackson Carter.

I lock eyes with my husband across the room as we watch our son demonstrate the events of the morning. Jackson drags his thumb across his bottom lip in that familiar way of his as he watches me, humor lighting his rugged features.

"Always you," he mouths for me only.

I don't shush my heart, the way I may have done years ago. Instead I curl my hand into a fist and kiss my first knuckle, then mouth back, "I love you too."

Want to know a secret?

We won't be seeing the end of one character from *Body Check…*

Dominic DaSilva, the analyst from Sports 24/7, has his own story! You first get a glimpse of him in *Hold Me Today*, Book 1 of my *Put A Ring On It* series, but *Kiss Me Tonight* (featuring Dominic himself) is now available too! Flip the page for a sneak peek after the Author's Note.

AUTHOR'S NOTE

BEHIND THE BOOK: THE NHL & CTE

The Blades is the series that was never meant to be a series—but I don't think I've ever been so grateful for inspiration striking me like a shovel to the face. (Elegant, I know). Of all the couples I've written—and this is my 10th book!—Holly & Jackson truly spoke to me on so many different levels.

More specifically, this book needed writing for so many different reasons. We've all been in Holly's position, fighting for our happiness and discovering who we're meant to be. As for Jackson . . . from page one, I knew that I wanted to bring light to a controversial topic that has been a "plague" to the NHL (and other sports) for a number of years now.

Players like Larry Zeidel, Gary Leeman, Derek "Boogeyman" Boogaard, Dave "The Hammer" Schultz, Stephen Peat, Steve Montador, and so many others, have all suffered TBI or CTE to varying degrees. In 2016, 100 former and current NHL players sued the league when the NHL refused to acknowledge the link between concussions and CTE. Some players joined the petition, then dropped out, no doubt fearing that linking their name to a cause such as this might have a negative effect on their careers.

As Gary Leeman once put it, "'The protocol was, 'Can you

go? If not, we'll replace you. The team's response was, they asked me if I could play . . . You felt like you needed to retain your spot in the roster, or you're going to lose it. If you got hit in the head, there was no time for you to figure out what was going on'" (*The Washington Post*).

Below, I have attached a list of sources about the NHL and CTE, should you find your interest piqued and would like to know more.

For now, I just wish to say that—as this is fiction—I'd like to think Jackson lives a long, healthy life where he makes a change within the NHL. He has a voice, as Holly said, and he intends to use it. Writing *Body Check* was always meant to focus on the psyche of Jackson as a player, and not on the medical treatments that no doubt follow his diagnosis.

This is a romance, after all, and I so hope you enjoyed Holly & Jackson's love story!

Sources about the NHL & CTE

"After Former Player's Death, Concussion Litigation Against N.H.L. Gains Heft." John Branch. *New York Times.* 18 February 2015. Access here: https://nyti.ms/2wR6iZX

"Derek Boogaard: A Boy Learns to Brawl." John Branch. *New York Times.* 3 December 2011. Access here: https://nyti.ms/2Q7WoeF

"Former Players are Suing NHL over Concussions but Remain Loyal to Hockey." *The Washington Post.* 25 May 2016. Access here: https://wapo.st/2NtDBfv

"I Love Everything About Hockey…Except for the Preventable Traumatic Brain Injuries." Lisa Patrick. *The Good Men Project.* 8 January 2017. Access here: http://bit.ly/2NSZSQK

"I Punched Out: The Death of Derek Boogaard." *Times Documentaries, New York Times*. Access here: https://nyti.ms/2QbGAaW

"The Fight to Save My Brain | Daniel Carcillo." *The Real Athlete*. Spring 2018. Access here (Facebook only): http://bit.ly/2M6wPr7

For more information on CTE - its symptoms and the research that exists on the disease - there is no better source than the CTE Center at Boston University. You can access the website at the following link and learn more about brain injuries. Access here: http://www.bu.edu/cte/

She's a single mom. He's a retired football player.
It could be love…if they don't kill each other first.

Dominic

She knows who I am.

Inside the candlelit world of the Golden Fleece, there was no doubt in my mind that the cute, drunk blonde didn't recognize me. We'd sat side by side with her mouthing off about how much of an asshole Dominic DaSilva was.

Is.

Shit, does it really matter? End of the day, the anonymity gave me an unexpected thrill. Like an adrenaline junkie watching the ground rise up fast, just before the release of the parachute, I'd done nothing to reveal that I was the same "asshole" clutching his leg on the TV.

Had it been uncomfortable to watch the lowest point of my life play out on screen while a bunch of strangers hollered their joy from every corner of the pub?

Yep.

Had I cared, especially once she ditched the prim and proper attitude and loosened up?

Not even a little.

There's a special circle of hell reserved for people like you.

A visual of her calling me an asshole just like him—*me. Just like me*—springs to mind, only to be cast aside by the memory of her landing face-first on my dick.

Embarrassment had pinkened her cheeks and sharpened her tongue, and there'd been one heavy, electric moment when I nearly said "screw it" to my mission of staying in my own lane and away from women and dating and relationships.

Because those pink lips of hers had beckoned. Strongly.

Now, standing mere feet away from her, I'm glad for resisting the urge to lean in and discover how she likes to be kissed. Aggressive, with warring tongues and nipping teeth? Or slow and soul-wrenchingly sweet?

Doesn't matter.

Considering how she's gaping at me, *oblivious* is no longer her middle name. She knows exactly who I am.

I shouldn't have taken off the damn hat.

Too late now.

Her jaw is hanging open and her eyes are the size of saucers.

One slender hand lifts to clutch her shirt collar—the same one I'm wearing—and an ominous feeling slicks through me.

Red-and-white London High polo.

The Wildcat mascot, paired with a football in motion, is printed over her left breast.

My gaze drifts south, over her loose shorts and the neon-pink tennis shoes on her feet. She's decked out in workout gear. Her blond hair is tugged up into a high ponytail, the tips of which brush her right shoulder. Unlike the other night, her face is completely devoid of makeup.

Though her lips are still the same berry shade that made me think twice about turning her down. *Au natural.* They're full and plump and instead of curving up in a smile like she's excited to see me, they're shaped in an *O.*

"Fuck me."

At her hushed whisper, I jerk my eyes away from her mouth like I've been caught with my hand inching toward the proverbial cookie jar. "What did you say?"

Her hand drops away from her shirt to point an accusing finger at me. "No."

It's all she says. *No.* And yet that one syllable rocks my entire world.

Because if she's here at London High, dressed like that, at seven in the fucking morning on a Monday, there's only one conclusion to be made here and we both know what it is:

"Levi."

Blue eyes, the color of San Francisco Bay at sunrise—so deep a shade they almost don't appear blue at all—blink back at me, her throat working hard with a swallow. "You know my name."

I rest a hand against the still-warm grill of my Ford 1-50. "I didn't then."

We both know what "then" I'm referring to.

"You let me think you were someone else."

And I enjoyed every second of stepping out of "Dominic DaSilva's" size sixteen shoes. Enough that I wouldn't change a single thing about the hour we spent talking at the pub, including the tense moment when we went from strangers to the intimately acquainted.

I've spent the last three days picturing her blond head buried in my lap.

Not that I'll ever admit that out loud.

Grasping my old hat off the truck, I swipe it against the outside of my thigh. Then shoulder past her so I can check out how much damage we're looking at here. "A slip of the tongue," I tell her, fitting the ball cap on my head and squaring off the brim. "We'll call it even."

"*Even*?"

"Even," I confirm smoothly. "You jacked up my car."

"You let me call you an asshole and didn't even have the decency to clue me in that I was making a complete fool of myself!"

"Are we talking about before or after you used my lap as a personal pillow?"

Want to keep reading? *Kiss Me Tonight* is now available in ebook, audio, paperback and hardback.

DEAR FABULOUS READER

Hi there! I so hope you enjoyed *BODY CHECK*, and if you are new to my books, welcome to the family!

In the back of all my books, I love to include a Dear Fabulous Reader section that talks about what locations from the book can be visited in real life or what sparked my inspiration for a particular plot point. (I like to think of it as the Extras on DVD's, LOL).

As always, we're hitting it up bullet-point style. Enjoy!

- There are so many snippets in this book that I've tried to be selective—otherwise we'll be here for days! To begin, it's best to admit that Trinity Church, where Zoe and Andre marry, *is* a real church in Boston! It is stunning and should you ever have the chance to visit, I hope that you will! Fun fact: in the 70s when the towering John Hancock building was erected, its glass windows were - ahem - *not* so secure. Many of them crashed down on the church!
- *Getting Pucked*, anyone? My inspiration came straight from *Hard Knocks* over on HBO and also

my love for reality TV. It seemed like a perfect fit to bring the two of these lovebirds back together after all they'd been through!

- Do you remember that crazy tale Jackson tells Holly about the *Playboys* and Christmas lights? Well, I'm here to admit that . . . the story is true. Well, *partly* true—I had to take fictional liberties, obviously. The owner of those Christmas lights and *Playboy* magazines? Mr. Luis' father. Two years ago, Mr. Luis and I were helping his dad move when Mr. Luis propped a massive box at the top of the attic ladder and told me to ease it down. There was no easing, let me just tell you that. It burst apart from old-age within seconds and the next thing I knew, it was raining glass bulbs and breasts *everywhere*. I don't think Mr. Luis has ever laughed harder and to this day, I like to remind his dad that he tried to do me in. Don't worry, all parties are aware the story made it into the book! His dad, one of the funniest people I've ever met, laughed and said, "Not exactly the way I thought I'd be remembered, but I'll take it."

- At one point in the book, Jackson mentions a video he watched where a NHL player breaks down in a mini-documentary while talking about the effects of brain injuries. That video is one I watched in real-life, narrated by former NHL player Daniel Carcillo about his personal experiences, and can be found here (https://www.facebook.com/TheRealAthleteTPT/videos/194857287884620/). It is heartbreaking but well worth a watch if you have the time. (Please note that the video is exclusive to the Facebook platform).

- If you're in the mood for some late night diner food while visiting Boston, I *highly* recommend South

Street Diner, where Holly & Jackson went after their shenanigans in the parking lot. The food is on point *and* it's open twenty-four hours, seven days per week.

- Random fact: the Safe Space thread with the Blades boys actually came from a group chat that Mr. Luis belongs to. It's his video game peeps but it *is* titled "Safe Space" and you can bet I put it in this book just as my little amusement. Now you're on in the inside joke too!

- And, lastly, Newport, Rhode Island. It is *magical* and by far one of my favorite places in the world! I've made many a stop at the Dunkin' Donuts mentioned in the book, and have walked the Cliff Walk more times than I count. Should you ever have the chance to visit, please do so! Also, to all my fellow Massachusetts people reading these notes, just know that we can stand strong against the #Masshole stereotype together, LOL.

As always, there are many more but here is just a sampling! If you're thinking…that seems rather fascinating and I want to know more, you are always so welcome to reach out! Pretty much, nothing makes me happier :)

Much love,

Maria

ACKNOWLEDGMENTS

Thank you for reading *Body Check!* It's almost impossible to think that, a little over a year ago, I was writing *Power Play* just for fun. I had no plans to publish it, no plans to create a series off the Blades boys, and yet here we are—four books later! Will there be a fifth? It's up in the air right now but Weston Cain is calling my name.

Launching a book is a team effort from start to finish, and I couldn't do it without my team/family/support system. Najla, Kathy, Tandy, Dawn, Brenda, Viper—thank you for making this book look beautiful on the inside and out!

Thank you to the bloggers, my VIPers, every reader in BBA for shouting from the rooftops about wanting Holly & Jackson. I think it goes without saying, if it weren't for you wanting more of the Blades, then this book wouldn't even exist.

To my girls in 30 Days to 60k and BF Accountability, it's safe to say that, without you prodding me to sit my butt down and write, this book wouldn't be finished. To Tina, Sam, Terra, and Joslyn—I adore you guys!

To Jami Albright, for letting me steal your characters and your town of Zachsville when I said, "My hero is from Texas and I want his mom to be best friends with Honey. Can we make this happen?" You said yes. And now the Blades will forever have their mark in your Brides on the Run series— which is pretty much a dream come true.

And, lastly, to you Dear Reader, for giving me a chance

and picking up this book. Thank you for helping me to live my dream of storytelling.

Much love,

Maria

ALSO BY MARIA LUIS

ABOUT THE AUTHOR

Maria Luis is an Amazon Top 25 Bestselling Author.

Historian by day and romance novelist by night, Maria abandoned the cold winters of Boston for hot and humid New Orleans (with a pit stop in England, along the way). When Maria isn't frantically typing with hot chocolate in hand, she can be found binging reality TV, going on adventures with her better half and two pups, or plotting her next steamy romance.

Stalk Maria in the Wild at the following!
Join Maria's Newsletter:
https://geni.us/MariaLuisSubscribe

Join Maria's Facebook Reader Group:
Book Boyfriends Anonymous

Printed in Dunstable, United Kingdom